Jeanne Whitmee began her career as an actress. After her marriage she became a speech and drama teacher and began writing in her spare time. She has written numerous short stories and several romantic novels under different pseudonyms.

Jeanne Whitmee has two daughters and four grand-children and lives with her husband in Wisbech, Cambridgeshire. Her previous novel, *Wives and Mothers*, is available from Headline:

'Virtually unputdownable for anyone who likes to enter the complex web of other people's lives'
Peterborough Evening News

The Long Way Home

Jeanne Whitmee

KNIGHT

First published in 1993
by Judy Piatkus (Publishers) Ltd

First published in paperback in 1993
by HEADLINE BOOK PUBLISHING PLC

This edition published 2003 by Knight
an imprint of The Caxton Publishing Group

10 9 8 7 6 5 4 3 2 1

ISBN 1 86019 6624

Typeset by Keyboard Services, Luton

Printed and bound in Great Britain by
Mackays of Chatham plc, Chatham, Kent

Caxton Publishing Group
20 Bloomsbury Street
London WC1B 3QA

For Lynn Curtis.
In gratitude for her help and
encouragement.

Chapter 1

Marie looked again at her watch. Liam had given it to her. It had a small oval face and it was made of real gold. It was her most precious possession. The tiny hands pointed to the half hour. Half-past six. She had been here almost three hours now and still there was no sign of Bridget, the woman who was supposed to meet her. If only she knew what Liam's sister looked like. Her troubled eyes raked the sea of bustling travellers in search of a woman with Liam's features, but the faces all around her were alien. Preoccupied with their own lives, they hurried past the young fair-haired girl standing so patiently by the bookstall without giving her a second glance.

Marie moved the new blue suitcase out of the way as a woman almost stumbled over it and glared crossly at her.

It was a cold, unfriendly place, she decided, Paddington Station. No one had smiled at her or asked if they could help as they would have done back home. She'd already double checked that she was in the right place. 'Wait by the bookstall,' Liam had said. There was no other bookstall, so she must be right. Marie watched the taxis that drove right into the station to park in a line down the middle. She watched the wheeling pigeons that swooped for crumbs and waddled precariously among the heedless

1

feet. She watched the ebb and flow of people surging back and forth like the waves of the sea whenever a train came in. But most of all she watched the time – both on the tiny face of her watch and on the big white face of the station clock. But Bridget didn't come.

It was cold. Only September, yet the gusty draughts that swirled around her legs made her shiver. She drew her inadequate coat more closely around her. The buttons wouldn't fasten any more. Although there were four months still to go before the birth of her baby her stomach was already large. Her back ached from standing so long, and so did her legs. She was hungry too. She hadn't eaten anything today, except for the sandwich she'd bought on the train this morning and she longed desperately for a cup of tea. There was a buffet bar a few yards away. She caught the savoury whiff of hot food from time to time as the doors opened to let customers in or out. It tantalised her nostrils and made her mouth water, but she was afraid to move from this place in case Bridget might come and go away again, thinking she hadn't come.

Marie shifted her weight from one leg to the other, wishing there was somewhere to sit down. The crossing from Belfast to Liverpool had seemed endless and the sea had been so rough. She'd been dreadfully sick on the ferry – and so relieved when the train finally arrived at Euston. She'd got a bit muddled over the Underground and worried in case she'd be late at Paddington Station and keep Bridget waiting. But she'd arrived ten minutes early. She remembered her relief; thinking that at last her journey was almost over. Yet here she was three hours later. Still waiting.

The station was quiet again now, in the lull between trains. What should she do? Soon it would start to get dark and it was beginning to look as though she must face the fact that Bridget wasn't coming. Panic made her heart lurch. She had no address. No telephone number to contact. She hadn't enough money for an hotel either. Where would she sleep? Liam had been so positive that Bridget would be here to meet her – to take her home and look after her until he could join them. But now she was alone and helpless in this strange unfriendly place.

Then suddenly she spotted a woman coming towards her, smiling. She had blue eyes and dark curly hair. Marie's heart leapt with relief as she stepped forward.

'Please, would you be Bridget?'

The woman looked startled. 'No. I'm sorry.'

Despair hit her like a hammer blow. The station began to tip sideways. The press of hurrying people seemed to crowd in on her suffocatingly. In her head the voice of the public address system echoed and boomed. *The train now standing-standing-standing . . .* The platform came rushing up to meet her – and everything went black.

When Marie came round she was sitting in some kind of office. The woman with the blue eyes whom she'd taken for Bridget was bending over her, a glass of water in her hand.

'Here, dear. It's all right. I'm a nurse. Have a sip of water. You'll soon feel better.' She glanced at Marie's rounded abdomen.

'When's the baby due, dear?'

'December,' Marie whispered.

The woman looked surprised. 'Not till then?'

Marie frowned as the memory of where and why she was here filtered back. She tried to get to her feet. 'I must – I've got to go. Someone is waiting . . .'

'No. You mustn't. You're not – *Oh*!' The woman

3

cried out as Marie gave a groan and sank to the floor again.

In the moments that followed there was general confusion as people crowded around, arguing over what best to do. Someone suggested sending for an ambulance, but the woman with the blue eyes said that they should first try to find out who she was and locate this person who was supposed to be waiting. Maybe it was her husband and he'd be worrying. Marie could only groan uncomprehendingly when they questioned her. Her small handbag yielded nothing helpful except the sailing ticket that showed she had arrived from Belfast that morning.

The staff in the station master's office looked at one another doubtfully and a feeling of silent apprehension settled over the place like a pall. Someone lifted the telephone and sent for the police.

While the woman with the blue eyes helped Marie into an adjoining room and sat with her, a railway policeman opened her case – and it was then that he found the explosive device, hidden away at the bottom wrapped in the shawl she had knitted for the coming baby.

'Miss O'Connor, I'll ask you again – what was in the suitcase?'

Sitting in the interview room at the police station, her heart drumming with fear and bewilderment, Marie repeated her description of the few clothes packed in the new suitcase, and the baby clothes she had made herself.

The other policeman asked: 'So who made the bomb? Who put it there if you didn't?'

Marie looked up, her eyes wide with fear. 'I've told you, I don't know anything about a bomb. I don't know what you're talking about.'

4

'Where did you stay the night before you left Ireland?'

'With Liam.'

'And who is Liam?'

'My boyfriend.'

'So it was his idea? Where were you to plant it?'

'*Nowhere*. There wasn't . . .'

'Why did he send you – in your condition? Is he completely heartless? Did you realise that when we found it there was only another half an hour left before it was timed to explode? Perhaps he had a reason . . .' The policeman leaned closer. 'Perhaps he was trying to kill two birds with one stone.'

She stared at them, open-mouthed with horror. '*No*. He wouldn't. We were going to be married.' She shook her head disbelievingly. It wasn't possible. They were saying – implying – that Liam had sent her to England with a bomb, hoping that she and the baby . . . She closed her eyes and bit hard on her lip, trying to shut out the unspeakable suggestions they were putting into her mind.

'All right, what's his full name?'

'Costello – Liam Costello. But he isn't the kind of person you say. Not at all. You're wrong about him. *Wrong*. This is all a mistake – a terrible mistake.' Tears trickled slowly down her cheeks. It was a nightmare. Surely she must soon wake and find it had all been a bad dream.

The policeman leaned towards her again. 'Then you're saying that you agreed to do it for him, Marie?'

'*No*.' She shook her head. 'I didn't. I *didn't*.'

'He sent you without telling you about the bomb then?'

'No. He wouldn't do that – not to me.'

'Right, let's begin again from the beginning. Why did you come to England? Where were you going?'

5

'Who were you to meet?'

'Come on now, Marie, why don't you tell us the truth? Who are you shielding?'

'If it's Liam, he isn't worth it, you know.'

'Maybe there's someone else. Did he have friends? Were there more than one?'

The relentless questions hammered into her brain and the men's faces loomed over her, so close that they became distorted, ugly in their intensity. She shook her head, her throat swelling painfully and her eyes scalded by tears.

'No – no. It isn't true.'

'How many, Marie? Just give us their names. No one will blame you for something you've been tricked into and you've nothing to be loyal to, now have you?'

The voices hardened, became impatient: 'Come on now. You'd better tell us the truth. It'll be easier for you if you do.'

Her head ached unbearably and she covered her face with trembling hands. The room began to spin and the darkness began to close in on her again, folding its thick black wings suffocatingly around her.

Marie's eyes snapped open. She was gasping for breath. Her heart was thumping and her nightdress clung damply to her body. In the darkness of the room she could hear the calm familiar sounds of the clock ticking and the deep regular breathing of Ralph, her husband, sleeping beside her. She lay very still, waiting for her heartbeat to steady and her breathing to return to normal. It was a long time – twenty years since it happened. At first the dream had haunted her frequently, but it was a long time now since it had come to revive the hateful memories. Yet no matter how long the interval between it was always the same. Always bad.

What had triggered the dream? She didn't have to ask herself that. It was Hannah's letter. She visualised it, lying at the bottom of her underwear drawer, hidden beneath the lining paper. It was almost a week since it had arrived, to fill her with excitement overlaid with fear. If Ralph were to find out . . . She felt her heart lurch sickeningly at the thought.

After a while she slipped silently out of bed, put on her dressing gown and went through to the kitchen. It was just getting light and as she waited for the kettle to boil she looked out at the view of the sea. She loved the view from the flat. The sea could look so blue and tranquil when the sun shone, but now, in the cold grey light of an early winter morning it looked bleak and hostile with angry waves crashing on the sandy beach. Even from their flat on the top floor of the clifftop hotel, she could hear its boom and roar. She paused for a moment to watch the flying spray, imagining the rattle of the shingle as the ebbing tide dragged it inexorably back into the seabed.

It was only a few weeks till Christmas, she reminded herself. Everything would be all right then. The Ocean Hotel was booked solid for the holiday. The thought warmed and cheered her. She loved the bustle of organisation; managing the staff, planning menus and entertainment – generally making sure that people had a good time. It had been her life, her whole existence for the past fifteen years. It was still all she really lived for.

The kettle boiled and she made tea and sat on one of the stools at the worktop, her still trembling hands cupped around the mug. The dream had shaken her badly. She could go for whole months at a time without even thinking of Liam and of all that had happened all those years ago – of his betrayal and the terrible thing he had done to her. Then something would happen to remind her and the dream would come again to drag her back, just as the tide dragged the pebbles back into the sea. However much she tried to put it behind her there was no escape. It was always there on the fringes of her life, waiting in the shadows. And now – now perhaps the time had come when she must turn and face it, she told herself with despairing resignation.

She had been sixteen when she first met him. The nuns at the convent children's home where she'd grown up had obtained a job for her as chambermaid at a Belfast hotel. She'd been happy there. For the first time in her life she had a small room she could call her own and a little money to spend as she wished. Most of the people she met were kind. Sometimes they gave her tips or small gifts. Then came Liam. He was something else. Something *quite* else. Never in her life had she met anyone as attractive. He could have charmed the proverbial birds out of the trees with his fascinating Dublin accent, his ready smile and that infectious, devil-may-care laugh. He had the brightest brown eyes she had ever seen, and his hair was as shiny and black as a raven's wing. He was tall and handsome, but, most miraculous of all, Liam seemed as smitten with her as she was with him.

He took her out on her days off – to cinemas and restaurants, places she had never seen the inside of before. He bought her presents, things she had only ever seen in shop windows: flowers and chocolates, the tiny gold watch and a ring with a pretty blue stone. He was the first man she had ever allowed to kiss her. Very soon Marie was head over heels in love; so much in love that it sometimes hurt her just to look at him. So much in love that she would have done anything – anything at all not to lose him.

When she had discovered that she was pregnant

8

she'd been so afraid. Perhaps Liam would be angry. What if he abandoned her? What would she do if she lost her job and had nowhere to go? But she needn't have feared. Liam had been surprised, even a little shocked at first, but he had soon recovered and started to make plans. He decided that she should work for as long as she could, then he would buy her a ticket and send her to England – to his sister Bridget in London who would look after her until he was able to join her. He would get a job easily enough, he told her confidently. They would buy a little house and live in England; beside the sea perhaps. It would be better for the baby to be brought up somewhere peaceful – away from all the troubles. Marie was happy and so relieved. How could she ever have doubted Liam? It all sounded so wonderful.

When the time came he bought her a new suitcase. Marie gave in her notice and left her job at the hotel, then she moved into Liam's flat until her sailing date. In those few idyllic days she knew more happiness than in her entire life before. She packed the new suitcase with her own things and the baby clothes she had made with such loving care. She listened carefully to all Liam's instructions, wishing they could go together but accepting that he must stay for a while. On the day he took her to catch the ferry he promised he would be with her within the month. It was the last she ever saw of him.

Marie was charged with 'conspiracy to cause an explosion' and remanded in custody to await the birth of her baby. It was while she was in the remand home that she met Hannah Brown, the social worker assigned to her. She was the first person Marie had met in England who believed in her innocence. And she truly believed that it was Hannah who saved her sanity.

9

'You have to think of the future, Marie. What are you going to do when the baby comes?'

'I won't part with it,' she said vehemently. 'They can't take it from me, can they?'

'Of course not. But you must make plans. If you intend to keep your baby you must pick yourself up and start again. You'll need to be able to earn enough money to keep the two of you. But you're young. You can do it.'

She persuaded Marie to think about training for a job, so that when she was discharged she could have a better life than she had before.

'Find out what you're good at,' she urged.

'But if they find me guilty – if they send me to prison?' Marie asked fearfully.

'They won't. You must think positively.'

'Liam will come forward when he hears about it, won't he? He'll tell them it's all a terrible mistake.'

'Of course he will.'

'I *have* to keep my baby.'

'And so you shall. You'll manage somehow, if you really want to.'

But when Marie was six and a half months pregnant the prison doctor told her during a routine examination that she was carrying twins.

'Had you thought about letting them go for adoption?' The middle-aged woman doctor faced Marie across her desk. Her attitude was pragmatic but not unkind.

'I've made up my mind – I want to keep my baby,' Marie met the doctor's eyes appealingly.

'Without support it's not really viable. You'd do better by yourself and the children if you let them go.'

Marie nodded numbly, but deep inside the words hadn't sunk in. The doctor could be wrong. Maybe it was just one baby after all. Everything would be all right. It had to be.

She went into premature labour one night in late October, giving birth to a healthy baby girl at ten minutes to midnight. Another daughter, tiny and underweight but yelling lustily, was born twenty minutes later. Marie's heart sank. The joy and accomplishment of birth was shadowed by crushing, overwhelming defeat. Now she had to face reality. She might just have managed to keep one baby, but two? It would be impossible. The doctor had been right. It was impractical and unfair – to herself and to the babies. Much better for them to be adopted by loving parents who would give them a good start in life; all the things that Marie herself had never had. She had nothing to offer them; no home, no money, no father. She faced the fact that she had no real choice in the matter.

She asked for the little girls to be baptised and to be allowed to give them names and her request was granted. She called them Sarah and Leah. Good names from the Bible, but without the Catholic label. Because they must have their own lives – make their own choices. At least she could give them that much. She held them once only; Sarah, fair like her, and Leah, as dark as her father had been. Marie looked down at Leah's furious little face and waving fists and wondered what life held in store for her daughters.

By the time they were two days old they had gone out of her life for ever; like rosebuds picked for a bouquet, Marie told herself with an aching heart, the morning dew still on their innocent faces.

Hannah had been over-optimistic about the outcome of Marie's trial. Charged with an act of terrorism, she stood trial six weeks after the birth of her babies. Liam had not come forward and could not be found.

She was told that no such person existed. Her counsel said that he must have given her a false name, but the prosecution accused her of fabricating the whole story in order to shield someone else. The evidence was circumstantial. She was found guilty and sentenced to five years' imprisonment.

Life in prison was hard, but not so very much harder than she had known before. Hannah came to see her and urged her to study.

'All right, you've lost your babies and that's terrible,' she said. 'But you must try to put the past behind you. You still have a future, Marie. You can still survive. You must. You know you're innocent and maybe one day you'll get the chance to prove it. Make a firm decision to make up for all that you've missed out on. You're bright, Marie. Why not finish your education – learn a skill?'

But for the first weeks Marie was too despondent, too heartsore to bother. She worked at her allotted job in the prison laundry, ate and slept like an automaton. Looking neither forward nor back, speaking only when she was spoken to. The only future she could see gaped before her like a deep, dark chasm, filled to the brim with black despair.

But Hannah never gave up. She visited Marie every week. She persisted in her encouragement and after a while Marie began to come out of her depression. She began to see that Hannah was right; the time would drag unless she took an interest in something. She'd always enjoyed and done well at her lessons at the convent, so in the months that followed she studied for and passed five 'O' levels. Encouraged, she went on and added two 'A' levels to her achievements. A correspondence course in business management was Hannah's next suggestion. Marie had proved herself to be good at figures, and she found that the idea of ordered planning and organisation excited and fascinated her. As time passed life began to look just a little less bleak.

She served a little over three-quarters of her sentence and on the day of her discharge Hannah was waiting for her at the prison gates. She was driving her eight-year-old red Mini and wearing a big smile as she opened the car's passenger door.

'Guess what. I think I've found you a job.'

'Where?' It was a bitterly cold January day with an icy north wind blowing sleet against the windscreen. As the car pulled out into the main road Marie looked out apprehensively at the traffic speeding frighteningly past. She was preoccupied with the thought that being on the outside was going to take some getting used to.

'It's at the seaside – a little place called Cromer. It's on the east coast. You've always said you liked the sea, haven't you?'

As they drove Hannah told of the family guesthouse she and her parents had visited every summer when she was a child. 'Mr and Mrs Evans were kindness itself, more like an aunt and uncle,' she went on. 'I used to think they were quite old but I don't suppose they could have been more than thirty at the time. I don't know why, but I had a yen to go down there and see them recently. I went for the weekend. Mr Evans was just the same, but his wife died a short while ago. He was saying that he didn't want to give the place up, but didn't know how he would manage without her. That was when I thought of you.'

'Of *me*?' Marie looked at Hannah, apprehension stirring in the pit of her stomach. For all her achievements, her self-confidence was still at a low ebb. Passing exams was one thing. Putting what she had learned into practice, quite another.

'Yes, *yes*.'

'But I don't know anything about the hotel business.'

'Of course you do. You worked in a hotel, didn't you?'

'Only as a chambermaid.'

'It's still experience.'

'I was hardly more than a child,' Marie said. 'It all seems a lifetime away – another world.'

Hannah glanced at her and guessed at the thoughts that were going through her mind.

'No reason why you shouldn't use past experience to help you make a new start,' she said brightly. 'You've got a business management qualification under your belt now, and that's what he needs – someone who can help him manage.'

'A qualification on paper is one thing,' Marie said. 'How do I know that I can do it for real?'

'You don't 'till you try, and now's your chance to find out.' Hannah smiled encouragingly. 'Anyway you can stay at my place tonight and we'll drive up to Norfolk tomorrow, then you can see what you think. If you don't fancy it, fair enough.'

'Does he know?' Marie looked warily at her friend. 'Did you tell him – about me, I mean?'

'Yes. I had to, Marie. You'd want to start with a clean slate, wouldn't you?'

'What did he say? Does he really want to employ a jailbird like me?'

'He's willing to give you a job, Marie,' Hannah said. 'The rest will be up to you.'

Marie looked at Hannah. She was a sturdily built young woman in her early thirties. Her long brown hair was scraped back and fastened with an elastic band, making no concessions to current fashion. She had a rosy, open face and clear blue eyes that always

14

looked directly into those of the person she was talking to. She was the kindest, most honest person Marie had ever known, yet she realised suddenly that although they had known each other for years she knew hardly anything about Hannah at all, whereas Hannah knew almost everything there was to know about her.

'You mentioned your parents just now,' she said. 'You've never spoken of them before.'

'They were killed in a plane crash six years ago,' Hannah told her. 'On their way out to Australia to see Dad's sister. They'd been saving for the trip for years.'

'Oh, God. I'm sorry.'

Hannah's eyes were on the road as she said: 'Having troubles of your own sometimes helps in my job. I believe in looking on the positive side. Everything has one if only you look for it.'

'Is that why you've always been so good to me?' Marie asked quietly.

'No.'

'Why then?'

'Because I believe in you,' Hannah said simply. She turned with her characteristic grin. 'So you'd better be sure not to let me down, eh?'

'Homeleigh' stood in a quiet tree-lined road not far from the seafront at Cromer in Norfolk. The brochure boasted that it was five minutes' walk from the beach, had separate tables in the dining room and wash-hand basins in all bedrooms.

Being the off-season David Evans was busy decorating. He answered the door to them, a white painter's apron tied around his stocky figure. He wore an old cardigan with darned elbows and his greying hair was liberally spattered with flecks of emulsion

15

paint. His kindly face lit with pleasure when he opened the door.

'Hannah, my love. Come along in. And this must be the friend you told me about.' He held out a hand to Marie. 'How do you do, my dear? Welcome to Homeleigh. I'll put the kettle on. Excuse the mess, won't you?' He led the way through a wide hallway draped with dustsheets, to the private regions at the rear of the house. Here Marie found the kind of kitchen she loved, cosy with the warmth from the Aga sitting in its tiled recess. One wall was almost filled with a huge dresser, its shelves filled with blue and white willow pattern plates. In the centre stood a large table.

'Sit you down, both of you,' David said. 'I'll have tea made in no time at all.'

'I hope we're not interrupting your work,' Hannah said.

He turned to grin at her. 'Any excuse to stop for a cuppa. You know me, Hannah, love. At least, you should do by now.' He smiled at Marie. 'When this young lady first came to stay with us she was knee high to a grasshopper,' he said proudly. 'That was our first year. Megan and I had just opened this place. Such plans we had.' He paused thoughtfully as he took a tin of biscuits from the dresser cupboard. 'Thinking about it, I suppose that means it's time I considered retiring,' he said pensively. 'But, do you know, I feel almost as young as I did then.'

'And you don't look a day older,' Hannah said. 'Why should you retire when you obviously enjoy your job?'

'Precisely. Have a biscuit.'

After tea David showed them over the house. There were fourteen bedrooms on the two floors above, a large lounge and a spacious dining room on the ground floor, as well as the kitchen and breakfast room and another tiny room which David used as an office. On the very top floor were three attic bedrooms.

'These are what I call our summer quarters,' he explained. 'Not good enough to let so we've always used them ourselves in the high season. Megan and I used the big one and the other two are for staff.'

Marie peeped into the quaint little rooms with their sloping ceilings and dormer windows. A bedroom like this of her very own would be sheer luxury to her. Even the smallest was bigger than the room she had at the hotel back home. She loved the house with its air of faded Edwardian grandeur, and David Evans was so kind, just the kind of man she had always fondly imagined her father might have been.

Hannah was looking at her. 'Well, what do you think? Will you take the job?'

Marie blushed. 'That's for Mr Evans to say.'

He laughed. 'If you'll come and work for me I'll be delighted,' he said. 'I can't pay you a great deal, but you'll have your own room and I'm not a bad cook, though I do say it myself.'

'I'll vouch for that,' Hannah said with a smile.

'You can have the use of the car too, if you drive of course,' David went on. 'But before you decide anything I think you'd better look at the mess I've made of the books first.'

As it turned out David Evans was right. The one year he'd run the place on his own seemed to have been pretty chaotic. On her first evening at 'Homeleigh' Marie went through the books carefully, reflecting that it was no wonder he found himself unable to retire. In the whole of the previous year he'd made hardly any profit at all.

'You don't charge much, do you?' she observed.

David laughed. 'Wouldn't be much point. I'd find the place empty if I put up the charges.' He sighed. 'You see, people have started to expect much more than they used to when they go on holiday. The newer hotels have extras like private bathrooms, or at least en-suite showers.' He cocked a quizzical eyebrow at her. 'People bathe much more often than they used to, you know. The weekly tub is a thing of the past. They don't want to queue up for a communal bathroom any more. Anyway, if they did it would take too long. We'd never get them down to breakfast. When you're running with a small staff time and routine are important.'

Marie took in all that David told her. She didn't say anything at the time, but she stored it all up to think about later as she lay in her snug little room under the eaves.

For the first two weeks she helped David finish the decorating and spring cleaning. They got along well and worked together harmoniously. David found Marie hard-working and willing to turn her hand to anything; she in her turn found him easy-going and pleasant. He made no mention of her past and it wasn't until she'd been there a week that she was able to steel herself to bring it up herself. They'd just finished their evening meal when she finally found the courage.

'Hannah told you about me – what happened?'

'Yes.'

'If there's anything you want to ask me about it, please do. You've a right to know,' Marie said.

David shook his head. 'Hannah told me that she's never doubted your innocence. If that's what she believes, it's good enough for me.'

'You're very kind.' Marie's throat thickened. 'She told you about – about the babies too?'

'Yes, love. She told me. And I'm very sorry. It seems so cruel. He must have been a very wicked man to do that to you. You little more than a child at the time too.'

Marie got up from the table, afraid that she might cry and make a fool of herself. 'It's over. I have to put it behind me – make a new start. I just wanted you to feel free to ask me about it, that's all. I'll put the kettle on, shall I?'

'You should go out,' David told her thoughtfully. 'Make some friends of your own age. You shouldn't be around an old man all the time.'

Marie laughed. 'You're not old.'

'I've got a son a good ten years older than you.'

Marie looked at him in surprise. 'A son? Hannah never mentioned him.'

'She wouldn't. I don't think she ever met him. I was married twice, you see. Very young the first time. Ralph was only three when the marriage broke up. He stayed with his mother, of course. Meg and I never had any family.'

'So where is your son now? Do you see him?'

'He's in the regular army,' David told her. 'I used to see him now and again when he was younger, but since he went into the service we've lost touch a bit. His mother died five years ago. I haven't seen him at all since then.'

'I daresay you'd have liked him to join you here in the business?'

David shook his head. 'This is no life for a young man. The army now . . .' He smiled reminiscently. 'I was in the army, you know. The war was on then. I went in almost straight from school.' He smiled. 'That was where I learned to cook.'

'Really?'

'When I came out after the war I decided to make a

19

career of it. Army cooking was pretty basic, as you can imagine, so I had to train. I've worked under some of the best chefs in the country in my time.'

'I'm not surprised. You're certainly a super cook.' Marie stirred her tea thoughtfully. 'David, I've been meaning to talk to you. You said the summer bookings would soon start to come in. We're into March now and they aren't coming very fast.'

'I know.' He sighed. 'I've been trying not to think about it, but I'm very much afraid this might be the last season for "Homeleigh". People have been going abroad for holidays these last few years – standards have been going up. They expect more now, and they can pay for it. Places like "Homeleigh" just aren't posh enough any more. After this summer I might have to sell up.'

'If you'll excuse me, I think you're wrong.' Marie leaned forward, suddenly confident. 'I've worked in a big hotel and I'm sure there are lots of people who like to stay in a small, friendly place like this, where they can get personal service. They'd have to go a long way to find a friendly atmosphere and food as good as you provide here. Even if you charged twice as much you'd still be cheaper than the hotels on the seafront.'

David was amused; pleased too that the girl should take such an interest in the business after such a short time. 'But we're not on the front, are we? And let's face it, we can't give them the same services, however much we might want to.'

'We could go more than halfway towards it.'

David's eyebrows rose. Marie, usually so shy and diffident, was suddenly animated and alive. There was a glint in her eyes and her pale cheeks glowed with sudden colour as she leaned eagerly towards him across the table.

'So what would you suggest?' he invited.

'Well, you're probably thinking I've got a cheek, talking to you like this, but I've been doing a lot of thinking.'

'I don't think it's a cheek at all. Please go on,' David prompted.

'Well . . .' She leaned her elbows on the table. 'Some of the bedrooms on the first floor are huge. Much larger than necessary. Why not have part of each made into a bathroom? Then, on the second floor, there are three doubles and three singles. Turn the singles into bathrooms. I know it would mean fewer rooms to let,' she went on, anticipating his next question, 'but you could charge more for rooms with private bathrooms.'

'I daresay, but where is the money to come from for all this work?'

'Maybe the bank would lend you some,' Marie suggested tentatively.

'Maybe it would.'

'And you needn't do it all at once. Do the first floor and see how it goes.'

'Any more ideas?'

'Well, yes. I've been looking round the town – finding out what the big hotels charge and what they give their customers for the money.' She fetched her handbag and took out several brochures. 'Look, most of them do half board nowadays. You do lunch *and* dinner. If you did breakfast and a good meal in the evening – maybe with a couple of choices on the menu – you'd save quite a bit both in time and money. People with children probably like to stay on the beach all day anyway.'

'Point taken. Anything else?'

Marie bit her lip. Was she overstepping the mark? 'Well, there are all sorts of things. Morning tea, for

21

instance. If you put tea-making machines in the rooms you wouldn't have to toil up the stairs with trays of morning tea. Then eventually you could put in TV sets.'

David's lips were twitching. 'Anything else?'

'A reception desk in the hall – just a small one where guests could check in and out and pay their bills. There's plenty of room and it would make the place look more professional.'

'You've really thought it all out, haven't you?' David said, impressed in spite of his amusement. 'I'd like to think about all this. Tell me all of it again and I'll write it down.'

'No need.' Marie took a notebook out of her bag. 'I've done it for you. I've costed it all roughly too and made a few notes. I even enquired about the cost of the alterations. The rooms already have the plumbing, so it wouldn't be too bad. Of course . . .' She bit her lip. 'You might need planning permission, I don't really know, but that shouldn't be a problem. I'll make enquiries about that too if you like.'

David took the notebook from her and looked in admiration at the neat figures. That night he went to bed with a feeling of tingling excitement and an interest in the business that he hadn't felt for years. He was beginning to think that Hannah Brown had done him a bigger favour than she knew. He'd found a treasure in Marie O'Connor.

Chapter 2

Leah walked in the Mayoral procession, her eyes demurely downcast. She wore a cream linen jacket over a citrus yellow silk skirt and top and her long dark hair was dressed in a sleek French plait.

It was ten years since she had walked in the procession for the first time. At eight years old it had been a special occasion and fun. She'd walked proudly, her head held high, convinced that everyone had turned out just to see her. She'd been with Jack and Hilary Dobson just six months then. They'd adopted her two years after the tragic death of their only child in a road accident, mainly – and misguidedly – because she bore an almost uncanny resemblance to their daughter. She'd worn a cream straw hat and a pale blue voile dress for that first Mayoral procession. She'd never had anything so nice in all of her life and she'd thoroughly enjoyed herself. But that had been before she'd discovered the reason why the Dobsons had adopted her – and the fact that she fell hopelessly and heartbreakingly short of their expectations.

The Mayor-making was a tradition that went back several hundred years in Nenebridge, and over the years Leah's view of it had gradually become cynical and jaundiced. After the Mayor's ceremonial investiture the councillors and their wives and families walked in a long procession from the Town Hall to the parish church for the service of commemoration, and then back again afterwards for wine and canapés in the Council Chamber.

At the front of the procession walked past Mayors wearing robes. Leah's adoptive father, Jack Dobson, was one of these. His smallish stature was flattered by the purple velvet robe trimmed with brown coney fur, making him look almost distinguished. The centre section of the procession was made up of the new councillors, both male and female, looking, in Leah's opinion, self-conscious and rather silly. But, bringing up the rear in regal splendour was the new Mayor, his deputy and entourage. Dennis Mason wore the red, ermine-trimmed robe and foamy lace jabot with a certain panache. The cocked hat suited him too, covering up his shiny bald head, but he wasn't quite corpulent enough to show off the magnificent chain to its full glittering advantage. Leah looked at him with half-closed eyes and amused herself by imagining him wearing it to slice bacon behind the counter of his grocer's shop. Not that he did that any more since the shop had been turned into a supermarket. The bacon, once expertly sliced by his father-in-law wearing a long white apron, now came in hygienic hermetically sealed plastic packs. Nevertheless, the image gave her a certain pleasure.

Glenis Mason, the new Mayoress, was a little bird of a woman in a frumpy green dress and a brown straw hat. The heavy consort's chain hung uneasily about her shoulders, making her look as though she were shackled. People said Dennis had married her for her money, and the shop that had once belonged to her father; it was probably true. Leah certainly couldn't imagine him marrying her for anything else. She tried to visualise them in bed together, limbs entwined in a lusty panting embrace, and had to bite her lips hard to keep from giggling.

Accompanied by the town band, inappropriately playing 'When the Saints Come Marching In', they marched through the streets, passing groups of shoppers who paused to glance in desultory fashion at the pompous display.

As she walked, Leah made up her mind firmly that this year would definitely be the last that she would do this. Last year her father had been Mayor. She'd sworn that would be her last year, but her mother had insisted on her accompanying them this year as the Masons were family friends. She comforted herself with the fact that if she played her cards right next year would see her far away from Nenebridge. There was nothing to stay here for. She'd promised herself some time ago that the moment she was eighteen she would do two things. First she would get herself a job in London – any job that would get her away from Nenebridge and into the heart of things. Then she would set about finding her real mother, something that had been an obsession with her ever since she was old enough to realise that she must have one.

As the years passed she'd grown more and more convinced that the woman who had given her birth must have been someone quite special and different. As a child she fantasised endlessly. In one favourite daydream she saw herself as having been born into an aristocratic family and stolen away by gypsies. In another her mother had been a titled lady who had fallen in love with a woodcutter's son and been driven from her home and inheritance in disgrace. Later she visualised a scenario of even higher melodrama. She was the result of an affair between a poor but

25

beautiful young woman and a member of the royal family. She had royal blood in her veins and should by right carry a title. But her poor mother had been forced to give her up and to live in exile for the rest of her life. One day, she promised herself . . . one day when she had become rich and famous, as she certainly meant to. She would make it her business to uncover the truth. She would find her mother and make it all up to her. She would buy a lovely house by the sea where they would both live happily together forever.

Leah had celebrated her eighteenth birthday last October. Already she had allowed six months to go by without making a start on her grand plan. But she had it all in hand. Oh, yes – she was working on it.

The walk to the church seemed boring and endless. They took the familiar route, over the bridge and along the High Street, past Dennis Mason's 'Qualimarket' where the staff had turned out to watch – it was more than their jobs were worth not to – past Clayton's, the town's one and only department store. Then came the post office, the ironmonger's, the television shop, and finally Woolworths. Leah reckoned that most of the councillors could have walked it in their sleep.

It had been different when she was younger and able to take refuge in her own private daydreams. At past Mayor-makings she'd been many things: a beautiful princess on her way to be married to the richest prince in the world; a tragic French *comtesse* on her way to the guillotine, where she would be rescued at the last minute by a handsome Sydney Carton figure (usually played by her current heart-throb); an Olympic swimmer, returning home in triumph with a dozen gold medals. In those days it had been fun. But as she grew up Leah found that daydreams no longer satisfied her. For some time now she had been restless. She wanted something more substantial than a fantasy world and now that she had come of age she was determined that nothing would stop her getting it.

The years Leah had spent in the children's home had left their mark on her. Year by year she'd seen other children find new families and homes, or kind friends who'd visit and take them out at weekends, but somehow her turn never came. As a child she was small and underweight, with stick-like arms and legs and poker-straight dark hair. Her pixyish little face with its high cheekbones was dominated by the huge dark eyes, and premature disillusionment mixed with longing had turned her expression from wistful and waiflike appeal to glowering sullenness. Within her hearing, someone had once unkindly likened her to a bad-tempered bush baby and prospective parents with images of blonde curls, rosebud mouths and laughing baby blue eyes passed her by without a second glance. She'd been fostered out twice, but on each occasion the family had returned her to the home in a matter of weeks. She was branded 'difficult', 'troublesome' and 'uncooperative', the main objection being that she tried to push out other children in the family and claim all the attention for herself. No one seemed to realise that Leah was starved of love; that all she longed for was just one person to call her own – someone to love, who in return would love and care only for her. They saw her as selfish and spiteful. A self-centred little attention-getter who didn't deserve all the trouble people went to for her. She'd lost count of the number of times that had been said to her.

When Hilary had first seen her she couldn't believe her eyes. The child was so like Fiona, their beloved

27

daughter. Fiona had been the only casualty in a car accident they'd been involved in on their way home from a holiday. She'd died of her injuries after lying in a coma for three weeks. Jack blamed himself mercilessly and the couple mourned their daughter's loss for almost two years before their family doctor had suggested adopting a child to save them both from severe clinical depression.

He'd recommended the children's home and they'd visited the place to oblige him, without enthusiasm, but from the moment Hilary set eyes on Leah her mind was made up, and any misgivings Jack had were quickly forgotten when he saw his wife smile again as she had not smiled since Fiona's death.

Fiona's room had been kept exactly as it was during her short life, with its shelves of toys and books, its sprigged wallpaper, pink carpet and frilly bed cover. Leah could hardly believe her luck. Jack and Hilary were so attentive too, showering her with gifts and treats. Lulled into a false sense of security, Leah revelled in it all. It was only some weeks later that she overheard Hilary telling a friend that although her husband had had misgivings, to her it was 'as though our darling Fiona had come back to us'. Only then did she realise that it was second-hand love – not intended for her but given *through* her to the little girl in the many photographs that were scattered around the house. She hadn't taken much notice of them before and certainly hadn't noticed the likeness to herself. But now she begun to study them, comparing them with her own reflection in the mirror. And it was on the day that she deliberately smashed then jumped on the big one that stood on Hilary's dressing table that the rot began to set in.

'Are you going to send me back?' she asked defiantly after the shocked scolding she'd received.

The reply had been more devastating than anything she had ever experienced. Beside himself with rage, Jack had taken her by the shoulders and shaken her, staring at her with eyes that glittered with hurt and anger.

'We can't take you back,' he'd told her in a voice that grated on her senses like sandpaper. 'We've legally adopted you. You know what that means, don't you? You're our child – our *child*, Leah. You're not, and never will be our daughter, but by God I'll make sure you behave as though you are. The three of us are stuck with each other now and we've got to make the best of it. But what you've just done, my girl, is going to take a lot of forgiving.'

Hilary had protested at Jack's harshness, making an instinctive move to comfort the child, but Leah had held out her hand as though to fend off a blow. 'I don't *want* to be your daughter,' she cried out, her eyes bright with the tears she refused to shed. 'I don't want to be like Fiona. I *hate* your stupid Fiona. I want to be *me*.' The expression in the huge dark eyes made Hilary recoil. She saw only stubborn defiance and ingratitude in the child she had so hoped to make their own. The spiteful reference to her beloved Fiona had cut her to the heart. She turned away with a muffled sob and left the room clinging to her husband's arm. They left Leah there, in the pink, frilly room, closing the door behind them without seeing the hopeless crumpling of the child's face. Their own hurt and disappointment blinded them to the fact that she was desperate for their love, not their forgiveness.

Eventually she was forgiven. In their own way Jack and Hilary tried to make up to her for the sticky beginning to their relationship. They made sure that she wanted for nothing. She was well fed and clothed;

29

well educated. But the love Leah craved so much was the one thing they could never give her. As the years went by she learned to live with it, getting her own back in child-like ways; raiding the fridge for goodies, pilfering the loose change Jack was in the habit of leaving on the dressing table. It was her way of coping until the day when the quest for her own true self could begin.

The church was packed and the procession advanced down the centre aisle to their reserved pews at the front. The congregation turned to look at them, the women curious to see what the councillors' wives were wearing; the men, to see if the councillors they had voted for looked worth their salt. The Town Constable, resplendent in his beribboned knee breeches, placed the mace on its stand beneath the pulpit and the service began.

Leah had taken good care to be on the end of the pew. Glancing to her left she saw that Councillor Tom Clayton was across the aisle from her. She gave him the slow, smouldering smile that she had learned was lethally effective, and was rewarded by the dark red flush that spread up from his neck and into his cheeks above his dark beard.

In the early days Leah grew used to being teased at school – for her smallness and her thinness mainly. Academically she was quite bright and could keep up with the best. She never minded the teasing. It was better than being ignored. As she grew into puberty she became interested in swimming and tennis, both of which helped develop her. By fourteen she had filled out and begun to grow taller. The pinched, triangular little face became heart-shaped; its sharp cheek and jawbones softened; the large eyes now enhanced her face instead of dominating it. With her glossy dark hair and sweeping lashes she had blossomed from an ugly duckling into an attractive teenager, a fact which gave her a great deal of satisfaction. She felt she deserved it.

By fifteen she had developed a slender but shapely figure and it wasn't long before she discovered her sexuality and the appeal she held for the opposite sex. She recognised it as a powerful and potent weapon. Not something to be used carelessly. With a shrewd perception far beyond her years, Leah valued it as an asset, not to be tossed away lightly but stored away to be used later to its full advantage.

Tom Clayton was forty-five. Born and bred in Nenebridge, he had attended the local grammar school and finished his education at the Technical College where he studied commerce. He then joined the staff at his father's department store and learned the business from the bottom up, in the time-honoured way. He'd inherited Clayton's five years ago when his father died. Since then he'd not only brought the Nenebridge shop up to date with his considerable business acumen and flair, but opened two more branches in a nearby town.

At twenty, Tom had married Angela Reed, the daughter of a prosperous local farmer. Angela was five years his senior; a tall, rather gaunt-looking woman whose energies, both emotional and physical, were lavished on the horses she trained and bred. There were those who said that she preferred her horses to her husband and that she had refused to give him any children. She never accompanied Tom to Civic occasions. Next year he would be Deputy Mayor, taking the full office the year after, an achievement which, as all his friends knew, was close to his heart but which Angela clearly and openly despised.

Leah noted Tom's flush with some satisfaction and lowered her eyes to her hymn book. The service droned on, seeming to last for several hours, but at last it was over and time to leave. The Mayor and Councillors were first to leave, filing out, one pew at a time, to walk past the standing congregation, passing the Rector who waited to shake their hands in the porch, finally emerging into the sunshine to pose for the waiting press photographers. Leah contrived to walk out of church with Tom.

'I'm glad you were able to come,' he said quietly as they waited to file past the Rector.

'Wouldn't have missed it for the world. I always enjoy the Mayor-making,' Leah lied, giving him her sultry smile.

'You're looking very attractive this morning, Leah.'

'Thank you. You look very distinguished yourself, though not nearly as distinguished as you will next year in Deputy Mayor's robes.' She glanced up at him under her lashes and noted triumphantly that his cheeks were flushed again.

One of the journalists waiting in the churchyard was Terry Grant. Leah had known Terry for some time. He'd come to her school when she'd won the tennis tournament two years ago, and after he'd interviewed her for the local paper he'd asked her for a date. They'd been seeing each other on and off ever since. Leah liked and admired Terry because he knew where he was going. He had the same single-mindedness as herself. He was the only person to whom she had confided her dreams and plans of the future. Terry had dreams too. His ambition was to be a reporter on a national newspaper. Last autumn he'd been made assistant editor of the local rag and he'd confided to Leah that he meant to leave for pastures new as soon as he felt he had enough experience. He waved across the sea of heads and began to make his way towards her.

'Hi. Enjoying yourself?'

'Get lost, Tel,' she told him out of the corner of her mouth.

He raised an eyebrow at her. 'Oh, charming. I love you too. What's up?'

'I'm busy,' she hissed. 'I thought you were too. Someone else will scoop your story if you're not careful.'

He laughed. 'Call this a story? Now – I bet you could tell a much more interesting one if you chose to.'

'What do you mean?'

He waved a hand round the churchyard. 'All these so-called civic dignitaries. I bet you've got the inside dirt on a few of them.'

Leah smiled sweetly. 'If I had I wouldn't give it to you. I'd be too busy using it myself.'

'Mean little cow, aren't you?' The easy, good-natured banter was typical of their long friendship and they both laughed. Terry looked at her. 'By the way, what did you mean when you said you were busy?'

'Never you mind. Just do me a favour and get lost. The Mayor is looking over here. I'm sure he's dying to be interviewed by the town's most dynamic young reporter.'

'Flattery will get you nowhere.' Terry glanced across at the Mayoral party. 'Mmm, maybe you're right. Cheers, Leah. I'll bell you.

As he walked off Tom quietly rejoined her. 'Is young Grant a friend of yours?'

She glanced up at him. 'Terry? I've known him a long time.'

'Quite a go-ahead young reporter,' Tom said, watching the loose-limbed young man in his jeans and leather jacket thoughtfully as he chatted up the preening Masons. 'Good-looking too.'

'Is he? I can't say I've noticed. Personally I prefer older men.' Leah raised her eyes to his in the way she'd perfected, practising in her room in front of the mirror. It consisted of a suddenly bold, direct and utterly disarming look. The effect on Tom was instant. He was mesmerised. She watched as he ran a finger round the inside of his collar.

'It's warm, isn't it? Shan't be sorry to get back to the Town hall for a drink.'

The Council Chamber with its heavy oak furnishings, crimson velvet drapes and portraits of past Mayors could be stuffy, but today the windows had been thrown open and it was welcomingly cool. Leah took a glass of wine from one of the waitresses and looked around the room. Her parents were busy talking to the Mayor and Mayoress. Suddenly Tom was at her elbow again.

'Can I get you anything?' he asked. 'These little sandwiches look nice.'

'No thanks.' She watched as he helped himself from the silver tray and munched hungrily. 'I expect you'd like to get off home for your lunch,' she observed.

He stopped, his mouth full of half-chewed sandwich. 'Oh lord, is it that obvious? Between you and me I didn't have any breakfast and I'm starving.'

'Poor Tom.' She smiled at him. 'Never mind. I daresay your wife will have a lovely roast waiting for you at home.'

He swallowed. 'Actually she's away for the day at a gymkhana. I was going to drive out somewhere for a pub lunch later.' He glanced surreptitiously round the room. 'I – er – suppose you wouldn't like to join me? Just for the – er – company, of course.'

She flashed him her most brilliant smile. 'Oh, Tom, what a lovely idea. I'll just go and tell my mother.'

He grasped her arm, his eyes anxious. 'No. Wait. It might be better if you didn't mention that you're going with me. You know how tongues wag.'

She nodded conspiratorially. 'Right. I'll just say I'm going to have lunch with a friend. Look, I'll leave now and wait for you in the little car park at the back of the cinema. No one will see you pick me up there.'

'Right.' Tom ran a finger round his collar again. 'It's not that there's anything wrong about it, of course. Just that . . .'

'I know – tongues wag.' She smiled. 'Don't worry, Tom. I'll be discretion itself.'

The car park at the back of the Astoria was deserted apart from a dusty tom cat raiding the dustbins. Leah hadn't been waiting long before Tom's dark blue Jaguar XL bumped across the rutted surface and stopped beside her. He leaned across and opened the passenger door for her. She got in without a word.

The cinema was on the opposite side of the river from the Town Hall which was why Leah had suggested it and, as she had guessed he would, Tom set off smartly, heading south away from the town centre towards the border with Northamptonshire. As they drove she glanced at him. He was quite well preserved for a man in his forties. Studying her parents' contemporaries, she had noticed that women wore much better than men. Men tended to develop paunches and sagging jawlines somewhere around their late-thirties. For some chauvinistic reason they seemed to feel there was no need for them to make the same effort as women to keep their youthful appearance. But Tom was still quite presentable. He was tall and his body appeared quite firm still. He wore good clothes and still had plenty of hair. Even the touches of silver – something a woman of his age would take pains to disguise – were attractive. Leah liked his sharply trimmed beard too. It gave him a slightly rakish air which she found sexy. No, seducing Tom wouldn't be too much of a bore, she decided with a sigh of satisfaction.

They lunched at a tiny thatched pub on the outskirts of a Northamptonshire village. Tom pored fussily over the wine list and eventually chose a light fruity Moselle, pronouncing its name and vintage with panache. He had learned about such things on the course he had taken before he opened the new food hall at Clayton's.

He's showing off, Leah told herself with a secret smile. He was trying to impress her. That was a good sign. As they ate he relaxed visibly and seemed to lose his sheepish air. Afterwards, as they strolled back to the car in the afternoon sunshine, he turned to her.

'It seems a shame to go home. Would you like to go on somewhere else?'

'Fine.' She smiled up at him eagerly, lips slightly parted. 'A walk in the country would be nice.'

Tom nodded eagerly and with not a little relief at her choice. No one would be likely to spot them in the heart of the country.

He drove to a quiet leafy lane and they got out of the car to explore. They found a stream and Tom took off his jacket, spreading it for Leah to sit down under the shade of a willow tree. She slipped her arms out of the cream jacket to reveal the lemon camisole top she wore beneath. It was made of a silky material that clung to her body in a way that made it obvious she wore very little, if anything, underneath. Tom's eyes were drawn as though magnetised to the delicate outline of her breasts. He coloured and looked away hurriedly.

'It's very good of you to keep me company like this.' He pulled at a blade of grass and shredded it thoughtfully. 'I often spend my Sundays alone. Angela is invariably away at shows and gymkhanas.'

'It's not good of me at all,' Leah said boldly, her eyes on his face. 'I didn't come out of kindness. I'm not that virtuous.'

He looked at her, aware of the challenge in the dark eyes. 'Then why did you come?'

She threw back her head and laughed lightly. 'I came because I like you, of course, Tom. You're different.'

'Different?' He was clearly flattered. 'How do you mean? In what way?'

She shrugged. 'You're not stuffy like the others. You're witty – good company.' She gave him a sidelong glance. 'I don't spend my Sunday afternoons with people who bore me,' she added.

'I'm sure you don't.' He looked pleased. 'Though I must say I've never thought of myself as witty.'

'You're sophisticated too,' she told him. 'Not like the awful yobbish boys of my own age. You know how to order food and wines. And what clothes to wear.'

'I'd have thought you'd prefer casual clothes,' he said, thinking of Terry Grant in his skin-tight jeans and leather jacket.

'Oh, Tom.' Leah laughed again. Her neck arched elegantly as she threw back her head and he longed to unplait her hair. To free it from the smooth discipline and see its glossy length tumble luxuriantly down her back. He was struck by the poetic thought that the sound of her laughter was as sweet and silvery as

37

birdsong. She was quite lovely, her lips pink and luscious and her teeth so white and even. He realised he was staring and looked away. Clearing his throat, he said: 'I daresay you'll be leaving Nenebridge soon, to find a job.'

Leah sighed. 'If I can't find one here, yes. There's nothing to keep me here now. What I really want is to be a fashion buyer,' she lied, glancing at him from under her lashes. 'But I'll have to train somewhere and I don't suppose I'd ever get a job like that in Nenebridge.'

Tom's heart began to beat faster. 'There's always Clayton's,' he said rashly. 'We run a day-release training scheme for buyers.'

Her eyes widened in mock incredulity. 'Clayton's? That would be marvellous. Oh, but I wouldn't want to accept any favours just because you and my father are fellow councillors.' She sighed and lay back on the grass, closing her eyes and linking her arms behind her head. 'But don't let's talk about work now. It's heavenly here. Let's just enjoy ourselves.' She opened her eyes and looked up at him. 'Oh, Tom, do relax. You're all tense.' She patted the grass beside her and after a moment's hesitation he lay down beside her.

She smiled. 'There, that's better.' She turned her head to look at him. 'Oh dear, I forgot. I'm spoiling your expensive jacket.' She made to sit up but he reached out a hand to stop her. As he did so his fingers brushed against her and he felt the exciting firmness of one breast. She sank back again slowly, looking at him with eyes huge and limpid and full of promise.

'Leah – oh, Leah. You're so . . .' Leaning over her, he kissed the soft, full lips, hesitantly at first, then, as excitement loosened his inhibitions, with mounting passion till she pushed her hands gently against his chest. At once he released her, shaking his head.

'I'm sorry. I shouldn't – didn't mean . . .'

But she laughed softly. 'I was thinking about the creases in your jacket, silly.' She slipped the garment out from beneath her and reached up to draw him down to her again. When his lips found hers again he found them opening for him eagerly and her little pointed tongue darting provocatively into his mouth. His hand found its way daringly under the loose camisole top and he caught his breath, heart racing, as it closed around one firm, naked breast. After a moment he allowed the hand to travel the length of her body, over the curve of her waist, pausing on one thigh then progressing to hitch up the hem of her skirt.

'No, Tom. Not here – not now.' Leah pushed him away and sat up, stroking her hand over her hair to smooth back the loosened strands.

He flushed hotly and stammered: 'Leah – I'm sorry.'

She put her fingers against his mouth to stifle the apology. 'Don't keep saying it, Tom. There's no need, really.' She looked around, shaking her head. 'It's just that – here, like this . . .'

'I know.' He helped her to her feet and together they brushed the loose grass from their clothes. Leah slipped her hand into his as they walked in silence back to the car. Tom's mind was in a whirl as he held the small, cool hand in his. *Not here – not now*, she had said. Did that mean that at some other time – in some other place . . .? God, but she was gorgeous. And so sexy. He wanted her so badly.

In the car he looked at her. 'You're sure you're not angry?'

She gave him her smouldering smile and reached

out to cup his face and draw it down to hers. Her sharp little teeth teased his lips tantalisingly and she whispered against the corner of his mouth: 'You'll have to let your beard grow a little longer. I'll be getting a terrible tell-tale rash.'

His arms closed around her, drawing her close, and his breath was ragged in her ear. 'When can I see you again? Soon, Leah. Please. It has to be soon.'

'Well – I don't know.'

'About that job . . .'

'I've been looking in the Situations Vacant column in the paper,' she said innocently. 'I'll probably have to move away from Nenebridge to get one.'

'I told you, I can arrange it.'

'Really? I haven't seen Clayton's advertising for staff.'

'Look in the paper next week,' he said, nuzzling her neck hungrily. 'We'll be advertising then.'

She smiled up at him. 'Will you really? Good, then I might apply.'

Chapter 3

1978

David Evans decided to take Marie's advice. After poring for several days over the information she had given him he went to see his bank manager. To his surprise his request for a loan was granted. Mr Shelton, who had advised David and Megan Evans on financial matters ever since they'd first opened 'Homeleigh', agreed that the advent of cheap package Continental holidays had brought about a crisis in the hotel trade in small seaside towns. But he had faith in the traditional British seaside holiday and felt confident that, once the public's appetite for holidays abroad had become jaded, they would gradually drift back to the 'Homeleighs' and the 'Sea Views'. But they would drift back with higher standards. What they would be looking for would be an updated version of what they had enjoyed in earlier years.

'You're right not to be complacent about it,' he told David. 'It's the town's main industry and it's worth a little investment. The local councils all round the coast have recognised the necessity. They are planning to build indoor leisure centres to make up for our unreliable weather. There'll be swimming pools complete with mock waves for the children. Restaurants and coffee bars. Indoor bowling and tennis – everything.' He chuckled. 'No more trailing about in streaming macs with whining children in tow. What you're contemplating fits in well with all that, Mr Evans, and I'm sure it will be worthwhile.'

After that things began to move fast. David found a builder who agreed to convert the rooms on the first floor in time for the coming season. Marie wrote letters to all the 'Homeleigh' regulars, announcing the new refurbishment and enclosing one of the new brochures they had printed.

But once the wheels had been set in motion David began to worry. He was afraid that when they saw the increased prices his regulars might turn elsewhere. But to his surprise and delight they didn't. Bookings began to roll in and very soon 'Homeleigh' was booked solid for the summer season. The new half-board arrangements went well too. Marie even persuaded David to go up to London for a weekend course in Continental cooking so that he could expand his menus.

The summer season that year was a hotelier's dream – week after week of sunny warm weather. The visitors kept coming right through to the end of September and by the time the doors of 'Homeleigh' finally closed for the winter David had paid back his bank loan and put enough money by to refurbish the second floor.

'I owe it all to you,' he told Marie on the day they closed. 'And I want you to take a holiday yourself now. You've deserved it.'

But she would have none of it. 'We've work to do,' she told him. 'There are still the top floor single rooms to convert into bathrooms. It won't be as costly as the first floor and we can do the decorating ourselves.'

David laughed. 'Hang on. I need a holiday first

even if you don't. I'm not as young as I was, remember? And I can actually afford one this year.'

'Then you go and let me get on with things here.'

David had protested but Marie was adamant, insisting that she preferred to be working. She didn't tell him that a holiday would give her too much time to think. All that summer the sight of couples happily holidaying with their children had torn at her heart. Wherever she walked, on the beach or the promenade, she seemed to see children playing: paddling, digging holes in the sand, sailing boats. Each time her heart contracted. They haunted her, those children. Superimposed on all their faces, she saw those of her two little girls, one dark and one fair – her own children. The aching longing for them, that she had been promised would fade, grew stronger and more painful as the time passed. She wondered constantly where they were and what kind of people had adopted them. They would be going to school now? Would they be clever – pretty – gifted in some way perhaps? It never occurred to her that they might still be without families. So many people were childless – wanting to adopt. Surely her little ones would have found caring, loving homes where they would be well provided for. She wished she could see them – just once to satisfy herself that they were happy and that she'd done the right thing in letting them go. And the knowledge that this was impossible only served to deepen the ache in her heart. But Marie never confided any of this to her employer. She owed him a lot and she would repay him in the very best way she could.

The following season was even better than the first. During the winter months while the builders were hard at work on the second floor, Marie studied all the magazines and papers advertising holidays. She contacted them all and negotiated the best terms. She went carefully through the file of past years' bookings, meticulously kept by Megan ever since the Evans had started the business. Making a list of all past visitors, she composed a standard letter and sent a copy, along with one of their new brochures, to each and every one of them. To her delight, more than half of them responded by writing to book. Many of them were now on their own again after bringing up their families and welcomed a return to the quiet homely hotel they had such happy memories of, now refurbished with modern comforts.

Two years later David acquired an acre of land at the rear of the house and built an extension and small swimming pool. Once again it had been Marie's idea. A licence was applied for and granted and a small bar was included in the new extension. It had an intimate, restful atmosphere with soft lighting and comfortable furniture.

'Not everyone wants to go to the pubs where they can't hear themselves think for the juke boxes and the game machines,' Marie pointed out. 'And the older folk and parents with young children would be pleased not to have to go into town for a drink of an evening.'

Once again, David had to admit that she was right.

Marie had been working for David Evans for just six years when 'The Marina' came on the market. It was a rundown hotel at the wrong end of the seafront; a four-storey, wedding cake of a place with a roof of gleaming blue glazed tiles and a wonderful view of the sea from all its balconied front bedrooms. Marie went to look at it on her day off. She stood looking up at the crumbling stucco and rusting wrought iron. The sea air had taken its toll. The name 'Marina', once proudly emblazoned in gilded letters across the sea-facing façade, hung crookedly from corroded nails, and the letter 'M' had fallen off, leaving its outline behind it like a green ghost. But Marie saw past the sad neglect to the rich potential beneath. From the agent's handout she saw that 'The Marina' had forty bedrooms, an impressive entrance hall and a terrace overlooking the sea. Certainly it was badly run down. To Marie's own knowledge it had stood empty for two years. She wondered why.

Making discreet enquiries, she learned that the previous owner had put in a manager who had absconded with the takings. 'The Marina's' rundown state had nothing to do with lack of business. She obtained permission to view and as she went from room to room excitement grew within her like a bubble. She could see enormous possibilities for the place. That evening she went to David with an idea that almost took his breath away.

'Suppose we were to sell "Homeleigh" and buy "The Marina" – do with it what we've done here, only on a larger scale.'

David gasped. It was a gigantic risk; one that terrified him. Marie seemed to have looked into it carefully enough and by now he had come to trust her judgement, but he found the thought of starting all over again at his age daunting to say the least. Looking at her sparkling eyes he wondered how he could refuse without disappointing her.

'I don't know, love,' he said, rubbing his chin. 'It'd be a mighty big project. We don't want to bite off more than we can chew. I'm the wrong side of sixty now, you know. By rights I should be thinking about retiring.'

'But it's such a marvellous opportunity,' she urged him. 'The place is going really cheap.'

'Anyone happen to tell you that the country's economy is in a bad way?' David asked wryly.

'Yes. And that's why this is the right time,' Marie insisted. 'Because of the recession that drift back to British holidays is coming, just as Mr Shelton said it would, and we want to be ready for it, don't we?' When David looked doubtful she asked gently: 'What is it, David? It's more than just your age and the financial risk that's stopping you, isn't it?'

He smiled. She knew him so well, this girl who had come to be as dear as a daughter to him. 'You know how I feel about this place, love,' he said. 'It's more than just a business to me. It's home too. Look, you're bright. You're still in your twenties, and you have a good business head on your shoulders. You could get a good job in hotel management anywhere. Why, at your age you could even take out a mortgage and buy "The Marina" for yourself. I'll even lend you some money if you like. You don't want an old man like me dragging you down. Why don't you just let me retire?'

'Retire?' Marie stared at him incredulously. 'David, you're not old yet. You're still fit and well and you love the hotel business, you know you do. If you retired you'd have to leave here anyway. Sell up and buy a bungalow, spend your days going to the public library and mowing the lawn – is that really what you want?' She leaned towards him in that persuasive way of hers and he knew even then that he was losing the fight.

'All right then,' he said with a resigned smile. 'Let's hear this plan of yours.'

'Right. Well, to begin with, if we bought a place the size of "The Marina" we'd have to employ a full staff, including a chef. You could put your feet up and live

46

comfortably. It'd be a kind of retirement, but you'd still be in the business.' She looked at him. 'I don't want to do it alone, David. I could never leave you. You're my family – the only person I've ever known who didn't let me down.' She covered his hand with hers and looked at him, her dark blue Irish eyes full of appeal. He was deeply touched.

David went along with Marie's plan. They sold 'Homeleigh' at a profit that staggered him, and put all of the money into 'The Marina'. The builder's estimate for the refurbishments caused him many a sleepless night but Marie didn't turn a hair. She was so sure that what they were doing was right. And when at last the work was all finished he had to admit that it had been worthwhile. Newly plastered in gleaming white, with the sign freshly gilded, it looked smart and inviting. On the sea-facing terrace, now sheltered from the elements by a glass roof, coloured umbrellas fluttered like a crop of bright flowers. Inside, all the rooms were tastefully furnished, each with an en-suite bathroom. They had everything from tea-making facilities to hair dryers, and in each of the two honeymoon suites a bottle of champagne waited to welcome the happy couple.

But it was the dining room that was Marie's pride and joy. Situated at the rear of the building it lacked the benefit of a sea view and decoration had posed a problem but Marie had hit on the idea of mirrored walls, which gave the required illusion of space and light. The floor was carpeted in deep blue, and glittering crystal chandeliers, their twinkling light reflected again and again in the mirrors, gave it an ambiance of glamour. Double glass doors opened into it from the lounge where guests sipped their pre-prandial drinks.

It was because she was so proud of the dining room

that Marie hit on the idea of launching 'The Marina's' re-opening with a champagne dinner. David was doubtful about the expense. The project had already cost more than they had bargained for. But Marie convinced him that they would not lose. She invited all the town's most influential people, and journalists – not only from the local press but some from the nationally published magazines they had advertised with during the past years. Not all of them came, but those who did were clearly impressed.

The evening was a great success and was rewarded by a centre-page spread in the local paper and an article in *Leisureways*, the popular holiday magazine. In spite of David's misgivings the two articles brought them enough business to pay for the dinner twice over; but it was the article in *Leisureways* that indirectly brought them a surprising and unexpected visitor, one who – although she didn't realise it at the time – was to have a far-reaching and fateful effect on Marie's future.

She was manning the reception desk herself when he arrived. It was mid-afternoon and the receptionist was taking her break. Marie looked up from typing bills to find a tall broad-shouldered man facing her across the desk. He had a compelling presence and the moment Marie looked into the piercing dark eyes she recognised that here was a man who commanded attention wherever he went.

She smiled. 'Good afternoon. Can I help you?'

'I'm looking for Mr Evans. Mr David Evans.'

Marie lifted the house telephone and began to dial. 'I'll ring and see if he's available. Your name, sir?'

'Ralph Evans. I'm his son.'

'*Oh*!' Shocked, Marie stared at him. 'In that case, I'm sure he'd want . . .' She broke off as David's voice spoke into her ear.

'Hello?'

'David, it's Marie. I'm in Reception. You have a visitor. It's . . .'

Ralph held up his hand, frowning and shaking his head. 'I'd like to surprise him,' he whispered.

But Marie was uneasy. It was some time since David had seen his son. Certainly not in the six years that she had been working for him. It could come as quite a shock. At the other end of the telephone, puzzled by the long silence, David asked: 'Is everything all right down there, Marie?'

'Yes – yes, fine.'

'Okay, I'm on my way down.'

Marie put down the receiver and looked at Ralph. 'He's coming.' For the first time she looked properly at Ralph Evans, her employer's son. He wore civilian clothes, a tweed jacket, well-cut trousers and expensive-looking casual shoes, yet he failed to look relaxed in them. Marie felt instinctively that he would feel and look happier in uniform. He was handsome in a dark, slightly predatory way, with thick curling dark hair and a well-trimmed moustache. She observed that he wasn't in the least like his father, either in looks or stature.

'Would you like to take a seat over there, Mr Evans?' she invited. 'Frankly, I don't feel surprising your father is a good idea. I think I should warn him. It's been some time since he's seen you, hasn't it?'

'He's all right, isn't he?'

'Oh, yes, he's fine. I just think it would be kinder.'

His brows came together and for a moment she thought he was going to ask her what business it was of hers. Then he seemed to change his mind. With a shrug he walked across the reception lounge, picked up a magazine and sat down behind a bank of leafy plants. A moment later the lift doors opened and

David emerged. He looked around the reception hall then looked at Marie enquiringly.

'David.' She leaned across the desk. 'This may be a slight shock for you. A pleasant one I'm sure. Your visitor – it's your son.'

David's eyes widened. 'Ralph? Here? But – how?'

'I read the article about you in *Leisureways*. In the dentist's, of all places, would you believe?' Ralph stood up and began to walk towards them. 'It made me feel guilty for losing touch – for letting things slide between us, Dad. I had some leave due, so I thought I'd come and see you.'

Almost beside himself with delight, David grasped his son's hand and shook it warmly. '*Ralph* – Ralph, my boy. It's good to see you. You must come upstairs. Have you had lunch? Have you booked in anywhere? You must stay here of course, mustn't he, Marie?' She and Ralph exchanged a look and smiled warily at each other.

Suddenly David stopped speaking, looking from one to the other. 'Ralph, I'm sorry, I haven't introduced you properly. This is Marie. She's my right-hand woman. If it wasn't for her I'd be . . .' He laughed. 'Heaven only knows where I'd be by now. On the dole most likely.'

Ralph's eyebrows rose a fraction and he eyed Marie with a grudging respect. Up till now he'd taken her for a receptionist, and a slightly officious one at that. Holding out his hand, he said: 'Well, glad to know you, Marie. We must have a talk. I can't wait to hear the inside story of this new venture you and Dad have embarked on.' He looked around him with approval. 'I must say I'm impressed.'

Marie glowed with pride. 'Well, we like it, but then we're a little bit prejudiced.'

'It's all her work,' David put in generously. 'The

credit is all Marie's.' He took his son's arm and led him towards the lift. 'Come upstairs to the flat, son.' Over his shoulder he said to Marie: 'When Jenny comes back from her break you will join us, won't you?'

She nodded, lifting the telephone. 'I'll have some tea sent up for you and I'll be up as soon as I can.'

When Marie joined them in the flat on the top floor, David and Ralph were chatting as though they'd been together only last week. The prodigal's return, she thought to herself. To her surprise she felt a pang of something approaching jealousy. Much as she loved him, David was not her father, he was Ralph's, and blood was thicker than water, in spite of neglect. But as soon as he saw her David drew her warmly into the conversation, making her resentment quickly fade away.

'You'll never guess what,' he said excitedly. 'Ralph is leaving the army. He has just three more months to serve and then he'll be looking for a job. I've told him he must come and work with us, mustn't he?'

Must he? Marie saw no earthly reason why. She looked from father to son and back again. Quick to sense her resentment, Ralph laughed.

'I don't think your—partner shares your enthusiasm, Dad,' he said.

The slight hesitation before the word 'partner' and the speculative way he looked at her made her cheeks burn. The dark eyes seemed to strip her of everything. It was as though she stood before him, not only naked but transparent too; as though he saw right through her and knew everything there was to know about her – and more.

'Oh, n-no,' she stammered. 'I was just surprised, that's all.'

'With the season just starting we need all the help

we can get,' David hurried on. 'Another pair of hands won't come amiss, eh?'

'No. No, of course not.' But Marie was put out. They had engaged all the staff they needed, discussing each appointment thoroughly. Their first season's budget was balanced on a knife-edge. With the loan to pay back and some of the bills still outstanding, this year they'd be lucky to break even. That David should impulsively offer his son a job – especially when there *was* no job – irked her more than a little. To hide her flushed cheeks she bent forward to pour the tea.

'You're Irish, aren't you?'

Her head snapped up at Ralph's sudden observation. 'Yes. But I haven't lived there for a long time. I thought I'd lost my accent.'

'You have – almost.' Ralph smiled at her, his eyes narrowing like a cat's. 'But I've been serving in Ireland for several years, so you see I have the advantage of being specially attuned to it.'

'What part of Ireland?' As she passed David a cup it took all of her control to keep her hand from shaking.

'Belfast – with the military police. And I'll be glad to wave it goodbye, I can tell you.'

'It can't be easy, being a British soldier there.'

Ralph smiled again, and the hard, dark eyes suddenly warmed and melted, totally disarming her. 'Don't worry, Marie,' he said softly. 'I shan't be taking up Dad's offer of a job. I've already got one lined up. I'm off up to London tomorrow to make the final arrangements.'

'Oh, but I wasn't – I didn't mean . . .'

He reached out to pat her arm. 'You have Dad's business interests at heart. I can see that. No doubt it would have upset your book keeping. I understand.'

Marie glanced surreptitiously at her watch. 'You'll stay for dinner though – and for the night? We do have room.'

'Of course he will,' David put in. 'I've already made sure of that. We shall all dine together.'

'And afterwards you two must go out for a drink together,' she added, eager to compensate for the gaffe she had made. 'You must have so much to say to each other.'

Ralph Evans was impressed with everything he saw that evening. It was early in the season and the hotel was only about half full, but everything, from his comfortable, well-appointed room with its little wrought-iron balcony overlooking the sea to the excellent dinner the three of them shared, made it clear that his father was on to a winner. It was also clear to Ralph that Marie O'Connor was the brains behind it all.

Later, as he sat beside David in the car, he said: 'So all this success of yours is down to Miss O'Connor?'

David smiled proudly. 'It certainly is.'

Ralph looked at his father speculatively. 'Last time I came to visit you were running that little boarding house place.'

David nodded. 'And I'd have been there now if someone hadn't come along to give me a much needed shot in the arm. Business was falling off alarmingly after Megan died and when Marie came to work for me she made me realise that I had to do something drastic to save this place from going under. We refurbished and extended "Homeleigh", built it up as a very profitable small hotel. Then Marie found "The Marina". It was rundown and neglected – going at a bargain price, so we sold up and took a chance on it.'

Ralph was silent. 'You make it all sound very simple and straightforward,' he said. 'I suspect there was a lot more careful organisation to it than you say.'

David nodded, his eyes on the road. 'You're right there. Marie's got a good business head and she's young – ready to take risks.'

Take them with someone else's money, Ralph mused. Unless . . . He watched his father's profile thoughtfully. 'I hope you won't take exception to me asking, Dad, but just what is your relationship with Marie?'

David shot him a startled look. 'Good God, there's nothing like *that* between us. Marie came along needing a job and a home just when I needed help. As it happened we suited each other down to the ground – business-wise, I mean.' He smiled wryly. 'I suspect I got the better side of the deal though. I don't know what I would have done without her.'

They drove in silence for a while then Ralph said: 'You referred to her as your right-hand woman. Am I to take it that she has a financial interest in the business?'

'No. Marie hasn't any money except what I pay her. But it is something I've been thinking about a lot lately,' David said. 'She's invested more than mere cash into my business. Maybe I should make her position more attractive before someone tempts her away with a better offer.'

Sitting in the quiet lounge bar of a small pub later with drinks before them on the table, Ralph asked: 'Tell me – how did you find Marie? After all, she isn't a local girl.'

David took a long pull of his beer. 'It was through a girl who used to come for holidays at "Homeleigh" with her parents when she was a kiddie. She came down for a weekend on her own. I happened to mention that I needed someone and she suggested Marie.'

'I see. I take it she was a friend of hers?'

'That's right. Hannah is a social worker.' David was a little uneasy, wondering if he had said too much. Could Ralph possibly suspect something about Marie's past? After all, he had been in Ireland for some time. He shook off his anxiety. Old habits died hard, he told himself. Once a policeman, always a policeman.

'You're quite sure you wouldn't like to work with us?' he asked.

Ralph shook his head. 'As I said, I have this job in London lined up. Anyway, you seem very nicely set up for staff at the moment.'

'There's always room for a member of the family,' David said. 'Blood is thicker than water, after all.'

Ralph studied his glass in silence for a moment. 'What kind of work did you have in mind for me, Dad? Barman – porter or something?'

David looked shocked. 'Good heavens, no. Look, I'm getting on a bit now. I'll soon be wanting to take a back seat. It occurs to me that you and Marie would make a good team. Eventually you could run the place together.'

Ralph's eyes flickered with interest, then he shook his head again. 'Better wait and see, eh? I've a feeling that Marie isn't so keen to have me aboard as you are.'

David smiled. 'When I was your age I'd have seen that as a challenge. She's an attractive girl after all.'

Ralph was silent. Marie wasn't his idea of an attractive girl. He liked a woman who dressed in up-to-the-minute fashions; one who wore sexy make-up and had her hair done regularly – put herself out to please a man. But Marie had potential, he'd give her that – naturally blonde hair and good features. She just needed taking in hand . . .

'When we get back, why don't you and she have a chat?' David suggested. 'Ask her to make you some coffee – get to know each other. I'm sure you'll hit it off.'

'And all this business flair. How did you come by that?' Ralph sipped the coffee Marie had made when David made his excuses and retired to bed.

'I took a business management course. I worked in a hotel in Ireland when I was younger.'

'Really, which hotel would that be?'

Marie smiled to hide her uneasiness. 'This is beginning to sound a bit like an interrogation.'

'Forgive me,' Ralph laughed. 'It's habit, I suppose.'

'I didn't know you were in the military police,' she said. 'But then David hasn't talked much to me about you.'

'Fair enough.' Ralph shrugged. 'No reason why he should. We've never been close.'

'But you are the only blood relative he has,' Marie pointed out.

'I've neglected him, you mean?'

'Not at all. I'm glad you came to see him, though. It made his day. Are you planning to see more of him now that your army career is over?'

He gave her the disarming smile she'd experienced earlier. 'Do you think I should?'

'It's not for me to say.'

'I suppose what I'm really asking is, would it bother you?'

She looked at him. 'Why should it?'

'You tell me.' He smiled again. 'I'd like to think that maybe *you'd* quite like to get to know me better.

I might not be such a bad guy once you got me house-trained.'

She laughed in spite of herself. 'I'm sure you're right.'

He regarded her for a moment. 'So – what are your plans, Marie? What do you intend to do with your life?'

She looked surprised. 'Well, this.' She held out her hands. 'I love the hotel business.'

'Will you persuade Dad to expand further then?'

'I'd like to. I'd like to see a chain of hotels around the coast. Small hotels with big hotel service and luxury. That's my dream, I suppose you could say.'

'And will it come true?'

'Who can tell? You never know your luck.'

'I happen to think we all have to make our own luck in this world.' His eyes swept over her in a way that made her blush. 'Do you ever take any time off? Do you have any other interests besides the hotel?'

She looked up in surprise. 'No. Not really.'

'What – no boyfriends?' He shook his head. 'I can hardly believe that.'

'The work and the hours we put in here don't leave much time for a social life.'

'But you should make time.' His eyes held hers. 'You're too young to submerge yourself in work. Letting your youth slip away – wasting yourself – that's a crime.' He moved closer. 'You asked if I'd be seeing more of Dad from now on. I think you can count on it.'

Hot colour burned Marie's face. 'I – I'm sure he'll look forward to that.'

'And you, Marie – will you look forward to seeing me again?'

She turned away and began to gather up the cups. Ralph reached out to touch her arm.

'I've embarrassed you. I had no right, I'm sorry. It's a sure sign that I'm in need of rehabilitating into civilisation.'

'It doesn't matter.'

'Oh yes, it does. I like you, Marie. I admire you too. And I'm grateful for what you've done for my father.'

She was silent, unable to think of a suitable answer.

'I wish we could get to know each other better.' Bending closer, he peered into her eyes. 'So would you like it if I came to visit again?'

'When?'

The dark eyes lit up. 'Ah, that's distinctly encouraging.'

'I only meant, if you come to see your father I'd naturally be happy – for him.'

'I think you know that I'm not talking about Dad now, Marie. I'm talking about us – you and me. As for when, I'm not sure exactly but soon. Because I'd really like to see you again. I mean that.'

'I see.'

He cupped her chin with his hand and turned her face towards his. 'This is where you're supposed to say you'd like to see me too.' He prompted gently. 'But you're too shy, aren't you?'

'I'm not shy – not normally.'

'Then how about telling me how you feel about seeing me again?'

Marie swallowed. Her heart was beating fast. She was so acutely aware of this man standing so close to her.

'Well, Marie?'

'Yes,' she whispered. 'Yes, I'd like to see you again, Ralph. I – I think.'

He bent and kissed her swiftly. 'You think too much. I can see I'll have to take you in hand.'

It's just . . .' She swallowed hard. 'There was someone – once. He . . .'

'Let you down?' Ralph tipped her face up to look into her eyes. 'I'd never let you down, Marie. You can depend on that.'

Alone in her room, Marie scrutinised her face and figure critically in the dressing-table mirror. It seemed a long time since she'd given much thought to her appearance. Ralph had said she was attractive, but she didn't think so. She was too thin for a start, and she didn't bother much with clothes or make-up. Perhaps she should. She turned this way and that. But what sort? Fashion was something she'd never had the chance to learn about. At the convent she'd dressed exactly like all the other little girls. Later as a hotel chambermaid it had been the same. One off-duty dress was all she could afford. Then later – in prison . . . She shuddered and thrust the thought from her, her skin crawling at the memory of the coarse stuff of that uniform and its characteristic smell. Getting into bed quickly, she switched off the light.

Lying in the dark, her thoughts returned to Ralph. There was no denying that he was attractive. In some way she couldn't quite describe, he reminded her of Liam. He didn't look at all like him, but he had a similar personality – the same kind of charisma; charming, funny and exciting, all at the same time. Just the type to sweep a young impressionable girl off her feet. But she wasn't a young girl any more. And Ralph wasn't Liam. Even if he were she'd promised herself long ago that she'd never trust that kind of man again. But Ralph was different. He was no stranger, he was David's son.

A worrying thought occurred to her. If David saw

59

that his son was interested in her, would he tell him about her past? She turned over, telling herself that she was worrying for nothing. Ralph had only been flirting with her. And anyway, David would never betray her confidence. That was the one thing in life that she could be sure of.

Chapter 4

From the moment Mavis and Ken Payne set eyes on Sarah they had been enslaved by her. The baby girl's blue eyes and blonde hair, already showing the promise of curl even at six weeks old, and the tiny, perfect hands and feet were everything they had ever dreamed of. It was almost impossible to believe that she was the twin of the other baby, the little dark monkeyish-looking child who seemed to scream all day long.

The process of adoption was set in motion; the interviews and the research into the finest details of both their backgrounds were carried out while the Paynes waited, hardly daring to hope, through anxious days and sleepless nights. At one stage there had been some doubt about their age. Were they too old to adopt at thirty-two? But finally everything was cleared and the day came when they were allowed to take Sarah home to their trim little semi-detached house in Leicester. It was the proudest day in their lives.

Already the nursery was ready and waiting with its shell pink walls painted by Ken and the rose-sprigged curtains and cot quilt to match that Mavis had spent hours sewing. On the white-painted chest that contained all the baby clothes, collected over the years of hope, a row of soft toys stood to attention, awaiting their new owner.

Mavis laid the baby girl tenderly in the cot and she and Ken stood together, hand in hand, looking down at the unbelievable miracle that was their daughter. This time there would be no disappointment. The circumstances were such that the mother had given her babies up unconditionally at birth. For Mavis and Ken the years of hoping and longing – of painful, embarrassing examinations and tests; of raised hopes and heartbreaking miscarriages – were over and done with. Now they would have a child in their arms at last. And if she wasn't of their blood then she would be of their hearts. No child would ever receive more love than little Sarah. Ken would take snaps of her with his specially bought camera to show proudly round the office, and Mavis would no longer have to envy her sister-in-law Jean her brood of three healthy youngsters. They were parents at last.

Mavis was a little disappointed that Sarah was already christened. She would have liked to have chosen the baby's name herself. She had always favoured Shirley, Marilyn or Cheryl. Sarah was such a plain name, but after discussing it they had decided to compromise and call their daughter Sally. It suited the dainty little girl better than Sarah, they both agreed on that.

Throughout her babyhood Sally Payne was loved and cared for as no other child in the neighbourhood. From picture-book baby she developed into a chubby toddler then into a bright, engaging five-year-old, taking her first wide-eyed look at the world outside the garden gate. Her first day at school was a big adventure for Sally, a traumatic ordeal for Mavis. But the Paynes soon became accustomed to their new status as parents of a schoolgirl.

The happy, rewarding years flew for Ken and Mavis. When Sally was eight they made two important decisions. The first was to tell Sally that she was adopted – news which, much to their relief, she received without a glimmer of distress. The second was to send her to an exclusive private school where she would receive individual attention. This was no small decision for the Paynes. Ken had to put in all the overtime he could in order to pay the fees. For a few years the trim little house at the end of Beech Lee Close went without its bi-annual coat of paint and they postponed the purchase of the new car they had budgeted for, resigning themselves to keeping their five-year-old Consul another year or two. Sally always came first. Ken's sister Jean, on one of her frequent visits from nearby Hinkley, looked sceptical.

'You'll spoil the child,' she warned, repeating her favourite maxim: 'If they've got it in them, it'll come out, I always say. I don't believe in private education. I wouldn't mind betting that half the teachers at that place are unqualified anyway.'

But Mavis and Ken were not to be moved. Mavis was privately of the opinion that Jean was jealous. Her children were all boys with great dirty knees and terrible table manners. None of them had ever been as attractive as Sally, even as tiny babies. They couldn't hold a candle to her. Ken refused to be annoyed by his sister's remarks. He just shook his head good-naturedly.

'She means well,' he told his irate wife after one of Jean's visits. 'She's only trying to help. But we've adopted Sally. She's ours, and it's up to us to do what we feel is the best for her.'

But for Mavis it was more than that. She wanted Sally to be accomplished and talented; to have a brilliant career; to be looked up to and admired – even famous perhaps. She wanted her to achieve all the things she herself had had neither the brain nor the opportunity to achieve. That was her dream for her daughter.

As Sally grew up her promise of beauty was fulfilled. Her hair curled softly and retained its flaxen purity of colour, and her complexion was like milk and roses. From the age of four she had attended ballet classes and music lessons and although she wasn't especially talented at either, she had proved herself proficient. At school she remained in the middle of her class, though Mavis insisted that if she really tried she could have been top.

The Payne family did everything together. In summer they spent a fortnight's holiday at a quiet holiday camp in Cornwall. At Christmas they shared the festivities with Jean, her husband Jim, and their three boys, who grew larger and noisier with each successive year. On weekday evenings Ken helped Sally with her homework and Mavis taught her to knit and sew. On Sundays the three of them attended Chapel, where Mavis took Sunday School and played the organ. For fifteen years life was rewarding and good. Then Sally began to grow up.

The first sign of trouble was when Jason, Jean's youngest, asked Sally to go to a disco with him. Mavis was appalled when a starry-eyed Sally announced that she had a date for the following Friday evening. The moment Sally was out of the way she was on the telephone to her sister-in-law.

'What does your Jason think he's doing, asking a girl of Sally's age to a disco? She's only a child.'

Jean laughed. 'In case you haven't noticed, Mavis, your Sally is growing up fast. She's a very pretty girl. And like it or not, the boys are going to be around in hordes from now on.'

Mavis went hot and cold all over. Surely they'd

brought Sally up to be different from other girls? She loved her home and the quiet things they'd taught her to appreciate. She went prickly with annoyance as she answered crisply: 'Sally isn't one of your dolly birds, Jean. I'm sure she wouldn't like this disco thing anyway. I don't think she even realises what it is.'

'Rubbish! Of course she knows what it is – and she'll love it.' Jean chuckled maddeningly at the other end of the line. 'And, Mavis love, you're a little behind the times if you don't mind my saying so. Dolly birds went out with flared trousers. Let the kids enjoy themselves. They're only young once. Anyway, it's only a little do at the youth club, not some den of iniquity as you seem to think.'

Mavis hung up in disgust.

To her dismay, Mavis found that Jean had been right. Sally knew exactly what a disco was, and she *did* want to go with Jason; she wanted to go very much indeed. So much so that there was quite a scene about it. They had never denied their daughter anything before and the argument devastated them. After she was in bed, Mavis and Ken had a serious talk about it.

'We're going to have to let her go out on her own some day, love,' Ken had pointed out reasonably. But Mavis sat twisting her handkerchief round and round her fingers till it looked like a piece of chewed string.

'The things you read about in the papers nowadays,' she wailed. 'Suppose something awful happened to her?'

'It won't. Look, at least we know Jason, and he's not a bad lad. He's always had a soft spot for our Sally. He'll look after her all right.'

'That motor bike,' Mavis murmured, picturing Jason recklessly taking bends on the wrong side of the road, her precious Sally clinging to the pillion.

Next morning at breakfast they told Sally she could go. But her delight was short-lived when she heard that there were to be conditions. She would not be allowed to be picked up by Jason on his motor bike. Ken would take her to the youth club in the new Ford Escort and he would collect her again at ten o'clock sharp. Sally wailed her protests. The others would all think her a spoiled baby. They'd laugh at her. She'd die of shame. But Ken and Mavis stuck to their guns. It was that or nothing.

But that was only the beginning. Sally loved the disco. It gave her a taste for teenage fun and showed her the freedom that other girls had. When she saw the way the others dressed in their leisure time she refused to wear the home-sewn dresses Mavis made for her any more. As soon as she was old enough she took a Saturday job in a florist's shop and saved up to buy some clothes of her own choosing. The first time she appeared in a tiny flounced ra-ra skirt and low-cut lurex top there was such a fuss that she took to smuggling her party clothes out to a friend's house and changing there before she went out. The strict curfew imposed upon her by her parents earned her the hated nickname of 'Cinderella'. Ken still collected her from discos and parties, patiently waiting outside in the family's blue Ford Escort – derisively labelled The Purple Pumpkin, and killing stonedead any chance of her being walked home by a boy.

As Sally's sixteenth birthday drew nearer Mavis tried to persuade her to put her name down at the Technical College for a typing and shorthand course.

'It's all computing and word processing nowadays, Mum,' Sally told her. 'We've done a bit of that at school and it's *stultifying*.'

It was Sally's current favourite word and it set Mavis's teeth on edge. 'Well, whatever you think it is, it's a good training for a well-paid secretarial job,' she said doggedly. 'Do you have anything better in mind?'

'Yes. Horticulture,' Sally said.

Mavis stared at her. '*What* did you say?'

'Horticulture. Well, floristry really. I've always loved helping Mrs Jessop on Saturdays.'

'Yes, but – that's only a little pin money job, a hobby,' Mavis protested. 'Besides, it's so dirty. You'd get your hands all messed up and break all your fingernails.' She peered at her daughter. Was this just another fad? 'Anyway, what kind of a career could that possibly lead to?'

'I've thought it all out,' Sally said. 'I'd like to have a garden centre or a florist's shop of my own someday. I could hire myself out – go around creating floral displays for hotels and theatres, places like that.' She leaned forward, her arms on the table and her pretty face earnest. 'Look, Mum, I'm not exactly "Brain of Britain", am I? I only passed two of my 'O' levels. And, besides, I really want to do this.'

Mavis gave a lot of thought to Sally's ambition as she prepared the evening meal. It was right enough what she'd said. Sally's exam results had been disappointing. They had hoped she'd stay on for another year and sit them again, but her headmistress hadn't seemed optimistic about further academic success. Maybe she and Ken could save up whilst Sally trained and set her up in a little shop eventually? A business of her own would keep her occupied and out of harm's way. Mavis began to warm to the idea. She didn't really have much to occupy her these days. Maybe she could even work with Sally – help her get the business on its feet.

Later she talked to Ken about it and he agreed; if that was what she really wanted, then Sally should train in floristry. He would look into it. They told her of their decision the following evening after their meal.

'Oh, that's *great*.' Sally jumped up to hug both parents. 'And Mrs Jessop says she'll find a place for me at Floral World in the High Street. I can start as soon as I leave school. She says I've got an eye for colour and design and she isn't interested in "O" levels or boring old crud like that.'

'Just hold your horses a minute.' Ken put on his stern face. 'If you're going to do this, you'll do it properly. Now – I've been along to the careers centre today and had a word. They've given me all the information.' He reached for his briefcase and drew out a prospectus. 'It's a two-year course at the Technical College. You'll take the Society of Florists' Diploma, and a City and Guilds Certificate.'

'Not more *exams*?' Sally wailed. 'It'd be like going back to school for two more years. I couldn't bear it.'

The inevitable argument ensued amidst tearful protests from Sally. She'd cherished fond hopes of leaving school behind her, joining the world of adults and becoming financially independent. Now, as always, her parents were trying to ruin it all for her.

It was quite the worst row they'd ever had, especially when Sally began to see that Ken and Mavis were not going to give in or even compromise this time. Although it hurt them to see her disappointment, they stuck to their guns as they'd promised each other they would. But her angry protests that they were only doing this to her because she wasn't their true child and they didn't want her to have any fun cut them both to the quick.

'You only adopted me because you wanted to make me do the things *you* wanted,' she sobbed. 'You've never trusted me, not even to go to the youth club like other girls do. You can't possibly love me – and I certainly don't love *you*.' Having delivered this crushing parting shot, she slammed the living-room door and ran upstairs sobbing noisily, to shut herself in her room.

Jean, who infuriatingly happened to walk in at the climax of the row, saw it all happening with a smug smile and an 'I told you so' expression. She and Jim had brought the boys up with few restrictions, yet *they* were turning out all right. She'd always known that Ken and Mavis were storing up trouble for themselves, taking on someone else's child and then wrapping the girl in cotton wool like that.

'Hold them too tight and you're asking for trouble,' she said with a shake of her head. 'But then, say what you will,' she added darkly, 'blood will always out.'

Stifling a scream of exasperation, Mavis gave her sister-in-law a red-faced, withering look. 'Oh – *go and boil your head, you smug bitch*!' she shouted as she slammed out of the room.

Chapter 5

The Dobsons had lived in the house in Acacia Grove ever since Jack's printing business had become successful in the early seventies. Jack had gone to work for Joseph Gibson straight from school as a sixteen-year-old apprentice. He'd risen through the firm steadily, finally taking over as manager at the age of thirty-five. Then, when old Joseph Gibson had died and the business had come up for sale, Jack had taken his courage in both hands, taken out a loan and bought the firm out.

Nenebridge was growing and Jack had had the foresight to see it coming right from Britain's entry into the Common Market. Over the past twenty years Nenebridge had developed from a sleepy little East Anglian market town into a hive of small businesses, most of which, in spite of two recessions, had continued to prosper. As a result of EEC restrictions, what had once been a rural area of small holdings and fields of waving wheat had become a sprawl of industrial estates and trading parks. Hilary, the only daughter of a local farmer, had inherited several hundred acres of farmland on her father's death and had sold out to the developers, making herself a considerable fortune. Factories producing everything from agricultural machinery to computers seemed to spring up, mushroom-like, almost overnight, and red-brick and cedarwood housing estates pocked the once idyllic country-side.

Due to Jack's foresight, Dobson's was the only up-to-date printing firm within miles and all the new businesses used them. Jack and Hilary and others like them were made, whilst others – those who'd tried to cling to the old ways – went under.

Twenty-one Acacia Grove had grown from a modest detached villa to what the estate agents described as a 'desirable executive residence'. Over the years the Dobsons had added more rooms at the side and back. Jack's thriving business and, more lately, his Council work had made it necessary to entertain. The garage had been doubled to accommodate Hilary's BMW sports car, and above it Jack had installed a games room with a full-sized snooker table. An elegant pinnacled conservatory full of cane furniture and exotic plants was the latest addition. It opened straight on to a paved terrace with steps down onto a manicured lawn.

Hilary was proud of her beautiful home. She cared for all of it herself, with the help of a daily woman and a man who came to do the rough work in the garden twice a week. She was a small woman, slender and still attractive, younger looking at fifty than most of her contemporaries, a fact which she exploited with secret satisfaction on every opportunity. She had never yearned for a career of her own. When she and Jack had first married they had planned to have a family of at least three children, but Fiona's birth had been difficult and later attempts at increasing their family had come to nothing.

Losing their beloved only child had been an overwhelming tragedy and finding Leah had seemed at first to be the perfect answer. When things hadn't worked out quite as they'd hoped, Hilary had thrown herself wholeheartedly into her position as the wife of one of the town's foremost businessmen and councillors. She campaigned tirelessly at election time and turned her morning room into the ward committee room to monitor the votes on the day. Her year as Mayoress had been a delight. She had carried out her duties with queenly charm and grace and she still basked in the admiration of the townspeople who acknowledged her respectfully when they met her in the street.

Always exquisitely dressed herself, her dark hair expertly cut by a London hairdresser on her monthly shopping trips to Town, Hilary deplored the casual clothes and hairstyles worn by her adopted daughter. Whenever Leah attended formal functions with them, she insisted that the girl dressed in a manner befitting her position.

As she prepared for a dinner party in her gleaming kitchen she thought about Leah. The girl had been a sad disappointment to them. When they had gone in search of a little girl to adopt they should have looked for a totally different child – maybe even one of the opposite sex. Jack had pointed this out at the time, and in restrospect Hilary saw that he was right. But the child had looked so uncannily like Fiona that she had found her totally irresistible. They had been acquainted with the child's background, of course, and this had made Jack even more doubtful. But hearing of the tragic circumstances in which Leah had been born had only made Hilary all the surer that they and the child were destined for each other.

Sadly, things had not worked out as they had hoped. Almost from the very beginning Leah had proved difficult and uncooperative. As a small child she threw tantrums, lied and stole things she need only have asked for. Even now she took everything for granted and was far from grateful for the many advantages they had given her. Not that Hilary wasn't fond of Leah. One couldn't raise a child, care for her for twelve years and nurse her through all the childhood ills without growing attached. It was just that she couldn't help but know deep in her heart that Fiona would have turned out so very differently. She cared about Leah's future, of course. She wanted what was best for her. The trouble was that Hilary's idea of what was best and Leah's didn't match.

The girl had always seemed to live in a world of her own, but lately she had become worryingly secretive. She went in and out as though the house was an hotel, never saying where she was going or with whom; it was something that Hilary was quite sure Fiona would never have done. But there, Leah was not Fiona and never would be, she told herself with a sigh.

She was pleased with Leah's looks at least. She had blossomed into a very attractive girl. The scowling, pinched look she had worn as a child had gone. Obviously she was more confident now that she had emerged from the 'ugly duckling' stage. And getting the position of trainee buyer at Clayton's must surely make a difference. Tom would keep an eye on her, Hilary told herself with a smile. Maybe they would make something of her yet. She slipped the crown roast into the oven and turned her attention to the creme brûlée.

'So you didn't fancy eating with your folks tonight?' Terry slipped another compact disc into the machine and Simply Red filled the room with rich sound. He poured more wine into Leah's glass and pushed aside the foil dishes which had contained their take-away meal.

'God, no. Executive dinner party – bor-*ing*.' She leaned back in her chair and stretched her arms out.

'So I get to enjoy the pleasure of your company instead.' Terry grinned good-naturedly. He glanced at his watch. 'I can't be any later than half-past nine, mind. I've got to drive over to cover a programme of wrestling in Peterborough. A local lad is having his first bout there.'

'That's okay. You can drop me off on the way. By then they should be busy having their coffee and I can slip upstairs unnoticed.'

Terry laughed. 'Anyone interesting there?'

Leah pulled a face. 'The Claytons: Tom, my boss and Angela the amazing talking horse. Their Worships the Mayor and Mayoress, and the Thompsons.'

Terry raised an eyebrow. 'Who're the Thompsons?'

'Bill and Janet Thompson. They live next-door – moved in about a month ago.'

Light dawned on Terry's face. 'Oh, *that* Thompson. He's my landlord.' He threw out an arm to encompass the eighteen by twelve room he called home. 'Rumour has it that he owns most of this street – left to him by his grandfather. Savemore Supermarkets have bought the site from him. He's made a fortune out of it.'

'Really?'

'Oh, yes. I'm expecting my notice to quit any week now.' Terry poured the last of the wine into his glass thoughtfully. 'As a matter of fact there was a rumour about an overturned preservation order, and a public outcry about building a hypermarket this close to the town centre. I thought I was on to something big a couple of months back. A buzz about a backhander to

75

the chairman of the planning committee when the plans went through unopposed in a hurry. But needless to say I couldn't get enough concrete evidence on it to persuade my editor to print. Even sworn enemies close ranks on issues like that.' He raised an eyebrow at her. 'What are they like – the Thompsons?'

'Jumped up and boring. They've only been invited because another couple dropped out at the last minute and Hilary needed to make up the numbers. You should have seen Mrs T's face when I went round with the invitation. She practically *wet* herself with excitement. She didn't even notice Hilary's deliberate slight in not inviting her personally.'

'Surely there was someone else she could have asked from her elevated circle of friends. Why the Thompsons?' Terry asked.

'Short notice,' Leah said succinctly. 'Besides, don't you know that the next best thing to a VIP is someone who thinks *you* are one? It's all to impress. That's Hilary's favourite pastime. She never loses an opportunity to queen it over people.'

'You're a bit hard on them, aren't you?'

'They deserve it. Actually I think Bill Thompson is hoping to put up for the council at the next election. The snag is that Janet – *isn't*, Mrs Thompson, if you see what I mean.'

'You mean they aren't married?'

'Precisely.'

Terry raised an eyebrow. 'So?'

Leah sighed. 'This is Nenebridge, Tel. You should know by now that unless you follow the rules here, the big boys won't let you play.'

'So maybe he'll make an honest woman of her in the nick of time.'

'I don't think so. Rumour has it that the rightful

Mrs T is clinging like a leech.' She grinned at him. 'Makes sense in view of the packet he's picked up for this crumbling heap, doesn't it?'

'Watch it. You're talking of the slum I call home.' Terry laughed but Leah looked suddenly depressed.

'Oh, Tel, I've got to get out of this place soon. It's driving me bananas. It's like living in a time warp. The town is growing all the time, it's turning into a modern industrial city but they won't face up to it. They're letting it happen – cashing in on it even – but they're all still parading around in fancy dress just as their ancestors did a hundred years ago.'

Terry drank the last of the wine and looked at her wryly. 'It's what's known as tradition, love. It's what gives the place its unique character.'

'It looks more like hypocrisy to me, and they can have it as far as I'm concerned.'

Terry's flat was little more than a bedsit. It was on the top floor of one of a street of mouldering Victorian houses on the wrong side of the river. A curtained alcove contained primitive cooking arrangements, whilst the rest of the room formed his living area. There was a bed, two armchairs, two dining chairs and a gate-legged table. Under the dormer window stood Terry's most prized possession, his compact disc player, and next to that stood a card table holding the battered typewriter on which he hammered out his copy. Compared to Leah's luxurious room in Acacia Grove it was depressingly shabby. The room was so dark that it was necessary to have the light on all day; it was un-warmable in winter, hot and stuffy in summer. But in spite of all its drawbacks, Leah would cheerfully have swapped places with him any time. She knew that material things meant nothing to Terry. At least not for the present. He knew where he was going. He had talent and ambition and he'd get there in the end. One day he'd be able to afford luxuries, but it would be because he'd earned them – because of who he was and what he'd achieved. Leah admired and envied him.

'You can't imagine what it's like,' she said pensively. 'All that pretentious socialising; all that dressing up and putting on an act. No one ever really *knows* anyone else. They all gossip behind each other's backs and there's no such thing as real friendship.'

'Feeling as you do I can't understand why you took that job at Clayton's,' Terry said. 'Why didn't you look for a job somewhere else? Look, tell you what, if you're really fed up you can move in here with me.' He grinned at her. 'It's only a single bed but it could be cosy – and kind of interesting.'

Leah sighed, ignoring his offer, which she knew was more than half serious. 'I've got to get myself trained for something first, haven't I? That's why I applied for the job at Clayton's. It's just that it all seems to take so long. I get fed up with waiting sometimes, but once I can get myself to London it'll all start happening. I know it will.'

Terry looked at her, recognising the slightly obsessive look in her eyes. He'd seen it many times before. 'Why London?' he asked. 'There are plenty of nice cities.'

She lifted her shoulders. 'It's the hub, isn't it? The centre of everything. Anything you're looking for starts from there.'

'I see.' He nodded understandingly. 'You're still planning to find your real mother then?'

'Of course.' Her eyes focused on his face. 'She's got to be out there somewhere, and I've got this really strong feeling that she wants me to find her.'

He reached out to touch her hand, his blue eyes concerned. 'Look, Leah, she might not want you to find her. She might not even *be* out there. She could be dead or she may have gone abroad – married and had ten more kids. Anything. Anyway, why are you so obsessed with finding her? You're *you*, nothing can change that.'

She got up and walked restlessly to the window. 'You don't understand, Tel. I don't belong here. I don't belong anywhere. I never have. Jack and Hilary didn't want me, they wanted Fiona back. They tried to turn me into her and it didn't work. They should have left me where I was.'

He got up and came to stand behind her. 'They've tried to give you every opportunity, Leah,' he said gently. 'You've got things other girls'd kill for.'

'They've never given me love, Terry,' she said quietly. 'They've never made me feel wanted. Sometimes I think they hate me – just for not being like their precious Fiona.'

'There'll be plenty of people wanting to love you, Leah.' He wanted to add: *If you'll only let them*, but he knew better than to spoil things between them. Leah needed him as a friend and that was better than nothing – for the time being at any rate. Putting his hands on her shoulders, he turned her towards him. 'Look, sweetheart, maybe your own mum didn't want you either. If she had . . .'

She looked up at him, her eyes huge, dark and swimming with hurt. 'Don't say that. She did want me. She *must* have. If people don't want babies they have them aborted, don't they? No one has to have a baby they don't want in this day and age. Something awful must have happened to her. She *thinks* about me, I know she does, I can feel it, and I'm going to find her if it's the last thing I do.'

He pulled her against him and held her tenderly. 'Of course you are. I'm sorry, love. I don't mean to pour cold water on your dreams. It's just that I don't want you to devote your whole life to something that may not be worth it.' He pulled her down to sit beside him on the narrow bed. 'Look – my mum walked out on my dad and me when I was nine. Nothing terrible happened to her, unless you count boredom. She had a good man, a kid who needed her and a decent home – even though it was a council house. Okay, I used to cry for her sometimes as a kid, but I grew out of it and I've never wanted her back. In my book a woman like that isn't worth losing any sleep over.'

'But you still had your father,' Leah argued. 'You had someone to belong to. You had each other. Right?'

The look in her eyes disturbed him slightly and he looked away.

'Well, yes, but . . .'

'Don't you see, *I* don't know what it is to have that special kind of love,' she told him quietly. 'Real unconditional love, I'm talking about. Not the kind you only get if you've been good. Having someone who's on your side even when you're wrong.' She glanced at him. 'And I don't mean sex either. That demands more back than it gives. There's only one person who can ever give you that special kind of love, and I mean to find her, no matter what.' She pushed him gently away and sat up very straight, her eyes dreamy. 'I have this feeling about her. I've always had it. She's different and special, and I have her blood in my veins.'

'You want to know who you are,' Terry said. 'That's what you're really saying. You can do that without finding your mother, you know.' She shook her head impatiently and he went on: 'Look, Leah, all

I'm saying is that you might be disappointed. Suppose she's someone you wouldn't want to know? Suppose she doesn't want to know *you*? There are all kinds of pitfalls to what you're planning to do, you know.'

But Leah was shaking her head. 'Ever since I was little I've known – just *known*, Tel, that there was something unusual in my background. I need to find out – to find *her*. I need to know.'

He nodded resignedly. 'All right then. I can see there's no changing your mind, so if there's anything I can do to help . . . *Hey*, don't strangle me.' He laughed as Leah threw her arms around his neck and hugged him hard.

'Terry Grant, you're beautiful,' she announced. 'You're the nearest thing I've ever had to a real live brother.'

'You're beautiful too.' He held her away from him, smiling down at her wistfully. 'And that's the biggest, back-handed-est compliment I've ever had.'

It was half-past nine when Terry dropped Leah off at the corner of Acacia Grove. It was a warm June evening and the scent of dewdrenched honeysuckle and newly mown lawns filled the air evocatively. He watched for a moment from the bright green 2CV as she swung down the tree-lined road in her jeans and tee-shirt, her denim jacket slung over one shoulder and her long dark hair swinging loose. On the outside she looked so confident, so cool and self-assured; the side of herself that she presented to the world. Terry believed that only he was privileged to know the real Leah; lost and bewildered, alone and yearning for that special love she'd spoken of. He thought about the remark she had made about sex: *It demands more back than it gives*. It was an oddly cynical remark for someone so young. As he slipped the car into gear and headed back towards the main road he allowed himself to dwell briefly on what it would be like if their relationship grew to be more than platonic. He sighed. Little chance of that. Leah saw him more as a older brother and friend. Still – maybe one day. In the meantime he was touched by her trust; grateful for it too. It was something not too many rising newspaper reporters could boast of. Leah and he were two of a kind and he promised himself that he would never betray her trust.

Leah climbed the stairs to her room as quietly as she could. She could hear the muted buzz of voices coming from the lounge, and through the half-open door of the dining room could see the debris of the meal on the table, awaiting the arrival of Mrs Lamb tomorrow morning. Hilary would probably stack the dishwasher herself and switch it on before she went to bed, if she wasn't too tired. Mrs Lamb would do the rest.

   Leah closed the door of her room with a sigh and threw herself down on the bed. The pink frills she had inherited from Fiona had long since gone. The room was now starkly plain: white walls with one or two pop posters; a plain blue duvet cover and blue velvet curtains. There had been various styles of decoration during the twelve years she had occupied the room. With a mischievous grin she recalled her punk phase. The time when she had decorated the room herself whilst Jack and Hilary were celebrating their wedding anniversary with a weekend in Paris. They had returned to find she had painted the walls in matt black paint and hung up old posters of the Sex Pistols. Hilary had almost had hysterics when she saw it and Jack had been white-faced and tight-lipped with suppressed fury. He had given her ten minutes to dispose of the posters and called in a man to redecorate the walls in aggressively pink-sprigged

Laura Ashley paper. Leah would rather he had remonstrated or shouted at her – hit her even. Anything but that tightly reined control of his – and the pink wallpaper.

But she had given up trying to pay them back for not loving her for herself. Her plans were made and all her energy was channelled into carrying them through. If only they didn't take so long.

She got up from the bed and undressed, peeling off her jeans and pulling the tee-shirt over her head. Then, taking her towelling robe from the hook behind the door, she padded across the landing in her bra and pants. Her hand was just reaching out for the bathroom door when it opened suddenly and Tom Clayton came out. He looked distinguished and well groomed in an expensive-looking dark grey suit. His eyes widened with shocked surprise as they came face to face.

'*Leah*.' His eyes devoured the firm young body and bare, tanned legs, then shifted his gaze guiltily to look past her towards the stairhead.

She slipped her arms into the robe and wrapped it round herself. 'Whoops! I thought everyone was downstairs in the lounge,' she said.

'I hope you're liking your job, Leah,' he said pointedly.

'The job's fine, thank you, Tom.' She avoided his eyes. She'd been working at Clayton's now for over a month and so far she'd managed to avoid Tom and the unspoken bargain that hung between them.

'I'm sure you know how much I want to see you again.'

'Do you?' She edged towards the bathroom door but his hand came out and grasped her wrist. It felt cold and clammy on her warm skin.

'You know I do. I quite thought I'd see you here this evening. I hope you're not avoiding me.'

83

'Of course I'm not. I'm sure you didn't really want me sitting opposite you at dinner tonight. Not with your wife watching.'

'So you went out.'

'Yes.'

'With a boyfriend?'

'With a friend.'

He regarded her with smouldering eyes for a long moment. 'Let's fix a time now,' he said breathlessly. 'Which day do you go to college?'

'Wednesdays actually.' Leah found the days she spent at college unutterably boring. Any diversion would be welcome. 'But I couldn't *possibly* play truant, could I?' she said provocatively.

His grip on her wrist tightened. 'Don't play around with me, Leah. A promise is a promise. I kept my side of it.'

She looked up at him swiftly, slightly taken aback by his suddenly assertive tone. 'All right then. Next Wednesday.' She tried to move past him but he held her wrist tightly.

'Wait. Look, go to college as usual and register first, then slip out and I'll pick you up outside the rear entrance in Gooch Street.'

'Gooch Street?' She giggled. 'All very cloak and dagger, isn't it? Just like something out of one of those old James Bond movies.'

He looked at her, his eyes flickering with uncertainty. 'You will be there, won't you?'

She looked up at him. It was exciting, this feeling of power. If she refused there was nothing much he could do about it, but he had given her a job – and he might be useful to her again if she played her cards right. Besides, he was quite attractive. With a quick glance towards the stairhead, she stood on tiptoe. Taking his chin in her hand she kissed him full on the mouth, her lips warm and moist and slightly parted. 'I'll be there, Tom,' she whispered huskily, then she slipped into the bathroom and closed the door firmly, turning the key with an audible click.

When Tom returned to the lounge downstairs the Thompsons were just taking their leave. Hilary was thanking them effusively for coming.

'I hope we'll be seeing much more of you now that you've moved in next-door,' she said as she ushered them out. 'And do try to drop in on Sunday, won't you? We're having a barbecue lunch – from twelve till three.'

Bill and Janet Thompson smiled and nodded, thanking Hilary for the delicious dinner and backing out of the room as though they were in the Royal Presence. When Hilary had seen them out she returned to the room with a sigh of relief.

'Well, thank goodness they had to leave early,' she said, subsiding elegantly into her chair. 'That man is the biggest bore I've ever encountered, and as for her . . .' She raised her eyes to the ceiling. 'That awful local accent – and the *dress*. I don't know if she'd run it up herself but it looked more like a set of floral loose covers.'

The others laughed politely but Angela Clayton, who was herself wearing a floral two-piece, flushed unbecomingly at the snide remark. She decided to get her own back via her husband.

'You've been an awfully long time, Tom. Aren't you feeling well?'

He frowned, glancing round at the others. 'Of course I'm well.'

She shrugged her angular shoulders. 'You look rather flushed. I wondered if the pâté . . .' She looked at Hilary pointedly. 'I never buy the stuff since

85

the listeria scare. One can't be too careful. Tom has such a delicate stomach.'

It was Hilary's turn to flush. 'As it happens it was home made, Angela,' she said between clenched teeth. She looked at Tom. 'You *are* all right, aren't you, Tom darling? I'd never forgive myself if I'd given you anything that upset you.' Her tone was placatory but the look in her eyes challenged.

'I'm perfectly all right, thank you, Hilary,' he said firmly. 'You'll have to excuse Angela. She thinks all women serve up ready cooked supermarket food like she does.' He glanced at his watch. 'I think it's time we were leaving too.' He stood up and held out his hand to Angela. 'Shall we go, dear? You know you have to be up early to muck out.'

As the three couples said their goodnights, going through the dutiful ritual of kissing the other's spouses, Tom wondered if it was his imagination that Hilary's lips lingered on his rather longer than the customary friendly embrace required.

The following Wednesday morning Leah was filled with nervous excitement as she travelled to college. Life was so dull. Meeting Tom would make a welcome little diversion as well as furthering the plan that was simmering away inside her head. He'd be sure to take her somewhere nice for lunch and afterwards . . . She didn't let her mind dwell too long on afterwards. She'd play that by ear.

Waiting in Gooch Street at the back of the college she felt like a mysterious woman spy and was reminded of all the fantasy games she used to play as a child. It was a mean little street, due for demolition. Weeds poked their tenacious heads through cracks in the pavement and rotting gates hung lopsidedly on rusty hinges. Most of the terraced houses were boarded up but some still housed the elderly occupants who had lived most of their lives there. Still clinging to their feeble government-subsidised independence, they were determined to retain their dignity until the time came for them to be sacrificed to the developers. Here and there a patch of dusty grass and a few dispirited geraniums struggled for survival among the discarded fish and chip papers and empty drink cans. On any other day it would have depressed Leah, but today it seemed to have just the right atmosphere for an illicit assignation.

When Tom's Jaguar turned in at the far end of the street it looked incongruously shiny and opulent. He stopped and leaned quickly across to open the door for her, darting a sideways glance before reversing into an empty space and heading for the main road again.

Leah looked at him, one eyebrow raised enquiringly. 'Would you like me to lie on the floor till we're clear of the town,' she asked with a sarcasm which he failed to pick up.

'No, it's all right. I don't know anyone on this side of town.'

She'd been right about the lunch. Tom clearly had it all planned. After driving south for about an hour on the A1 he drove on to the forecourt of a motel and country club. There were three restaurants and he ushered her into the smartest where a waiter showed them to a secluded corner banquette and handed them an oversized menu each. His discreet eyebrows rose a fraction when Leah ordered smoked salmon followed by lobster thermidor, but the man seemed not to mind his young companion's extravagance, even though he ordered only an omelette and salad for himself. When the waiter had gone Leah looked at Tom.

'What's up? Aren't you hungry?'

He shook his head. 'I've got a civic dinner to attend tonight. I don't normally eat lunch anyway.'

'Neither do I, but this is an occasion, isn't it?' She looked at him questioningly.

'Is it?'

'Aren't we celebrating?'

'Celebrating what?'

She poured herself a glass of water and sipped it, looking at him over the rim. 'You tell me. I take it we're spending the afternoon together.'

Tom cleared his throat and lowered his head. 'Keep your voice down.'

She looked around. 'But there's only one other couple in the place and they're too far away to hear. Well – are we?'

'You know damned well we are.'

She leaned towards him across the table. 'Why are you so jumpy, Tom? Are you nervous?'

'Of course I'm not nervous.'

'If you're regretting it, it's all right. You can just take me back after lunch and I'll . . .'

'*Leah*! Please, will you stop it?'

'Stop what?' She stared at his red face with huge innocent brown eyes.

'Just let's talk normally.' He looked up with obvious relief as the waiter appeared with their food. 'Ah – here comes lunch.'

Leah lay on her side, her back towards Tom who was lying on his back and snoring loudly. She didn't know quite what she'd expected but it certainly wasn't the fevered groping that had begun the moment the chalet door had closed behind them. She hadn't expected it to be romantic exactly, but neither had she visualised the inept and painful coupling that had occurred almost before they'd had time to undress. Tom couldn't wait – *hadn't* waited. The whole thing had been over almost before it had started. Tom had achieved what he'd come here for, but for her the feeling of power had been short-lived. She had expected to get something out of it herself. She'd been right about sex; it did demand back more than it gave. And it was certainly overrated.

She shifted her position and Tom stirred and opened his eyes. He lay blinking for a moment as though momentarily wondering where he was. Then his eyes focused on her.

'Oh, I must have dropped off for a moment.' He slipped an arm around her and drew her close. 'Not exactly surprising, eh?' he said archly.

Leah said nothing. If *that* had exhausted him then he must be older than she'd thought.

He raised himself on one elbow to look down at her. 'Are you all right, little one?'

She winced at the coy endearment. 'Of course.' She rolled away from him sulkily and sat up with her back towards him.

'I'm sorry if I hurt you,' he said, stroking her back. 'You know, you really should have warned me it was the first time for you.'

She shot him a black look over her shoulder. 'What did you take me for?'

'Oh, God, Leah, I didn't mean that. It's just that you young women nowadays . . . I mean – you're all so liberated.'

'So you thought I jumped into bed with just anyone, did you? Just like some grubby little back street hooker?' When he didn't answer she added: 'I wonder what my parents would think of your opinion of their daughter?'

He sat up and leaned forward to peer into her face, anxiety creasing his brow. 'Leah, look, come on, sweetie, don't be like that. Lie down again and relax. Be nice to me. Tell me what's really the matter. I want to please you too, you know. Was it too quick – is that it?' He began to fondle her. 'That's a compliment, you know. You excited me so much I couldn't wait for you. Better next time, eh?'

He pushed her back against the pillow and to her horror she realised that he was becoming aroused again. Gritting her teeth, she made herself submit to the clumsy gropings once again; pretending to enjoy the exploring fingers, the damp kisses and heavy breathing of his mounting excitement. This time it did last longer, but Leah found the laboured heaving no less revolting than before. At last he collapsed groaning on top of her, a dead weight, breathing hotly into her ear, his face twisted into a contortion that seemed to suggest agony rather than pleasure.

She closed her eyes tightly against the sight and swallowed hard at the lump in her throat. Two tears squeezed out at the corners of her eyes to trickle slowly down her cheeks. Where was the mind-blowing ecstasy you read about in books? Was all that a con-trick too? Was everything in life a cheat? It wasn't fair.

Tom stopped the car at a bus stop on the outskirts of town, reaching across to take her hand and search her eyes before she opened the car door.

'You're very quiet. Sure you're all right?'

'I'm fine.'

'It's been wonderful, darling. I can't tell you how wonderful. I have to see you again, Leah. Is that what you want too?'

Again? How much did he expect in return for

giving her the beastly job? Biting her lip she thought
of her plan. The thought of it shone like a beacon.
The achievement of it made anything seem worthwhile.

She made herself smile at him. 'Of course I do.'

He squeezed her hand. 'Christ, that's marvellous!
Next week? Same time and place?'

'I don't know. What about college? I can't keep
ducking out.'

'Come off it, Leah. You hate college.'

'But I want to be qualified. I want to earn more
money.'

'I'll give you a rise. Double your present salary.
How does that sound?'

She brightened. 'Well – all right then.'

'It'll be between ourselves, of course – wouldn't do
for everyone to know. About your rise, I mean.'

'If you say so.'

'So is it a date then, next week?'

She nodded resignedly.

Leah didn't go straight home. Instead she crossed the
road and took a bus going in the opposite direction –
to the village of Smallfield. It was still called a village
even though the town had swallowed it up more than
a decade ago. Now it was what the local estate agents
called a 'garden suburb'. The original cottages had
been surrounded and outnumbered by rows of
modern bungalows and small housing developments;
brash new mock Tudor pubs with plastic beams and
reconstituted stone fireplaces.

Kate Dobson, Jack's mother, lived in the bungalow
she and her late husband had bought for their
retirement. It had a large garden at the back where
she grew all her own fruit and vegetables, a lawn and
roses at the front.

91

Granny Dobson was neutral ground as far as Leah was concerned. The old woman was gruff and outspoken. When the two were first introduced to each other twelve years ago, both had been openly doubtful. Kate made no secret of the fact that she didn't hold with any adoption, particularly Leah's, and Leah had resented what she interpreted as the old woman's hostility. But at least they had both known where they stood. Since then they had developed a special kind of relationship. Kate plainly saw through the posturings of her son's friends and colleagues. She considered Jack's rise to a position of power in the town to be nothing more than 'putting on airs and graces', largely due, in her opinion, to the influence of Hilary, the daughter-in-law she had never liked.

Over the years she had come to feel sorry for the child on whom her son and his wife had tried to impose their broken dreams. She had made her home a refuge for Leah, who often found her footsteps turning towards her adopted grandmother's bungalow when things troubled her.

Although their respective views were at odds the two had an odd kind of affinity. Kate mourned the passing of the old town; its hardworking life and slow pace. She loved to talk of the old days when Jack's father was station master at Nenebridge, and Leah was the only person left who liked to listen. Kate often reminisced of how the fruitgrowers would bring their produce to the station at first light in horse-drawn carts, ready to be sent to market. She told of the struggle it had been for them to send their only son to the local grammar school.

It was another world to Leah. A world where people really cared about each other. She shared with Kate the wish that Jack could have been satisfied with his old life.

When Leah appeared unexpectedly in the kitchen doorway the old woman looked up and greeted her with characteristic bluntness.

'Oh, it's you.' She sat at the newspaper-covered kitchen table shelling peas she had just picked from her garden. She wore a print wraparound pinafore, lisle stockings and an old pair of tennis shoes. Her grey hair was cut short and caught back with a kirbygrip and her face was as wrinkled and weather-beaten as a walnut from long hours spent in the garden. 'What wind blew you in then?'

Leah sat down opposite and began to help with the peas. She loved Granny Dobson's old-fashioned kitchen, with its deep white sink and wooden draining board. The shelves beneath were concealed by a blue and white gingham curtain that matched the ones at the window. Above the large kitchen table a row of blue and white jugs hung on the wall in a row, diminishing in size from a quart to a gill, and there was a Victorian pine dresser. It was a far cry from Hilary's clinical fitted kitchen at Acacia Grove.

It was in Kate Dobson's kitchen that Leah, enveloped in one of Kate's pinafores, had learned to cook and perform other domestic chores. Kate understood that little girls learning to cook got into a mess and spilled things. Unlike Hilary she never minded, knowing that squishing your hands about in beaten egg and having flour in your hair was half the fun.

This afternoon Leah found it soothing sitting at the table shelling peas. Sometimes she felt that this was the only place where she could truly be herself.

'You all right, my old sugar?' Kate asked.

Leah shook her head. 'Just thought I'd like to see you.'

Kate Dobson got up from the table and filled the

93

kettle. Lighting the gas, she sat the kettle on the ring and turned to look at Leah, one hand in the small of her back. 'Blasted rheumatics,' she said, grimacing. 'Always gets me when I sit too long.' She resumed her seat at the table and went on stoically shelling peas.

'I suppose you went to the Mayor-making as usual,' she said with a sniff. 'Dennis Mason! Fancy him being Mayor. I remember him when he was a ragged-arsed kid, running errands for tuppence a time. His mother used to work in the market selling fish to make ends meet. Had to, poor cow. Her old man gambled away almost every penny he earned.' She shook her head. 'Dennis knew what he was on to when he married that Glenys Watts.' She chuckled hoarsely. 'Funny-looking girl, she was, used to sit in the cash desk in her dad's shop. Red nose and little piggy eyes – looked like she had a permanent cold.' She rose to her feet as the kettle began to whistle, wiping her hands on the front of her pinafore before spooning tea into the big brown pot. 'Not much handsomer now by the look of the photo in the *Clarion*.' She nodded towards the paper on the table as she poured water into the pot. 'Still, she had what *he* wanted all right. And I *don't* mean oomph.'

Leah laughed. Already she could feel the tightly coiled tension inside herself beginning to unwind. 'I know what you mean, Gran.'

Kate viewed her adopted granddaughter shrewdly as she poured two cups of strong tea. 'What is it then? You look a bit down in the mouth.'

'I'm okay. Just a bit fed up.' Leah swallowed the lump that suddenly rose in her throat.

Kate sucked up her hot tea noisily, gnarled brown hands cupped round the cup. Her shrewd bright eyes peered at Leah over the rim. 'Thought so. Want to talk?'

Leah looked up and said impulsively: 'What would you say if I told you I wanted to find my real mother?'

There was not so much as a flicker of surprise in the steady gaze the old woman directed back at her. 'I'd say it was perfectly natural,' she said. 'But I'd say you might well be heading for trouble too, mind.'

'So you think I shouldn't try to find her?'

'I don't think anything. And if I did I'd keep quiet about it just for once.' One of the wrinkled hands reached out and covered Leah's. It was warm and rough and reassuring. ''Cause I know you'll do it anyway if you've made your mind up to,' she said. 'My Jack and that snooty Hilary made a big mistake when they adopted you. I told them but would they listen? Would they 'ell as like.' She shook her head at Leah. 'Oh, not only a mistake for them – for you too. For one thing you were too old to take Fiona's place, and for another – I believe that if it's God's will to take your child, He will, one way or another.' She sighed. 'He took two of mine. I just had to bear it. Well, you wantin' to cut and run proves I wasn't far wrong, doesn't it? It's no more than they deserve.'

She reached for the teapot and filled her cup again. 'People can't help but be what they are. That's what it comes down to in the end. You can't fly in the face of nature. Look at this puffed up lot.' She swept a pile of pea pods from the newspaper that covered the table. Dennis Mason's bland countenance smiled smugly up at her above full Mayoral regalia. 'They've made a pile of money out of killing the town and now they parade its corpse around pretending nothing's happened. Look at 'em. Kings of a dung heap, that's all they are now,' Kate said scathingly. 'So if you want to try and find out who your mum was, you have a go, girl. And good luck to you. At least you're prepared to look truth in the face.'

'Thanks, Gran.'

Kate's hand held on to hers. 'But don't go doin' anything you might be ashamed of,' she said perceptively. 'And try not to hurt anyone who's been good to you. Never cut off your retreat, my Bert always used to say. You never know when you might need it.' She smiled. 'That's not bad advice, you'll find.'

Leah drank the last of her tea thoughtfully, watching as Kate carried the colander full of peas to the sink and set about clearing up the table. She didn't need to ask herself what Granny Dobson would say if she knew about Tom Clayton. That would come under the heading of 'something to be ashamed of'.

'I'll remember,' she said. 'I'd better go now. Thanks for the tea – and the advice.' At the door she stopped, a thought suddenly occurring to her. 'Oh, I almost forgot.'

'Yes?'

'There's a barbecue at home on Sunday. It's from twelve till three. Why don't you come?'

Kate cackled. '*Me*? They won't want me there, girl. I'm not swanky enough for them any more.'

'But *I* want you, Gran. I've been told to invite a friend and I'm inviting you.'

Kate nodded, her blue eyes dancing. 'All right then. I'll come if you want me to. Damned if I won't,' she said rebelliously.

Chapter 6

When Ralph Evans returned to 'The Marina' just two weeks after his first visit his father was delighted. The hotel was fully booked so he stayed in the flat, sleeping on the settee in the living room. He gave no indication of how long he would be staying and David didn't ask, so, after his second night Marie felt obliged to ask about his immediate plans.

'When do you start your new job, Ralph?'

They were having coffee in the flat after her morning round of the hotel and she had seized the opportunity to speak to him while his father was out.

He gave her a slightly wounded look. 'In other words, when do I intend to leave?'

'I didn't mean it to sound like that,' Marie said quickly. 'I just thought you must be uncomfortable on the settee and there's no prospect of a room being vacant for some weeks.'

'As it happens I have to leave tomorrow,' he said with his disarming smile. 'You might as well know – the job I applied for and felt sure I'd get, fell through. I'm off to try for another tomorrow. This time in Manchester.'

'I'm sorry. Well, good luck with the new one then.'

'Thanks.' He regarded her for a long moment. 'Actually I've been disappointed that you were so busy. Selfish of me, isn't it? I did hope we might see something of each other while I was here. As it's my

97

last night, could you spare some time to have dinner with me this evening?'

Marie's heart gave a little skip. 'I suppose that could be arranged.'

'Good. I hope you haven't forgotten that you promised we'd get to know each other better.' He smiled, assessing her in the way that made her colour rise. 'I see you've had your hair restyled since I was here last. It suits you.'

Her hand went involuntarily to the new hair-do. She'd visited one of the town's best hairdressers a couple of days after Ralph's last visit. The stylist had cut it in a short, bubbly style, leaving longish tendrils that curled into her neck. The effect had been quite startling. With the weight taken from the heavy mass that she usually wore tied back, the natural curl had sprung to life, framing her face in a flattering way that made her look seventeen again.

'Thank you. I fancied a change,' she said.

Ralph smiled. 'It makes such a difference. You've changed your style of dress too.'

It was true. On the same day that she had had her hair done, Marie had taken an afternoon off to go shopping for clothes. Knowing next to nothing about fashion herself she had taken the advice of the manageress of a little boutique whose window displays she had often admired. The woman had transformed her, encouraging her to try things on that she would never have dared even to consider before. She had advised her tactfully about make-up too and the result was quite magical. From a rather ordinary girl with a good complexion and naturally blonde hair she had become a sophisticated, attractive woman overnight. She had been surprised at the effect on business too. Now that dark classic suits and tailored shirts had taken the place of the baggy tweed skirts and cardigans she wore for work, she found that her staff treated her with more respect. The visitors too seemed to look up to her, never taking her for one of the staff as they once had, but acknowledging her authority as manageress.

As well as working clothes there were two or three off-duty outfits in Marie's wardrobe too and it was one of these that she chose to wear for her dinner date with Ralph that evening – a plain black dress with a deeply scooped neckline. The skirt was expertly cut and flared out flatteringly over her hips. When he saw her, Ralph smiled his approval.

'You look beautiful.' He reached into his pocket and brought out a small package which he handed to her. 'This should make a pretty finishing touch.' Inside was a fine gold chain on which hung a single pearl. Marie gasped.

'Oh – is it *real*?'

He threw back his head and laughed. 'Well, it isn't made of plastic. And it won't turn your neck green.' He took it from her and fastened it around her neck, his fingers lingering on the smooth warm skin. 'I saw it and knew it would look perfect against your skin.' Hands on her shoulders, he turned her towards him and smiled down into her eyes. 'And I was right. It's lovely – like you.' He looked at her enquiringly. 'Do I get a little kiss?'

Shyly she lifted her face and accepted the kiss he planted on her mouth. 'Thank you, Ralph, though you really shouldn't.' She looked at herself in the mirror. 'It's beautiful. It must have cost the earth and I know you can't . . .'

He put his finger against her lips and shook his head at her. 'Never mind all that. Wear it for me.' He drew her arm through his. 'Now let's go and paint the town red. I want everyone to see my stunning girlfriend.'

Marie had not known that it was possible to enjoy herself as much as she did that evening. They drove to Norwich and dined at a popular nightspot, dancing afterwards till the small hours. Marie hadn't danced since Liam had taken her out. At first she was stiff and tense in Ralph's arms, but he held her close and guided her steps expertly and soon she found herself relaxing. By the end of the evening she was beginning to wish that Ralph had taken the job David had offered him.

On the way home he stopped the car in a quiet lane and kissed her till she was breathless and dizzy. Gazing up at the star-filled sky she wondered at the miracle of finding such happiness again, then reminded herself that this was Ralph's last night. He would be gone tomorrow. She was going to miss him.

Back at the hotel they went up in the lift to the top floor flat, whispering so as not to wake David as they tiptoed in.

'I'll make you some coffee,' Marie said, opening the kitchen door.

As they sat on stools at the breakfast bar, sipping their coffee Ralph asked her: 'Well, how are the plans going?'

She shook her head. 'We have to go slowly. Save some more money before we go in for another place.'

He looked surprised. 'Why? You could get a bigger loan with two successful hotels doing business. Why wait?'

'David likes to be cautious,' she told him. 'He's afraid of failure. Sometimes I wonder if he'll ever want to progress further than this.'

'But *you'd* like to.'

She sighed wistfully. 'Yes. I still dream about that hotel chain. But then, I'm only an employee.'

100

'It's a great idea. What makes you think Dad wouldn't want to do it?'

'He's getting on in years now. I wouldn't blame him if he wanted to take things easy. It wouldn't be fair to press him.'

He looked thoughtful. 'Maybe you're right. Have you talked about it to him?'

'No. He's worked hard over the past years. He deserves a rest now.'

Outside her bedroom door, Ralph kissed her goodnight.

'Well, this is it, sweetheart. I'll most likely be gone by the time you wake up. I've no idea when I'll be back again.'

She clung to him. 'Oh, Ralph, I . . .'

He held her away from him and looked down into her eyes. 'What, love? What is it?'

She shook her head. 'Nothing. Just that I wish you weren't going away.'

He drew her close again. 'You don't know what it does for me, hearing you say that. And things are going to work out for us, sweetheart. Just you wait and see.'

She lifted her face to his, her eyes misty and her mouth soft and inviting. 'Oh, Ralph.'

He kissed her, crushing her close, his mouth hungry and excitingly passionate.

It was only after Ralph had left the following day that David told her about the conversation they'd had in the early hours of the morning.

'He woke me before he left,' he said with a smile. 'Said he didn't want to go without saying goodbye. He brought me some tea and we had a little chat.' He looked at Marie a little sheepishly. 'I – er – I offered him a job.'

Marie was taken aback. 'But he's gone up to Manchester for an interview.'

'I know. He's too independent to say yes right away, but I've a feeling he'll take it all right. The job he's applied for up north is nothing more than a door-to-door salesman. I'm sure you'll agree that my son is worth more than that. And we have all this.' He spread his hands. 'It would be foolish not to take him into the business, wouldn't it? I'm getting on after all, and you and he . . .' David beamed. 'You should hear his ideas,' he said excitedly. 'This could be big business, you know. Big hotel luxury coupled with small hotel personal service. That's how Ralph sees it. He thinks we should expand. Says he can see a whole chain of Evans Hotels in ten years' time, all round the coast. Doesn't the idea excite you?'

Marie was surprised. So this was what Ralph had meant when he said that things would work out for them. He had done this for her – for them.

David was looking closely at her. 'You two are getting along really rather well, aren't you?'

Marie blushed. 'Quite well, yes.'

'You know, with someone like Ralph working with us we might just be able to do it.' He looked at her, his head on one side. 'You've blossomed since you met him. I used to worry about you never getting out to have fun. But since Ralph came home . . .'

'Oh, David, do you really think he'll take you up on your offer?' Marie interrupted.

He grinned at her knowingly. 'Well, let's put it this way – I've a feeling he isn't going to want to be away from you for too long.'

Marie felt a tingle of excitement, then she said: 'David, he doesn't know – about me and my past, does he?'

'Good heavens, no.'

102

'You haven't – wouldn't ever tell him, would you?'

He took both of her hands in his. 'My dear girl, all that is ancient history. Whatever you did in the past was over long ago. I see no reason why anyone should know.'

She squeezed his hands gratefully. 'Thank you, David.'

'No. Thank *you*, my dear. If it wasn't for you there'd be no business for Ralph to join, would there?'

He didn't add that since his talk with Ralph he saw Evans Hotels Limited as a large and prosperous family business; a bright future stretching decades ahead, with his grandsons eventually at the head of a huge national concern rivalling nothing less than Trust House Forte. But the starting point to that dream, its trigger, was to get Ralph and Marie safely married.

In all the years that Marie had worked for David Evans she'd kept in touch with Hannah regularly through letters, but her career had prevented her from visiting very often. She'd been pleased with the success that Marie had brought David and when she received Marie's letter, inviting her to her engagement party she had dropped everything and telephoned 'The Marina' at once.

'Marie, I've just got your letter. Congratulations.'

'Thank you. You can come, can't you, Hannah? It will only be a little dinner party – just the four of us – but it wouldn't seem right without you there. After all, if it hadn't been for you, Ralph and I would never have met.'

'Of course I'll be there. Just try and stop me. You know, it's funny but I didn't even know David had a son.'

'You wouldn't. Ralph is David's son by a previous

marriage. They haven't been close for years – till recently.'

'I'm still reeling.' Hannah laughed down the line. 'David must be absolutely over the moon. Tell me all the details – no, better still, save it all up till I get there.'

'I will. It'll be wonderful to see you and catch up on all our news.'

'Great. I can't wait to hear all about it. See you on Friday evening then.'

'And you'll be able to meet Ralph. He'll be here too. He arrives on Saturday.' There was a pause then Marie said, 'Oh, by the way, Hannah, Ralph doesn't know – about me and what happened. He doesn't know anything. David promised not to tell him so . . .'

'God, you didn't think *I'd* say anything, did you?' There was a silence then Hannah said: 'Look, Marie – maybe you'd rather I kept away, for the time being.'

'Oh, no. I didn't mean that. It's just . . .' She chewed her lip and after a moment Hannah said: 'You're afraid I'll start prodding your conscience – telling you you *should* tell him. Is that it?'

'*Do* you think I should?'

'Look, love, it all happened a long time ago. It's none of my business any more, but in my opinion it's a closed book. You paid a terrible price for something you didn't do and now it's over and done with. David clearly doesn't feel it's necessary and I certainly won't let you down.'

'Oh, Hannah, I know you won't.'

'Sure you still want me?'

'Don't be silly.'

They laughed together and Hannah said: 'Right, that's done with then. See you Friday.'

They stayed up late on Friday night, chatting and

giggling like schoolgirls. It was as they were making a last cup of coffee in the kitchen of the top floor flat that Marie said: 'Hannah, I suppose you don't know what happened to the twins, do you?'

She frowned. 'What makes you ask?'

'I can't help thinking about them,' Marie said. 'I've never stopped really. I don't suppose anyone who's given up a child ever does. But it's at moments like this – of deep happiness, and unhappiness too, I suppose – that the feeling is strongest.'

Hannah went to her and laid a hand on her arm. 'You have to try to forget, Marie, to let go. The babies are part of the past you want to put behind you. You can't put it aside unless you do it completely. That segment of your life must be cut clean out if it's going to work.'

'I know, I see that. I just wondered if you knew.'

'Yes, I do know,' Hannah said softly.

Marie's eyes searched hers. 'Are they – did they find nice parents?'

'Yes.'

'Together?'

'Marie, what did we just agree?'

She bit her lip and turned away. 'I just wanted to know that they're happy so that I can be happy too; so that I'll feel I have the right and I don't have to feel guilty any more.'

'Guilty?' Hannah took Marie's shoulders and looked into her eyes. 'You must put all thoughts of guilt out of your mind, Marie. You did the best – the *only* thing you could have done for your babies at that time. Try to see the positive side. Some good did come out of it all, didn't it?' She spread her hands and looked around the room. 'You'd never have had all this if you'd kept the children. So try to start your new life with a quiet heart.'

'Yes, you're right.' Marie smiled. 'I will. I promise.'

But long after she was in bed that night her thoughts were with the little girls she had parted from ten years ago. Did she truly deserve to be happy? she asked herself. Could she ever really let go of the bitter memories, forget the injustice that had taken her liberty and her children from her? And was Hannah telling the truth when she said the children were happy? She could never be a hundred per cent certain of that, could she?

Ralph arrived the following day, along with all his luggage and personal possessions. This time he would not be leaving again. This time there would be no more goodbyes, Marie told herself joyfully. For the time being they would share the flat with David, but already they were making plans for a place of their own. David had offered to move out and let them have the flat to themselves, but Marie wouldn't hear of it. At his time of life any change was an upheaval and she knew he loved the little four-roomed apartment they had created, with its sunny rooms and sea views.

Marie could hardly wait to introduce Ralph to her oldest and best friend. Hannah was out when he arrived, taking a walk on the cliffs. They were having tea when she returned and the moment she walked into the room Marie jumped up, her cheeks pink with excitement.

'Ralph, this is Hannah, my oldest friend.'

He stood up and turned to face the tall slim woman with the tanned face and blue eyes. Hannah had turned forty now, but maturity had bestowed a special kind of beauty on her, a serenity and poise that was all the more effective because she was unaware of it. The sea breeze had loosened her long brown hair from the coil she wore low on her neck. Strands of it lay on the shoulders of the violet cashmere sweater she wore, and as she smiled at him she brushed more straying tendrils away from her forehead.

Ralph offered his hand and when Hannah put hers into it he held it firmly. 'So you're Hannah. I've been looking forward to meeting this paragon I've heard so much about.' The way his eyes held hers felt like a kind of contest and she knew instinctively that to look away would be to allow him to win.

'We've been shopping all morning,' Marie told him excitedly. 'And Hannah has helped me choose my wedding outfit. But you're not to see it till the day, is he, Hannah?'

'Certainly not. I believe it's supposed to be bad luck.'

'I'm sure Hannah has excellent taste,' Ralph said, holding her eyes. 'I'm sure you're going to look lovely, darling.'

Gently but positively, Hannah withdrew her hand from Ralph's grasp and moved to the table to pour herself a cup of tea. She was oddly disturbed. She didn't know quite what she'd expected. A younger version of David perhaps, certainly not a hunk of a man with such a compelling presence. In her job she was used to meeting and dealing with people; used to the kind of man who would exploit his sexuality – use every trick in the book to exert power over a woman. She'd met the challenge many times – and won. But this one . . . Did Marie know what she was letting herself in for? She had come such a long way since her prison sentence – had become an astute, competent business woman – but she was still under thirty and a child when it came to relationships with the opposite sex. She glanced across the room and saw the way the girl's eyes followed Ralph's every move adoringly. Clearly it was too late – much too late to warn her.

Later, when they were alone, Marie asked Ralph what he thought of Hannah. 'She's my best and oldest friend,' she told him. 'I do so want you to be friends.'

He gave her a long hard look. 'How did you come to be friends with a social worker, Marie?' he asked directly. 'Have you been in trouble of some sort?'

She flushed a deep red. It was no use. If they were to be married she couldn't keep it from him. 'Yes. I should have told you before, Ralph.' She glanced apprehensively at him. 'I – I went to prison once. Someone I trusted hid a bomb in my suitcase when I first came to England. Luckily it was discovered before it went off.'

'My God! When was this?'

'A long time ago now. In 1970. I was only seventeen. You probably read about it in the papers, but didn't remember my name.'

'No.' He was frowning. '1970, you say? I'd be serving in Germany at the time. I didn't finish my stint there till '73.'

'I was arrested and charged with terrorism,' she went on. 'It was terrible. I was found guilty of attempting to cause an explosion. Hannah was the only person who believed in my innocence.' There was a long pause before she dared raise her eyes to his. 'I'm sorry, Ralph. Now that you know, I suppose you won't want to . . .' Before she could finish the sentence he had pulled her into his arms and crushed her mouth with his.

'It's all over,' he said against her hair. 'I don't want to hear you mention it again. Understand?'

She sighed and relaxed against him, weak with relief. 'Of course. Thank you, Ralph.' She'd been about to tell him that she'd been pregnant at the time of her arrest, but it seemed foolish to press her luck too far. She'd confessed to her conviction and prison sentence. That was the worst part. There was no point in telling him any more.

The wedding took place the following spring at the local register office. Ralph knew that Marie was a practising Catholic, but he would have none of it. He was an atheist, he told her. If she had seen the things he had seen, she would have stopped believing in God long ago too, just as he had. He convinced her that she would be just as legally married in a register office as she would in a church and although she was disappointed she finally had to give way.

The day of the wedding was fine and sunny, a crisp spring day with a sky of azure blue and air like chilled wine. Hannah helped a nervous Marie to dress in the softly flowing blue dress and white picture hat trimmed with forget-me-nots. She carried a posy of white rosebuds and more forget-me-nots and looked more beautiful than Hannah had ever seen her. For a fleeting instant she saw again the thin little waif she had first met in the remand home eleven years ago, her young face haggard beyond her tender years with worry and the pain of betrayal. Marie had been through so much. She'd fought for her own survival and won. And Hannah prayed with all her heart that her instinct about Ralph was mistaken – that this might be the happy ending that Marie truly deserved.

After the brief ceremony and a small reception back at 'The Marina', attended mainly by staff, Ralph and Marie left for their honeymoon. David had lent them his car to drive to the airport. On the front steps of the hotel he stood beside Hannah as they waved the happy couple off in a hail of confetti.

'This must be the happiest day of my life,' he remarked, his eyes bright and moist. 'Don't they make a handsome couple?'

'They do indeed,' Hannah said.

'And they look so happy,' David went on, blowing his nose. 'The two people I care most for in the world, and they've found each other.'

Hannah took his arm. 'Let's go inside and have a nice cup of tea, David,' she said gently. 'It's been a long day.'

The little town of Rimini was a source of wonder and joy to Marie. She had never been abroad before and she loved the little cobbled square with its medieval buildings and strutting pigeons. Having coffee at the pavement cafés, watching the life of the busy town going by, filled her with childlike delight. The beach too, with its golden sand and warm shallow water, was everything she could have wished. Under the warm caress of the sun she lay with eyes half closed, watching her handsome husband as he sunbathed, his skin golden and taut over rippling muscles. I'm so *lucky*, she told herself over and over.

The first time they had made love Ralph had discovered that he was not her first lover. Marie was upset. It was something she hadn't bargained for. He had asked if her lover was the man who had betrayed her and she told him briefly and tearfully about Liam, admitting that he had been the man who had betrayed her. Ralph had kissed her, assuring her that it wasn't important – that like her prison sentence, what had happened in her life before they had met was past history.

He was a passionate, eager lover. She told herself that he made her feel desirable, disregarding the bruises he left on her body, covering them with make-up when they went to the beach, and telling herself that his impatient ardour would settle down once they became accustomed to each other. But one day towards the end of their two-week honeymoon, something happened to sow the first seeds of doubt in her mind.

She woke early and couldn't go to sleep again. Hearing a church bell she had risen and dressed, quietly and carefully so as not to wake Ralph, and gone out into the cool of the morning to join the early worshippers for mass at a little church nearby. In the tranquil hush of the church with the familiar scent of incense and the assurance of the brightly coloured statues around her, Marie felt calm and peaceful. The simple mass was like a benediction and she told herself that it was no accident that she had wakened early this morning. It had happened so that she could come here and give thanks for her newfound happiness.

After the mass she stayed on for a few minutes to absorb the peace and tranquillity. On her way out she paused by the statue of the Virgin then, on a sudden impulse, she put a handful of lire into the box and lit two candles, one for each of her children, kneeling for a moment at the Virgin's feet to say a prayer for them. Then, feeling happy and refreshed, she hurried back to the hotel, her heart as light as a bubble, eager to tell Ralph about the little church she had found. Maybe one day before they went home he would join her; maybe some day she would make him see that it was wrong to turn one's back on God.

He was standing by the window wearing his bathrobe when she arrived. When she opened the door of their room he swung round to face her and the black fury on his face stopped her in her tracks. His

111

eyes blazing like hot coals, he demanded: 'Where the bloody hell have you been?'

'I – I woke early, Ralph. I heard the church bell, so I went to mass.'

He crossed the room and grasped her shoulders. '*Mass*? You mean you went to church – when you knew how I felt about it?'

'I – know you don't like to go, Ralph, but I thought you wouldn't mind if I . . .'

He shook her. 'You thought wrong then. I won't have my wife bowing and scraping to that superstitious rubbish, understand? You can forget all that now that you're married to me, Marie. And while we're on the subject, you'd better forget you're Irish too.'

Her eyes filling with tears, she stared up at him. 'How can I forget? I am what I am.'

He glowered down at her. 'I'm beginning to wonder just who I've married, Marie. You plead your innocence but then you're off secretly behind my back, doing the things you know I hate. How can I ever trust you?' His fingers bit deeply into her flesh through the thin cotton dress she wore. 'You're mine now. I woke up and I wanted you. And where were you?' He flung out an arm. 'Out there fiddling with beads and muttering a load of mumbo-jumbo.'

'Ralph . . .'

'Did you confess to the priest while you were at it? Did you tell him all about the dirty things you'd been doing? Did you tell him you once tried to blow a lot of innocent people to Kingdom Come? That you slept with another man before you were married? I bet that gave him a kick. A real sinner to forgive for once.'

She felt the colour drain from her face. 'I told you, Ralph, I was innocent. You said we wouldn't mention that again.'

112

'I said I didn't want to hear *you* mention it,' he shouted. 'But if you insist on grovelling to priests – confessing!'

'No, I wasn't. I didn't . . .'

'Well, here's something else for you to confess.' He threw off his robe and began to tear at the fastenings of her dress. 'You belong to me now. Not to a lot of old men in black robes. When I wake up I want you here beside me.' He kissed her brutally till his teeth ground against hers, then picked her up and tossed her on to the bed, throwing himself down on top of her. Ignoring her cries he tore into her. His anger seemed to have aroused him almost to the point of madness. What he did could not be called love-making. It was more like punishment – rape – an ordeal that seemed to go on and on, painfully and endlessly. And what was worse was that her helplessness and distress obviously heightened his arousal, adding to his manic energy and giving him unimagined potency. But at last, mercifully, it came to an end. Ralph rolled away from her with a groan and lay with his back towards her, sated and seemingly senseless, while she lay bruised and motionless, too shocked to speak or move.

After a moment he got up and without a word went into the bathroom. He came back a few minutes later wearing his robe and crossed the room to kneel beside her. The anger had gone from his face and he looked contrite and ashamed.

'Oh, my God, Marie, I'm sorry,' he whispered, taking her hand and pressing it to his lips. 'I don't know what came over me. Can you ever forgive me?'

A great sob rose in her throat and burst from her in a choking cry. He reached out and gathered her to him, holding her close and rocking her to and fro.

'I was so scared when you weren't there,' he said. 'I

lost someone once, you see. I couldn't stand it if I lost you too, and I couldn't help thinking about the other man. The one you loved before. But I shouldn't have done what I did. It was cruel and wrong.' He held her from him to look into her eyes. 'My poor baby, I've hurt you. Forgive me – please?'

Gulping, she nodded wordlessly. Would he ever really believe in her innocence? In that moment she knew, once and for all, that she could never tell him about her babies now.

He crushed her trembling body close again, kissing her bruised mouth tenderly, and after a moment he looked at her. 'Come on. Have a nice bath and get dressed. You'll feel better after breakfast. I know, I'll take you to San Marino. You'll love it there.' He sat beside her on the bed and put his arm around her. 'Listen, Marie. It's going to be good, our life together. We're going to make a go of it, you and I. When we get back we're going to set about building that chain of hotels. Dad will go along with it and I'll do all the work. He won't have to do a thing. He needn't even move if he doesn't want to. He can stay on at "The Marina" where he's happy.' He hugged her. 'With you beside me I'm going to make a fortune, Marie. Together we can do anything – right?'

She smiled up at him tentatively. 'Right.'

'And you forgive me? Oh, say you do, sweetheart.'

'I forgive you, Ralph.'

'It won't happen again, I promise.'

'I know it won't.'

They went to San Marino for the day. They saw the three towering peaks, drank the sweet local Muscato and climbed the steep, winding streets to breathe the intoxicating mountain air. By the end of the day Marie felt relaxed again and as Ralph made love to her later that night, tenderly and with his fiery passion firmly under control, the memory of that morning's horror seemed like a half-remembered dream. Lying awake in the velvet warm darkness she thought of their future and the promises he had made. Evans Hotels – her dream could – *would* become a reality with Ralph to help her. The sacrifice he had asked of her was nothing really. Nothing could alter the fact that she was Irish. And no one in the world, not even Ralph, could change what she truly believed deep in her heart. Could they?

Chapter 7

Leah was bored. Pandering to the sartorial tastes of Nenebridge matrons was the most stultifying occupation she could imagine. It wasn't that fashion didn't interest her, just that the Ladies' Gowns department at Clayton's had little to do with fashion, at least not the kind Leah was interested in. Known as the town's most exclusive store, it was popular with the well-heeled middle-aged female population. If it came from Clayton's then it would be sure to 'look right'. The more it cost, the more the buyer valued it. To shop at Clayton's was the 'done thing' and had been for as long as most people could remember.

But Leah wasn't just bored with her job. She was bored with Tom Clayton. The regular Wednesday afternoon liaisons were becoming a drag. As often as she could she found excuses to get out of them but it seemed that the more she made herself unavailable, the keener Tom became. Her arrangement with him was still a closely guarded secret, as was the inflated salary she was receiving. The additional cash did not come in her weekly wage packet but was usually passed surreptitiously to her by Tom himself at any convenient moment. She hated him for it. It made her feel like a tart, but she swallowed the feeling, justifying it by telling herself that the moment her accumulating bank balance had reached the target figure she would be off out of Nenebridge, leaving

Tom and all the rest of them to stew in their own juice. Then and only then could her quest, and her true existence, begin. There were only two people she'd be sorry to leave – Granny Dobson and Terry.

It was Monday afternoon and the dress department was quiet. Most of their regular customers were on their summer holidays. They had bought their collection of summer dresses, their evening skirts and tops and their beach wear several weeks ago, chatting animatedly about their plans to holiday in the Greek Islands, the Bahamas or the Caribbean, and now it was what Terry called 'The Silly Season', when very little happened and interesting stories were thin on the ground. Next month what Leah called 'The Sick-making Season' would begin; when the regular customers would be back for their autumn outfits, a size larger after their over-indulgence on holiday. They'd all be sporting leathery tans that gave them the appearance of crocodile handbags and trying to outdo each other with their name-dropping, boasting with studied nonchalance about the famous people they had met at their up-market holiday resorts.

Leah was in Designer Suits where Miss Jeffries, the manageress, had sent her, armed with a clothes brush to valet the batch of autumn outfits that had arrived that morning.

'Most trainee buyers are quite happy to learn everything from the bottom up, Miss Dobson,' she'd remarked spitefully.

As she brushed imaginary lint from well-padded shoulders Leah amused herself by wondering what the vinegar-faced spinster would say if she knew that she, Leah, was getting the same salary as she was herself. Not that I don't earn every penny, she told herself grimly. And if Angela Clayton ever found out about her husband's Wednesday afternoons she'd probably have him gelded, which was no more than he deserved.

Bored with her task, Leah's thoughts wandered back to the charity barbecue that Hilary had put on a few Sundays ago. Everyone who was anyone had been there, just as Hilary had planned. Leah had watched them all arrive from her bedroom window in their expensive frumpy summer frocks and hats. The men looked self-consciously casual in blazers and open-necked shirts. Some of the more adventurous among them had even squeezed their spreading haunches into jeans, their bellies cascading unattractively over the waistbands.

She had waited till they were all assembled then selected her own outfit and changed into it – a microscopic scarlet mini-skirt and almost non-existent white suntop. Tom Clayton almost dropped his G and T when he caught sight of her and Jack had given her a thunderous glare which she chose to ignore.

Granny Dobson had arrived in style with Terry who was covering the occasion for the *Clarion*. He'd spotted her as she was getting off the bus and offered her a lift to Acacia Grove in his 2CV. She sat ramrod straight in the passenger seat beside him, wearing her Sunday dress, a navy blue crepe with white lace collar. Her steel grey hair was crowned by an amazing hat with a predatory-looking bird wobbling precariously on the brim. Hearing the sound of the familiar 'sewing machine' engine, Leah went out into the drive to meet them, helping Kate out of the car whilst Terry extracted his camera and gear from the back seat.

'Gran, it's lovely to see you. You look great. Do come and let me get you a drink.'

Kate cast a critical eye over the front of the house. 'Well, well. Done a lot to the place since I was here last, haven't they? Those look like replacement windows. And that porch wasn't there last time. No wonder they don't ask me over very often. Tuppence to speak to 'em now, I shouldn't wonder.'

Leah winked at Terry and took Kate's arm, steering her round to the back lawn where a perspiring Mrs Lamb was serving the drinks at a 'bar' set up behind the garage. She got Kate a very large port and lemon, then looked around for somewhere for her to sit. A group of chairs had been arranged in the shade at the end of the garden, but on the way across the lawn Kate caught sight of her son who was chatting to a group of County Councillors under the cedar tree. She waved her arm vigorously and called to him: 'Oi – Jackie! When you've done maggin' you can come and say 'ello to your old mum.'

Leah smothered a giggle. '*Gran*! One of those gentlemen is the chairman of the County Council. Dad's hoping to get elected to the County next time.'

Kate grunted. 'Don't give a damn if it's King Dick 'imself he's chewin' the fat with. If he's too grand to talk to his own mother he's not fit to be in office at all.'

Jack joined them a moment later, looking daggers at Leah. He took his mother's other arm, escorting her rather hurriedly to the chairs in the shade. 'I had no idea you were coming, Mother,' he said between clenched teeth. 'Who invited you? Was it Hilary? She didn't say a word to me.'

Kate lowered herself into a garden chair with a grunt. 'Ah, that's better. Now – when you're serving the grub I'll have a nice steak. You can cut it up for me though. My teeth don't fit as well as they used to.' She opened her handbag and took out a set of pink and white dentures, which she popped deftly into her

120

mouth with a resounding *clop*. 'There, that's better,' she said, gleaming up at them. 'Ready for anything now.'

'I'll get you a plate of food, Gran. Shan't be long.' Leah made a dash for freedom in the direction of the smoking barbecue but Jack caught her up. He was clearly furious.

'Did you invite your grandmother here this morning?'

'I might have mentioned it to her, yes,' she said lightly. 'You never have her round for a meal. She never goes out at all. I thought she might enjoy it.'

'I don't doubt that she will,' Jack muttered under his breath. He looked Leah up and down. 'Couldn't you have chosen something a little more suitable to wear in front of my friends?'

She looked surprised. 'Look what some of *them* are wearing. Anyway, it's boiling hot. I thought this was suitable.'

'You know perfectly well what I mean. You're practically naked,' he growled.

'No one would turn a hair if this was a beach.'

'But this *isn't* a beach. So go and change into a dress at once.' He made off and Leah grimaced behind his back, gleefully ignoring his request. When she returned to Kate's side with a loaded plate she found Terry sitting next to her. The bird on her hat was wobbling animatedly as she regaled him with tales of old Nenebridge, pointing out various people she had known as children.

'Look at that stuck up Elizabeth Frampton. Councillor Mrs Frampton indeed! She grew up plain Lizzy Wiggins in Smallfield, you know. She puts it round that her father was a farmer but I know different. He was a railway porter who worked a market garden as a sideline. She and her brother used to come round the doors with a little handcart made out of an old orange box, selling vegetables.' Kate cackled as she looked across the lawn to where the elegantly dressed woman was holding court.

'Right little scruff, she was – always had a dirty face and a candle coming down her nose. Nits, too, I shouldn't wonder. A very indifferent mother, Ada Wiggins was.' She munched her steak with relish. 'To look at Lizzie now you'd think she'd been born with a silver spoon in her gob.'

Leah and Terry exchanged grins and Leah noticed that Terry was surreptitiously taking notes. Presently he put away his notebook.

'Can I come and see you some day soon, Mrs Dobson?' he asked. 'I've been thinking of doing an article on old Nenebridge and I'm sure you could help me a lot with the research.'

Kate beamed. 'Come whenever you've a mind to, young man. Kettle's always on.'

'I'll remember that.' Terry got to his feet. 'Well, better not outstay my welcome,' he said. 'I can see Councillor Dobson giving me meaningful looks. I've noted everyone's name and taken all the shots I can.' He stood up and looked at Leah. 'Come out for a drink later?'

She nodded eagerly. 'Love to. I'll come round to your place about seven, shall I?'

When he had gone Kate nudged her. 'Nice young feller, that. You could do a lot worse.'

Leah shook her head. 'He's just a friend.'

'He's a good lad, I can tell.' Kate leaned closer. 'That Tom Clayton now. He's a case. You want to watch him.'

Leah's eyes widened. 'Why? In what way?'

'Got a rovin' eye if you ask me. He's had his eye on you all mornin'. That Hilary's been watching 'im too.'

'Has she?' Leah looked across to where Hilary was chatting to friends. She wore a shocking pink sun dress which showed off her tan and complemented her brunette colouring. As she watched, Leah could see what Kate meant. Hilary's eyes kept straying towards Tom Clayton. They followed him hungrily now as he moved among the guests.

'Hilary's the perfect hostess,' she said lightly, taking Kate's empty plate. 'She watches everyone to make sure they've got something to eat and drink. Besides, she's fifty.'

'What's fifty these days?' Kate gave a short bark of laughter. 'Most of the women here are mutton dressed as lamb. There's no fool like an old fool, lass, believe me. And *he* wouldn't need much encouragement either with a wife like he's got.' She nodded towards Angela who had eschewed the summery clothes the other women wore in favour of jeans and a tee-shirt which emphasised her board-flat chest. 'Plain as a pudd'n and bony with it,' Kate said. 'Cold-blooded too or I'm a Dutchman.' She chuckled. 'I bet it's like getting into bed with a bundle of bean-sticks. Yes, any woman who gave Tom the glad eye had better watch her britches.'

'*Gran*!' Leah smothered a giggle. 'What would they say if they could hear you?'

'I don't care tuppence,' Kate said truculently. 'When you get to my age you can say what you like and to 'ell with the lot of them. Anyway, I know all there is to know about this lot, and most of 'em knows it too. There's not one of 'em here who's what they'd have you think, which is why they all crack on they don't know me.' She handed Leah her empty glass. 'Here, get me another o' them port and lemons, will you, my old sugar? After that I think I'll be off.'

Leah had taken Kate home in Hilary's car. When she returned the guests were beginning to dwindle away. Reluctant to join them again she went into the kitchen to get a drink of lemonade. She was in the pantry when she heard someone come into the kitchen and close the door. Standing still she heard Hilary's voice say quietly: 'Wednesday would be a good day. I could drive over to Huntingdon and meet you somewhere.'

'I can't make Wednesday. I'm sorry, Hilary.' It was Tom's voice that replied. He sounded edgy. Leah clasped a hand over her mouth and held her breath. She was trapped. If they found her in here . . .

'Please, Tom. I have to see you.'

Through the crack in the half-open door Leah saw Hilary stand on tiptoe and wind her arms round Tom's neck. 'Make it Thursday then. That's half closing day. You must be free then.'

'The shop might close but the office is still open. I don't know . . .'

'Oh, Tom, please don't be mean to me. I can't tell you what agony it is to see you and pretend to be indifferent.'

Tom reached up and removed her arms from his neck. 'Hilary, not here. Someone could come in at any moment.'

'I don't *care*.'

'But you *must* care. They'd be hell to pay if Angela found out.'

'You told me she wouldn't care. What are you doing on Wednesday anyway?' Hilary's voice was petulant. 'Last Wednesday I was shopping and I saw you going off somewhere in the car.'

'I had to meet someone on – on business. Look, Hilary, I can't make any promises at the moment. I'll have to give you a ring.'

At that moment there was movement and voices could be heard in the hall. They left the kitchen separately, Tom first and then Hilary. When she was sure they'd both gone, Leah let out her breath in a sigh of relief. So Gran was right. There was something going on between Hilary and Tom. And by the sound of it he was worried. Maybe at last Tom would let her go.

'Have you finished this rail, Miss Dobson?' Miss Jeffries' stiletto-sharp voice pierced Leah's reverie. 'I'm sure you've taken long enough to have the autumn collection quite immaculate. There are two customers waiting in the showroom. I think they'd appreciate some attention.'

'Tom, I really think we should stop meeting,' Leah said. It was Wednesday and they were having lunch at their usual restaurant. She had racked her brain to think of a way of telling him it was over but in the end had decided that telling him straight out was the best.

'If you're worried about being found out, I've got the answer,' he said with a smile. 'I've thought of a way we can be together quite legitimately.'

She looked up at him in alarm. 'Legitimately? What do you mean?'

'It's easy.' He smiled. 'Next year, as you know, I'll be Deputy. Angela has already announced that she won't support me and I'll have to look around for a consort.'

'So?'

'Well – isn't it obvious?'

Leah shook her head in disbelief. 'You don't – you *can't* mean me?'

'Why not?'

Leah cast around for a watertight reason. 'Well, I'm too young for a start. Consorts are usually middle-aged, aren't they?'

'There's no rule that says they have to be. I think you'd be a definite asset.'

'What about my parents?'

'Not a problem. I'll ask their permission first, of course, but I'm sure they'll give it.'

'But there's my job. It would cause bad feeling if I had to have all that time off. And it would look like favouritism, wouldn't it?'

'Hand in your notice then.'

She stared at him. There was nothing for it. She would have to give it to him straight. 'Suppose I don't want to?'

He assumed that she was talking about the job. 'You can have it back again afterwards, of course. That's not a problem.'

'I meant, suppose I don't want to be your consort?' Leah frowned. 'Do you realise that by the time you'd been Deputy *and* Mayor, two whole years would have gone by?'

'What's two years? We'd be together.'

Leah stared at him. She'd made a terrible mistake in getting involved with Tom and if she didn't get herself out of it quickly things would get worse. Consort! The very sound of the word was stuffy. She pictured herself dressed up in dreadful outfits from Designer Suits at Clayton's, accompanying Tom on all those dreary occasions – opening fêtes and making official tours of hospitals, schools and factories; Civic dinners with endless mind-numbing speeches. It would be like being buried alive. She'd *rather* be buried alive. She stirred her coffee thoughtfully, frowning as the germ of a suspicion occurred to her. Could it be that Tom was making an attempt to kill two birds with one stone? Was this his way of trapping her into remaining legitimately at his side, and in so doing ridding himself of Hilary's unwanted attentions at the same time? She looked up at his self-satisfied, smiling face and came to a sudden decision.

'Tom – I wasn't going to mention this today, but I'm leaving Clayton's anyway.'

His smile evaporated. 'Leaving? But why, Leah? Aren't you happy? I know Miss Jeffries is a bit of an old battle-axe, but she's only trying to help with your training.'

'She's a frustrated old bitch and sick with jealousy.'

Tom coughed. 'Well, that's probably true. But surely you can make allowances?'

'Frankly, I don't see why I should. I don't want the job any more. I'm not being allowed to train properly, am I? You don't give me the chance to go on my day release course. No, I don't want the job, Tom. And, to be brutally honest, I don't want our affair to continue either.'

He reached across the table for her hand. 'Leah, you're upset. I don't know why, but I'm sure it's nothing I can't put right. Look, let's go.'

'Go where?'

He flushed. 'Well, where we usually go.'

'To bed, you mean? No, Tom. It's all over. The whole thing was a dreadful mistake.'

He glanced round the restaurant. 'Please – keep your voice down. Look, let's get out of here. Go somewhere where we can talk.'

They left the restaurant in silence. Outside Leah made her way back to the car and stood waiting for Tom to unlock the passenger door. When they were both seated inside he turned to her.

'You don't mean what you said. Tell me what's happened to upset you.'

'I'm not upset, Tom. Just bored. Look, I wanted a job. You gave me one. You made it clear what you wanted in exchange and you got it. We're quits. We owe each other nothing.'

He flinched. 'You make it sound so sordid. It wasn't like that.'

'Oh? Then what was it like?'

'Have these Wednesday afternoons meant nothing to you?'

'No more than they have to you. Only *I'm* honest about it. I feel the time has come for both of us to move on.'

He flushed darkly and his eyes narrowed. 'You scheming little whore!'

'Thanks for that.' She looked up at him. 'I wasn't going to mention this, Tom, but I overheard you talking to Hilary in the kitchen on the day of the barbecue.'

He groaned and rubbed a hand over his beard. 'So *that's* what all this is about.'

'No, Tom, you're flattering yourself. It has nothing at all to do with my decision. That was already made. But if you were to persist in pestering me I'd have no choice but to tell her . . .' She eyed him. 'Or maybe Jack would find it more interesting.' His eyes widened with surprise, but before he could react she opened the car door and stepped out. 'I'll get a bus back to Nenebridge. Goodbye, Tom.

Kate was making jam when she arrived. Leah could smell the pungent aroma of hot sugar and plums as she walked down the path. She found it soothing and reassuring. As usual the old woman gave no sign of surprise at her arrival.

'Hello, my old sugar. Be a duck and put the kettle on? Been standin' over this 'ot stove all afternoon and I'm spittin' feathers.'

Leah made the tea and laid out cups, milk and sugar without a word, helping Kate to pour the hot jam into jars and tie on the waxed paper tops before they sat down. When they faced each other across the kitchen table Kate eyed her shrewdly.

'Somethin' up, lass?'

Leah sighed, swallowing the lump that suddenly rose in her throat. 'Oh, Gran,' she said thickly, 'I've done something really silly. I've been such an idiot.'

Kate poured two cups of tea. 'Only one thing a girl your age feels an idiot over, and that's a man. Not that nice young Terry, I hope?'

Leah shook her head.

'Someone older then – married?' Leah's eyes affirmed her guess. 'Don't tell me it's that lecherous Tom Clayton?' Kate shook her head from side to side. 'Oh, my dear Lord! I guessed as much when I saw the way he was eyein' you up at that there barbecue affair.' She reached for Leah's hand across the table. 'Come on, my woman, tell me the worst. Not pregnant, are you?'

Leah looked up with a rueful grin. 'Heavens, Gran, I'm not *that* kind of an idiot.' She looked down at her hands. 'And before we go any further, it was me who did all the seducing. I planned the whole thing. The mistake is all mine.'

'Bet he didn't need much seducin', though.' Kate sighed. 'What happened then? You underestimated him, eh? Saw him makin' sheep's eyes and thought you could have him on toast. What's the trouble then?'

'It didn't work as I meant it to. I want out.' She sighed. 'I wanted a job, you see. Anything so long as I could make some money and get away from here. Tom – well, he made it clear that he wanted me. It seemed so simple. We both kept the bargain. But now . . .'

Kate groaned. 'He's holdin' you to it – don't want to let you go?'

'Worse. He's just asked me to be his consort, would you believe, when he comes to office next year.'

Kate's eyes opened wide. 'He *never*. That'd set a few tongues waggin'.'

'Apparently his wife wouldn't mind. And he seems to think Jack and Hilary won't either.'

Kate snorted. 'The man must need his head testing if he thinks he could get away with that.'

But Leah knew different. Tom had thought it all through carefully. He planned to use her to get himself off the hook with Hilary. But Kate didn't know about that particular little complication, and she wasn't about to tell her. In any case, it wasn't the point at issue.

'I wish I hadn't done it, Gran. I feel so cheap,' she said quietly. 'I thought I could use my – my sexuality to get what I wanted. But he turned it round against me.'

Kate was shaking her head wisely. 'They always do, lass, his type. If you weren't so young you'd have known that. You got to get up early in the mornin' to get one over on the likes of Tom Clayton. He i'nt as green as he's cabbage-lookin'.' She gave Leah's hand a squeeze. 'Never you mind, my sugar. Some nice young man'll come along for you. You don't want to worry.'

'I'm not worried about that.' Leah's head came up defiantly. 'It's not romance I'm looking for. It's some way of making myself independent. I want to make a life of my own. There's no such thing as love anyway. It's just something people bargain with. Men only really want you for what they can get. In future I want to be independent enough to choose who I bargain with, and tell all the rest to go to hell.'

'No easy way to do that.' Kate looked at her gravely for a long moment then said: 'You know, you're wrong about love, though I suppose I can't blame you for thinkin' the way you do. Love's there if you look for it. Oh, you've got to earn it right enough. And maybe it is a kind of bargain too, in a way. But not the way you think, my sugar.' She held out one clenched hand. 'It's like a handful of sand, see? Grab it too hard and the grains'll slip through your fingers. You has to handle it gentle – hold it lightly and you'll hold it safe.' She brushed the imaginary sand from her hand and looked at Leah. 'As for this 'ere *sexuality* you spoke about – if you ask me it's used too freely these days. A woman's heart and body is something precious, to be guarded like a jewel and kept special for the right man. Not used for barterin' or tossed away like some cheap old rubbish! No, my sugar. The right man when he comes'll show you what love's really like. It's got nothin' to do with bargains or barterin'. And it's well worth waitin' for.'

Leah looked at the craggy face, grown suddenly soft and dreamy. Kate looked suddenly young again, her blue eyes faraway and the smile on her lips, gentle and unguarded. Her values might be old-fashioned but they had clearly worked for her. Leah gazed on the memory of deeply felt love on the old woman's face – and envied her.

Hilary watched from the kitchen window as Jack put the car away in the garage. The moment she saw the expression on his face she knew something had upset him. The evening meal was ready to dish up and she went through into the lounge to pour out the gin and tonic he always liked to unwind with when he came home from the works. She paused to look up, the glass in her hand as he came through the door.

'Hard day, darling?'

He stood facing her, his face pink and his hands

clenched in front of him, cracking his knuckles in the way that always made her wince.

'Tom Clayton came to see me this afternoon,' he said sharply. 'I wonder if you know what about?'

Hilary's heart seemed to freeze into a ball of ice inside her chest and she almost dropped the glass she was holding. 'Tom?' she said shakily.

'Yes, Tom.' Jack took the glass from her and took a deep draught from it, then walked through into the conservatory and stood staring out into the garden. Hilary followed anxiously. She waited for him to continue and when he didn't, cleared her throat and asked apprehensively: 'Well, what did he want?'

Jack rounded on her, his eyes bulging and his face suffused with colour. 'You might well ask. I tell you, Hilary, I can hardly bloody *speak* I'm so angry.'

'With – with Tom?' Her voice sounded unnaturally high and she cleared her throat again. Taking a sip from her own glass, she wished she'd had the presence of mind to add more gin.

'With him, yes, the damned fool – though at least he was man enough to come and lay his cards on the table. What riles me is that I've housed a woman like *that* in my own house all these years . . .' Suddenly he banged his glass down on the glass-topped table and strode through the lounge. Pulling the hall door open he shouted angrily: 'Leah, come down here at once.'

Hilary's heart sank. Surely he wasn't going to involve the girl – wasn't going to humiliate her in front of their daughter? Her heart was hammering sickeningly and her mouth was dry as she stammered: 'Jack, why bring Leah into it? For God's sake, surely we can discuss this in a civilised way – what – whatever it is.' Her nerves stretched to breaking point, she stared at him. 'Well, are you going to tell me or aren't you?'

He walked back into the conservatory, picked up

his glass and handed it to her. 'Get me another of these – a large one. I'm saying nothing till the three of us are together.'

Leah had been in the shower when Jack called. When she appeared she was wearing her bathrobe, her wet hair wrapped in a towel. She walked through to the conservatory on bare feet. 'Did you call me?'

'I most certainly did.' Jack turned towards her. 'Sit down. I've got something to say to you.'

Leah looked from Jack to Hilary and back again. Later she reflected that they'd looked like a judge and jury, waiting to pronounce sentence.

'Sit down,' he repeated.

Leah glanced at Hilary as she perched on the edge of one of the cane chairs. She saw the fear in the older woman's eyes and at that moment knew that something serious had happened.

'Tom Clayton came to see me this afternoon,' Jack growled. 'He came to confess a piece of madness he'd been led into and – and to beg my forgiveness.'

Hilary bit her lip hard and shot him a beseeching look, but Jack didn't even notice it as he ground on: 'What he told me was so incredible – so bizarre – that I didn't believe him at first. Perhaps *you* can guess what it was?'

He stared accusingly at Leah, but she shook her head.

'I've no idea.'

'Then I'll tell you. He claims that you offered him your *favours* in return for a job in his store. Is that correct?'

Leah vaguely registered Hilary's expression of shock mixed with relief before Jack went on: 'It seems that you've been sneaking off to meet him on Wednesdays instead of attending college – spending the afternoons in some seedy hotel room. He also

133

tells me that you've demanded extra money and that now you're making more demands. Blackmailing him, in fact.'

'That's not true!' Leah sprang to her feet but Jack silenced her with a look.

'Before you attempt to wriggle out of this by telling more of your wicked lies, Tom has already warned me that you have some outrageous story ready – that you'll stop at absolutely nothing to get yourself off the hook.'

'All I wanted was to stop seeing him,' Leah said. 'I just want to be rid of him.'

Hilary looked incredulously from one to the other. 'You mean – it's *true*?' she whispered.

Leah met her eyes. 'Yes, some of it,' she owned. 'But he's twisted it out of all proportion to save his own skin.'

'How dare you?' Jack thundered. 'How dare you slander the name of one of my oldest friends? Tom Clayton is a respected member of the community. A businessman and a councillor. Oh, I know he's been a damned fool, but I don't have to look far for the person who made all the running, do I?' He glared at Leah. 'He's been man enough to come and confess it all to me – admitted that he was wrong – begged my forgiveness. He was quite beside himself with remorse.'

'I bet he was,' Leah said defiantly. 'Tom Clayton is nothing more than a dirty old man. He's a sneak and a liar too. I told him today I was bored with him, if you want to know. This is his way of getting back at me.' She looked at them. 'And I'll tell you something else – I'm not the only woman he's been seeing.'

'Stop it. Oh, my God, *stop it*!' Unable to bear the strain any longer, Hilary got to her feet and rushed from the room, a handkerchief clasped to her mouth.

'You see what you've done to your mother, you little slut?' Jack bellowed as the door closed behind his sobbing wife.

She met his angry bloodshot eyes levelly. 'She's not my mother,' she said. 'Any more than you're my father. You've always hated me, both of you. I intend to find my own mother. And when I find her I'll leave you and Tom Clayton and all the other pompous, boring people in Nenebridge to play your little power games. When I find my real mother you won't see me for dust.'

'And believe me, the day can't come soon enough for me,' Jack hissed at her. 'Right from the first you've been trouble. I knew it when we first brought you home, but Hilary wanted you and no other child would do.'

'Only because I looked like Fiona. She never wanted me for myself.' Her chest and throat ached with the tears she refused to shed. 'You never even tried to love me for myself – even when I was little. I've been less than nothing to you. A pale copy of the child you lost. Like a shadow – something that isn't really there.'

Jack laughed mirthlessly. 'Oh, you've been *there* all right – more's the pity. A bloody nuisance from day one, that's what *you've* been. Flaunting yourself in your common clothes, embarrassing me in front of my colleagues. And now – *now* behaving like a prostitute with one of my oldest friends. You sicken me, girl. Go and find your "real mother" as you call her – if she's free, that is. See if anyone wants you. I'll be surprised if they do.'

'If she's *free*?' She stared at him. 'What do you mean, free?'

'If she's not back in prison for some other crime.' Seeing her shocked expression he took a step towards her, his mouth twisted into a triumphant smile. 'I'll even help you if you like. I'll give you your birth certificate. The real one, not the shortened version. You'll see from that just what your precious *real* mother was. Knowing you, I doubt very much if you'll still want to find her after hearing that, but if you do, good luck to you both. I'm sure the pair of you richly deserve each other.'

With a stifled sob, Leah ran past him, through to the hall and up the stairs. She didn't believe it. She wouldn't believe it. Her mother wasn't a criminal. She couldn't possibly be. She'd find her and show them – show them all.

On the landing Hilary came out of her room and stood barring her way.

'He – he says my mother was a criminal,' Leah said. 'He's just being spiteful. It isn't true, is it?'

Hilary's eyes were red with crying, her mouth distorted with bitterness. She didn't reply to Leah's pitiful question – didn't speak at all. Just raised her hand and struck her a stinging blow across the cheek. Then she walked back into her room and slammed the door.

She was all packed. It hadn't taken long because she had packed only the clothes she'd bought for herself with her own earnings. They filled one medium-sized suitcase. Now she stood looking round the room. She wouldn't miss it. It had never felt like hers anyway. This house had never felt like home. On the dressing table was the birth certificate Jack had thrust into her hand, knocking on her door before he retired to bed. Some weeks ago she'd written off to apply for it. She'd wondered why it hadn't come. Now she saw clearly that Jack must have intercepted it. It gave her mother's name as Marie O'Connor and stated that her father was 'unknown'. Her place of birth was down as the hospital wing of a remand home in East London. She had stared at it for a long time but finally had to admit that there was nothing more she could glean from it. Folding it carefully she put it into her handbag, then, propping the note she had written on the dressing table and slinging the strap of her bag on to her shoulder, she picked up the case and stood looking round the room for the last time.

'This is it,' she told herself. 'I've done it at last. For better or worse, I've broken free.' She caught sight of her reflection in the mirror and grinned back at it defiantly. 'And I won't come back,' she promised.

Chapter 8

Once she had settled down at college Sally found she enjoyed it immensely. She had already had some experience, working with Mrs Jessop at Floral World on Saturdays, but it was only when the course got under way that she could see just how little she really knew about the art of floristry. Not that she would have admitted this fact to her parents.

In the first months she learned how to wire flowers and how to 'moss' and 'de-thorn', how to make up simple flower arrangements and bouquets for different occasions. Later she learned more about the horticultural side of the business; how to grow and care for different flowers and plants; which ones could be revived after wilting and how to do this. She learned how to plant and maintain window boxes for hotels and civic buildings; which plants to use for minimum care and greatest effect. The course included early morning 'outside' visits to flower markets to learn the skills of buying and packing for transportation. Late night visits to parks and public buildings were made, to learn the maintenance of street displays, beds and hanging baskets, which had to be cared for when there were few people and the least possible traffic about.

Later in the course business studies would be covered. Sally looked forward to learning about the different ways in which a florist might work, and how to run her own business.

In the meantime she was learning to be a young adult as well as a florist and businesswoman. She was learning how to mix with her contemporaries on an equal footing in a way she never had at school. During her first days at college she made friends with Sharon Smith. Sharon was the eldest of five children. Her father worked in an engineering factory and her mother was an office cleaner. Sharon and Sally shared a wish to shake off the shackles of home and parents, but for different reasons. In Sharon's case overcrowding was the problem.

'If I moved out it'd mean less work for Mum for a start,' she told Sally one day as they shared their lunchtime sandwiches in the college grounds. 'I have to share a room with Liz and Kelly. Ours is a council house and we've only got three bedrooms. The boys have the other one. We're always rowing these days. Liz is only fourteen but she's getting to be a right little bitch. She's always taking my things without asking. I can't wait to have a room all to myself, Sal.'

Sally nodded. 'I'd like to get a place of my own too.'

Sharon looked at her in surprise. 'You would? Leave your lovely home? You must be mad. If I had a bedroom like yours and a mum who could cook like yours does, I'd be happy to stay put.'

'You don't know what they're like,' Sally said. 'They want to know every little move I make. "Where are you going? Who with? When will you be home?" It gets me down.' She looked sideways at her friend. 'They're not my real parents, you know.'

Sharon looked at her with new interest. 'No kidding,' she said, her mouth half full of cheese sandwich. 'You're adopted, you mean?'

'That's right.' Sally gazed into space. 'Sometimes I wonder what kind of life I'd have had if I'd gone to different parents.'

'You want to thank God you didn't get mine,' Sharon said with a laugh. 'Not that they ever needed to adopt babies. Mum always says she's only got to fold Dad's pyjamas to get pregnant.' She finished her lunch and scattered the crumbs to the waiting birds. 'Ever thought of trying to find your real mum?' she asked casually. 'You're allowed to now, you know. Once you're eighteen.'

Sally looked at her, aghast. 'One mother is more than enough for me, thank you,' she said. 'All my life she's seemed scared to let me out of her sight, and it just gets worse. I love her, of course,' she added awkwardly. 'But sometimes I feel almost desperate to get away from her. No, I need another mother like I need a hole in the head.'

Sally had taken Sharon home to a meal once. Ken and Mavis had been welcoming and polite to the girl, but afterwards Mavis had expressed her disapproval to Sally in no uncertain terms.

'Couldn't you find a nicer class of girl to chum up with than Sharon?' she asked as they washed up together. 'After all, there must be dozens of nice, well brought up girls at the college – even if they're taking different courses.'

'Like typing and shorthand, you mean?' Sally asked pointedly.

Mavis bridled at the sharp tone of her daughter's voice. 'No need to be sarcastic, Sally,' she said. 'I'm only giving you my opinion. Daddy and I have lived in the world longer than you, you know. You must allow us to advise you.'

'All right, what's wrong with Sharon then?' Sally challenged.

'Nothing's *wrong* exactly. It's just that she clearly hasn't been very carefully brought up.' She glanced at her daughter. 'From what she was saying I gather they live on a council estate.'

'So – what if they do?'

Mavis sniffed meaningfully. 'One only has to see her table manners and hear the way she speaks to know that little care has gone into her training.'

'Sharon can hardly help the fact that her parents are working-class.'

'Of course not. And there's nothing wrong with that,' Mavis said.

'And there are five of them. It can't be as easy as when you only have one.'

'I'm not criticising,' Mavis said patiently. 'As long as they stick to their own kind.' She untied her apron. 'Of course you can be *nice* to Sharon. Just don't get too friendly.'

'Why not? I like her. We get on well.'

'Because she comes from a different kind of background,' Mavis said with a sigh. 'What's wrong with trying to find someone of your own kind? You want to go up in the world, not down.'

Sally threw down the teatowel. 'And how am I supposed to know what my own kind is?' she demanded. 'I'd be grateful if you'd tell me. Or don't you know either?'

'Don't you dare take that tone with me, Sally.'

Hearing raised voices, Ken came into the kitchen. 'Now, now, what's all this?' he asked benignly. 'My two best girls arguing?'

'I've just been telling her to try and make friends among her own kind, that's all,' Mavis began. Ken stopped her from expanding on the subject with a frown and a slight shake of his head.

'Sally – my chrysanthemum cuttings are looking a

bit seedy,' he said. 'I'd like you to come out to the greenhouse and have a look at them, if you've got a minute. You did say you'd had a lecture on chrysanths last week.'

The row was diverted and the difficult situation defused, but Sally's resentment of her mother's interference in her life built up a little more with each passing day.

When at the end of the first year the college planned an end of term party and disco, Sally was determined to have the freedom to go as she pleased and not be delivered and collected by Ken. It was to this end that she travelled over to Hinkley one afternoon to ask her Aunt Jean's advice.

'If Dad insists on taking me there in the Purple Pumpkin and collecting me again at ten o'clock, I'll kill myself,' she said dramatically. 'I suppose I'll just have to tell all the others I can't go.'

Jean looked at her pretty niece with her halo of blonde curls and her wide blue eyes and smiled sympathetically. 'Why don't you invite Jason?' she suggested. 'He's bought himself a little car now. Surely Mum and Dad wouldn't mind if he took you and brought you home in that?' She saw the girl's hesitation and guessed at what was going through her mind. 'It'd just be a convenient arrangement, love, not a date,' she said. 'Once you were there you needn't be tied to each other. You could dance with anyone you wanted to.'

Sally's face brightened. 'Do you think Jason would like to go, though?'

Jean glanced up to see her son coming through the gate. 'Here he is,' she said with a smile. 'Why don't you ask him?'

Much against their better judgement Ken and Mavis

agreed that Sally should go to the college dance with their nephew as her escort. Jason was working now, as a trainee with a firm of estate agents, and seemed to be turning out quite respectable. But when he called for Sally wearing his best jeans and brand new leather jacket, Mavis looked him over disapprovingly. She managed to hold her tongue till the two young people had departed in Jason's second-hand Fiesta.

'He could at least have worn a suit,' she said with a sigh. 'I'd have thought your Jean would have made sure he got himself up nice to take Sally to a dance.'

Ken shook his head. 'Things are different nowadays, love.'

'They were *different*, as you call it, when we were growing up,' Mavis reminded him. 'We had the permissive society then, but it didn't mean we had to join in. And we didn't, did we?' She shook her head. 'I just hope that all our careful upbringing will stand her in good stead.'

Ken lit his pipe thoughtfully. He hoped so too, but he wouldn't let Mavis see his concern.

'Course it will, love. She's got a good head on her shoulders, our Sally. Don't you worry.'

In the car Jason glanced at Sally's neat skirt and sweater in amusement.

'Like the outfit, Sal.'

'Don't be funny. Look, drop me off at Sharon's, will you? It's twenty-four Station Walk. I've left my gear there.'

He groaned. 'You'll be all night, nattering and slapping stuff all over your face.'

'No, I won't. Then you can give Sharon a lift too – if you don't mind.'

He shrugged. 'No skin off my nose. As long as you

144

don't keep me waiting more than ten minutes. After that I'm going and you can find your own way there. All right?'

When they drew up outside Sharon's house he reminded Sally that he wasn't about to be kept waiting. 'I mean it,' he called after her as she hurried inside. But when Sally emerged fifteen minutes later, his mouth dropped open in surprise. She wore a skintight mini dress in shocking pink and green. The top was deeply scooped and the skirt was stretched tightly over her shapely hips. Sharon had painstakingly 'spiralled' her hair into gloriously wild disarray and her make-up was sexily sultry, with heavily lined and shadowed eyes and glossy pouting lips. Jason suddenly saw his cousin with new eyes. Rendered temporarily speechless, he got out and opened the door for her.

'Thanks, Jase. This is Sharon,' she said, climbing into the passenger seat.

'Hi, Sharon,' Jason said without so much as a glance towards the other girl.

'Hi,' said Sharon. 'And pardon me while I kill myself,' she added dryly.

The new image seemed to have given Sally a different personality. Along with the colourful dress she seemed to have acquired confidence and a brash sophistication that was an obvious emulation of Sharon's. At the party she was greatly in demand and once there Jason hardly saw her. She was constantly on the floor, dancing with wild abandon as the disco pounded and the lights flashed. Jason caught himself looking round the room for her all the time. He told himself that was what he was here for. He was responsible for her, here to look after her, wasn't he? What'd they say to him if she went and got herself into some tricky situation? When she had first asked him he'd thought it a bit of a cheek. Sally was a pretty girl, but she was three years younger than him after all. Just a kid really. But now . . . When he lost sight of her towards the end of the evening he asked Sharon where she was.

'How should I know?' Sharon asked moodily. She was looking fed up and he could guess why. She'd got her friend up for the party, only to find all the guys flocking round and leaving *her* out in the cold. It must seem unfair.

'I'm not her keeper,' she told Jason tetchily. 'And she won't thank you for sticking your nose where it isn't wanted either.'

He went outside to the car park for a breath of fresh air. Drawing his cigarettes out of his pocket he slipped into the shelter of the bike sheds to light one, and it was then that he heard it – a cry of distress from behind the wall that separated the car park from the sports field. On the other side of the wall he found Sally struggling in the clutches of a boy with long dark hair. She was crying and he could see that one of the shoulder straps of her dress was torn. He threw down the cigarette and began to run towards them.

'*Hey*! What do you think you're doing? Leave her alone,' he shouted.

The boy turned an angry face in his direction. 'Clear off. What the hell's it got to do with you?'

'She's my sister.' Jason squared his broad shoulders aggressively. 'You gonna let her go or do I have to teach you a lesson?'

The boy gave Sally a shove that sent her staggering into the wall. 'Aw, take your bloody kid sister home then,' he said. 'Nothing but a little tease anyway.' He slouched past Jason, brushing roughly against him as he passed. Jason lunged towards him and grasped him by the collar.

'If I ever see you so much as look at her again, I'll make you wish you'd never been born,' he growled.

The other boy snarled. 'Oh, yeah? You and who else?'

As Jason helped Sally to her feet he smelled alcohol on her breath. 'How much have you had to drink?'

She pushed him away. 'Mind your own business, Jason Harris. Who asked you to come rushing up like a cardboard Rambo? And since when have I been your sister?'

He stepped back, stung by her ingratitude. 'That guy – he was *attacking* you. If I hadn't come along . . .'

'Who says he was attacking me?' Sally made an attempt at straightening her ruined dress. 'How do you know I didn't like him?'

'If you did, you had a funny way of showing it. Just look at you. You're not going to tell me you *like* being roughed up like that? Anyway, you were protesting loudly enough for the whole college to hear.'

Suddenly she burst into tears and began to beat her fists against his chest.

'Oooh – I *hate* you. I hate everyone. First it's Dad, following me around and spoiling everything. Now you. You're all as bad. *Families!*' She stamped her feet angrily. 'Who needs them?' The tears streamed down her cheeks, making dark mascara rivulets on her pale cheeks. Her shoulders heaved with a mixture of shock and anger. 'W-why don't you b-bugger off and leave me alone?' she sobbed.

'Okay, if you're going to swear at me you can get on with it.' Jason turned proudly and walked a few steps, then he halted, looking round at the pathetic tattered figure leaning against the wall. Walking back, he took off his leather jacket and slipped it round her shoulders. 'Come on, kid, better let me take you home now. The car's not far away. No one'll see you.'

In the car Sally seemed to crumple. Leaning against his shoulder, she sniffed into her handkerchief.

'I feel such a fool, Jase,' she mumbled.

He slipped his arm around her shoulders. 'Forget it. It's not worth upsetting yourself over.'

'I just wanted to *live* a bit,' she said, blowing her nose hard. 'To find out what it was like to go out by myself – without Mum and Dad breathing down my neck.' She looked up at him with brimming blue eyes. 'I expect you think I'm a silly kid who shouldn't be allowed out?'

Jason looked down at his cousin and wondered how he could possibly have given her that idea. He'd always thought her pretty, but now she was beautiful – even like this with her make-up running and her hair tangled. Looking up at him so trustingly, she brought out all his protective instincts. Suddenly he wanted to kill tigers for her, preferably with his bare hands. Bending his head to hers, he kissed her gently and experimentally.

'I don't think that at all, Sal,' he whispered, his lips brushing her damp cheek. 'I think you're gorgeous. I always have.'

Chapter 9

Ralph was as good as his word. Within months of his marriage to Marie he had persuaded David to buy another hotel, this time further south at Great Yarmouth. Two years later they opened another in Clacton-on-Sea, and by the time their fifth anniversary came round the Evans chain consisted of three hotels and had reached as far south as Hastings.

Everything had moved much too fast as far as David was concerned. He was very much aware of the vast amounts of money being laid out and the debts Ralph was taking on. The precarious knife edge on which the business's finances were balanced terrified him. He was constantly afraid that they would fail and lose all they had worked for. He was worried about Marie too. She seemed under a strain, working all the hours God sent and looking thinner and more stressed week by week. But he had to admit that Ralph certainly made things hum. It was he who made all the fact-finding trips. He had a talent for finding rundown properties going at knock-down prices and getting them even cheaper. It was Ralph who negotiated with owners and agents and talked them into selling, arguing that a quick sale was money in the bank, even at the price he was willing to pay.

After completion Marie took over. It was her job to move in and plan the decor and furnishings; to supervise all the work and engage new staff. Then later, once they opened, it was Marie who stayed on with the newly appointed manager for the first few months, ironing out any teething problems as they arose.

David stayed on in Cromer, enjoying his semi-retirement in the top floor flat at 'The Marina', though sometimes he felt guilty about letting his son and daughter-in-law do all the work. He was lonely at times too, though Ralph frequently visited him – more frequently sometimes than he might have wished. Ralph had a disconcerting habit of bringing up the subject of money – broadly hinting that he was dissatisfied with his salaried position as business manager and that he would be respected more if Evans Hotels were to be made over completely to him. David had already suggested forming a company in which the three of them would have equal shares, but Ralph wasn't keen on the idea, insisting that he should have sole charge of the business himself. But David held out, reluctant to relinquish the reins himself, and as Ralph refused to accept compromise there was deadlock between them. David's stubbornness on the matter irked Ralph intensely but he kept his patience firmly under control. He could wait, he told himself. He'd make his father see sense in the end. And if all else failed – well, he couldn't live for ever, could he? And Ralph was his only living relative.

Marie threw all of her energy into her work. Although life was hectic she could see the dream she had never really believed would come true rapidly becoming reality. But she was also being made to realise that there was a price to pay for it all. She missed running the business. Ralph had taken everything over now, insisting that she would never handle the high-powered financial deals that were now necessary. Sometimes she felt herself weakening under the strain and worry of the new life that Ralph had imposed on them all. It was as though the business was gathering momentum to an extent where it was only barely under control. But that was Ralph. That was the way he liked to do everything. He hated standing still.

Since their marriage Marie had discovered a lot about her husband, not least of which was his temper, which could be triggered off by the slightest thing. In the early days she had tried to stand up to him, but she had soon discovered that it was better not to goad him. Answering back, she had often found herself the butt of that temper and more than once Ralph had lost control and struck her. He was always apologetic afterwards, begging for her forgiveness and bringing her expensive presents or flowers to make up. But Marie dreaded his unpredictable outbursts and had grown used to devising ways of avoiding them.

Ralph's life-style had altered radically since leaving the army. He had shaved off his moustache and grown his hair longer. He'd acquired a whole new wardrobe of expensive clothes and invested in a fast sports car which he drove at break-neck speed, insisting that time was of the essence. In business he applied the same breathtaking roller-coasting methods as he did behind the wheel. Sometimes the risks involved frightened Marie, but there was little she could do but close her eyes, hold her breath and pray for good fortune. Ralph's business methods were all his own. They consisted of a mixture of charm, tenacity and extreme pressure, in that order. But there was no denying that they got results, and in any case, Marie was sure that there would be little point in trying to interfere. Ralph wouldn't listen to her suggestions any more than he would listen to David's.

It had been Ralph's decision that they would have no children.

'Business and kids don't mix,' he told her soon after their honeymoon. She'd been disappointed. Another baby would have helped fill the void left by the twins – a void she could never speak of to anyone, not even David and least of all Ralph. But she had to agree that if they were to build up their hotel chain a young family would only hamper them. Sometimes she longed for a settled home – somewhere to retreat to. She mentioned this to Ralph, thinking that all his years in the army would have made him long to put down roots too. But he only laughed derisively at her.

'Here you are, living in hotels, being waited on and cooked for, having the best food and wine and the most luxurious room in the place,' he taunted her. 'A choice of homes in beautiful seaside resorts to move between as the mood takes you. And all you crave for is some cosy little suburban semi where you can mess around in the kitchen in a frilly pinny. You must be mad, woman.'

He had laughed dismissively and Marie hadn't brought up the subject again.

She tried to visit David as often as she could. Since she and Ralph had married he seemed to have grown visibly older. He'd had one or two attacks of severe bronchitis in recent winters, and over the last couple of years walking and climbing stairs seemed to take it out of him. Each time she visited him he seemed a little more frail, though he really wasn't an old man by modern standards. She mentioned her worries about him to Ralph, but he seemed unconcerned.

'None of us can live for ever,' he said with a shrug.

Ralph had never made a secret of the fact that he liked women. Marie had noticed early on that he couldn't keep his eyes off an attractive woman but the first time she discovered definite evidence that he was having an affair she was devastated. She had taken one of his suits to the dry cleaners and found, in one of the pockets, a letter which could only have been written by a woman with whom he had been on intimate terms. Taxing him with it, she had found him unrepentant.

'So what? It means nothing.'

Marie held out the letter. 'But she – this woman – sounds as though she's in *love* with you.'

He shrugged. 'That's her problem. I told you, she means nothing to me. There's only you, Marie.'

'But if what you say is true . . .'

'Listen, Marie, it's nothing to concern yourself about. I always come back to you, don't I?'

'You mean this isn't the first time?' she asked.

'It's not the first and it won't be the last.'

She stared at him. 'Does your father know about this?'

He laughed. 'What's it got to do with him? Look, Marie, I've said – I always come back to you, don't I?'

She frowned. 'Suppose I don't want a husband who sleeps around, Ralph?'

He stared at her for a moment, his eyes hard and angry, then he pulled her to him and kissed her hard. 'You'll always need me, Marie,' he growled. 'We're too tied up together, what with Dad and the business, for you to want to run away. You know which side your bread is buttered.'

Picking her up effortlessly he carried her to their bedroom and began to make love to her, allowing his passion full rein. She sensed that he was angry and finding an outlet for that anger in sex. It frightened her. Violent sex seemed to give him a perverted kind of satisfaction. The involuntary cries that escaped her lips were more of pain than pleasure but as always they only served to heighten his arousal.

When it was over he refused to let her escape, holding her close in an almost suffocating embrace, her face pressed against his chest.

'You should know by now that I've got insatiable appetites, Marie – for everything. For money and power and success. And for sex too. Sometimes I have problems holding back, as I think you know. These little diversions of mine – and that's all they are – could be thought of as a safety valve, so maybe you should be grateful for them.' He grasped her chin and forced her to look into his eyes. 'So shall we forget all about it now? Believe me, my only real concern is *us*. Evans Hotels are going to be a big success. You'd better believe that.'

Marie did believe it. What she wasn't so sure about was the survival of her own self-esteem.

In the meantime Ralph continued to press his father to hand over the business to him.

'Can't you see how humiliating it is for me?' he said, standing over David. 'How do you think it feels, having to come to you for everything? I'm making the decisions, surely I should be able to sign the cheques too.'

'I've told you the answer to that,' David said. 'We'll form a company and you and Marie can be directors. That would make good sense.'

'And who's going to be managing director?' Ralph demanded.

'Why – me, of course.'

'And suppose we want to expand even further? Suppose we needed a substantial loan? What bank is going to extend a loan to you at your age?'

'It wouldn't be to me, but to the company. That's why it makes sense.'

'But it would mean all decisions being put before board meetings.'

'Yes, it would. Ralph – I don't want you to take this the wrong way, but I do feel that you're already taking too many of the decisions. This whole thing is accelerating too fast. It's getting out of hand. We don't want to run before we can walk. If we're going to form a hotel chain this is the only way to run it properly.'

Ralph's eyes glittered with suppressed anger. 'And what use do you think *you're* going to be as MD?' he snapped. 'All you've ever run is a tin pot boarding house in Cromer. And you had to get Marie in to help you with that after Megan died.'

David frowned. 'Marie and I were doing fine. We were quite content with things as they were.'

'Till I came along, you mean? Well, I've got news for you. *You* might have been quite content, but Marie was fed up with the set up. She told me so. She said she felt you were holding her back. I've got a lot of time to make up and I intend to go places. How can I do that with you dragging on the reins like some old cart horse?'

David's face paled as he stared at his son. 'It's thanks to Marie that there was any business at all for you to step into. Maybe I have held her back. All the more reason for her to have a share of the business now, and a hand in making the decisions too.'

Ralph snorted impatiently. 'Marie is a woman – with a woman's limitations. She's fine on the housekeeping side, but . . .'

'I'd like you to go now, Ralph,' David interrupted. 'Before one of us says something we might regret. I thought when I offered you a job . . .'

'*Ah*! I was wondering when you were going to throw that in my face,' Ralph shouted. 'All the work I've put in on this business, all the grafting I've done, and that's all the thanks I get. All right, I'll go.'

He flung out of the room, leaving David shaking. There was something dark in his son's character that he didn't understand – something that was almost menacing. Where did it come from? he wondered. Not from him and certainly not from Ralph's late mother. He seemed to use these browbeating tactics to sweep all before him. And David could see it leading to trouble before too long.

It was in the winter of 1984 that David had a bad bout of 'flu. It turned to bronchitis and then to pneumonia, which put him into hospital for a few days. The manager of 'The Marina' telephoned Marie to tell her about it and once David had recovered enough to come out of hospital, she went up to Cromer to nurse him. She was shocked by his appearance. The flesh seemed to have fallen off him, making the bones of his face prominent and giving him a gaunt appearance. He looked ten years older than his seventy years. Marie felt guilty at not having come to look after him before.

'Why didn't you let me know how ill you were?' she chided him gently. 'Every time I talked to you on the phone, you insisted that you were on the mend.'

David squeezed the hand that held his. 'I know how busy you are. There are plenty of people to cater for my needs here.'

'Cater for your needs, but not look after you,' Marie said. 'Anyway, I'm here now. And I'm not leaving till you're on your feet again.'

He smiled. 'Well, I won't pretend it isn't good to

have you here,' he admitted. 'It'll be quite like old times again. Just you and me.'

She cooked all his meals herself in the kitchen at the flat and kept him entertained with news of the latest hotel Ralph was negotiating for down in Dorset.

'When it's finished you must come down for a long visit,' she told him. 'In fact, it wouldn't be a bad idea if you were to leave here and come down to Dorset permanently. The cold air from the North Sea can't be good for your chest in the winter. It's so much milder down there. Apparently they hardly ever have any snow. What do you say?'

David gave her a rueful smile. 'Don't you think you should ask Ralph first?'

'Ask him? But you're his father.'

David shook his head. 'I must confess, Marie, that I don't feel much like his father, and I'm sure he doesn't see me as such. I think I annoy – no madden – him at times.'

'Whatever makes you think that?' Marie asked.

'He hasn't told you?' David looked at her quizzically.

'Not about your annoying him. What has he been saying to you?'

David sighed. 'He wants me to hand over to him.' He ran a hand wearily across his brow. 'Maybe I've acted like a stubborn old man. Maybe I should do as he says. But I wanted you to have a share in the business, Marie. And to be honest I don't feel ready to hand everything over to him. Not yet.'

She was disturbed. Ralph had mentioned none of this to her. 'You mustn't consider me, David,' she said slowly. 'You mustn't quarrel with Ralph because of me. He's your son and blood is thicker than water.'

He reached for her hand and held it tightly. 'I'll be

honest with you, Marie. *You* feel much more like family to me than Ralph does. He might be my son but I hardly know him. The worrying part is that the longer I know him, the further apart we seem to get. I worry about his business methods too. We seem to be taking too much on, and since he took over the financial side from you I'm not completely convinced that he does things as ethically as he might. I don't understand where some of the money comes from. I just hope it's all above board.'

Although Marie had her own doubts on this score she had no real way of knowing. Ralph never let her see the books. He confided nothing to her and allowed her only the same salary as the other managers. She didn't mention this to David, but tried to reassure him. 'I'm sure Ralph wouldn't do anything you wouldn't approve of.'

'Then there's you.' David looked into her eyes. 'You're not happy, are you, love?' He waved away her look of protest. 'No, don't deny it. I've seen the sadness in your eyes. You're just not the same Marie I used to know.'

'I'm older, David,' she made a brave attempt at lightness. 'I'm thirty-one now. I'm not a carefree young girl any more.'

'Let's face it, love, you've never been a carefree young girl, more's the pity.' He patted her hand. 'But I had such high hopes for you and Ralph. I thought he'd be good for you. Take care of you and make you happy. I was so delighted when the two of you married. If I'd known then . . .'

'All this is in your mind,' Marie interrupted. 'You're having morbid thoughts because you've been ill. You're still tired and low. Off you go to bed now and I'll bring you a hot drink. At the weekend I'm going to take you back to Hastings with me and keep you there till I'm good and sure you're fit to be on your own again.'

David enjoyed his stay in Hastings, and by the time he had departed for Cromer again Marie was satisfied that he was on the way to being his old self. She had enjoyed looking after him, personally cooking his favourite meals – dishes that he himself had taught her to cook in the old days at 'Homeleigh'. When she drove him to the station and waved him off she felt a pang of sadness. It had been nice to feel needed; so satisfying to see David's cheeks rounding out again, the firm, healthy flesh filling out his spare frame and the vitality returning into his eyes.

Ralph had been away for most of David's visit. As well as combing the coastal resorts for new properties he liked to spend a regular night or two in each of the Evans Hotels, just – as he said – to keep them on their toes. The third time he came home to find his father still there he had expressed irritation at the length of the convalescence. He accused Marie of neglecting her other duties and allowing the staff to become sloppy. He clearly resented the time she spent with David and made sure he received her whole attention whilst he was home, virtually ignoring his father.

Marie dreaded her father-in-law's departure, knowing that she would miss him. But by the time David was fit enough to return to Cromer contracts had been exchanged on the Dorset hotel and it was almost time for her to appoint a new manager for the Hastings hotel and travel down to Dorset to take over there.

She'd never been this far south and the moment she saw the place she fell in love with it. The hotel stood on high ground overlooking the beautiful Studland Bay. The views were spectacular and she set about planning the decor and furnishings with enthusiasm.

She had already made up her mind that David should make his home here in this tranquil place with its mild climate, and set about the conversion of the top floor into a large apartment with four bedrooms where the three of them could make a permanent home together. Ralph was furious. He argued that half of the top floor rooms could have been made into a smaller manager's flat, leaving the others free for guests. For once, Marie put her foot down.

'Once your father has moved out of "The Marina" you can do that with the apartment there,' she said. 'I want this to be our home, and a home for your father too. I want to have him where I can keep an eye on him now that his health is failing.'

To her surprise Ralph had given in and she congratulated herself on making a stand and getting her own way. But Ralph had his own reasons for giving way to her. He told himself that maybe it would be as well to keep the old boy sweet. If he couldn't make him see sense, maybe Marie's fussing over him would do the trick. Later, when the time was right, he'd get her to talk him into handing the business over to him. She'd do it. He'd make sure of that.

'The Ocean' opened three months later, just in time for the summer season. David found the move from Cromer an exhausting upheaval, but once he was installed in his spacious room he had to agree that it was worth it. In the first weeks he and Marie explored the area, enjoying long walks through the chines and along the cliffs. They took most of their meals in the hotel dining room, but sometimes in the evenings Marie would cook for them both in the small kitchen of the flat. Occasionally David would play chef, as he had in the old days, and they would eat at the table by the open window and enjoy the sparkling sea air and the wonderful view of the bay.

At the weekends when Ralph came David made himself scarce, taking himself off for day-long excursions or keeping to his own room. Ralph refused to eat in the flat. He liked to play 'boss'; to be seen in the restaurant by staff and guests and to keep an eagle eye on the waiters, making sure that they were not slacking. He insisted that it kept the chef and dining room staff up to scratch, but Marie privately thought that it made them nervous and resentful.

At the end of August Marie invited Hannah to take a week's holiday at 'The Ocean'. Hannah's work had taken her to the north-east soon after Ralph and Marie were married, and for the past few years she had lived in Newcastle. Although they'd corresponded regularly they hadn't met for some time. Marie wanted to show off the newest of the Evans Hotels to her friend and she knew that it would please David to be able to renew his longstanding friendship with Hannah too.

She arrived on a Friday afternoon at the end of the month. One of those mellow, golden summer's end days when the sea is like a sheet of shimmering silver and the sun shines through a gauzy golden haze. She had changed her car and now drove a smart little red BMW cabriolet. She looked tanned and fit from a recent holiday in Greece, and almost the first thing Marie noticed was that she had had her hair cut. The long brown tresses were gone, giving way to a smart highlighted bob which made her look younger than her forty-five years.

The two women hugged each other warmly and Marie took Hannah straight up to her room.

'I thought you'd like this one,' she said, throwing open the door. 'It has a view of the sea.'

'Oh, it's *beautiful*.' Hannah opened the window and took a deep breath. 'You really have done wonders, haven't you? What's this – your fourth hotel?'

Marie nodded. 'Yes, but don't let's talk about business now. Tell me all your news. How's your new job? And your holiday in Greece – did you have a good time? You look wonderful.'

Hannah chatted for a while about her holiday and the new job she was about to return to in London. But as she spoke she was assessing her friend. Marie didn't look well. She was too thin and there were dark smudges under her eyes.

'That's enough about me,' she said at last. 'Tell me about yourself. How's David? You said he'd been ill.'

'He's fine now – living here with us as I told you. I insisted,' Marie said. 'Besides, he's company for me, with Ralph away so much.'

Hannah saw the shadow that clouded Marie's eyes when she mentioned Ralph's name.

'Are you happy?' she asked.

'Yes, of course.'

'Ralph certainly doesn't seem to let the grass grow under his feet.'

'No.'

'And you – are you sure you're not working too hard? You're looking a little tired. Have you had a holiday this year?'

'Good heavens, there's no time for holidays. We haven't been away since – since Italy, our honeymoon. No, I expect the refurbishment here and David's illness has taken it out of me. I'll be fine now that the season's coming to a close.' She walked to the door. 'You'll excuse me if I leave you to unpack, won't you? Life gets hectic here around now. I'll join you for dinner later, of course. Any of the waiters will show you to our table. Oh, and do have a drink first, won't you? On the house, of course. I'll join you if I can. 'Bye.'

162

Hannah stood for a moment after she had gone. There was something wrong. Marie's cheerfulness seemed forced. She told herself it was tiredness after the season, but the niggling doubt at the back of her mind refused to rest.

After she'd unpacked and changed, Hannah went down to the bar. Marie did not appear but she got talking to a couple who had just checked in for a weekend visit. The man introduced himself and his wife as Mark and Barbara Summers and during the conversation Hannah learned that he had recently retired from the services and had just come out of hospital after surgery for injuries received during the Falklands War. She was still chatting to Mark and Barbara when Ralph walked into the bar. He greeted Hannah like an old friend, kissing her on both cheeks and turning his back pointedly on the couple she had been talking to. They moved discreetly away, making Hannah feel acutely embarrassed at Ralph's boorish behaviour.

Over the weekend Hannah felt that Ralph was putting on a special show for her benefit and was quite relieved to see him leave early on Monday morning. Over breakfast she noticed that Marie was quiet and later she excused herself, saying that she needed to work in the office for an hour. Hannah found her there later, opening and sorting mail. Tapping on the half-open door, she said: 'Hello – can I come in?'

Marie looked up. 'Hannah! Of course you can. It's the secretary's day off today. That's why I'm doing this. I've almost finished.'

'I thought we might have a day out together. If you can spare the time, that is?'

'Oh, that would be lovely.' Marie reached quickly for a cardigan that hung over the back of her chair, hastily throwing it around her shoulders, but not

163

before Hannah had glimpsed the livid bruises on her upper arms.

'Have you hurt yourself?'

Marie blushed scarlet. 'No.'

'But there – on your arms. Those bruises look nasty.'

'Oh, that? I – bumped into something. I'm always doing it.'

Hannah frowned but didn't pursue the subject further. They asked David to go with them but he said he had a dental appointment. They took Hannah's car and drove out to the New Forest, stopping for lunch at a quiet little pub. It was there, sitting outside in the late summer sunshine, that Hannah gently probed Marie about Ralph.

'Are you sure everything's all right between you and Ralph?'

'I told you – yes.'

'You're happy?'

'Of course. You never stop asking.' Marie laughed, but Hannah noticed that she couldn't quite meet her eyes.

'I know I keep asking, and frankly, Marie, it's because you look downright afraid of him,' Hannah said in her forthright way. 'And the bruises on your arm . . . they weren't caused by bumping into anything, now were they?'

Marie sighed. 'He doesn't mean to. Sometimes he's – sometimes he gets . . .'

'Violent?'

Marie shook her head. 'No. He's just a little – excitable at times. He doesn't seem to realise how strong he is.'

Hannah was seriously worried now. 'Has he always been like this with you?'

'I suppose . . . no.' Marie shook her head unhappily.

'You shouldn't be asking me these things. It's private.'

'I know. I'm sorry, Marie. But you don't have to put up with that kind of thing, you know. A marriage certificate doesn't give a man the right to abuse you.'

'He doesn't. Please – can we talk about something else?'

The warm colour and the look of shame in the other woman's eyes were revealing. Hannah had seen the same reaction so many times before in the battered wives she had dealt with. Reluctantly she let the subject drop but not before she'd covered Marie's hand with hers and said: 'Look, love, I'll say this once again and then we'll leave it. You don't have to put up with it, you know. You don't have to stay with him.'

Marie said nothing for a moment. It was as if she was struggling with herself inwardly. Then she said in an almost inaudible voice, 'And just where else do you suppose I'd go? This is the only home – the only work I know, Hannah. And I couldn't leave David. He needs me.'

'Does David know how things are?'

'No.' Marie looked up with an expression of appeal. 'Please don't say anything to him. He's not strong. I don't want him upset.' She tried to smile. 'It'll work itself out, Hannah. Don't worry.'

'I'm always there if you need help,' she said softly. 'You know that, don't you?'

'Of course.' Marie withdrew her hand, but her eyes were bright as she looked up. 'And thanks. But I'll be fine. Honestly.'

It was the same night, as Hannah was having a pre-dinner drink in the bar, that Mark Summers joined her. She turned to smile at him as he slid on to the bar stool next to hers.

'Said I'd meet Babs in the lounge,' he explained with a smile. 'But you know how long they take.'

She laughed. 'I should do.'

'Spotted you in here and thought I might as well join you.' He ordered a gin and tonic, looking enquiringly at her. 'What's that you're drinking?'

She shook her head, holding up her glass. 'I'm fine thanks. One's my limit.'

He paid for his drink and took a sip, looking hesitantly at her over the rim of the glass. 'Look – I don't know if I should say anything, but something's been bothering me ever since Friday night.'

She smiled. 'Really? Anything I can help with?'

'I wonder – it's just – the man who joined you in here on Friday evening. Who is he?'

'His name is Ralph Evans. His father owns this hotel.'

The man's eyebrows rose. 'Really?'

'What makes you ask?'

'I know – or rather *knew* – him. It was quite a while ago. I had a job to place him at first. Even then I wasn't sure. He's changed quite a lot since I knew him.'

'How long ago was it?'

'Oh – must be all of seven years now.' He rolled his glass between his hands, frowning as though trying to make up his mind about something, then he turned and looked at her. 'Close friend of yours, is he? Know him well?'

An intuitive caution stirred in the pit of Hannah's stomach.

'Not well,' she said truthfully. 'Hardly at all, in fact.'

'But you knew he was in the army?'

Hannah nodded. 'Military Police, wasn't it? That was before I met him though.'

'Tell you his reason for leaving, did he?'

'No.'

He looked uncomfortable. 'Look – maybe I should keep my big mouth shut. None of my business really. Babs is always telling me to keep my nose out of things that don't concern me, but we're leaving this evening and . . .' He looked at her. 'You're obviously a nice woman and I wouldn't like to see someone like you getting mixed up with his sort.'

'Mr Summers, I think you'd better tell me,' Hannah said quietly. 'It sounds as though it's something I should hear.'

'I think so too.' Mark took out a packet of cigarettes and offered it to Hannah. She shook her head but he lit one thoughtfully before he began: 'I served with him in Northern Ireland. It was some years ago, as I said. I knew him only slightly – mainly through the case because I was on escort duty at the time. He certainly wouldn't remember me.'

Hannah frowned. 'The *case*?'

He nodded. 'He was court martialled. Obviously, he never told you. Not surprising really.'

'No. What was he in trouble for?'

'Basically for being too handy with his fists; knocking prisoners around. Then there was an unsavoury business with a local girl. Apparently he beat her up quite badly. That was when things got serious. She accused him of passing information to . . .' He looked at her. 'Shall we say, a subversive organisation?'

Hannah let out her breath in a silent whistle. 'So – what was the outcome of the court martial? Was he found guilty?'

'He got a longish sentence for the assault charge, but the girl's accusations were never proved. There

167

was insufficient evidence that he'd been an informer. After he'd served his sentence he came out of the army. He'd served his time and I imagine he was left in no doubt that it was time for a change of career.' He looked at her. 'I hope I haven't put my foot in it?'

Hannah finished her drink and looked at him. 'On the contrary. I'm very grateful to you, Mr Summers. Thank you for being so open with me.' She looked past him through the open bar doors into the lounge and smiled. 'I think I can see your wife looking for you.'

'You mean to say you sat in the bar, discussing Ralph with one of the guests?' Marie's eyes were bright with anger and two spots of crimson flamed in her cheeks. 'I don't know how you have the gall to come to me and admit it.'

'Please, don't take it like this, Marie. I'm telling you as a friend.'

Marie stood at the open window, her face stony as she faced Hannah. 'A friend? Is that what you call yourself? It's rubbish – all of it. The man's a liar.'

Hannah took a step towards her. 'Don't bury your head in the sand, Marie. Mark Summers wouldn't have told me if it wasn't true. Why should he make it all up?'

'He was mistaken then. He must have taken Ralph for someone else.'

'No, he didn't. He remembered the name – everything. Marie, I'm telling you for your own good. I'm warning you, Ralph has a criminal record. He's been in prison.'

Marie spun round to face her. 'And in case you've forgotten, *so have I*!'

Hannah winced. 'But you were innocent.'

'How do you know that?'

168

Hannah stared at her. 'You *were*. I know you were.' Suddenly she was afraid. 'Marie – what's the matter with you, for God's sake?'

'You say you know I was innocent, but you can't know for sure, can you? Maybe Ralph was innocent too.'

The two women stared at each other for a long moment. Marie's eyes were like ice, cold and glittering, expressionless, and suddenly Hannah felt that she was looking into the face of a defiant stranger, someone too far away to reach. She said: 'I think perhaps I should leave in the morning.'

Marie shrugged. 'That's the most sensible thing you've said so far. I agree. I think you should go. But I must ask you to promise me one thing. Please don't mention any of this to David.'

'Of course I won't. What do you take me for?'

'I *took* you for a friend,' Marie flung back at her. 'I'm beginning to doubt it.'

'Look, Marie, will you at least *ask* Ralph about it?' Hannah pleaded.

'If there was anything he wanted me to know he would have told me when I told him about my trouble,' Marie said defiantly.

Hannah stared at her. 'You told him?'

'About my conviction and going to prison. He believes in my innocence.'

'So – he knows about the twins?'

'*No*. Not that. I couldn't bring myself to tell him that.'

There was a pause as Hannah looked at her. 'Look, if you believe he's innocent, why not give him the chance to tell you so?'

'I told you – no.' But Marie shook her head, her face pale. 'Why should I stir up a whole heap of trouble that no one can do anything about? We're all right as we are. Just leave it alone, can't you, Hannah?'

'You're afraid of him, aren't you?' Hannah shook her head. 'Oh, Marie, don't you see? I'm worried about you. That's the only reason I'm telling you this. I don't want to see anything bad happen to you.'

'It *won't*,' Marie said, turning away. 'Please, will you go now?' She stood looking out of the window, her back towards Hannah. After a moment she heard the door open and quietly close behind her. Only then did she allow her shoulders to sag and the tears she'd held back to fall. She covered her face with her hands. 'Oh, Mother of God help me,' she prayed silently. 'Please – tell me what to do.'

Chapter 10

When Terry answered the ring on his bell that night and went downstairs to open the door, he was more than a little surprised to find Leah standing outside.

She picked up her suitcase and looked at him hopefully. 'Can I come in?'

'Of course you can. What's happened?' he asked, looking at the case.

'I've left,' she told him. 'There was a row. I'm not going back, Terry – ever.' She stood in the dark hallway looking up at him appealingly. 'Terry, can I stay with you for a couple of days, please? Just till I sort out where I go from here.'

'Here?' He frowned. 'Haven't you got a girlfriend you could stay with?'

'You know I haven't – not one I could trust. All my old schoolfriends' parents are friends of Jack and Hilary's.' She peered at him. 'Why, is it a problem?'

Terry raked a hand through his hair. 'Look, love, any other time it'd be fine, but I've had notice to quit the flat by this weekend. The building is coming down next week. I've got some holiday due to me so I'm going away tomorrow.' Her forlorn look tugged at his heart. It was so unlike Leah to show the slightest hint of vulnerability. Something serious must have happened. Relenting, he reached out and took her suitcase. 'Come upstairs, kid. We'll talk about it over a coffee. You look as though you could do with a cup.'

She climbed the three flights of stairs behind him and when they reached his top-floor room she closed the door firmly behind her and stood with her back against it.

'Can I stay just for tonight then?' she asked. 'I wouldn't ask but I haven't got anywhere else to go. I'll sleep on the floor – anywhere. And tomorrow I'll be gone before you're awake. I'll get a train and go to London.'

He sighed. 'And just what do you think you're going to do when you get there?' he asked, switching on the kettle. 'It's a dicy business, you know, a girl of your age, alone in London.'

She grinned mischievously. 'Do you think the white slavers'll get me? Terry, you're a stuffy old fusspot. I'll be all right. There are hostels for single girls, aren't there?'

'And do you know the addresses of any?' He looked at her. 'Before you set off I think you should make enquiries and organise yourself a bit better. You can't just take off. You're not nearly as grown up as you think, you know.' He held out his hand for her coat and indicated his best chair. 'Sit down and get it off your chest, whatever it is. Have a row with the folks, did you? I expect it'll all have blown over by the morning.'

'Not this time, it won't.' Leah threw herself down in the chair.

'Serious, eh?' He was busy spooning instant coffee into two mugs.

'You could say that. I've been really stupid, Tel. I mean – *really* stupid.'

He poured boiling water onto the coffee and added milk. 'Well, I'm all ears if you want to unburden yourself.'

Leah sipped the scalding coffee gratefully. 'You won't like me much when I tell you.'

'Risk it,' he said with a grin. 'Nothing you could do would shock me.' Or put me off you, he added to himself.

'You might change your mind when you know what I did.'

'Well, neither of us is going to find out unless you tell me, are we?'

She swallowed another mouthful of coffee and took a deep breath. 'I seduced Tom Clayton.'

Terry spluttered over his coffee. '*Councillor* Tom Clayton?' he asked, wide-eyed. She nodded. 'Of Clayton's department store?'

'The same.'

'But he must be old enough to be your father. Why did you do it?'

She shrugged. 'I could see he fancied me and I wanted a job in his shop. I knew there were no vacancies . . .'

'And you thought he might create one for you if you were nice to him,' Terry finished for her.

'That's about it.'

He studied her for a moment, then asked: 'So what went wrong?'

She stirred restlessly in her chair. 'Oh, lots of things. He became too demanding for starters. I was supposed to go to college on day release but I ended up with him instead on those days. It was impossible to get any proper training, and anyway I hated the job. Anyway, to cut a long story short, today I tried to finish it. We had a row and I suppose his precious ego took a battering.'

'What did he do?'

'He went to Jack.'

Terry stared at her incredulously. 'He went to your father?'

'My adoptive father,' she corrected. 'My ex-adoptive father. Yes. Apparently he came over all pious and contrite – told a whole pack of lies and made me look like a blackmailing little tart.' Her face suddenly crumpled and she began to sniff back the threatened tears. 'Which I suppose I am.'

Terry watched her for a moment, torn between sympathy and exasperation. 'Leah, you little fool. Whatever possessed you?'

'I was bored,' she groaned. 'Bored and fed up.' She sniffled into the handkerchief he passed her. 'And I suppose, if I'm honest, it was nice – having someone wanting me.' She grimaced. 'But I soon found out that it wasn't worth it.'

Terry frowned. 'I still don't understand why he went to your father. Surely he didn't have to go that far? And where did the blackmailing part come in?'

She looked at him. 'When I could see he was going to be hard to shake off, I told him that I'd discovered he was seeing someone else. I threatened him that I'd spill the beans if he didn't let me go. *That's* why he ratted on me.'

'And was it true that he was seeing someone else?'

'Yes.'

'Who?'

'That's the awful part . . .' she hesitated. 'Promise it's only between the two of us?'

'Of course.'

'It was Hilary.' Unconsciously, her fingers touched her cheek. 'I overheard them talking in the kitchen – after the barbecue that Sunday.'

Terry gave a long, low whistle. 'Phew. You weren't kidding when you said you'd been stupid. You've landed yourself right in it this time, haven't you?'

Leah straightened her shoulders defiantly and took a deep breath. 'I don't care. In fact, I'm glad. I'm going to find my real mother now – whatever Jack says. I've saved some money. I'll be all right for a while, even if I don't get a job right away.'

Terry took the empty mug out of her hands and stood looking down at her thoughtfully. 'Look, I don't like the idea of your going off to London all alone, Leah. You haven't thought it through properly, and you'll find it a lot harder to get work than you seem to think.'

For the first time she looked doubtful. 'Well, what shall I do then?' Her face brightened. 'I suppose I couldn't go with you, could I? Just to give me time to think what to do next.'

Terry bit his lip. He'd walked right into that one. 'I don't know, Leah. You see, it's more of a working holiday really,' he said. 'I'm going to Cleybourn-on-Sea. It's a little fishing village in Norfolk, on the Wash. A mate of mine has a holiday cottage down there and he's renting it to me for a couple of weeks. The idea is to have some peace and quiet to write a series of features for the paper. You'd probably be bored out of your skull.'

'No, I wouldn't. Oh, Tel, it sounds great. Can I come – please?' Her eyes began to shine again and he felt his resolve melting. 'I won't be a nuisance,' she urged. 'I could even be a big help – cook your meals and do the housework. I could be a kind of housekeeper-cum-rotweiler – keep intruders away.'

He began to laugh. 'I wasn't anticipating any intruders.'

She looked at him with eyes as brown and melting as treacle toffee. 'Does that mean yes? Can I come? Please?'

The drive to Cleybourn-on-Sea took a little under two hours. It should have taken much less, but the little 2CV was loaded to the gunnels with all Terry's worldly possessions and he had to keep stopping to rearrange the load. He hadn't allowed for Leah and her luggage as well.

Before they left Nenebridge they called in on Kate Dobson so that Leah could say goodbye. The old woman was pleased to see them both, but when Leah explained the reason for her call, Kate's face fell.

'It's not too late to go back, sugar,' she said. 'I'm sure your mum and dad will have forgotten the silly squabble by now.'

Leah shook her head. 'They're not my mum and dad, Gran. Let's face it, they never have been, not in any way. And it was more than just a silly squabble, I'm afraid. This time it's serious. I shan't be coming back again.'

'Is there anything I can do?'

'No.' Leah shook her head. 'And don't ask me what happened, Gran. I can't tell you. It's over. That's all.'

Kate's eyes filled with tears. 'I shall miss you. You'll come back and see your old gran, won't you? There'll always be a place for you here, you know.'

'I do know.' Leah hugged her. 'And of course I'll come if I can.' She swallowed hard. 'Oh dear – I'm going to miss you too, Gran.'

'We've had some good laughs, eh?'

'Yes, some good laughs.'

Kate held her at arms' length. 'So you're going to try and find your real mother like you told me. Is that the plan?'

Leah nodded. 'I hope so.' She glanced at Terry. 'When I get myself organised. I'm going . . .'

Kate stopped her with a shake of her head. 'Don't say any more, my old sugar. The less I know, the less I'm likely to let something slip. They're bound to come asking.'

'She'll be all right, Mrs Dobson,' Terry put in. 'I won't let her come to any harm.'

'I know you won't, lad.' Kate pulled Leah close and kissed her. 'Off you go then. Nothing an old geezer like me can do to stop you, is there? Not sure I would even if I could. Drop me a postcard now and then if you get time.'

'I will, Gran, I promise. Take care of yourself, won't you?'

In the car she was silent and Terry left her to her own thoughts for a while. When they crossed the Norfolk border and the countryside began to rise and fall, he turned to look at her.

'Shall we stop for a pub lunch somewhere?'

She turned to him with a smile. 'Yes, please. I'm starving.'

It was mid-afternoon when they reached Cleybourn-on-Sea. Turning off the main road they ran down into the winding main street of the little fishing village with its flint and shingle-built cottages. Hazel Cottage was at the bottom of the street, almost on the quayside. It stood in a little courtyard shared by three other cottages. Hazel Cottage had a white-painted front door sheltered by a small porch over which a purple clematis climbed. Under the front window stood a stone trough out of which a profusion of dahlias exploded, splashing their vivid pinks, yellows and reds against the grey-shingled wall.

Leah exclaimed with delight. 'Oh, Terry. It's lovely.'

'Yes, nice, isn't it?' He began to unload the car. 'The key is at number three.' He pointed to the cottage facing. 'Will you go and collect it while I shift some of this stuff, Leah?'

Number three had a long low building at one side.

Through the window Leah could see that it was in use as an artist's studio. A table under the window was littered with tubes of paint and other artists' materials. A large canvas, supported on an easel, was positioned under a skylight towards the back of the studio and she could see a pair of denim-clad legs protruding from beneath it. At her tap on the window the owner of the legs emerged from behind the easel and came to open the door. He was thirtyish, she estimated, and a paint-splattered tee-shirt completed his rather grubby ensemble. He had long dark hair which he wore tied back in a pigtail and his face was swarthily tanned – she guessed from long days spent painting in the open. His hazel eyes twinkled with interest as he looked out at her.

'Hello there.'

'I'm sorry to disturb you.'

'Don't be. You're a very pleasant diversion.'

'Er – apparently the key to number four has been left here for us.'

'Oh, that's right. Hang on, it's in the kitchen. I'll get it for you.' He slipped into the cottage and re-emerged almost immediately with the key. 'I'm sorry,' he said as he handed it to her. 'I'm Colin Mays. I should have introduced myself before. Living alone down here all summer, one tends to forget the social niceties.' He frowned. 'I was told to expect a young guy – a journalist or something.'

'Oh, yes.' Leah laughed. 'That's Terry. He's unloading the car. I'm Leah Dobson. I'm afraid I imposed myself on him unexpectedly at the last minute, but I've promised to work my passage.'

'Well . . .' He smiled. 'You can impose yourself on me any time.' He caught sight of a laden Terry and gave him a friendly wave, which he was able to acknowledge only with a nod of his head. 'Anything you need, just give me a yell. The door's always open. If I've got it, you're welcome to it. If not . . .' He shrugged. 'See you later then, Leah.'

The inside of Hazel Cottage lived up to its romantic exterior. There was a spacious living room with an ingle-nook fireplace, a minute kitchen with an even smaller bathroom leading off it. And upstairs, two roomy bedrooms.

'Do you want the one with the view of the Saltings?' Terry asked.

'No, you have it. It's your holiday.'

Terry grinned. 'After the view of the railway line and the cemetery I had at the flat any view looks picturesque,' he said. 'No, I'm not planning to do much view-gazing. You have it.'

After they'd unpacked Terry went to the village shop and bought supplies. They made a meal of eggs and chips, over which Leah asked for the first time what Terry's future plans were.

'I've had my name down for a flat in that new block down by the river,' he told her. 'The one they've converted from an old warehouse. They're rather good – sheer luxury after my last abode; a proper bathroom and kitchen all to myself. Can you imagine? By the time I get back from here mine'll be ready to move into.'

Leah sighed wistfully. 'You are lucky, Tel. You have a job you like and a home of your own. You're achieving your ambition. You're independent.'

'And so can you be.' He leaned towards her. 'Try to make use of this time by sorting yourself out – making some sensible decisions about the future, Leah,' he urged. 'Don't get bogged down in obsession. You have your own life to live. Make up your mind what you want from it and where you're going.'

'I suppose by obsession you mean looking for my

mother?' she said stiffly. 'It's all right for you. You know who you are. Can't you see, Terry? I have to find that out before I know where I'm going. I feel I can't begin to *exist* till I know.' She pushed her hair behind her ears and looked at him dolefully. 'The trouble is knowing where and how to start.'

He sighed and looked at her with a mixture of exasperation and pity. 'Oh, Leah. All right then . . . I can see you're not going to give up. If it's really what you want . . .'

Her eyes lit up. 'You mean you'll help me?'

He raised his eyes to the ceiling. 'I must be out of my tiny mind, but, yes, okay, I'll do what I can.'

Her shining eyes clouded. 'Oh – er – Terry, there's something I haven't told you.'

He shook his head impatiently. 'Look, Leah – if I'm going to help you, you have to be completely honest with me. It's essential. What is it this time?'

'Last night, when we were having that awful row, Jack said something.' She paused to look up at him uncertainly.

'Right, go on.'

'He said – that my mother had been in prison.' She reached for her handbag and rummaged in it. 'I didn't believe him at first. I thought he was just being spiteful. But he gave me my proper birth certificate. The one with all the details on it. And look.' She spread the certificate on the table between them. 'See – it gives my place of birth as this remand home place.' She looked up at him. 'It means I have to find her even more now. Tel. It must all have been some terrible mistake. I know it must.'

Terry studied the birth certificate for some minutes, his mind heavy with apprehension. 'Look, Leah,' he said at last. 'Are you really sure you want to go through with this?'

'I have to, Tel – *have to*.' Her eyes were huge and full of pathos.

God help me. I must be mad, he said inwardly. Aloud, he heard himself saying: 'Okay then. I'll do what I can to get you off the ground with it.'

Her eyes lit up. 'Oh, Terry. When can we start?'

'Hang on a minute.' He held up his hands. 'I have to get these features done first. It's what I'm supposed to be here for. It's my job, right?'

She nodded. 'Right.'

'So will you promise to leave me alone to get on with them?'

'Yes. Yes, of course I will. I told you, I'll do all the chores and cook your meals so that you needn't do anything but concentrate on your work.'

'Right. After that I have another couple of weeks' leave. I was going to use the time to move into the new flat and get settled, but I do have to go to London anyway for . . .' He paused to look at her. Her eyes were shining with anticipation again and he had a sudden pang of serious doubt. Was he really doing her a favour? She seemed so confident that it would all end well, even though she knew her mother had given birth to her in prison. The woman could be anything from a murderess to a petty thief. He wouldn't want to be responsible for bringing more trauma into her life. Suppose the woman was someone undesirable and, once found, could not be shaken off?

'Look, kid,' he said, taking her hands. 'You're sure – *really* sure – this is what you want, aren't you? Because once we unlock the box it could be hard to get the lid back on, you know.'

'I don't care. I have to find her. Look, I've told you, Tel. I can't start living till I do. If you don't want to help me it doesn't matter. I'll . . .'

'Okay, okay then. On your own head be it.' He gave her a wry grin. 'After this fortnight my expertise as bloodhound extraordinaire is all yours.'

The first days at Cleybourn were halcyon days for Leah. Whilst Terry was busy she explored, walking on the quay where friendly fishermen nodded and gave her the time of day. She walked the rough paths out to the point to breathe the salty air and watch the seabirds. Once she took a trip run by a local boatman out to Blakeney Nature Reserve to see the seals. There were almost as many artists as there were fishermen at Cleybourn and on her walks she often came across Colin Mays seated at his easel, but although she always smiled and nodded, she never stopped to talk to him, afraid of intruding on his work.

The cottage didn't take long to tidy in the mornings and she had finished the chores and the day's shopping by ten. In the evenings she would happily prepare a meal in the sunny little kitchen while Terry worked on. Then they would eat together. Sometimes after supper they would stroll down to The Mermaid Inn by the quay for a drink and a chat with the locals, but more often than not Terry was yawning his head off by ten.

'I never knew that writing was so tiring,' Leah remarked one evening, halfway through the first week.

'It's the most tiring occupation I can think of,' Terry replied through another gaping yawn. 'Which is why I never bring anyone with me.'

Leah grinned. 'Point taken. I'm not complaining.'

'I'm not complaining either.' He grinned. 'I never knew you were such a good cook.'

She smiled, pleased with the compliment. 'Granny

Dobson taught me. I've never really had the chance to cook for anyone before though.'

'Well, I must be the best fed guinea pig around.' He smiled wryly at her. 'Poor Leah. Are you horrendously bored?'

'Not really. I do sometimes wish I could paint or something though. Then I'd have something positive to do.'

'You wouldn't fancy a job as a barmaid, would you?' Terry said, half joking.

Her eyes lit up. 'Do you know of one?'

'The landlord of The Mermaid was saying yesterday that he's short-staffed. I daresay he wouldn't turn down an offer of temporary help. The season will be over soon so he won't want anyone permanently.'

Leah called in at The Mermaid next morning. The pub wasn't open so she knocked on the side door. It was opened by the landlord, a middle-aged man who surveyed her with a rather dour expression. He wore a grubby white apron tied round his rotund figure.

'Yes?' He looked her up and down suspiciously.

'I'm sorry to intrude, Mr Johnson.' She'd taken careful note of the name over the door at the front before knocking. 'But I heard that you were looking for bar staff and I wondered . . .'

'There's no permanent job goin' here, miss.' He started to close the door, but Leah quickly put in: 'It was *temporary* work I was looking for.' The man hesitated, the door still open a crack. 'I'm here with my friend, you see. He's working all day and I'm at a loose end. If you could do with some temporary help, I'd be glad to oblige.'

'Ah – well . . .' He opened the door again. 'In that case maybe you'd better come in.'

The bar of The Mermaid, so quaint and cosy in the

evenings, looked shabby in daylight and not all that clean. It was dim and stuffy and it smelled of beer and stale cigarette smoke. Dick Johnson was obviously in the process of giving the place a perfunctory lick and promise. A mop and a bucket half full of dirty water stood by the bar. Another close to it contained the contents of the ashtrays, now stacked up on the bar ready for washing.

'No one here but me at the moment,' he explained. 'My wife passed away last year. I've got a daughter, Sharon. She used to work with me, but she got married two months ago and moved over Suffolk way.' He shook his head. 'You never realise what your family means to you till they've gone.'

'I'm sure you're right.' Leah looked round her. It was sadly obvious that the place had lacked a woman's touch for some time.

Dick Johnson moved behind the bar where he suddenly looked much more at home. He peered at her enquiringly. 'Like a drink, Miss – er . . . ?'

'Dobson,' she supplied. 'Leah Dobson. A lemonade would be nice. Thank you.'

He flicked off the cap of a bottle of fizzy lemonade and poured it into a glass for her. 'So, you're looking for a spot of work to fill your time?'

'That's right.'

'How long for?'

She shrugged. 'We're only here for another ten days, but I've nothing to rush back for. I daresay I could stay on a bit longer if I could find some accommodation – and if you needed me.'

'Well, let's see how it goes first, shall we?' He looked at her speculatively. 'Done bar work before, have you?'

'No, but I'm sure I'll soon pick it up.' She sipped her lemonade.

184

'I dare say you will at that. Won't take long to show you how to pull a pint and work the till, and I can write up all the prices for you.' He rubbed his hands. 'Well, come and see where everything is. And if it's agreeable to you, you can start this lunchtime.'

'Hadn't we better decide what I get paid first, Mr Johnson?'

Dick looked at the girl perched on the stool on the other side of his bar and for the first time his face broke into a smile. 'Thought you said you'd never worked in a bar before?'

'I did say that,' Leah agreed. 'But I didn't say I was going to work for the benefit of the experience.'

Dick threw back his head and roared with laughter. 'Bugger me if that don't sound just like my Sharon talkin'. Reckon you'n me is going to get along fine, girl,' he said.

Leah was on her way back to the cottage when she met Colin Mays. He was piling all his equipment into an ancient Mini, parked outside the courtyard gate.

'Oh. You're not leaving?'

He looked up at her with a grin. 'No. I borrowed a car from a friend in the village. I'm just off to Blakeney to paint. The light on the water is wonderful at this time of year.' He pushed his folded easel into the back of the car and straightened up. 'Haven't seen much of your boyfriend since you've been here. Don't you go about together in the daytime?'

'He's working,' Leah said. 'Doing a series of features for the paper he works for.'

'And neglecting you? Shame on him. I've seen you walking by yourself. Why do you never stop for a chat?'

To her intense annoyance Leah found herself blushing under the scrutiny of the frank hazel eyes. 'I like being alone,' she said defensively. 'And Terry's a *friend*, not a boyfriend. I just came along with him on this trip because I was at a loose end.' She looked at him. 'As a matter of fact I've just got myself a job at the pub. I start this lunchtime.'

His eyebrows rose. 'At The Mermaid? Well, you won't get much solitude there. Old Dick Johnson's trade will go up by leaps and bounds when word gets around that he's got a pretty new barmaid.' He regarded her with an amused expression, one hand on the car's roof, his long sinuous body perfectly at ease. Everything about him spoke of sensuality as Leah was acutely aware. 'You still haven't explained why you never stop to speak to me,' he said, his eyes holding hers.

'Simple. I don't like interrupting people at work,' she told him. 'Especially artists. Terry hates interruptions.'

'The man must be mad,' Colin muttered under his breath. 'Well, I hereby give you formal permission to interrupt me any time you feel like it,' he said as he opened the car door and folded his length into the driving seat. 'See you later, Leah. 'Bye.'

That first lunchtime Leah hardly knew whether she was on her head or her heels. She hadn't realised that there were so many tourists in Cleybourn – or so many locals either, for that matter. She was kept busy right till closing time. As she and Dick were tidying up after closing he congratulated her.

'You did well, girl.' He eyed her sky blue cotton dress appreciatively. 'Nice to have sumthin' good to look at behind the bar again. Several people said so.'

'Thanks.' Leah polished a glass thoughtfully. 'One thing I noticed though. You don't serve any food. Lots of people asked me if we did lunches.'

Dick shook his head. 'We did when the wife and

young Sharon were here. Couldn't manage it on me own though.'

'You could if you had a microwave. You could buy in pies and frozen veg and just heat them up, and salads are easy. Have you got a freezer?'

He looked surprised. 'Well – yes.'

'Then you could always have a supply of fresh sandwiches and other quick savoury foods. It would increase your profits.'

Dick laughed heartily. 'You're a caution, girl, and no mistake. Tryin' to teach your grandmother to suck eggs, are you?'

Leah looked at him haughtily. 'Mr Johnson, my name's Leah not "girl" and if my grandmother needs teaching how to suck eggs, then I'll be only too happy to teach her.'

Dick stared at her, open-mouthed, and while he was recovering she hung up her tea towel and began to get ready to leave. 'Tell you what,' she said. 'Pay me extra and I'll spend the afternoon making sandwiches for the freezer. I could go down to the quay for fresh crabs if you like. The cafes on the coast road charge a bomb for a fresh crab sandwich.' She looked at him, her head on one side. 'What do you think then, Dick? Are you on?'

His surprised face broke into a grin. 'All right then gir – er, Leah. We'll give it a try, buggered if we won't.'

Leah's bar food was a great success. By the end of the week Dick was doing a roaring trade at lunchtimes. Trade picked up considerably in the evenings too when customers realised they could buy a light supper snack to go with their evening drinks. Leah found she was enjoying herself enormously. She enjoyed creating attractive meals and thinking up new ideas. She

187

soon got to know a lot of the regulars by name and enjoyed meeting the visitors and chatting to the many artists who patronised the pub too. As the time for departure grew nearer she found herself wishing that she could stay on. She voiced the thought to Terry a couple of nights before he was due to go back to Nenebridge. He looked thoughtful.

'Maybe I could get the cottage for you for another couple of weeks,' he suggested. 'I'll give Paul a ring and see, shall I?'

He went out to the public callbox and came back ten minutes later, his face wreathed in smiles.

'Guess what? The place is yours for as long as you want it. Paul says it isn't booked any more till next Easter and you can have it for a peppercorn rent just to look after things for him. It means I'll be able to come down from time to time and report on what I've managed to find out for you.'

'Oh, Tel, you are clever.' She threw her arms around his neck and gave his cheek a resounding kiss. 'What would I do without you?'

He reached up and took her arms from round his neck. Holding them firmly to her sides he looked into her eyes.

'Don't do that, Leah,' he said gravely.

'Sorry. Why not?'

Because I like it too much, he wanted to say. Instead he smiled wryly. 'Better not.'

'But why?'

For a moment he looked into the melting brown eyes and was almost lost. 'Because – if we're to remain friends, if I'm to help you to do what you've set your heart on, better not to let things get complicated.'

'I don't see why they should.'

'No, I don't suppose you do.' He smiled at her wistfully. 'But they would. Friendship is one thing, a relationship another. We're happy as we are – yes?'

'Yes.'

He smiled. 'Exactly.'

Dick was more than pleased that Leah could stay on to help out for a few more weeks. She worked hard after Terry had left, filling the freezer at The Mermaid with sandwiches of every kind. She also made various kinds of soup from some of Granny Dobson's favourite recipes, poured it into neatly labelled plastic pots and stacked the freezer with them too.

'Even if you don't sell it all you can eat it yourself in the winter,' she told Dick. 'But I've an idea that my gran's soup will go down well in the winter here, even with the locals. It's all made from traditional Norfolk recipes.'

Dick was more than pleased. When this saucy young woman had first presented herself at his side door, asking for work, he'd taken her for a flighty young fly-by-night, but he'd been wrong. She was a real worker, and interested in the business too. He only wished he could offer her enough money to keep her on all winter, but trade fell sharply in the off-season. He only kept the place ticking over. Besides, he shrewdly guessed that she'd soon be restless and wanting to move on anyway.

Since Leah had been working at The Mermaid Colin Mays had become a regular lunchtime customer, and one day towards the end of the first week after Terry's departure he waited for her to come off duty and walked back to the cottage with her.

'You must miss what's-is-name – Tommy?'

'Terry? Yes, I would have, but I've been too busy.'

'So I've noticed. What do you do with yourself in the afternoons?'

'So far I've stayed on to work at The Mermaid, but I've filled the freezer now so I'm at a loose end.'

'Come painting with me this afternoon instead.'

She looked at him in surprise. 'But I don't paint.'

'That needn't stop you.' He looked up at the sky, his eyes narrowed against the sunlight. 'Look at that cloud formation. I thought of going out to the point this afternoon, in the hope of catching a spectacular sky.'

'Sounds nice.' She smiled at him. 'All right then, I'll pack a picnic.'

He grinned and dropped an arm across her shoulders. 'I was hoping you'd say that.'

Leah lay in the long wiry grass, her eyes closed and the sun warm on her face. She loved working at The Mermaid, but just for once it was sheer heaven to be idle and she was enjoying it. She'd watched Colin paint for the first hour, but now she was luxuriating in sheer laziness. She wrinkled her nose as something tickled it and opened her eyes to find Colin trailing a piece of grass across her cheek.

'I wasn't sure if you were asleep,' he said, stretching his length beside her, folding his arms behind his head. 'Aah – wonderful, isn't it?'

Leah stretched like a cat. 'Mmm, gorgeous. Hard to believe it can ever be cold and blowing a gale out here.'

He turned, supporting himself on one elbow to study her face. 'You have the most beautiful bones,' he remarked, trailing one finger down her jawline.

She laughed. 'What a corny old line. That's what artists always say in books.'

He shook his head. 'I mean it though. And your

190

hair – so thick and black. Do you always wear it plaited like that?'

She sat up and pulled the pins out, shaking it loose. 'There, is that better?' Released, her thick dark hair blew about her shoulders, giving her a wild, gypsy look. Colin smiled and nodded.

'That's how I'd paint you, if I were a portrait painter. As it is I'd never do you justice so I won't even try.'

'What about *your* hair?' Leah reached round to the back of his head and untied the leather thong that held his hair in place. As it hung down on either side of his face she regarded him. 'Mmm. If you had a beard as well you'd look like one of those Old Testament prophets.' She laughed, and he took her face between his hands. For a moment he looked at her, studying her features intently, then he kissed her. The kiss left Leah breathless. It was like no other kiss she had ever experienced; long and searching and deliberate. He explored her mouth sensuously, drawing from her a response that was totally irresistible. At last their mouths parted. For a moment she looked up at him, all her surprise and delight shining in her eyes, then she reached up and drew his head down to hers again. As their lips met again he lay back and pulled her close, running his hand down the length of her spine until her body was moulded to his. She felt his hardness against her thigh and excitement stirred urgently within her. She murmured against his mouth:

'Colin – oh, Colin.'

'Not here. Let's go back,' he whispered. 'I want to make love to you properly – in bed.'

In the little bedroom under the eaves they lay together, naked on the big brass bed. It was cool and dim under the low ceiling and the only sounds that drifted in through the open window were birdsong and the rustling of leaves. Leah lay with her head on Colin's chest. Her hair spread across his body like a black silken cloud. How could she ever have imagined that sex was overrated? she asked herself dazedly.

When they returned to the cottage they had climbed the stairs silently, hand in hand. In the bedroom Colin had undressed her slowly, as though he were unwrapping some precious gift, examining her body with delighted appreciation. His firm cool hands and the light kisses with which he had covered every part of her, had driven her to a frenzy of desire, encouraging her to respond with a boldness that had surprised them both. She found herself stirred urgently into a need to please him as much as he pleased her, and some deep primeval instinct seemed to imbue her lips, her hands and body with the age-old secrets of love. He hadn't hurried. There had been no urgent, frantic coupling as with Tom Clayton, but a slow mounting of passion, heightened by long kisses and sensual caresses. He had held back to bring her almost to fever pitch. And when at last their bodies had joined she had heard herself cry out; a cry of pure joyous animal ecstasy.

Now they lay together silent, warm and close among the tangled sheets. Heart beating against heart, limbs entwined. Leah stroked the dark curls on Colin's chest, her eyes trying hard not to see the hands on the bedside clock creeping round to five o'clock.

'I'll have to go in a minute,' she said at last, stirring reluctantly. 'It'll be opening time soon.'

His arm around her tightened. 'Ring Dick – tell him you're sick.'

She raised her head to look at him, sorely tempted. 'I can't. He relies on me.'

'He can cope for one evening.' He smiled lazily. 'I'd like to make love to you from now till morning.'

'Do you think you could?' she asked with interest.

He laughed and pinched her bottom playfully. 'Stay and find out.'

'Oh, I *wish* I could.' She sat up and looked down at him. 'But I mustn't. A job's a job.' She regarded him, her head on one side. 'I could come back later though. If you wanted me to.'

He grasped her round the waist and pulled her down on top of him. 'Of course I want you to.' He kissed her. 'You're sensational, Leah, do you know that?'

She smiled down at him mischievously. 'You're pretty sensational yourself.'

He ran a hand down the length of her body, making her shiver with pleasure. 'Tell me, your friend – is he gay?'

She shrugged. 'How would I know?'

'He must be or he couldn't keep his hands off you.'

Leah felt a sudden pang of disloyalty. Terry was a good friend. She'd have been lost without him and he'd promised to help her. She slid off the bed and began to pull on her clothes. 'I must go now, Colin.'

He lay back, watching her lazily through half closed eyes. 'I'll walk down and meet you at closing time,' he promised. 'I'm taking no chances of losing you to some other guy. Not after this afternoon.'

Leah spent most of her off-duty time with Colin after that. In the afternoons she accompanied him on painting trips, returning with him to the cottage in the late afternoon to cook a meal. And it was to Colin's cottage that she returned each night after The Mermaid closed, to sleep with him in the big brass bed, making love till the small hours. In a very short

193

time she knew without a shadow of doubt that she was in love.

Suddenly her whole existence was filled with Colin. His vibrant shadow eclipsed everything. Nothing else seemed to matter. She longed for time to be suspended so that their summer idyll could last for ever. Colin's appetite for her seemed insatiable, as hers was for him, and their lovemaking grew more imaginative and adventurous as the night followed night. Each day was merely the happy prelude to a night of delicious sensual pleasure in the arms of the man she loved.

Once or twice she tried to broach the subject of what would happen when the summer ended and his tenancy of the cottage came to an end, but Colin always managed to steer the conversation on to a different track. She didn't mind too much. What they had was much too good to spoil. Living from day to day, happy in her job at The Mermaid, returning joyfully to Colin each evening was all she wanted from life. She had never felt so happy or so well. Even Dick noticed the change in her. Her eyes and hair shone and her skin glowed, golden with vitality. She sang as she went about her work and her radiant smile was a joy to behold. The customers adored her and the trade at The Mermaid broke all records. As Dick remarked confidentially to one of his regulars: 'If there was some way to bottle that girl and sell her by the pint, I'd be a millionaire by now.'

One afternoon after closing she walked home alone. Colin hadn't put in an appearance at lunchtime, but she wasn't worried. Sometimes he became too engrossed in his painting to notice the time. Letting herself into the courtyard, she was immediately aware of an odd feeling of emptiness. The door of number four stood open as usual and as she walked in she could hear the vacuum cleaner going upstairs. She opened the door to the stairs and shouted Colin's name.

The vacuum stopped, but it was Mrs Penn, the cleaning woman from the village, who clumped red-faced and heavy-footed down the steep stairway to look round the kitchen door.

'Can I help you?'

'Oh, I – is Colin – Mr Mays around?'

The woman shook her head. 'I'm sorry, miss. He left this morning.

Leah frowned. '*Left*?'

'That's right. He's gone home – to Surrey, I think he said. His wife came to collect him in the car. About eleven o'clock it'd be.'

Leah's heart seemed to freeze. 'Oh – I – I see,' she managed to stammer. 'Thank you. Goodbye.'

She backed out of the door and hurried across the courtyard to Hazel Cottage. Closing the door behind her, she stood with her back pressed against it and her eyes closed, trying to force her numbed mind to absorb the shock of what she had just heard. It was a mistake. It *had* to be. Colin wasn't married. He would have told her. And he would surely not have left for good without saying goodbye – without arranging where and when they'd meet again.

It was when she opened her eyes that she caught sight of the folded scrap of paper on the floor, half hidden under the edge of the rug. Bending eagerly, she picked it up and opened it.

In Colin's flowing artist's hand two brief sentences were scrawled: 'Thanks for everything. Sorry to be such a bastard. C.'

Chapter 11

Marie regretted the end of her friendship with Hannah. She had no other close woman friend and she missed the long letters they exchanged and Hannah's visits. Although they had been infrequent she had looked forward to seeing her, hearing her news and gossip and getting a glimpse of a world outside of which she had little experience. But although she missed her friend, Marie could not bring herself to heal the rift between them. Hannah's honesty had made her afraid. The truth about Ralph's past stood between them like an insurmountable barrier. If she faced that, she would have to turn around and come face to face with her own past again. There was that other secret in her own background. If she began digging into Ralph's the truth might come out about her babies and she knew instinctively that Ralph would not be tolerant when it came to her dishonesty. He would hold it in reserve; a weapon to use ruthlessly and without hesitation to bring her into line should she rebel against him.

So life went on at The Ocean Hotel. David's health improved with his move to Dorset. Although he still suffered breathlessness at times, the bad chest colds that had plagued him in Norfolk did not return and his general condition improved.

He did worry about Ralph's spending though. The

bank overdraft, taken out to pay running costs, would clearly take years to repay and the maintenance bills were astronomical. All Ralph would say when his father tried to discuss the cash-flow problem was: 'You have to speculate to accumulate, Dad. You'll never get anywhere in this world by standing still. Owing money is a fact of life in business.'

But David continued to worry. He often shared his anxieties with Marie when they sat together on weekday evenings when Ralph was away. She tried to reassure David as best she could. But in spite of her outward reassurance she was deeply worried herself. She felt they had overreached themselves and she didn't see how they could possibly be free of debt for years to come, even if all the hotels did outstandingly well.

It was when a local plumber who had done a small emergency job for them came to her with a bounced cheque one Monday morning, that her worst fears were confirmed. She rang to make an appointment and that afternoon she went to see the bank manager. When he told her bluntly that he was calling in their overdraft, she was appalled.

'Please could you just wait till my husband gets home at the weekend?' she had pleaded. 'I'm sure there must be some mistake.'

'Mrs Evans, do you realise just how large your overdraft is at this bank?' the man asked patiently.

She shook her head, ashamed to admit that Ralph kept her so much in the dark about their finances. The manager opened the file that lay on his desk and passed it to her, his finger pointing to the outstanding figure. She gasped.

'*Oh*! I hadn't realised it was so much. But as I said . . .' She trailed off as she looked up to see the manager shaking his head.

'I'm sorry, Mrs Evans. In spite of our warnings the cheques continue to be presented. I'm afraid you've gone way beyond the limit already. I've warned your husband time and again to curb his father's spending but he seems to have no control over it. It's a very strange way to run a business, as I've said many times, and this time I'm afraid we must foreclose.'

Driving home Marie puzzled over what could have happened. Officially the business was still in David's name. He was the one who signed the cheques and settled the household accounts; and David hated to be in debt. Everyone must be paid the moment the bill came in – it had always been his way. But he was a careful man. She felt sure he would not have signed cheques as recklessly as the bank manager implied. True, his health had been below par over the past couple of years, but nevertheless his brain was still alert enough. One thing was certain. There was no way she could keep the problem from him and as soon as she got back to 'The Ocean' she took a tray of tea to his room where he was resting and broke the news to him as gently as she could. As she had feared, he took it badly.

'How could we have overstepped the overdraft by that much?' he asked. 'All the hotels have been doing good business. We're not overstaffed and I know you balance the catering accounts carefully. I've kept such a careful check. Unless . . .' Doubt creased his brow. 'Sometimes I think I'm getting too old for all this, Marie.'

'You don't make mistakes, David.' she said firmly. 'The maintenance bills have been costly. I suppose you took them into account.'

He shook his head. 'I know what money I've paid out and it can't have come to that figure. There's some mistake. There has to be.'

'I'm afraid there isn't, David. The bank manager showed me their figures.' She patted his arm. 'Don't worry. I'm sure that when Ralph comes home at the weekend he'll be able to sort it out. In our business it's a matter of juggling. We'll find some way to cut down in another area.' She was thankful that David seemed placated, but privately she wished she felt as confident herself. She had not reminded him that Ralph was capable of spending large sums of money on himself without a qualm.

When he arrived home that weekend Ralph was in a good mood. He announced to Marie almost as soon as he arrived that he had seen a rundown property on the outskirts of Harrogate that he hoped to begin negotiating for.

'Ralph, I think you should see this first.' She handed him the official letter of foreclosure from the bank which had arrived that morning. As he read it his good mood evaporated and his brows gathered in an ominous frown.

'What the hell do they mean by it?' he stormed, flinging down the letter.

'I went to see the manager last Monday,' she told him. 'Mr Taylor the plumber came to see me with a cheque that had bounced.'

He glared at her. 'So what happened?'

'To Mr Taylor? I paid him out of my own money. It's all right.'

'Sod Taylor. I'm talking about the bloody bank.'

'The manager was adamant. He said he'd warned you but that cheques continued to be presented. As I hadn't access to the books I couldn't argue with him.'

'It's Dad,' Ralph stormed. 'I told him to show every bill to me first before paying it. The stubborn old fool refused to hand over the business to me and this is the result. Trying to run a business like this is ridiculous.

I'm tied hand and foot. I'll talk to him.' He strode towards the door. 'Where is he?'

Marie stepped forward and took his arm. 'Please, Ralph, don't. Not in this mood. Calm down first. I don't want him upset.'

He spun round to glower at her, his face a mask of fury. 'You don't want *him* upset? What about me? What about you, if it comes to that?' He shook off her hand. 'This is our livelihood, woman. Do you want to see all I've worked for slide down the drain just because that old fool can't loosen the reins and let me handle things my own way?'

'I know, but . . .'

'But nothing. I'm going to sort him out once and for all.' He strode out of the room, leaving the door swinging on its hinges. Marie wanted to follow, to try to mediate between father and son, but she knew it would only inflame the situation even more. Hovering anxiously in the hallway she heard the boom of Ralph's angry voice and the rise and fall of her father-in-law's replies. She felt helpless and inadequate.

David did not appear for dinner that evening but had a tray in his room. Marie was worried about him and wanted to eat upstairs in the flat, but Ralph was determined that they would eat in the restaurant as usual. Over the meal he put on his public face and behaved like the jovial mine host, but once they were alone upstairs again his anger returned.

'Didn't you realise he was laying out all that money?' he demanded. 'Couldn't you have stopped him?'

She shook her head. 'He was only paying the outstanding bills. I can't tell your father what to do with his money. Since we married you've kept me completely in the dark about the finances. When I kept the books I could tell you off the top of my head where every penny was. David looked to me for advice then. We consulted each other. Now . . .'

'He should have handed the business over to me.'

'Be fair, Ralph. He wanted us to form a company – share the decisions between the three of us,' Marie pointed out. 'That way we'd all have had the power to sign cheques.'

'If you two had had your fingers in and out of the till we'd have been bankrupt long before this,' Ralph said scathingly.

'We never had an overdraft of that size before you came into the business,' Marie said quietly. 'And the bank never bounced one of our cheques either.'

'And why? Because all you had then was a tacky little boarding house in Cromer.'

'"The Marina" wasn't a boarding house.'

'And it wasn't exactly "The Hilton" either, was it?' He stared down at her angrily. 'It's *me* who developed this business, don't forget. You wanted a chain of hotels; *I* built it for you. It's all my hard grafting that's got us where we are. But just because a stupid old man in his dotage has to pay every bloody bill the minute it falls through the letter box, I'm landed in this mess.' He glared at her. 'You make me tired, you and him. You're two of a kind – small-minded and incompetent. You can't see any further than the end of your noses. You've undone everything I've tried to do.'

'We've expanded too quickly,' she said crisply. 'We're trying to run before we can walk. The answer is simple. We'll just sell one of the hotels and pay off the debt. We'll still have three. Then we should hold off for a while till we're in the black again.'

'Sell?' He stared at her. 'Sell, did you say? I'm in the business of buying, not selling. What the hell do you know about it? Just you take care of the curtains and crockery department. That's *your* province.'

Marie flushed with sudden anger. 'It might help if you cut down on some of your personal spending,' she said. 'Perhaps if you bought fewer new clothes – if you traded the car in for a cheaper model – maybe if you spent less on your women . . .'

Without warning he lunged and struck her hard on the cheek with the back of his hand, sending her reeling sideways across the room. Her shoulder hit the wall with a painful crack that knocked all the breath from her body and she sat down ignominiously on the floor. Ralph strode across the room to stand over her.

'Get up,' he growled. 'Get up, you snivelling bitch, and don't you ever tell me what to do again.' Grasping her by the shoulders he dragged her to her feet and pushed her against the wall. 'Now listen to me. I owe you and him nothing, do you hear? *Nothing*. Maybe you should know something. That old man . . .' He jabbed a finger towards the door. 'That old idiot who's got me into this mess – he isn't really my father at all.'

Marie stared at him, her mouth agape with shock. '*Not*? But I – I don't understand . . .'

He propelled her roughly across the room and shoved her into a chair. 'My mother told me just before she died – David Evans was the man she married, but she was already pregnant by another man. She never told him that and the bloody fool never twigged it. So you see, when I came out of the army and took the job he offered me, it was out of *pity* for the pair of misfits you were. It was out of the goodness of my heart – because I felt sorry for the poor old bugger, being taken in like that all those years. I felt I owed him something.'

'Are you saying that was the reason you married me too?'

He pushed his face close to hers. 'Well, it wasn't for your charm and beauty, was it? And it certainly wasn't because you're great in bed.' He laughed coarsely. 'Talk about doing it with a sack of potatoes! And then you wonder why I look around elsewhere. Neither you nor Dad live in the real world. You don't know what life is all about – either of you.'

'Do you want a divorce?' she asked.

His eyes flickered. 'Divorce? Don't make me laugh. What would you do if I said yes? Where would you go then? Who'd employ *you*, do you think? You'd be lucky to get a job as a skivvy in some back street dosshouse. Anyway,' he sneered, 'Catholics don't hold with divorce, do they? Or can they conveniently change their minds about that when it suits them?'

Marie knew she was defeated. Clearly Ralph had married her to get at his father's business, but it was too late to turn back the clock now. It was true that she had never worked anywhere else. The thought of leaving the security of the only home she had ever known frankly terrified her, and Ralph had sensed that right from the beginning. Then there was David. He was the only family she had ever had. She owed him so much. What would become of him if she left? Now that she knew that Ralph was not his son at all, she realised that he had no feeling of loyalty towards him, let alone affection. If she were not here to look after David, Ralph would probably bundle him into some old people's home and leave him there to rot. No, somehow they must sort out their problems. Make the best they could of a bad job and stay together. The business was their only source of income. They were all three committed to it – and to each other, bound together by unspoken secrets like handcuffed prisoners.

David stayed in his room for the remainder of the weekend. Marie took his meals to him, but he ate little and refused to discuss with her what had passed between himself and Ralph. He looked ten years older and seemed to feel the strain of it badly. She was deeply worried about him.

Long after Ralph was asleep on Sunday night Marie lay thinking, her mind running over the problem again and again. Now there were two things she was forced to keep from David and she wondered if she were doing the right thing. Not only had Ralph lied about his army record, he was not entitled to be here at all if what he said was true and David was not his natural father. But the more she racked her brain the more tangled the problem became and by the time she fell into an uneasy sleep no solution had presented itself.

The dream wakened her at dawn. Her face and body were damp with sweat and with the strain of reliving the experience that had changed her life. Now she knew that what she wanted more than anything else was to go to church. She thought longingly of the quiet peaceful atmosphere; the mingled scents of flowers and incense, the comfort of prayer and the soft light of the candles, until the urge was too powerful to resist. Creeping out of bed she stood for a moment at the window looking down at the view she loved, but this morning it brought her no comfort. The sea looked cold and unfriendly in the grey dawn light. She turned away to pull on her clothes.

In the little church of St Joseph she found the peace she longed for. She knelt in a pew near to the front where she could see the altar clearly. She said her rosary and then put some coins in the box and lit a candle, then she sat staring up at the statue of the Virgin. The words just wouldn't come. Her mind was an arid void.

'Are you troubled, my child?'

The soft voice startled her and she turned to see the elderly priest standing nearby. He slipped into the pew beside her.

'You look as though you need to talk. If that's the case, I've plenty of time to listen.'

She shook her head. 'I wouldn't know where to begin, Father.'

'Can it really be so bad?' He smiled gently.

'I haven't been a good Catholic, Father. But the punishment – the penance sometimes seems . . .'

'More than you can bear?'

'This is the first time I've been in church for years.'

'But you're here now. That's what matters.'

'This morning I woke early and knew this was the only place I'd find peace.'

'I'm glad. And are you comforted?'

Marie bowed her head. 'I'm afraid it'll take more than one candle to solve my problems, Father.'

'Would you like me to hear your confession?'

She thought longingly of the confessional – the comforting dimness and the grill between priest and sinner that made it so easy to say what was in your heart.

'I haven't time. I wish I had.'

'Then come when you can – any time you feel the need to talk. Ring the presbytery bell. It's what I'm here for.'

'Thank you, Father. I will.'

He laid his hand gently on hers then turned and walked away.

Marie watched him go, a tall, soft-footed figure in

his black soutane. Inside her head the words she had tried so hard to find were forgotten. Repeating over and over were the names of her children: Leah and Sarah. 'Please forgive me for giving you away, my little ones,' she whispered. 'Oh, please, Holy Mother, let them one day understand and forgive me.'

When she got back to the hotel Ralph was pacing the room angrily.

'Where have you been? You're never damn' well here when you're needed.' He shook an impatient hand in her face to prevent her from answering. 'Never mind now. I haven't the time to listen. Look, I've had a talk with Dad. He's agreed to have a power of attorney drawn up in my name, just until we get this mess sorted out. I've managed to make him see what a hash he's making of things. I'll ring the solicitor as soon as it's nine o'clock and we'll get the whole thing settled before I leave.'

'Does that mean you'll have control of his money?'

He glared at her challengingly. 'It does. Any objections?'

'It's just that after what you told me, it seems to me that you don't really have the right . . .'

'Listen!' He reached out to grasp her arm but when she shook it off and faced up to him, he drew away, his eyes wary. 'Listen, Marie. I was angry when I told you that. It was . . .'

'Are you telling me now that it was all a lie?' The boldness in her own voice surprised her. Maybe going to church had helped to give her strength after all. Ralph was clearly surprised at her tone too. His eyes widened.

'Not exactly. My mother did say that, but she was dying at the time. She'd been saying a lot of things. She was out of her head – rambling. I've no way of knowing for sure whether it's true or not. None of us will ever know. He gave me his name and he's the only father I've ever known, so I'd be grateful if you'd forget it, right?'

She looked at him levelly. 'I think you know that I'd never do anything to upset David,' she said quietly. 'But if you make him unhappy – jeopardise his health and his future . . .'

'Don't push your luck, Marie.' His face hardened again. 'Don't think you've got anything on me because you haven't. I could chuck you out just like that if I chose to, so don't you forget it.' He grinned malevolently. 'And don't go getting a power complex.'

The solicitor arrived at eleven o'clock with the necessary forms and Ralph signed them before leaving. When he had gone Marie went to her father-in-law's room.

'David, are you all right?'

He sat slumped in his chair. 'He thinks he's won,' he muttered. 'He thinks he's got the better of me, but he'll find out, Marie. He'll see.'

She went to him and took his hand. 'Don't upset yourself. It wasn't your fault.'

'I don't care what anyone says, I didn't run up that overdraft. I'm not senile yet,' he said. 'I should have made changes long ago.'

'Never mind. It's done now.' She sat beside him, stroking his hand. 'Let me cook for you this evening. We'll have dinner together. Or would you like to come down to the restaurant? You haven't been out of your room for days.'

He smiled up at her. 'You're a good girl, Marie. You won't ever leave me, will you?'

'Of course I won't leave you, David. No matter what happens.'

She'd been asleep for some time when she woke suddenly. In the dark she lay listening, wondering what could have wakened her so abruptly. Then she heard the sound again. It was unmistakable this time: half groan, half cry. Instantly she was out of bed and pulling on her dressing gown.

In the corridor she listened at David's door. 'David – are you all right?' When there was no reply she opened the door and looked in. He was lying half in and half out of bed, gasping for breath, his face contorted with pain.

She made him as comfortable as she could, then went out into the hallway to telephone. As she began to dial, she suddenly remembered. There was a doctor staying in the hotel. He was attending a medical conference and had checked in yesterday. She rang down to Reception and spoke to the night porter.

'John, Mr Evans has been taken ill. There's a doctor in number twenty-two – Doctor Hodges. Will you ring and ask him to come up to the flat, please? Tell him it's urgent – an emergency.'

Doctor Philip Hodges was there in minutes. Even though he wore a dressing gown he looked calm and efficient enough to bring her reassurance. Marie explained briefly what had happened. He examined David carefully and turned to her.

'Can you get me the number of the local hospital, please? I'll speak to them. I think we should get him in without delay.'

'Is it serious?' she asked as she dialled the number.

'I'm afraid it looks like a coronary,' he said, taking the receiver from her. 'They'll know better when they've done an ECG.'

Doctor Hodges stayed with David while Marie

dressed, and when the ambulance arrived she went along to the hospital, travelling inside with him. In the accident and emergency department she waited anxiously until he was assessed, trying hard to concentrate as a nurse filled in details on a seemingly endless form.

'Next of kin?' The young nurse was looking at her expectantly.

Next of kin. After what Ralph had told her she hesitated to give his name. But there was no one else. 'His son,' she said. 'Mr Ralph Evans.'

After what seemed an age the sound of footsteps echoing along the corridor heralded the arrival of a doctor. He told her that David was being admitted to the coronary care unit.

'Mr Evans has suffered a moderately severe heart attack, but his condition isn't critical at the moment.'

'Can I see him?'

The doctor looked at Marie's worried face. 'Are you his daughter?'

'Daughter-in-law,' she told him.

'Is it Marie?'

'Yes.'

'Just for a moment then. He's been asking for you. It may reassure him to see you.'

As she followed him along the corridor she asked the question that had been worrying her ever since she found David stricken in his room. 'Could it have been caused through stress of some kind?'

'It could,' he agreed. 'Although it looks as though he's had a heart condition for some time. You didn't know?' She shook her head. 'Has he been under stress?'

She nodded unhappily. 'There was a disagreement earlier today – well, yesterday morning now. It upset him.'

210

He smiled kindly. 'Well, I wouldn't worry too much about it. An attack was on the cards anyway, I'm afraid. Anything could have triggered it off.'

Yes but it wasn't anything, Marie told herself grimly. It was Ralph. His next of kin.

She was shocked to see David wired up to a frightening assortment of equipment in the coronary care unit, but the sister reassured her.

'The wires are to monitor his heartbeat,' she explained. 'And the oxygen is to help his breathing. I must ask you not to stay too long. He needs rest.'

Marie took David's hand and pressed it. 'Don't worry,' she whispered. 'I'll take care of everything. You're going to be all right – home in no time.'

He managed a weak smile and his fingers tightened around hers before he closed his eyes again. After a moment she tiptoed out.

On her way back to the hotel in a taxi Marie did some thinking. Suddenly she felt strong and her mind was crystal clear. The moment she got in she went to David's desk. She hated going through his things without asking his permission, but she told herself that this was an emergency. She gathered together all his spent cheque stubs and paying-in book, also the file in which he kept all his bills and receipts. Ralph kept the books locked away in a safe in his office, but she was fairly sure that from what she had, she could piece together enough information to prove that David had not gone over the limit on the overdraft. In her room she checked the amounts paid out with the cheque stubs and compared the figures. It was just as she had thought. Even though David had paid the bills promptly he had not exceeded the limit. So was it the bank's mistake? Or had someone else been signing cheques in David's name – forging them?

She sat for perhaps half an hour, mulling over the problem and thinking what to do. But David's illness was the first priority and suddenly she remembered the admittance form. It was her duty to inform his next of kin, whatever the relationship. Ralph had mentioned that he was staying overnight at the Hastings hotel. She picked up the receiver and dialled the number. The night porter answered.

'Can I help you?'

'It's Mrs Evans speaking. I believe my husband is staying there. I must speak to him immediately, please. It's a matter of some urgency.'

'Certainly, Madam. I'll ring his room.'

There was a long pause and Marie began to wonder if Ralph was out, then there was a click and a drowsy female voice said: 'Hello – yes?'

Marie's fingers tightened convulsively round the receiver. So he was even taking his women to their own hotels now. 'It's Mrs Ralph Evans,' she said briskly. 'Can I speak to my husband, please?'

There was a muffled buzz of conversation in the background, then Ralph came on the line.

'Marie?'

'Yes, it's me.'

'What the hell do you mean by it – ringing me here in the middle of the night? Are you checking up on me now?'

'Ralph, your father has had a heart attack. He's in hospital. As you are his next of kin I thought I'd better let you know.' She dropped the receiver on to its rest and sat staring at it. It was up to him now but she guessed he'd be here post haste. The prospect of possible inheritance would be too strong to resist.

The following morning she breakfasted in the restaurant. It had been past five o'clock when she had

212

finally fallen back into bed and this morning her eyes smarted and her head ached dully. She was drinking her third cup of black coffee when someone stopped by her table and she looked up to find Doctor Hodges looking down at her.

'Good morning, Mrs Evans. I was wondering how your father-in-law is this morning.'

'I rang the hospital as soon as I wakened. He's still in the coronary care unit, but holding his own.' She smiled. 'I didn't get the chance to thank you for what you did last night, Doctor. Will you join me for a cup of coffee?'

He took a seat opposite her. 'Thank you. I do have a little time to spare this morning.' He was a tall man in his early forties, well groomed and good-looking. His smooth dark hair was brushed back from a high forehead and his grey eyes were kindly but perceptive. They studied her as she poured him a cup of coffee.

'Mr Evans is your father-in-law, I believe?'

'That's right, but I've worked for him for the past seventeen years so he's more like a father to me. I never knew my own.' She sighed. 'Last night was a shock.'

'You didn't know he had a heart condition?'

'No. He's been troubled with chestiness over the past few years and he gets breathless at times, but we'd no idea there was anything wrong with his heart.'

'Try not to worry. I'm sure he'll be all right.'

'I hope so.'

He looked at her. 'You're looking rather peaky yourself, Mrs Evans. That's a nasty bruise on your cheekbone. An accident?'

Her hand flew to her cheek and the tender place over the bone where Ralph had hit her. Since the bruise had come out she'd disguised it with make-up and a pair of dark glasses but this morning, in her haste, she'd forgotten. 'This? Oh, yes. I slipped. Clumsy.'

He looked unconvinced. 'Perhaps you should have it X-rayed. It's quite swollen.'

She shook her head. 'I'm sure it's all right.'

'I like your hotel very much,' he said, changing the subject. 'I'm giving a series of lectures at the conference this week and I wanted somewhere quiet to study my notes and prepare. This is ideal. Every comfort yet a homely atmosphere.'

Marie smiled. 'That's exactly what we aim for. Your wife doesn't come with you on these occasions then?'

'My wife was killed in a car accident some years ago.'

'Oh – oh, I'm so sorry.'

Philip Hodges smiled. 'It's all right. You weren't to know. It was a long time ago now. Almost ten years.'

'Then you couldn't have been married long.'

'Just two years.'

'Oh, how tragic.' She reached out in an involuntary gesture to touch his hand. Immediately she blushed crimson and withdrew it. 'I'm sorry,' she said, confused. 'All the trauma has made me rather emotional. My father-in-law's illness – everything.'

But he was smiling at her gently. 'Please don't apologise. People are so impersonal nowadays. No one wants to get involved in other people's lives, especially their tragedies. I appreciate your concern, believe me.'

'And I yours, Doctor.'

'Philip, please.'

Smiling, she held out her hand. 'And I'm Marie.' He pressed her fingers briefly. 'I'm afraid I'll have to be going now,' she said, looking at her watch. 'I have to talk to the staff and then I want to go along to the hospital.'

'I must go too.' He stood up then hesitated, looking back. 'I wonder – perhaps you'd have dinner with me this evening? It's not much fun, eating alone, and it would be nice to hear news of your father-in-law.'

'That would be nice. I'd love to.'

At the bank the manager agreed to see her again with open reluctance. As he closed his office door he looked stern.

'I thought I'd made it clear, Mrs Evans. There's nothing else we can do . . .'

'I want you to look at these if you don't mind.' Marie put David's file on the desk. 'My father-in-law is a very methodical man. I feel sure that he did not exceed the limit on the overdraft. Would it be possible for me to look at the cheques that have been presented over the past months?'

'This is rather irregular.' The man frowned. 'Why doesn't your father-in-law come in and speak for himself?'

'Because he is in hospital,' Marie said. 'He was taken ill late last night with a heart attack. I'd like to get this worry sorted out for him as quickly as possible. I'm sure it will help his recovery.'

'I see. I'm extremely sorry, Mrs Evans. Please accept my sincere condolences.'

The change in the manager's attitude was dramatic. He rang through to his secretary and within minutes Marie was looking at the bundle of cheques that had caused all the trouble. One by one, she went through them. They all bore David's signature, but on close examination she could see that although skilfully done, many of them had been written with a hand

215

other than his. They were made out to people she had never heard of, and who certainly had nothing to do with Evans Hotels. She looked up at the manager.

'May I take these home with me?' she asked. 'I'm sure there is some reasonable explanation.'

He frowned. 'I don't know . . .'

'Perhaps if your secretary could photocopy them?'

He hesitated. 'Well, I don't see why not. If it would help your father-in-law.'

'Thank you. And I can assure you that the money we owe will be paid back in full as quickly as possible. I shall see to it personally.'

Ralph arrived late that afternoon. Marie found him pacing the living room of the flat like a caged tiger when she got back from the hospital.

'Oh, there you are,' he said the moment she came into the room. 'What's all this about Dad? It'd better be important, dragging me back like this.'

'David is much better, I'm happy to say,' Marie told him. 'And I wouldn't bother going to see him if I were you. He needs rest and quiet and I don't think the sight of you would help his recovery.'

'Then why did you drag me back?' His lip curled. 'Was it just to gloat at catching me out last night?'

Ignoring the jibe, Marie opened her bag and took out the bundle of cheques, spreading them on the table. 'I'd like you to look at these,' she said. 'Some of them bear your father's signature. And some of them *don't*.' She looked up at him meaningfully and was rewarded by the sight of his colour draining.

'I don't know what you mean,' he blustered.

'Oh, I think you do. You forged those cheques. I don't know what for but it certainly wasn't anything to do with Evans Hotels. You forged them and then you made your father believe that he was responsible for the bank foreclosing. The worry of it caused his heart attack. It was a despicable thing to do.'

He stared at her defiantly. 'What choice did he give me? He's always treated me like a schoolboy – someone not to be trusted.'

'And it seems he was right.'

'It was an emergency – money I had to pay quickly. It would have come right if only I'd had time. If only he hadn't been in such a hurry to stuff tradesmen's pockets with our money.' His eyes narrowed. 'Where did you get those cheques? You haven't been meddling at the bank again? You haven't said . . .'

'I've said nothing – except the money will be paid back in full.' She took a deep breath and looked him in the eye. 'I won't have David's name dragged through the mud, Ralph. I won't have him disgraced. I don't care what happens to you, or to me either for that matter, but for David's sake I'll see that you pay back every penny. If not . . .'

Ralph took a step forward, his hand outstretched towards the cheques.

'Take them if you like,' she said. 'Those are only photocopies. The originals are still at the bank. I don't doubt that an expert would spot the forgeries in seconds once suspicion was aroused.'

'Damn you,' Ralph growled. 'You wouldn't do it. You wouldn't dare.'

'You've got a month. Four weeks,' she told him. 'Pay by then and no one need know. Fail and I go back to the bank – and if necessary, the police.'

He walked to the door and opened it, then he slammed it shut again and turned to look at her.

'All right. You've got me over a barrel this time, but I'll get even with you, Marie.' He walked towards her, raw hate burning in his eyes. 'I wouldn't mind betting that there's more to your past than you've admitted.' He grasped her chin painfully between thumb and forefinger and stared into her eyes. 'Funny, isn't it, that your only woman friend is a *social worker*? Your bit of trouble was over years ago, so what held the two of you together all these years? And why did you fall out with her so abruptly? Did she threaten to tell me something about you, Marie?' He thrust his face close to hers and his breath rasped in her ear as he said: 'If I ever find out the answer to that one – and I'm pretty sure you wouldn't want me to – I'll make you regret the day you ever left Ireland. And that's a promise.'

Chapter 12

Sally had mixed feelings about Jason's obvious feelings towards her. On the one hand it was flattering to have someone in love with her; on the other hand she didn't really want to be tied down. Sharon went out with a different boy every week. 'Playing the field' she called it. 'If you don't have a damn good time when you're young, you never will,' she told Sally. Sharon was streetwise. She'd been allowed to take charge of her own life since she was ten years old and her fund of worldly knowledge and her self-awareness impressed Sally profoundly.

Not that Sharon disapproved of Jason. On the contrary, she thought he was dishy and 'quite a hunk'. 'But you don't want to let him think he's the only pebble on the beach,' she warned. 'You don't want him taking you for granted. Go out with a few more guys before you make up your mind.'

Sally promised that she would – and she could have done. There were always plenty of boys asking her out. It was just that she knew her parents would be horrified at the mere sight of some of them, and the idea of their agreeing to let her go out with them was laughable. The thought of Ken trundling round after her in the Purple Pumpkin now that she was nearly eighteen was enough to make her turn them all down flat and stick to Jason. At least that way she got a little freedom.

Mavis and Ken had resigned themselves to their daughter's 'going steady' with Jason. Better the devil you know was how they looked at the situation. Jason was clearly extremely fond of Sally. He had fairly good prospects and seemed to be a hard worker. Of course they were both far too young to think of marriage, but in the meantime Jason would take good care of Sally and see that she didn't get into the wrong kind of company.

Jean's view of the situation was far less complex. She was frankly delighted that the two young people had got together. She never stopped talking about their romance, irritating Mavis to distraction with her plans for the wedding and the little house they would live in afterwards. She even had her own wedding outfit all planned.

'Good heavens, there's plenty of time for all that,' Mavis told her with a disapproving sniff. 'Our Sally's not much more than a child yet, even though she does like to play the grown-up woman.'

Jean smiled to herself. Sally was no child, not in any sense of the word. With her film-star looks and her curvaceous figure she was enough to turn any male head. You'd have thought Mavis would have been pleased to get her safely married off to a decent lad with a good career in front of him. But no. She would have kept the girl cooped up in the house if she could. Pity she hadn't lived in the days when they still had chastity belts. She longed to say all this to her sister-in-law but knowing of old the explosive reaction she would get, she confined herself to the bland remark: 'I suppose having two of my lads already married I'm used to looking ahead.' But she couldn't resist adding mischievously: 'Before we know it, Mavis, you and I will be grandmothers.'

Mavis turned away with a shudder. The idea of her

dainty Sally swollen and bloated with pregnancy shocked and appalled her.

Sally was reasonably content. She was almost at the end of her course and soon after the exams were over she would be eighteen. She could see the torch of independence beginning to glimmer at the end of her tunnel. She and Jason went out together twice a week and she enjoyed the companionship of Sharon, who was always ready to fill in the gaps in her sketchy experience of life and sex.

Since the night of the college first year party Sally had compromised on her style of dress. Jason had assured her that girls who dressed as she had that night were certain to attract the wrong kind of boy. It was no wonder that the lanky youth who had wrestled with her in the car park had got the wrong idea about what sort of girl she was. He went shopping with her and helped her to choose clothes that he promised were more 'her'. Dresses in dainty Laura Ashley prints, a slim black skirt in a longer length, and some pretty tops trimmed with lace and broderie Anglaise. Mavis viewed them with pleasure and satisfaction. Grudgingly, she had to admit that Jason was a good influence on her daughter. Sharon, on the other hand, looked askance at the new clothes.

'Getting to be a regular little Julie Andrews, aren't you?' she said. 'Have you singing in the church choir next.'

It was at the end of the spring term that Sharon had her party. It was her birthday and her parents had agreed to go out, taking the younger children with them, and leave the house to Sharon and her friends till midnight. She told Sally excitedly about her plans in the cloakroom at college. Sally was wide-eyed with surprise. The very idea of Mavis and Ken going out and leaving the house to twenty marauding teenagers till the small hours was totally unthinkable.

'Why are you looking like that? Hey – you do want to come, don't you?' Sharon peered at her. 'You can bring Jase if you really want to, though I can tell you there'll be no shortage of crumpet there, I'll see to that.'

'Of course I want to come,' Sally assured her. 'It's just that Jason is going away on a course that week. I'm not sure if . . .'

Sharon groaned and raised her eyes to the ceiling. 'Don't tell me. Mummy and Daddy won't want you going out on your own.'

'Of course they won't mind,' Sally protested unconvincingly. 'It's just that – well, Jason and I are sort of engaged.'

'First I've heard of it.' Sharon said scathingly.

'Well, not engaged exactly. But . . .'

'Tell him if he doesn't like it, he can get stuffed,' Sharon advised. 'What's up? You're your own woman, aren't you?'

'Y-yes.'

'It's like I said – you've got to show them you can do without them. It makes them appreciate you more. Tell you what. If it's the late night you're bothered about, why don't you tell your mum you're going somewhere else and stay the night at our place?'

'Shouldn't you ask your mother first?' Sally asked apprehensively.

Sharon laughed. 'She won't mind. There'll probably be bodies crashed out all over the place by the time she and Dad get home anyway. They'll just step over them.'

The image that this conjured up was quite beyond

Sally's comprehension, but she promised she'd try to think of some way she could come to the party.

It was the following week when she was doing the Saturday shopping for her mother that she met Aunt Jean in the supermarket. As always Jean greeted her warmly.

'Hello, love. If you've finished your shopping how about joining me for a coffee?'

They sat in the supermarket snack bar and over coffee and doughnuts Sally confided to Jean her quandary over Sharon's party.

'I said I wasn't sure I could go because of Jason being away, but really it's Mum and Dad. They don't approve of Sharon at all.'

Jean shook her head. 'Well, I think you should go, love. Jason wouldn't mind. He's always saying you should get out more and he knows he can trust you.' She sipped her coffee thoughtfully. 'Look – maybe I shouldn't encourage you to be deceitful, but you could always say you were spending a night over at our place if you like – so as to be there when Jason gets home on Saturday morning.'

Sally's face brightened. 'Could I really?' She frowned. 'I hate lying to them, Auntie Jean, but honestly what else am I to do?'

Jean patted her hand. 'Don't worry about it, love. Just you go to the party and enjoy yourself.'

When Sally arrived at Sharon's house the other girl took one look at her clothes and laughed. 'You cannot be serious, man. You can't wear *that*!'

'Why not?'

'Because it's a rave-up, not the bleedin' vicarage tea party.' She grabbed Sally's arm and dragged her towards the stairs. 'Come up to my room. We'll soon find you something more suitable.'

Sally emerged half an hour later wearing a pair of silver hotpants and a black satin top with daring cutaway panels which she felt distinctly unsure of. Sharon viewed her with satisfaction.

'You look knock out,' she announced. 'Now come on down as they say and meet the gang.'

By nine o'clock the little house was crammed with people and the noise from the stereo turned up to full volume was deafening. Sharon had laid on plenty of lager and Coke and there was some gin and whisky too. Occasionally there was a loud thumping from the house next door, but Sharon told them to ignore it. The neighbours had been warned and they'd promised to stop at midnight anyway.

Sally began to enjoy herself. Sharon handed her a large drink.

'What is it?' Sally asked suspiciously.

'Gin and orange. Get it down you,' Sharon instructed. 'It'll put you in the party mood.'

Sally sipped the drink and found that Sharon was right. After she had drunk it she found that she felt great, really relaxed and confident. Everything blurred and softened at the edges, making the shabby room and the people in it look nicer and much more fun. Before long she forgot all about her parents, and the lie she had told in order to be here, and began to enjoy herself.

There were lots of boys there; some she knew and some she didn't. One in particular took a shine to her, hardly leaving her side from the moment he set eyes on her. They danced together, sat on the stairs to eat crisps and drink cans of lager, discussing the latest pop music and films, then danced again. He told her his name was Greg, and Sally decided that he was quite nice-looking. As they danced he whispered in her ear that she was beautiful and that he'd seen her at college and always fancied her. It was when Sharon put on a record of Chris De Burgh singing Diamond In The Dark and everyone began to hold each other close and sway to the music that Sally felt the first stirrings of excitement. Greg held her tightly against him and began to run his hands over her in a way that sent shivers up and down her spine. His mouth found her cheek, then the corner of her mouth. He bent his head to find the little hollow beneath her ear. Feeling the tremor of pleasure that went through her body, he looked into her eyes.

'Shall we go upstairs?'

Sally closed her eyes. She felt strangely excited in a way she had never experienced before. Her stomach was full of butterflies and her heart raced as though something special was about to happen. The rhythm of the music seemed to seep right into her very soul. As Greg repeated his question his hand found her breast, his fingers creeping through one of the cut away panels to touch her. She felt her skin tingle and her nipple hardened against his fingertips. She let her head fall back and a little gasp of delight escaped her parted lips.

'Come on, Sal,' he urged, edging her towards the door. 'I know you want to.'

No one noticed as they climbed the stairs together. In Sharon's bedroom coats were piled in a heap on the bed. Greg swept them on to the floor and drew her down beside him. She closed her eyes as he kissed her, her lips parting to allow him to explore her mouth with his eager tongue, thrilling to the cool touch of his fingers on her skin as he deftly removed the silver pants and top.

'You're gorgeous,' he murmured, his hands eagerly exploring her body as he moved over her. She half opened her eyes and smiled up at him, arching her body sensuously, too languorous to find the words to respond. As he entered her a razor-sharp dart of pain made her tense for a second then, as he began to move, something else took over – something so pleasurable that she found herself clutching at him convulsively, dragging her fingernails down his back, thrusting against him again and again.

'Hey – steady on,' he murmured. 'We don't want it over too soon.'

But something had taken possession of Sally. She couldn't get enough of this new sensation. It was as though there were some wonderful prize waiting for her – it was there – just out of reach. She must have it and she would – she *would* . . .

Suddenly Greg pulled abruptly away from her with a cry.

'*Christ*! You little fool.'

Sally stared numbly up at him, her eyes opaque, the pupils dilated. Her mind was fuddled. All she was aware of was a feeling of acute let-down. 'Wh-what's the matter? Why did you stop?' she moaned.

'Don't you know *anything*?' He sat up, avoiding her eyes, and turned away. 'Look, it's late. I've got to go now.' He stood up and began to drag on his clothes.

Sally felt oddly detached as she lay there watching him straighten his clothes and comb his hair in front of Sharon's dressing table mirror. The lovely floating feeling was beginning to wear off and the reality of what she had just done was beginning to dawn on her. She told herself that she didn't even know his second name and yet she'd made love with him – been as intimate as it was possible for two people to be. But they were facts she didn't want to face just yet. All she wanted was to blot it all out, curl up and go to sleep.

She woke to Sharon shaking her.

'Come on, party pooper. A fine party girl you turned out to be. A couple of drinks and all you want to do is come up here and fall asleep.'

Sally blinked up at her friend. 'I'm sorry. What's the time?'

'Half-past seven. You've missed the party, stupid. Time for little Cinderella to go home – or did you say you were going over to Hinkley?'

The events of the previous night had begun to filter back now and Sally sat up. Her head was pounding and her tongue felt thick and dry as felt in her mouth. She ached all over too, but worst of all was the guilt and self-disgust she felt. She'd made love with someone she didn't even know – allowed him to do things she'd never have permitted Jason to do. And what was worse, she'd enjoyed it – hadn't been able to get enough. It was as though some other girl had temporarily taken over her body, behaving in a totally alien way. Cheeks burning with shame at the memory of her abandoned behaviour, she got up from the bed and looked at Sharon.

'Can I have a bath?'

Sharon laughed. 'What do you think this is – the bleedin' "Dorchester"?'

Seeing Sally's crestfallen expression, she added: 'Sorry, kiddo, the boiler's out and there isn't any hot water. Why don't you wait till you get over to Hinkley and have a bath at your auntie's?'

In the bathroom there were damp towels on the floor and a dark greasy ring around the wash basin. Sally washed as best she could in cold water, then, feeling slightly better, said goodbye to Sharon and walked down the street to catch the bus to Hinkley.

227

By the time she sat for her exams Sally knew there was little doubt that she was pregnant. She told no one. Not even Sharon. And she was almost at the end of her tether. In the end, desperate to unburden herself to someone, it was Jason she told.

It was on a Saturday evening and they were going out for a meal to celebrate her exams being over. He'd booked a table at an Indian restaurant, but the smell of curry made her turn in the doorway, bile rushing into her mouth. Her face drained of colour.

'I'm sorry, Jase. I c-can't.' She turned and ran.

He caught up with her in the car park where she was leaning weakly against the side of the car, her forehead beaded with perspiration. 'Sal, what's the matter, love. Are you ill?' He helped her into the car and she burst into tears.

'Oh, Jason. I'm pregnant. I don't know what to do.'

He was shocked. 'You can't be pregnant, Sal. We haven't . . .' He broke off, staring at her in dismay as the realisation of what she was telling him sank in.

He listened patiently to her explanation of what had happened, his face darkening with anger and disgust. Sally looked at him.

'I can see that you hate me for it, and I can't blame you,' she said miserably. 'What I did was unforgivable.'

'I'm not angry with you, silly,' Jason said. 'It's *her* – Sharon. She shouldn't have given you strong drink when she knew you weren't used to it. And this guy – he must have known you didn't know what you were doing. The lousy creep took advantage.' His hands clenched into fists. 'I just wish I could get my hands round his rotten neck.'

'You can't, Jason. It wouldn't do any good. There's nothing anyone can do about it now. It's too late.' She wished she had the courage to confess to him that she had known what she was doing but just hadn't cared. The feeling of guilt she had suffered over the way she had thrown herself at Greg had tortured her ever since. It would help so much to share some of that guilt, but she knew she couldn't. Instead she asked weakly: 'Oh, Jason, what can I do?'

'Marry me,' he said decisively. 'I'm not earning much yet but we could live with Mum to begin with. There's room now that Paul and Mike have left home, and you and she have always got on well together.'

'Oh, Jason.' Hope and relief welled up in her heart as she looked up at him. 'Oh, but – even if we did, it'd be born too soon.'

'We'll let them think it's mine, naturally.'

They'd agreed to talk about it in detail very soon. But as she lay in bed later that night, Sally knew that she could not accept Jason's noble sacrifice. All her life she had been managed and manipulated; first by the rejection of her natural mother, then by her adoptive parents. Since she had been at college, Sharon had taken it upon herself to organise her life. Even Jason and his mother had influenced her in their own different ways. Finally there had been the unknown boy who had taken his pleasure of her body, used her, then walked away without a backward glance.

Suddenly she was angry. It was time she took charge of her own life. If she married Jason it would solve one problem only to create another – one that would last for the rest of her life. She liked Jason and respected him, but she didn't love him and wouldn't be governed by him. She'd go away by herself. With luck she'd be a qualified florist any day now. She'd get a job and a flat and start her life anew.

Then all at once in the darkness she felt the first

faint but unmistakable stirring of the new life within her. She stiffened at the strangeness of the new sensation and her hands moved to her stomach in a gesture of instinctive protectiveness. The sudden realisation that it was a new human being she carried inside her sobered her. Was this yet another person waiting to have a say in how she lived her life? She reminded herself that she wasn't – and probably never would be completely free now.

But free or not, she could take charge of her own destiny and that of her child. With a sigh she turned over and closed her eyes. The future held nothing but problems, yet suddenly she felt light and relaxed. She had made a decision; the first she had ever made without consulting someone else. Suddenly, for the first time in her life, she knew who she was.

Chapter 13

When Leah arrived back from The Mermaid the following Friday night she found Terry's 2CV standing in the courtyard. Her heart lifted as she hurried across the yard. He was in the kitchen, a teatowel tucked into the waistband of his jeans, making spaghetti Bolognese.

'Hi.' He looked over his shoulder. 'I've got supper all ready. How's that for service?'

'Oh, Tel, I'm *so* glad to see you.' She threw her arms around his neck and hugged him hard.

'What a welcome. I've only been gone three weeks.' He held her away from him. 'It's good to know I've been missed. I thought you'd be too . . .' He broke off as he saw that her eyes were bright with tears. 'Hey, what's all this?'

She turned away, brushing at the wetness on her cheeks with the back of one hand. 'It's nothing. I've been lonely, that's all.'

Frowning, he cupped her chin, searching her eyes. 'Are you sure that's all?'

'Of course.'

'Is it your job at the pub? Did something go wrong?'

'No, that's fine. I'm enjoying it. But you can be lonely in a crowd sometimes, you know.'

Still unconvinced, he turned back to the cooker and began to dish out two generous portions of spaghetti.

'Well, whatever it is, I hope it hasn't put you off your nosh. Here, get your chops round this and I'll tell you all my news.' He reached across to where his rucksacks hung on the hook behind the door and pulled out a bottle of chianti. 'Find me the corkscrew, will you?'

She found it and handed it to him. 'Does this mean we have something to celebrate?'

'You could say that.' He uncorked the bottle and set it in the middle of the table between them. 'Will the *signorina* be seated?' He pulled out her chair with a flourish.

'*Si.*' She took her seat and smiled up at him. '*Grazie, signore.*'

The spaghetti was good and they ate in silence for a few minutes.

'Well?' she said at last. 'Are you going to tell me this news or do I have to play Trivial Pursuit?'

Terry picked up his glass and leaned back in his chair. 'While I was here I wrote those features for the *Clarion* – right?'

'Right.'

'What I didn't tell you at the time was that I was doing something else too: a freelance article about corruption in local councils.'

'Wow.' She looked up at him with wide eyes. 'Controversial stuff, eh?'

'I offered it to one of the national dailies and I knew that if they took it I could forget my job on the *Nenebridge Clarion*.'

She smiled wryly. 'That goes without saying. But if it was such a gamble, why did you do it?'

'I've been getting restless lately – felt I was stuck in a blind alley. I got so sick of all the manipulation – all the cover-ups and the wasted money. Most of all I was sick of the way the local press was gagged by people with influence.'

'Good for you. Quite a crusade.' Leah helped herself to wine and looked at him enquiringly. 'So – was your article accepted?'

Terry's eyes sparkled as he took a slip of paper from his wallet and held it up for her to see. It was a cheque headed by the name of a well-known newspaper, made out to Terry for quite a generous amount of money.

'It'll be published next week and carrying my by-line. And that's not all. They've offered me a permanent job on the staff. Only a very junior job to begin with, but the prospects are good.'

'Tel, that's wonderful!' She paused to consider all the implications. 'But surely that means you'll have to move to London?'

'I hardly think my face'll be welcome around Nenebridge after next week.'

'Then what about your new flat?'

He laid down his fork and looked at her thought-fully. 'I wondered if you'd like it?'

'*Me*?' She stared at him incredulously. 'I'm never going back to Nenebridge again. Surely you know that.'

He sighed. 'I think you should at least let your parents know where you are, Leah. They're bound to be worried.'

Her mouth set in a stubborn line and she avoided his eyes. 'They're *not* my parents. And you wouldn't say they'd be worrying if you'd heard some of the things they said.'

'That was all in the heat of the moment. By now they're probably frantic with worry. Look, suppose they report you to the police as a missing person?'

She looked up at him, her eyes alarmed. 'They wouldn't, would they? I'm over age after all. Would the police come looking for me?'

He shrugged. 'They might, if the Dobsons laid it on thick enough. After all, Jack does have some influence.'

'I'll send them a postcard. Will that do?'

'I wish you'd go back, Leah,' he said. 'I'd know you were safe there.'

'I'm not going back, Terry.' She looked up at him accusingly. 'What you're saying is you don't want to have to feel responsible for me any more,' she said. 'Well, you needn't. I'm quite capable of fending for myself. You can go off to your new job and forget all about me. I'll be fine.' She looked at him. 'I suppose life's been too exciting for you to bother finding anything out for me?'

He sighed. 'Well, as you say – life has been pretty hectic.'

'I thought so.' She stood up and began to gather the used dishes together. 'I knew it was too much to hope for. After all, when you have such an exciting future of your own to look forward to, why should you concern yourself with my problems? I can see now why you want to dump me back in Nenebridge.'

He reached out and grabbed her arm as she passed him. 'Leah, before you fly off the handle sit down and listen a minute, will you? I was saving that bit of news up till last.'

Slightly mollified, she sat down again, looking at him intently across the table. 'All right then, what *did* you find out?'

He took her birth certificate out of his wallet and laid it on the table between them. 'I went along to this remand home place. I told them I was a friend of yours and that I was helping you look for your mother. At first they didn't want to tell me anything, but eventually they grudgingly looked up their records and let me have the name of the children's home you were taken to soon after birth.'

'And?' She waited for him to go on. 'Is that all?'

'That's all they'd tell me, I'm afraid,' he said. 'But if you were to go yourself, with proof of your identity, they'd probably tell you more.'

'I see.'

Her disappointed face tugged at his heart and he heard himself saying: 'I did go to the children's home though.'

'You did?' Her face brightened. 'Did they tell you anything there?'

'Not a lot, but more than at the remand home.'

She waited. 'Well, go on. What did they tell you?'

He chewed his lip. He hadn't meant to tell her. He'd meant to let her find it all out for herself. 'I think you'd better prepare yourself for a surprise, Leah.'

'Oh, do go *on*, Tel. Why must you keep me in suspense like this?'

'It seems that there were two babies born to Marie O'Connor, not just one. You have a twin sister, Leah.'

She stared at him, her brown eyes incredulous. 'That can't be true. I'd remember. I don't remember any sister. There was only me at the home.'

'Your sister was named Sarah, and she was adopted at a few weeks old. That's why you don't remember her.'

'You mean they – these people took her and not me? That's wicked. Twins shouldn't be parted.'

He reached across the table to touch her hand. 'I daresay that in cases like that it's better for one baby to get a good home than for two to be left.'

'*I* was left. Did they think that didn't matter?' She got up from the table and stood with her back to him, staring out of the window at the empty cottage opposite. 'All my life people have rejected me,' she said, half to herself. 'Now it seems they've been doing it right from birth. Is there something the matter with me, Terry?'

'Of course there isn't.' He got up and stood behind her, wrapping his arms around her. 'It's just bad luck, love. Damned bad luck.' He held her close, feeling the tension in her body, sensing the turmoil inside her – wishing there was something he could do to heal the deeply ingrained hurt he knew she felt.

'Okay, so I've got a twin sister,' she said at last. 'Sarah.' She said the name experimentally, feeling the shape and texture of it on her tongue, trying to imagine it as the name of the person closest to her, and failing totally. She turned to look at him. 'I want to find her. Where do I begin, Tel?'

'Now wait.' He looked down into her eyes. 'Finding your mother is one thing. Finding your sister is something else.'

'Why?'

'Well, to start with I'm not sure that you're even entitled to. Your mother yes, but . . .'

'Surely my *twin* sister? Why should I not be entitled to look for her? After all, we're both adults now.'

He sighed. 'It mightn't be a good idea.'

'Why?'

'All sorts of reasons. She might not know she's adopted. Even if she does she might not know she had a sister. You didn't. And her parents might not want her to know. Leah. Something like this could disrupt a whole family.'

'What about me though? My whole life has been disrupted. No one seems to care a damn about that. I just want to find someone who is close to me, Tel. I just need to find a place to *fit*.'

236

'It's hard for you, I know.'

'No, you don't,' she challenged. 'You just think I'm an impulsive, immature *kid*.'

'No, I don't. It's just that it's not always easy to see these things with a clear eye, Leah. Just go easy on it, that's all I'm saying. You do tend to – well, jump into things without thinking them through.'

'Maybe they won't tell me where she is anyway,' she said despondently.

Terry paused in an agony of indecision. Should he tell her? 'Look, I did get one more piece of information out of them – the name of the social worker who was working on the case at the time.'

Leah's eyes lit up with a naked hope that he could hardly bear to look at. 'Could I find her, do you think?'

He shrugged. 'I don't know. It's a long time ago. She could be anywhere now. Anything could have happened.' He was annoyed with himself for telling her so much more than he'd intended. There he'd stop. He wouldn't tell her he'd been to the library and searched through all the microfilmed newspapers published around the time of her birth. Or that he'd found the sensational story that had made headlines twice in one year – the story of seventeen-year-old Marie O'Connor, the pregnant teenager who'd arrived in London with a bomb in her suitcase. And who was later convicted of terrorism.

It was dark when Terry woke to find Leah creeping into bed beside him. He blinked sleepily.

'Leah, what's the matter? Are you ill?'

'No. I can't sleep.' She looked child-like and vulnerable in the moonlight shining in at the window. Her eyes were very bright and he suspected she'd been crying.

237

'It's all right. Go back to sleep,' she said. 'I just woke up and felt lonely. I wanted to be snuggled up warm with someone.'

Suddenly wide awake, he threw back the duvet and sat on the edge of the bed, his back towards her. She could be exasperatingly naive at times, this half-child, half-woman.

'Leah, just what in the hell do you think you're playing at?' he demanded. 'You can't *treat* people like this, you know. Do you think I'm made of bloody stone or something?'

His outburst shocked her. 'Are you rejecting me too now?'

She was sitting up, her cotton baseball-shirt nightdress clinging to her and her dark hair tumbled about her shoulders. He turned, relenting as he caught the unmistakable quivering of her lower lip. 'You can be crashingly unimaginative at times, Leah.'

'I'm sorry. I didn't mean to . . .' She reached for his dressing gown and pulled it round herself, then sat with her arms clasped round her knees, looking small and forlorn. 'Terry – you said earlier that I jump into things without thinking them through. You were right. And I did it again while you were away.'

Shivering, he reached for his sweater, looking at his watch as he did so. It was three-thirty and it was bloody cold. He reminded himself that summer was over. 'Go on,' he said, pulling the sweater over his head. 'What have you done this time?'

'Remember the artist across the yard at number four?'

'Colin thingummy. Guy with long hair – bit weird-looking?'

'He *wasn't* weird-looking.'

He shot her a look. 'I see. Like that, was it?'

She sighed. 'I let him make a fool of me, Tel. I – I

238

thought I was in love. I th-thought it was the same for him. I really did.'

He saw the bleakness in her eyes and reached out to pull her against his shoulder. 'Oh, Leah, what am I going to do with you? Go on, what happened?'

'It was so – so wonderful. At least, I thought it was. Then he suddenly left at the end of last week, one day while I was at work; didn't even tell me he was going – or that he was married.'

He groaned. 'And you wonder why I think you shouldn't be allowed out alone.'

'What's *wrong* with me, Tel?' she asked plaintively. 'Why do people treat me like this?'

'Because you sit up and positively *beg* them to,' he said. 'You're basically a strong person, Leah. It's just that you have this blind spot when it comes to people.'

'He left me this awful note,' she shuddered. '"Thanks for everything", it said. It was so – so *humiliating*.'

He pulled her close against his side. She hadn't heard a word he'd said. Maybe she'd been right all along. Maybe finding her identity was important. If she could sort out who she was perhaps she'd stop wanting love at any price and settle down to making a life for herself.

'I wonder what she's like, Tel?' she said softly.

'Who – his wife?'

'No. Sarah. Do you think we're identical? Do you think she's exactly like me? Isn't it strange to know that there's another person just like me walking around.'

He laughed shortly. 'God forbid.'

She jabbed him in the ribs with her elbow. 'Don't be such a pig. No, seriously, just think. Sarah is my other half. We must have started out as a single cell. I have to find her, Tel. I just have to.' She looked up at

239

him. 'Can I stay here with you now? It's almost morning. I don't want to be on my own again tonight. Please?'

He sighed resignedly. 'Okay, you win as usual. Stay if you want.' Lying back against the pillow he tucked the duvet round her. She was asleep in seconds, her head resting in the hollow of his shoulder, her lips slightly parted and snoring ever so gently with a sound like the purring of a cat. He lay there wide awake. Watching as the sky grew light, he smiled wryly at the irony of it all. Would this girl sleeping like a baby in his arms, who wanted so badly to be loved, ever know how much love was hers for the taking?

When he wakened the sun was shining and he was alone again. He found her downstairs in the kitchen, making breakfast. She wore jeans and an Aran sweater of his, which reached almost to her knees.

'Hi. I've been for a long walk,' she told him. 'Trouble is, I didn't bring anything warm to wear so I borrowed this.' She tugged at the neck of the sweater. 'Okay?'

'Fine. Be my guest. Breakfast smells good.'

'Eggs, bacon, tomatoes and mushrooms. I'm returning the compliment for last night's supper.' She held up a slice of bread. 'Fried?'

Terry grinned and rubbed his hands. 'Great. Two, please.'

'I always said you were a pig.'

He watched her as she expertly flipped the eggs on to a plate and put the bread into the pan. Her cheeks were pink from the fresh sea air and tendrils of hair, loosened from her plait by the wind, corkscrewed around her neck and ears.

'How long will you be working at The Mermaid?' he asked.

She shrugged. 'Till the end of the month. I don't think Dick'd mind all that much if I went sooner though. There aren't many tourists around any more and his takings must have fallen.'

He tucked enthusiastically into the food she put before him 'Look, Leah, I'll make a bargain with you. You let your folks know you're okay and I'll find you a place to stay in London.'

She spun round to stare at him. 'You *will*?' She took an impulsive leap towards him but he held out his hands to ward off her embrace.

'Okay. I'll take your thanks as read. No need to go over the top.' As she sat down opposite him with her own breakfast he reached for a slice of toast. 'There's this guy on the paper who has a house in Notting Hill. He was sharing it with two other reporters but they've both left, one to get married and the other to take up a job abroad. He's offered me one of the vacant rooms but as far as I know the other is still going begging.'

'You don't think he'd mind a girl?'

'Not at all. The one who's leaving to get married is a girl. I got her job.'

'I see. But could I afford it?'

'With your savings and what you've earned at the pub you should be okay for a few weeks. You can't have spent much while you've been here.'

'That's true. But I'll be needing some warmer clothes with winter coming on, and it's expensive living in London, isn't it? My money won't last very long. And then what?'

'Get a job. You got one here.'

She looked at him doubtfully. 'Do you think I could?'

'I don't see why not. Dick says you're great. I'm sure he'd give you a glowing reference. You've had some experience behind the bar now.'

She nodded thoughtfully. 'I like the catering best.'

'Well, there you are. London's full of restaurants and wine bars. You're bound to find something.'

'It sounds wonderful. I'll ask Dick about a reference this morning.' She jumped up and began to clear the table. 'Which reminds me, I promised to go in early this morning and help him give the place a good clean.'

'Leave the dishes then.' Terry got up and took the pile of plates out of her hands. 'You haven't forgotten what I said, have you?' His eyes were serious as they looked down at her. 'You either see your folks, or you ring them. Let them know what you're doing and where you are or it's no dice about the room. I mean it, Leah.'

Her face fell. 'Oh, okay then. I suppose you're right.'

'I know I am. It could save a lot of complications in the long run.' He grinned at her. 'I'll come down to the pub for my lunch, shall I?'

She smiled. 'Great. I'll make you a crab sandwich – on the house.'

By the time Terry left on Sunday evening it had all been arranged. Leah had given Dick a week's notice and he, in return, had given her a reference. Carefully written in glowing terms in his best handwriting, he had used The Mermaid's headed notepaper – only used, as he told her, for special clients. Arrangements had been made for her to travel up to London the following Sunday morning. Dick had promised to drive her to King's Lynn station and Terry would meet her train at Liverpool Street. She could hardly contain her excitement. There was only one thing left for her to do.

242

She used the telephone at The Mermaid, choosing a time just before opening in the evening. Both Jack and Hilary should be at home, and she didn't care which of them she spoke to. She wasn't expecting either of them to beg her forgiveness or urge her to come home. But, as Terry said, at least she'd have done the decent thing. As the telephone rang out at the other end she could hear the drumming of her own heart, and when she heard the receiver being lifted the breath seemed to leave her body.

'Hello? Nenebridge 54277.' It was Hilary's voice, crisp and cool.

'H-hello.' She swallowed hard. 'It's Leah.' The silence at the other end was so prolonged that for a moment she thought they must have been cut off, then Hilary said in a voice like breaking glass: 'So – you've finally condescended to ring, have you?'

'I did leave a note.'

'Yes. We found that after you absconded.'

'You make me sound like a criminal. Look, I just wanted you to know that I'm all right.'

'How good of you to think of us.'

Leah winced. 'I know you always did all you could for me,' she went on. 'And I appreciate the years that you looked after me, really I do. But if we're both honest, it never really worked out, did it?'

'Why are you *really* ringing, Leah? What is it you want?'

'Nothing. I just wanted you to know that I'm safe and well. I'm in Cleybourn-on-Sea at the moment, but I'm moving to London at the weekend. I'll send you my new address.'

'You must do as you think fit.'

'How is everyone?'

'Everyone here is fine – never better.'

'Good. I – I thought you might be worried.'

'We gave up worrying about you a long time ago, Leah. And you proved, I think, that you don't give a damn about anyone but yourself. And now, if you've nothing more to say I'd be grateful if you'd ring off. I'm preparing a dinner party and I'm rather busy.'

'Look, I'm sorry – about Tom Clayton and everything. I didn't know – didn't mean to . . .' There was a loud click and Leah found she was speaking into thin air. Hilary had hung up on her. She replaced the buzzing receiver. Well, at least she had kept her promise to Terry. She'd always known it would do no good. They didn't care where she was or what happened to her.

When she wakened on Sunday morning it was raining. Packed and ready, she wandered round the cottage as she waited for Dick. Although she would miss this little place, she somehow had the odd feeling that it had already cast her off. All her things were packed in the suitcase and it looked too clean and tidy – as impersonal as it had been on the day they had arrived. In the yard the cobblestones glistened in the rain. The rambling rose on the porch of number four looked straggly and unkempt, the last of its blooms hanging tattered overblown heads. And the dahlias in the trough under the window were nipped by early frost, their bright petals already turning brown at the edges. Leah shivered and drew her light jacket more closely around her. It was time to leave.

Dick arrived on time in his elderly Cortina, muffled against the rain in a raincoat and scarf. He opened the passenger door and handed her in, then threw her suitcase into the boot.

'You picked a right old day for it, my 'andsome,' he remarked as he settled his bulk behind the wheel.

'Another hour and I reckon you could ha' swum it to 'Lynn.'

The cross-country drive to King's Lynn took almost an hour. In the station booking hall Dick hugged her warmly.

'Well, this is it. Gunna miss you, girl,' he said, blowing his bulbous nose. 'Best little barmaid I've ever 'ad. Any time you want to come back to Cleybourn, just you drop me a line. Always a place for you at The Mermaid.'

She kissed him on both cheeks and promised to come back. The train came in and she climbed aboard. Finally she was on her way to London.

Melbury Street was close to the main road and five minutes' walk from Notting Hill Gate Underground. The houses were small, semi-detached Victorian villas with two storeys, basement and attic, and Terry told Leah that most were occupied by artists and actors. All of them had been treated to what estate agents call 'sympathetic restoration' which Terry described as 'twee'. Each of the new owners had tried hard to give their house individuality. They were painted in bright colours and most had window boxes, bay trees in tubs or plant-filled jardinières decorating the area steps. Number twenty-four vied with the best of them. The brickwork in the area had been painted white to reflect the light, and someone had painted a trail of ivy on the wall over the iron railings that wound down to the basement door. In the tiny flagstoned space at the bottom stood a cobwebbed conifer in a green and white painted tub.

'I'd no idea there were places like this in London,' Leah exclaimed. Her only experience of London was of the West End where she'd been with Hilary on shopping trips and occasionally to the theatre.

245

Terry laughed. 'All sorts of things in London that you don't know about. But I'm sure you're about to discover them.' He used his key to open the door at the bottom of the steps and they walked into a narrow hallway. To the right, a door led into the basement kitchen, a large warm room with an Aga. It was fitted with pine units and there was a fridge-freezer and an automatic washing machine. In the centre of the room was a round table with six wheelback chairs tucked under it. Leah looked around admiringly.

'I like this. It's cosy.'

'That's all there is down here,' Terry told her. 'It was two rooms but it's been knocked into one. We all share the cooking facilities and keeping the place clean. Bill's quite strict about that.' He gave her a wry look. 'And I warn you – he says that girls are the worst when it comes to clearing up after themselves.'

'I hope he isn't one of your chauvinistic types.'

'No. He's just had one or two bad experiences, that's all, so watch your step.'

'Does the house belong to him?'

'Yes. He used to live here with his wife, till the marriage broke up a couple of years ago. Come and see the rest.' He led the way upstairs. On the ground floor the two original rooms had been knocked into one again to form a spacious oblong room with shabby-comfortable furniture and an abundance of bookshelves. At the front a bay window looked on to the street and at the back there was a glazed door that gave onto a paved yard.

'We all use this room too,' Terry was saying. 'Though you can entertain in your own room if you want to be private.'

Leah stood looking out into the back yard at tubs of wilting plants. The whitewashed walls facing her held a trellis with a dead clematis still clinging to it. Strung from one side of the yard to the other was a washing line on which hung two greyish teatowels.

'How sad,' she muttered.

'What?'

'Everything's dying. It was the same at Cleybourn. Even the dahlias were wilting.'

Guessing that she was feeling a little unsure and disorientated Terry slipped an arm around her shoulders. 'It's just the season. Who was it said: "I saw the tree, eternity put forth the blossom, time"?'

She turned to look at him with a wistful smile. 'I don't know, but I like it. It's hopeful.'

He grinned and took her hand. 'Come up and see your room.'

Leah's room was at the back of the house. There wasn't much of a view from the window, just the back yard with its washing line and dead flowers and, over the wall at the end, the back yard of the house in the next street, which at first glance seemed to be half full of overflowing dustbins. It was certainly a far cry from the view of the Saltings and she had a sudden pang of nostalgia.

'It's great, Tel,' she made herself say, looking round at the single bed, the worn carpet and slightly sagging armchair. 'I'm really grateful to you for getting it for me. I only hope I can afford to stay.'

'You'll be fine. Just take it one day at a time,' he advised. On the landing he showed her the bathroom, which was next door to hers, and his own small room which led off the half landing.

Downstairs there was the sudden bang of a door and footsteps on the stairs, accompanied by cheerful whistling.

'That's Bill,' Terry told her. 'Come and meet him.'

Bill Fenton was tall and loose-limbed. He wore corduroy jeans and a leather jacket, scuffed at the elbows. His checked shirt was open at the neck, but Leah noticed that his shoes were expensive and well polished. He smiled at her, but she was well aware that the smiling grey eyes were assessing her shrewdly at the same time.

'Hello, Leah. Welcome to Melbury Street.' The hand he offered her was hard and strong and as she shook it briefly she sensed his restlessness. 'Has Terry shown you round?'

Leah smiled. 'Yes, and it all looks very nice.'

'You'll have to get used to the odd hours that journalists keep,' he said. 'No set mealtimes for instance. We pass each other on the stairs like ships in the night.' His accent was faintly cockney and Leah guessed that he had a quick wit and was probably quick to speak his mind.

'I won't get in your way, I promise.'

Bill looked at Terry, one eyebrow raised. 'What on earth have you been telling the girl about me?'

'That you don't trust girls to clean up properly,' Leah put in. 'But I'm no slut, as you'll hopefully find out.'

Bill gave a great shout of laughter. 'Good for you, girl. I might as well tell you that I don't like wet tights dripping down my neck when I'm shaving either.'

'I'll remember. I'm a good cook, by the way.'

'Oh, no.' Bill held up a prohibitive hand. 'Strictly sex equality here. We all do our own thing, right, Tel?' Terry nodded and Bill grinned at them both. 'Right then. You'll soon shake down. Be one of the guys in no time. Got to rush now. Cheers.' He clattered up the rest of the stairs and disappeared into the room at the front of the house.

'He's okay, Bill,' Terry told her as they went downstairs. 'Been in the business since he left school. What he doesn't known about journalism and newspapers isn't worth knowing, and he's got the best nose for a story in the business.'

'What went wrong with his marriage?' Leah whispered.

Terry shrugged. 'His wife was a journalist too. She landed a good job in TV though up north – Granada – Grampian or somewhere. The relationship couldn't stand up to being apart so much.'

Leah spent the days that followed getting her bearings. She bought herself a raincoat with a warm lining, a couple of sweaters and some new jeans, appalled at the way London prices gobbled up her money. She familiarised herself with the rambling spread of the capital city. Investing in an *A to Z* she studied the maps and Underground system carefully until she felt fairly confident that she could take herself about without getting lost. She even managed to fit in a little sight-seeing. On a visit to the Houses of Parliament she bought a picture postcard for Granny Dobson; then, on second thoughts, she bought another, wrote her new address on the back and addressed it to Jack and Hilary. She put them both into a postbox with a sigh of relief. She'd kept her promise to Terry. Now she could forget it.

In the evenings she studied Bill's stack of London telephone directories and excitedly pointed out to Terry that there were several Miss H. Browns listed in various parts of London.

He looked doubtful. 'It's not an unusual name. It could well be that none of them is the Miss H. Brown you're looking for.'

'But if I work systematically through them one by one . . .'

'That'd be time-consuming and it could also be expensive. Besides, it's a long time ago, love. Miss

Brown could have become *Mrs* somebody by now. I think getting in touch with Social Services direct might be a better plan. I expect they have some sort of register of all their employees.' He gave her a warning look. 'Oh, and better keep a record of all your telephone calls. Bill will hit the roof if you run up a big phone account.'

Alone in the house the following Monday morning Leah began her task. She drew an immediate blank at the local Social Services office when they informed her that they could not give out private whereabouts of any of their social workers on the telephone.

'Does that mean she is still working in London?' Leah held her breath. 'Look, if you could just tell me which area?'

But the female voice at the other end of the line cut her off short. 'I've told you. We can't give out that kind of information. If you have some kind of problem . . .'

'I'm trying to find my sister.'

'You mean Miss Brown is your sister?'

'No. My sister and I were adopted at birth. Miss Brown was the social worker on the case, so I'm told.'

'Why didn't you say? How long ago was this?'

'Nineteen years.'

'It's a long time, but you're perfectly within your rights to try to find her through the proper channels. Perhaps if you wrote to Social Services in the district where your birth was registered.'

'Thank you. I'll do that.'

Leah fetched her birth certificate – the original one that Jack Dobson had given her on the day she left Nenebridge. She already knew that Hannah Brown had long since left there but maybe someone would know where she was working now. It was worth a try anyway.

The voice at the other end was helpful and kind. 'Miss Brown left here years ago, I'm afraid.'

'I know, but I thought . . . I was adopted, so was my twin sister, you see, and I'm trying to trace them both. I'm not having much luck so far.'

'I know it can be difficult sometimes. Look, if you'd like to give me your number, I'll try and find out where she is and get back to you.'

'Oh, that would be marvellous. Thanks.'

Leah waited by the telephone all afternoon. Maybe the girl had had no more luck than she had. Maybe she'd been too busy even to try. She had almost given up hope when suddenly the phone rang. Snatching it up eagerly she said breathlessly: 'Hello. Leah Dobson here.'

'Hello, Miss Dobson. It's Marjorie Bates from Social Services. We spoke earlier – about Hannah Brown.'

'Yes – yes?' Leah tried not to sound impatient. 'Have you traced her?'

'I haven't been able to find out where she's working now, but someone here in the office used to know her socially. She's given me a telephone number. Whether she's still at that address I couldn't . . .'

'It's worth a try,' Leah interrupted. 'Go ahead. I've got a pencil.'

There was a pause at the other end. 'Look, we're not really supposed to give out private phone numbers so . . .'

'It's okay. I won't say where I got it. And it really *is* a genuine case.'

The girl read out the number and Leah wrote it down. At last she was getting somewhere. When she'd hung up she sat looking at the telephone pad with Hannah's number printed on it. At last she was within an ace of making contact. She had only to make one call. Should she ring now, or wait till this evening? Unable to wait she carefully dialled the number, then held the receiver close to her ear, the sound of her own heartbeats loud in her ears.

The telephone rang out three times at the other end, then there was click and a pleasant voice said: 'Hello, Hannah Brown here. I'm sorry I can't take your call at the moment, but if you'd like to leave your name and number, and maybe your reason for calling, I'll ring you back. It may be a few days as I'm going to be busy over the next couple of weeks. If it's an emergency please ring the office.'

After the bleep, Leah said quickly: 'My name is Leah Dobson. The name on my birth certificate was O'Connor. My twin sister and I were adopted and I'm trying to trace my mother and sister. I'd be grateful if you could help.' She just had time to give the telephone number when the time ran out. She replaced the receiver with a feeling of frustration. Now all she could do was wait.

Sitting disconsolately at her bedroom window when she was alone in the house, Leah watched the comings and goings of the neighbours. It was in this way that she discovered that the house whose yard backed on to that of number twenty-two was an Italian restaurant. A young man wearing a white shirt and black trousers frequently came out into the yard for a smoke. It wasn't long before he noticed her at the window and began to give her a friendly wave.

He had dark skin and curly black hair and soon, in addition to the wave, he began trying to mouth some kind of message to her. She couldn't make out what he was trying to say and at last, her curiosity getting the better of her, she went down into the yard and stood on a box to look over the wall.

'Is there something wrong?'

He laughed up at her. He had sloe-black eyes and his teeth were very white against his swarthy skin. 'Ah, no, *signorina*. Everything *right*.'

His accent was a fascinating mixture of Italian and cockney which made her smile.

'So why were you waving at me?'

He came closer to the wall. 'Because you sit at the window.' He pointed. 'You look so sad – homesick, maybe? Like me when I come to England.'

'Perhaps. A bit. Is that your house?'

'House? Ah, no. It is Bella's.' Seeing her bewilderment he added: 'Ristorante.'

'Oh – you're a waiter?'

He looked slightly indignant. 'No. Part-owner,' he told her proudly. 'With my sister Anna and her husband Franco. They come five years ago – from Bologna. I come three.'

'I see. Sorry, I didn't realise.'

He smiled again. '*Va bene*. Is quite all right, *signorina*.'

'I'm Leah.' She reached over the wall to hold out the tips of her fingers.

'*Come stà*?' He grinned broadly and shook the fingers. 'I am Giovani. But everyone call me Joe.'

'Nice to meet you, Joe. Or should I say, *come stà*?'

He laughed. 'You come soon to see our ristorante?'

She shook her head. 'No money, Joe. I'd love to but I'll have to find a job first.'

His eyes widened. 'You want job? You waitress – cook – serve bar?'

'Well, yes. Do you need someone?'

'You come and see my sister. She gonna have a baby – must rest more. She the boss. But she like you, I know.'

'Well, I'd love to. How do I get there?' Leah was quite excited now.

'Is Bella's Ristorante. Stermyn Street.' He pointed. 'You Melbury, okay?'

'That's right.'

'You go to top.' His arms waved like a windmill. 'Turn right and then right again, okay? This Stermyn Street. You see Bella's Ristorante pretty bladdy quick.'

Leah laughed. 'When?'

He hunched his shoulders. 'Any time. Now.'

When Terry came in that evening he found Leah fizzing with excitement.

'Hey guess what – I've got a job.'

'Great. Where?'

'Bella's, the little Italian restaurant in the next street. The woman who runs it is pregnant and needs extra help. I'm to work there in the evenings and at lunchtimes. That'll leave me afternoons to do my searching.'

'That's wonderful. Money good?'

She pursed her lips. 'Not 'specially, but apparently I'll make up on tips.'

Terry smiled. 'Well, anyway, it's a start. Good luck, love, and well done.'

Bill, who had overheard Leah's news on his way upstairs, told her later that Bella's was becoming an increasingly fashionable eating place among the local yuppy population.

'Quite the in place, in fact. You should do all right for dosh there, kid,' he told her with a wink. 'Just put on your miniskirt and flash those shapely pins.'

'Now who's being sexist?' she asked him.

Bella's Ristorante had a Georgian bow window with a frilled lace curtain, coach lamps and two bay trees in tubs on either side of the front door. It looked to Leah for all the world like an English tea shop – until she stepped over the threshold. Inside, the tables were laid with red and white checked cloths and in the centre of each stood a little candle lamp and a tall glass with bread sticks. The bar was decorated with trailing vines and bunches of plastic grapes and at the back was a mural of Napoli, complete with a benign-looking Vesuvius in the background. The piped music was soft and discreet, but mainly Italian too. Neapolitan love songs, popular arias from operas and the occasional burst of Vivaldi.

From the very beginning it was clear that Anna was, as Joe had said, the boss. She was small and plump and quite heavily pregnant, but her dark eyes were quick and shrewd and her hands and feet were never still. Her husband Franco was more placid. He had sleepy brown eyes with hooded lids and a deep velvety voice. He was in charge of the bar whilst Anna reigned supreme in the kitchen. They both spoke slightly better English than Joe.

When Leah asked Joe what he did, he told her with twinkling eyes that he was the maître d'. When Anna heard his description of himself, she laughed her husky chuckle.

'You better watch my little brother,' she warned. 'He is the youngest of the family. He's been bossed all his life. Now *he* got someone to boss is possible he get to be big pain-in-the-bum.' She wagged a finger at Leah. 'He try it – you tell him go to hell. Anna say so.'

In the kitchen Anna explained to Leah that she was six months pregnant with her first baby and that her blood pressure was high. The doctor had threatened that if she did not take more rest from now until the birth, he would make her spend the rest of her pregnancy in hospital.

'Then you must take care,' Leah told her.

Anna threw up her hands in frustration. 'Is so *stupid*. My mama, she have twelve kids and never go to hospital one time.'

'Not everyone is so lucky,' Leah said.

Anna hunched her shoulders resignedly. 'So – you help me cook in the mornings. Enough for evening too. Help Joe wait tables at lunchtime. In evening, woman come to help in kitchen. You help out in general wherever needed. Okay?' She looked at Leah hopefully, her head on one side, eyes bright as a robin's.

Leah nodded enthusiastically. 'Okay-fine. I've been working in a pub in Norfolk. I've got a reference.' She opened her bag and gave Anna the reference Dick had written. Anna read it quickly and passed it back with a smile.

'Sounds like he wish you stay there.'

Leah smiled. 'It's a beautiful place, but in winter it's too quiet for business.'

'In winter this place do good,' Anna said proudly. 'Businessman's lunches, romantic evening dinner for two.' She rolled her dark eyes. 'Executive dinner parties – teenage bashes. Sometimes people take whole ristorante.'

Leah smiled. 'Great.'

'Si – good. So you come tomorrow, huh?'

'You bet,' Leah told her.

In the first two weeks at Bella's, Leah learned a lot. The work was hard and she found she had little time for worrying that Hannah Brown had not contacted her. Now and again she thought about it and wondered whether to try ringing again, but Hannah had said a couple of weeks. Better leave it at least three before she began to push it.

Her new job helped to take her mind off things. She was learning to cook the regional Italian dishes Anna had made herself famous for. *Risi e peoci*, a kind of risotto with clams; *Fegato alla Veneziana*, calves' liver and onions; and several wonderful seafood dishes and soups, including the tasty and filling *Stracciatella*, with pasta, eggs and cheese. The Andretti family worked like slaves and Leah could see that they needed help, especially now that Anna was forced to take the evenings off and rest.

Leah did a bit of everything from cooking and waiting to serving behind the bar and taking bookings on the telephone. She soon grew fond of the noisy, volatile Andrettis with their fiery tempers and quick, uproarious laughter. She loved the work too; meeting people, serving them and seeing that they had everything they wanted. Franco taught her the correct way to serve wines: how to advise customers on what to order from the wine list and what to drink with what. By the time November came she could even speak a few sentences of Italian – enough to welcome the customers and pronounce the names of the dishes convincingly, though some of the words that Joe taught her caused Anna to throw up her hands in mock horror.

'He teaching you to *swear*, Leah,' she said, her eyes twinkling. 'Don't you listen to my bad little brother.'

The bustle of life at Bella's left Leah little time for looking for her mother or Sarah. Sometimes she wondered if she would ever get around to finding them, but she promised herself that she would make the time somehow – someday soon.

At the end of November Anna's baby was born. She went into labour quickly one morning almost two months earlier than the date given her for the baby's birth. Amidst much noise and excitement from all three Andrettis the midwife and ambulance was summoned and she was hastily despatched to hospital. Franco went with her and Leah and Joe managed as best they could in the lunchtime rush. By four o'clock Franco was back, his limpid brown eyes alight with excitement. He embraced them both and although his English seemed temporarily to have deserted him, Leah managed to pick up the facts that he was the proud father of a baby boy who had weighed in at six pounds, and that Franco now felt *molto meglor*.

'What about Anna?' Leah asked with smile. 'Is she *molto meglor* too?'

Franco placed his hands together under his cheek. '*Si* – she rest. Fast asleep.' He laughed and threw an arm around each of them. 'Tonight there will be glass of *vino* for everyone – on the house.'

They were about to open for the evening when the telephone rang. Leah answered it. The voice was Terry's.

'Leah, Hannah Brown rang here for you.'

Her heart leapt. 'Oh, Tel. Just my luck. I would be out when she rang back.'

'I told her where you worked and she asked if it'd be all right if she came round there to see you this evening. She said she had to come over this way. I said I'd check and ring her back.'

It was quite late when Hannah arrived but Leah spotted her the moment she came in. She stood just inside the door, glancing round her. She looked quite old. Late forties – older maybe, Leah decided, but quite smart and youthful-looking for all that; lean and well groomed with an air of authority and quiet assurance about her.

Leah approached her. 'Miss Brown?'

'That's right. And you're . . . ?'

'Leah Dobson. It's good of you to come. I'll be off duty quite soon. Then perhaps we can talk.'

'I'm sorry to have taken so long to get back to you,' Hannah said. 'I've been away on holiday, but I didn't want to advertise the fact that the flat was empty.'

Leah smiled. 'Of course. Can I get you something – a coffee, perhaps?' She pulled out a chair at the table nearest the window. Hannah sat down.

'Thank you.'

At the bar Franco nodded his head in Hannah's direction and asked; 'A friend?'

'Yes, she's waiting till I'm off duty. We have something rather important to discuss. Is it all right?'

He looked at his watch. 'You work long time today. You finish now. Give your friend a glass of *vino*. On the house.'

They sipped their wine and Hannah told Leah about her holiday in Provence. She hadn't mentioned the reason for their meeting and, realising that she was waiting for her to broach the subject, Leah said: 'So – do you think you'll be able to find my mother and sister for me?'

Hannah laid down her fork and met the girl's eyes. 'I'll be frank with you, Leah. Finding them isn't a problem. There are other things to be considered first though. First I'd like to be sure that you've examined your reasons for wanting to find them – and to reassure myself that they are the right reasons. And secondly I think it's important to discover whether *they* want to find *you*.'

Chapter 14

Marie folded the letter and stowed it away in her pocket. She'd been surprised and pleased to see Hannah's familiar writing on the envelope but decided to save the letter until her coffee break so that she could read it at her leisure. But after the initial paragraph, the news it contained filled her with a turbulent mixture of opposing emotions. Her stomach churning with mingled excitement and dread, she read it through several times till she knew every word of it by heart. And for the rest of that day the words rang out inside her head like a litany.

Dear Marie,

It is so long since we were last in touch. I hope all is well with you. I miss you and regret the quarrel that drove a wedge between us, and I hope you'll agree that it's time we buried the hatchet, as they say. My reason for getting in touch now is two-fold. I've been meaning to write to you for some time, but putting it off like a coward – afraid if I'm honest of your silence, or worse still, a rebuff. However, something has happened recently that has made up my mind for me. Marie – I have met one of your daughters. Leah has been trying for some time to find you. Also her twin sister, Sarah. I promised to help if I could,

261

but of course I warned her that I must first find out whether you were willing to see her.

She is a delightful young woman. I'm sure you and she would get along well, should you choose to meet. She has not found a happy family life with her adoptive parents and longs to have 'someone of her own' as she puts it. I do hope you will agree to let me set up a meeting. Think carefully about it and let me know your decision soon.

Love,

Hannah

P.S. I'd like to see you again soon too.

All morning Marie was acutely aware of the letter in her pocket. She found herself constantly feeling for the sheet of folded paper just to remind herself that she hadn't dreamed the whole thing. As she went about the familiar routine her mind was humming with all the possibilities suddenly open to her. For almost as long as she could remember she had wanted to see the daughters she had parted from at birth. Now a million questions buzzed through her mind like bees in a hive. What were they like? How had they grown up? Had they been happy, successful, clever? Hannah had said that Leah had not found a happy family life. Had she had a miserable, sad childhood? Did she blame the mother she had never seen for that? But above all, did she know the truth about her origin – her mother's past, and the circumstances that had forced her to give up her babies at birth? And if she had still to discover these things, could she ever come to terms with them and forgive?

And over it all loomed the bulky image of Ralph. If he should get to know about her reunion with her daughter, what would his reaction be? But that was something she had no wish to ponder over.

After the business over the forged cheques Ralph had been subdued but in a dangerous, simmering kind of way. He appeared infrequently at 'The Ocean' now, but when he did he brought with him all the tension of a tightly coiled spring. Marie felt nervous and edgy all the time he was around, knowing that he was only waiting for her to make one wrong move so that he could pounce.

After David's two-week stay in hospital he had been allowed to return home, but since his illness he was noticeably weaker and more vulnerable. Doctor Philip Hodge visited regularly. Since his visit to the medical conference he had decided to leave his practice in the Midlands and buy into a group practice in nearby Parkstone. During the negotiations and change-over he spent a lot of time at 'The Ocean' and he and Marie became friends. She found herself looking forward to his visits. He was pleasant and sympathetic, so easy to talk to that on more than one occasion she had asked his advice. Although he hadn't actually said so, Marie knew that he was concerned about David's health. She was careful to keep all worries and anxieties from him, and in Ralph's lengthening absences, shouldered most of the responsibility of the hotel's running herself. Not that she minded about the infrequency of Ralph's visits. She was glad for David's sake that they saw less of him. His visits seemed to have the same unsettling effect on her father-in-law as they did on her. When the letter came, she longed to show it to David and ask his advice, but knowing it would only worry him, she said nothing. Instead she went over and over in her mind the various actions she might take. That evening she waited until David was safely in bed before shutting herself in her room. Lifting the telephone she carefully dialled the number on Hannah's letter, her heart quickening as she heard the lifting of the receiver and the familiar voice at the other end.

'Hannah – it's Marie. I got your letter.'

'It's good to hear your voice, Marie. How are you?'

'I'm well, thanks.'

'And David?'

'Not too good. He had a heart attack earlier this year. It's left him quite shaky.'

'Oh, I'm so sorry. Give him my love, will you?'

'I will. Hannah – about Leah . . .' Marie twisted the telephone flex between her fingers. 'I'm sure you know that I'd love to see her. It's what I've always dreamed of. But . . .'

'It's Ralph?'

'He still doesn't know – about the babies.'

'Need he know now? You could come up to Town.'

'I suppose so. It's just . . .'

'You're afraid of what might be stirred up?'

'There was some trouble a few months ago. Ralph can be – well – difficult, as you know. I believe that what you told me about his army record could well be true. I'm sorry for the things I said at the time, Hannah.'

'Marie, you are all right, aren't you? If you need help . . .'

'No. I'm fine, for now, anyway. To go back to Leah.'

'Yes?'

'How much does she know?'

'Only that she has a twin sister. She'd somehow discovered that for herself. Nothing else though. It will be up to you to tell her the rest, or to keep it secret as you wish.'

'If I were to meet her, I'd want everything to be out in the open.'

'That's your decision, Marie. Do you want me to set up a meeting then?'

She sighed. 'Not yet. Look, I've been thinking. I'll write her a letter first – care of you. I'll try to put it all down: make her see how I felt all those years ago, that I had no choice but to let her and Sarah go. After that, if she still wants to meet me, then we'll take it from there.'

'I think that's a very good idea, Marie. I'll wait to get the letter and I'll pass it on straight away. But if I'm any judge of character, I've a feeling she'll still want to meet you.'

'Well, we'll wait and see. Tell her I shan't blame her if she wants to forget the whole thing once she knows.'

'You're sure you're all right, Marie?'

'I'm sure.'

'I've missed you.'

'I've missed you too.'

'I'll talk to you soon then, eh?'

'Yes. Soon, I hope. Goodbye, Hannah. And thanks.'

It was well after midnight when Marie finally put down her pen. The wastepaper basket at her feet was full of crumpled half-written attempts at telling her story in a way that sounded sincere. She had torn up her first efforts, seeing them as bizarre, self-pitying and melodramatic. She didn't want her unknown daughter to think of her as a victim, weak and ineffectual. She had loved Liam with all her young girl's heart. She would have done anything for him – anything except the act of brutal, suicidal terrorism he had so cruelly schemed to trick her into. Writing it all down proved to be painful as well as difficult. It brought back all the half-healed agonies and opened afresh the wounds. And yet looking back on it now she saw with startling clear-sightedness that but for her pregnancy she might well have died all those years ago. Blown to pieces along with God only knew how many other innocent victims. It was only her own physical vulnerability that had saved her life, the lives of her unborn children and untold others on that fateful day at Paddington Station. Seeing some good in the situation helped and, satisfied at last, she sealed and addressed the envelope, ready to post first thing in the morning. Now it was in the laps of the gods, she told herself.

It was towards the end of the Friday lunchtime rush that Hannah came into Bella's Ristorante. Leah's heart quickened when she saw the tall, slim figure take a seat at the table by the window. As their eyes met she knew instinctively that Hannah was not here to eat. She had news and Leah couldn't wait to finish serving so that they could talk.

Franco's young sister Asunta had arrived from Italy a few weeks ago, to take care of little Paulo so that Anna could resume full-time work downstairs. Sadly, the arrangement wasn't working out. Asunta was young and could be slipshod. There were constant rows over badly washed clothes and inadequately aired nappies. Poor Franco seemed in a permanent state of anguish as he tried to keep the peace between his wife and sister, and Leah was for ever closing the doors in an attempt to shut out the shrill exchanges between the two women that floated down from the flat above. Since Paulo's birth she found herself doing more and more of the cooking, which she enjoyed, but trying to divide herself effectively between the kitchen and restaurant was becoming increasingly difficult. To add to the stress of the situation, Joe had become totally captivated by the seductive, dark-eyed Asunta and repeatedly took her side, accusing his sister of bullying and unfairness. Upstairs in the flat the atmosphere became more and more Latin as the family quarrelled vociferously. And for Leah, life at Bella's became more fraught with every day that passed.

At last the two remaining customers paid and left. As was her custom, Leah saw them out, opening the door and bidding them '*Arrivederci*'. Then she turned her attention eagerly towards Hannah.

'Sorry to keep you waiting. Can I get you anything? Coffee or a glass of wine?'

'Nothing, thanks.' Hannah opened her handbag. 'I just came to give you this.' She passed Marie's letter across the table. 'I've been in touch with your mother and she has written this for you. She feels you should read it before you make up your mind about wanting to meet her.'

'Oh – but why?' Leah fingered the envelope apprehensively. 'Does this mean she doesn't want to see me?'

'On the contrary. She wants very much to meet you, Leah. But I'm sure the letter will make it all clear.' Hannah stood up and laid a hand on Leah's arm. 'What she has to tell you will probably come as a shock. Think carefully before you make your mind up.' She smiled. 'I have to go now. Give me a ring in a few days' time. Remember what I said. Don't let your emotions take control.'

Leah watched her go. In the short time she had known Hannah she had come to admire and look up to her. She always looked so cool and self-assured in spite of the stressful nature of her work. She invariably managed to look elegant too. Leah watched her pause in the doorway to put up the collar of her Burberry raincoat and open her umbrella against the icy November rain. Then, with a final wave, she was gone.

The square white envelope lay temptingly on the table. On it her name was written in a clear, round hand. Her mother's hand. How odd that this was the first time she had ever seen it. Leah fingered the envelope. It was thick with the folded sheets inside. The letter must be a long one. What could be in it? But she had no time to read it now. There were tables to clear and re-lay, as well as all the clearing up to do. Already she could hear the clatter of dishes from the kitchen as Joe helped Franco to stack the dishwasher. Then there was the preparation for this evening's menu. It would be at least an hour and a half before she could go home. Picking up the letter she tucked it into her apron pocket and went off to the kitchen.

At Melbury Street Bill and Terry were in the kitchen. She heard their voices as she let herself in at the basement door. Looking into the kitchen, she found them eating a late lunch together and wrinkled her nose at the smell of fish and chips.

'You two will ruin your digestive systems,' she told them.

Bill looked up with a grin. 'Leave it out, Lee. Best grub in the world, good old British fish and chips.' He waved his knife towards the Aga. 'More in the oven. Join us?'

'No thanks, I've eaten.'

Bill pulled a face. 'Foreign muck, I'll bet.'

It was their standing joke but this time Leah refused to be drawn. 'Got a few jobs to catch up on. See you later. Enjoy your cholesterol, boys.'

In her room she closed the door, shivering as she took off her coat. The room felt cold and unwelcoming. She switched on the electric fire, and drew up her one armchair close to its glow, then she settled down to read the letter. There were two sheets of paper in the envelope, both closely written on both sides. As she read, her eyes widened in astonishment. Hannah had warned that she could be shocked but she had expected nothing like this. It was like something out of a book or a newspaper story. The kind of thing that happens to other people, never to oneself. She read swiftly to the end then began again at the beginning, reading more slowly, taking in the words and all the depth of feeling that had gone into their writing. She felt herself deeply moved as, slowly, her eyes filled with tears.

But I want you to know, Leah, that I loved the man who was your father with all my heart. And I can only think that he must have truly believed that the cause to which he had pledged himself justified the terrible thing he did. Over the years I have tried hard to understand how he could send me on that terrible suicide mission. I have tried hard to forgive him, but I have to tell you that I've failed in both of these. However, I have come to realise that I would not be alive today if it had not been for my unborn babies. If I had not fainted when I did the consequences could have been devastating. So in a way, Leah, I have you and your sister to thank for my life. Parting with you was the hardest thing I have ever had to do. I hope you can understand that I had no choice but to let you go. I did it for your good – for the best. The chance of a good future was all I had to give you. I have never forgotten your dear little faces and in all the years between I have prayed for your happiness.

A sudden knocking startled her. It was immediately followed by Terry's head coming round the door. 'Hi there, I just . . .' He broke off as he saw her face and the letter in her hand. 'What's up, love? Not bad news, I hope.'

She held out the letter to him. 'I've just had this. Hannah brought it to me this lunchtime. It's from my mother.'

'Hilary? Trouble at home?'

'No. My real mother.'

He closed the door and came to her, his face concerned. Reluctantly he took the letter she held out to him. 'Look – are you sure? I mean, it's private, isn't it?'

'You can read it,' she told him. 'Please. I'd like you to.'

He sat down on the edge of her bed and read it through, then he looked up at her. 'I have to admit that I knew about the case,' he told her. 'When I was going through the newspaper archives I found the story.'

'You mean it was all in the papers at the time?'

'Of course. It made the headlines twice in one year. At the time of her arrest and then later when she came to trial. After – after you were born.'

Leah looked stunned. 'You didn't tell me.'

'I know. I don't really know why. I suppose I chickened out. It's not exactly the kind of thing one wants to hear about one's birth, is it?' He looked at her. 'What are you going to do?'

Her eyes suddenly focused on him. '*Do*? I'm going to see her, of course. Did you think all this would put me off?'

He gave a wry grin. 'No, not for a minute, knowing you.'

'She must be a remarkable woman, Tel. She got most of her education is prison. Imagine that. And since then she's made a career for herself in the hotel business. She's a survivor. I admire that.'

'So what is the next step?'

'I'll telephone Hannah and she'll fix something up.' Leah's face suddenly brightened. 'Isn't it exciting, Tel? Just think, I've actually *found* her. I'm going to meet my real mother at last. And it'll be all right. I know it will. After all, the past is dead and gone. We have the future to look forward to now. So much to make up to each other.'

'And your sister?' Terry asked.

Leah's smile faded. 'Ah, that's not quite so easy. Hannah says she was adopted at a few weeks old and it seems she's had an ideal upbringing; parents who idolise her – everything a girl could wish for. It doesn't seem likely that her parents will want that kind of disruption, and Hannah seems to think it might be better to leave well alone as far as she's concerned.'

He reached out for her hand. 'Look, I've got some news myself. The paper is sending me up north for six months, to another of the group's papers in Lancashire. It's to get more experience. I'm off on Friday, When I come back, if I make the grade, there may be a promotion in the offing.'

'Terry, that's great news.'

He smiled. 'It is rather. I haven't been home for a while and I'll be able to spend some time with the old man. We haven't seen each other for ages.'

'You must be looking forward to that.' She looked at him wistfully. 'I'll miss you.'

'Will you? I'll miss you too.' He looked into her

eyes for a long moment. 'We haven't seen a lot of each other since you've been here, what with the hours we both work.' He squeezed her hands. 'You will be all right, won't you?'

She laughed and ruffled his hair. 'Don't be daft. Of course I'll be all right. You don't have to feel responsible for me, you know. I'm a big girl now.'

'It's just that they seem to take advantage of you at that restaurant. You look whacked when you come home some evenings.'

'It's only since baby Paulo arrived. Everything'll be fine once Asunta gets used to Anna's ways. And now that I have this to look forward to . . .' She held up the letter.

Terry smiled ruefully. 'I hope it all works out as you hope, love.' He hesitated slightly, then leaned forward to kiss her.

She touched his cheek with her fingertips. 'You're the best friend I've ever had, Tel. I don't know what I would have done without you these past months.'

'Rubbish, you'd have managed fine.' He grinned. 'I quite like having you around anyway, even if you are a bit of a wally at times.' Suddenly serious, he looked into her eyes. 'Look, Leah, I don't know quite how to say this, but don't – well, just try not to expect too much from this reunion. I don't want you to be hurt. I suppose what I'm trying to say is, don't get your hopes up too high.'

'Hopes? Of my mother, you mean?'

'Basically, yes. You've built up such a powerful image of her all these years. She's only another human being, remember. And life does funny things to all of us, Leah. After all this time – after what you've both been through . . . She may not turn out to be what you think – what you want her to be.'

She sighed. 'I know, but I think I've got both feet on the ground. And I'll remember what you say.'

'I'll ring you,' he said. 'And I'll be home at weekends whenever I can.'

'I've told you, I can look after myself.'

He kissed her again. 'Just be careful.' He wanted to add: And please don't fall in love with anyone while I'm gone. But, wisely, he didn't.

Hannah had been reluctant to contact Sarah's adoptive parents. She had explained to Leah that the other girl's situation was very different from her own and that her enquiries might not be welcomed. However, the girl had been so eager that she had promised to try. She'd been surprised when Mavis responded promptly to her letter, inviting her to go up to Leicester to see them. Hannah's letter had explained briefly that Sarah's sister had been in touch and would like to meet her. She'd added that she would understand if it was against their wishes. The Paynes seemed such a closeknit family and she wouldn't have been surprised if they'd seen her request as intrusive.

She drove up to Leicester the following Saturday. Nothing had changed since she last visited the Paynes, soon after Sarah's adoption. The little house stood neatly in its corner of the cul-de-sac, the paintwork immaculate and the front garden trimmed and pruned for the winter. She parked her car in the drive and rang the bell, smiling to herself as the doorchimes played 'Bless This House' somewhere inside. Mavis answered the door. She looked much the same as Hannah remembered her, except that her hair was now touched with silver. She wore a demure navy blue dress with a white collar and as Hannah stepped into the hall the scent of beeswax and fresh flowers welcomed her.

'It was so nice to hear from you after all these years, Miss Brown,' Mavis said welcomingly. 'Do come in. We've been looking forward to seeing you again.'

'It's good to see you too.' Hannah stepped into the hall and took off her coat, laying it across Mavis's outstretched arm.

'Ken and I hoped so much that you'd find time to come.' The hint of desperation in Mavis's voice was unmistakable and for the first time Hannah had an inkling that there was more than hospitality behind the invitation. 'Do come into the lounge,' Mavis invited. 'Ken's out at the moment but he won't be long. We can have a little chat before he gets back.'

In the pleasant front room they faced each other across the glowing fire. Mavis sat on the edge of her chair, her hands tightly clasped in her lap. 'I must admit that your letter worried us a bit at first. You see, we never told Sally about her twin sister. Perhaps it was silly of us, but we really didn't see the point at the time.'

Hannah frowned. 'I see. In that case it could come as quite a shock to her.'

'I suppose it might.' There was a pause, then Mavis went on: 'To be honest with you, we – I felt a bit guilty about the other baby. We should really have taken them both, I suppose. They didn't really want to part them. But the other little baby was so different from Sally. They weren't at all like twins. It sounds awful of me, I know, but to be honest, I just couldn't take to her.'

'No use worrying about it now, Mrs Payne.' Hannah was puzzled by Mavis's obvious preoccupation with something that had happened so long ago. 'I'm sure things worked out for the best.'

'It's quite a coincidence that you should get in touch just at this time,' Mavis said. 'We've been very worried about our Sally lately.'

'Oh? In what way?'

'She's gone to work in London, you know – been there almost four months now.' Mavis sighed. 'All that way.'

Hannah smiled to herself. 'Young people have a habit of doing that kind of thing, Mrs Payne. I'm sure you've nothing to worry about. What kind of job is it?'

'Floristry. She's qualified, you know,' Mavis added proudly. 'At the local Technical College – City and Guilds and everything. Her teachers were ever so pleased with her. Well, she was always very artistic. The job is with a firm called Petals. It's in Edgware. They do flower arrangements for hotels – functions, you know the kind of thing. She got the job through the college. But the thing is, she could have had one here in Leicester just as easily. Ken's planning to take early retirement next year and we'd planned such lovely holidays together.'

Hannah hid a smile. 'Perhaps she wanted to strike out on her own.'

'That's the odd thing about it,' Mavis said. 'You see, she was almost engaged to be married just a few weeks ago.'

'Engaged?'

'Yes, to Jason, Ken's sister's youngest boy. I can't pretend that Ken and I were happy about it, with them both being so young. But everything seemed settled between them. Then, suddenly . . .'

'A quarrel?'

'That's what we thought, but not according to Jason,' Mavis said. 'but then he hasn't been very helpful either.' She bit her lip to stop its trembling.

275

'All these years we've brought her up as our own. She *was* ours, Miss Brown. We thought we knew her through and through. Then all at once it's like dealing with a stranger.' Mavis took out a handkerchief and dabbed at her eyes, glancing as she did so at a photograph of Sally on the mantelpiece.

Hannah followed her gaze and saw a pretty blonde teenage girl who looked almost uncannily like Marie. She was sitting on a swing and laughing up into the sunlight. Hannah looked back at Mavis's stricken face. She was beginning to see that the Paynes needed to see her even more than she needed to see them.

'When we got your letter saying that Sally's sister wanted to meet her we were shocked at first, then we got to thinking it might help to settle Sally – knowing she had a sister; might sort of bring her down to earth again. We wrote her a letter, telling her that you'd been concerned with her adoption and that you wanted to talk to her.'

Hannah wondered if this had been a wise move. She asked: 'And what was her reaction?'

Mavis shrugged. 'I've no idea. She hasn't answered the letter. It's almost as though she's trying to break off all contact with us. We haven't seen her for almost three months now.' Mavis wrung her hands. 'We did suggest once that we'd make the journey up there and pay her a visit, but it seemed to throw her into a panic. She almost begged us not to go.' She sighed. 'It's very hurtful, Miss Brown. We've always done our best for her. We've always been so close. That's why Ken and I appreciate your coming.'

'I take it you'd like me to go and talk to her?'

Mavis looked relieved. 'Oh, if only you would. If you could get to the bottom of what's wrong. We'd be so grateful.'

'All right. I'll try, but I can't promise anything.

Young people do grow up, you know. Sometimes they get to the stage where they need to break away and stand on their own feet. Sarah probably feels that if she came home or saw too much of you her resolve might begin to waver.'

'Oh. Do you really think that's all it is?'

'Well, let's just wait and see, shall we?'

Mavis looked up as the sound of a key was heard in the front door. 'Ah – that'll be Ken. I'll make the tea. The kettle's on.'

As they sat sipping tea together in the comfortable sitting room that Mavis called the lounge, Ken echoed his wife's anxiety over Sally and their shared feelings about a reunion with Leah, though his reaction was much more philosophical than his wife's.

'Mavis has felt very hurt and shut out these last weeks,' he said. 'Sally hasn't even given us her private address in London, you see. All we have is the name and address of the shop where she works. But as I see it, we have no choice but to go along with it all until she's worked it out, whatever it is. This might be just what she needs. I think we should give her the opportunity to decide for herself.'

Hannah smiled. 'That's very unselfish of you, Mr Payne.'

Ken looked at his wife. 'Get Miss Brown that address, love,' he said. 'Then perhaps she can drop into the shop and see Sally. I'm sure she'll know the best way to handle things.'

The moment Hannah set eyes on Sally she knew there was more behind her strange behaviour than a desire for independence. The girl standing behind the counter in the florist's shop looked gaunt and ill – very different from the happy girl in the photographs on Mavis and Ken's mantelpiece. The springy blonde hair was limp and dry, and her cheekbones stood out prominently. The gathered overall she wore could not conceal her thickening figure, and the profusion of bright flowers that surrounded her only served to accentuate her pallor. When Hannah introduced herself, hostile suspicion showed itself plainly on the girl's face.

'So they've sent a social worker to check up on me now?' she said angrily. 'Why can't they leave me alone? And why did you have to come here? Do you want me to lose my job?'

'As you haven't given your parents your private address, I didn't have much choice,' Hannah said. 'It is important that I speak to you. Perhaps we could arrange to meet somewhere later?'

Sally looked around, then seeing the manageress eyeing her, said quickly: 'Oh, all right. I get off at half-past five. I'll meet you in the Wimpy across the road if you like.'

Hannah arrived at the cafe a little before five-thirty and sat at a table in the window, watching the florist's shop across the road. When Sally emerged she saw that her earlier suspicions had been right. The loose coat she wore could no longer conceal the fact that she was pregnant. It explained everything. She stood up to wave as the girl stood just inside the door, but her greeting was received coolly.

'I haven't got long,' Sally said as she joined her. 'The trains get full up and I've got quite a long way to go.'

'It's all right. I'll give you a lift,' Hannah said.

'Oh no you won't!' The suspicion was back. 'You'll only go and give them the address.'

Hannah shrugged. 'Just as you wish. Sit down. I've got you a coffee. Do you want anything to eat?'

Sally shook her head. 'No thanks. I don't even want

the coffee really.' She looked desperately tired as she lowered herself into the chair opposite. 'Look, if you're here to lecture me, I'd prefer to get it over with as soon as possible.'

'Why are you treating your parents so badly?' Hannah asked. 'Surely they deserve better than that.'

'All I'm doing is saving them a lot of embarrassment if they only knew it.' Sally spooned sugar into the coffee and stirred thoughtfully. 'Except I suppose you'll go straight back and tell them now, won't you?'

'Is that what you want, Sally?'

'*No*.'

'Then I won't. They do care about you, you know. Have you any idea what you're putting them through?'

Sally glanced up and for a moment Hannah saw a girl immature for her years, fear and uncertainty in her blue eyes. Then, just as quickly, the brittle veneer returned. 'Look, I don't want to sound rude, but what does it have to do with you?' she asked. 'And if that's the only reason . . .'

'It's not,' Hannah interrupted. 'The reason I'm here has nothing at all to do with your parents. I wrote to them because I wanted to contact you, Sally. To tell you that your sister is anxious to meet you.'

'*Sister*?' The girl stared at her, uncomprehendingly. 'I'm not with you. We've got our wires crossed somewhere.'

'No, it's true. You do have a sister. A twin, actually. Her name is Leah. She's here in London and she would very much like to meet you.' There was a long pause. Hannah asked: 'Well – how do you feel about it, Sally?'

'How do I *feel*? You come here and tell me I've got a *twin sister*, right out of the blue, just like that. Then you calmly ask me how I feel . . . I suppose you could say that I'm shocked.' An ironic smile twisted the corners of her mouth. 'Gob-smacked, my friend Sharon would say.' She paused. Then: 'So – is she my double, this twin?'

'No. You're not identical twins. In fact, you're not at all alike.'

Sally was silent for a moment as she digested the information. Watching her face, Hannah said gently: 'This might be an ideal time for you to find someone close, Sally – you shouldn't be shutting your parents out, you know.'

For a moment Sally looked as though she were about to make another protest, then her belligerent attitude seemed to dissolve and she slumped forward wearily. 'I want to take charge of my own life. I have to now.'

'Do you? Your mother says that before you took this job in London you were practically engaged to – Jason, was it?'

Sally shook her head impatiently. 'Jason and I were never more than good friends.'

'Then he isn't the baby's father?'

'Oh, *no*.' Sally's head snapped up. 'If only he were.'

'You are fond of him then?'

'Yes. He's the only other person who knows. He even offered to pretend the baby was his and marry me. I couldn't have let him do that, could I? However tempting it was.'

'Do you want to tell me about it?' Hannah asked gently.

Sally bit her lip. 'It happened at a party. Mum and Dad didn't even know I went. They were always so stuffy about parties and so on. If they'd given me more freedom . . .' She broke off to push a straying lock of hair behind her ear. 'He – this boy – was a complete stranger. Somebody had given me a drink. Gin, I think. I'm not used to alcohol.' She looked up quickly. 'I'm not trying to make excuses, mind. I knew what I was doing.' She shook her head. 'I'm so ashamed and sickened by it all, I just couldn't tell Mum and Dad. I didn't know what to do at first. Jason made this offer and somehow that made me face things. I thought about it and I made up my mind. I intend to cope by myself.' She looked up anxiously. 'Promise me you won't tell them?'

'I've already promised. You didn't consider abortion then?'

'No. I hate the idea of killing something – of taking away its right to live. My own mother gave me up for adoption. I suppose I'll do the same.'

'But how will you keep it from them? It'll be Christmas soon. Your parents are bound to expect you home for that. I'm sure if you told them they'd want to help?'

'*No*.' Sally shook her head adamantly. 'I don't want that. I'll manage. I'll take it a day at a time. I'll get through somehow.'

'What about your job? Does your employer understand?'

Sally nodded. 'It's all worked out. I'm having a couple of weeks off when it's born. It'll go for immediate adoption.'

'And that's what you want?'

'Look, all my life I've been pampered and cosseted,' Sally said. 'I've had all my decisions made for me. This is *my* problem – *my* decision. I got myself into this mess. Now I have to see it through myself. And adoption is the only way.'

Hannah saw the soft young mouth harden determinedly and she thought she understood. 'Are you taking proper care of yourself?' she asked.

Sally nodded. 'I have the check-ups every month and take the vitamins and other gunge. I do want it to be healthy.'

'Good. Look, will you make me one promise? Will you get in touch with me if you need help?' Hannah took a card from her bag and passed it to Sally. 'Keep this somewhere safe. You can always reach me on that number.'

Sally glanced at the card, then slipped it into her pocket. 'Okay, thanks.'

'What would you like me to do about your sister? Would you like to meet her?'

Sally shrugged. 'Would she want to meet *me* when she knows? I shouldn't think I'm anyone's idea of the ideal sister.'

'That's something you'll have to work out between you. Here.' Hannah wrote down Leah's address and telephone number and passed it across the table. 'Think about it and contact her in your own time. If and when you decide to.' She watched as the girl looked at the paper, folded it and put it away. At least she hadn't refused to take it, that was something. It was up to Sally now. There was nothing more that she could do.

Hannah rang Leah on Friday evening to tell her that she had arranged a meeting between her and Marie. She didn't mention her visit to the Paynes or her meeting with Sally. The whole business was too nebulous as yet.

'I told Marie that Sunday was the best day for you,' she said. 'She'll come up on the ten o'clock train from Bournemouth Central this Sunday. It gets in to Waterloo just after eleven. Can you meet it?'

Leah's heart was beating fast with excitement. 'Of

282

course I can. Thank you, Hannah.' A thought suddenly struck her. 'Oh – but how will we recognise each other?'

'Marie is slim and fair. She says she'll be wearing a black coat with a blue Paisley scarf. I said I'd tell you to wear a red flower on your lapel.'

'Fine. I'll get one. I can't wait till Sunday. Thanks for fixing it up, Hannah.'

'Not at all. I hope everything goes well for you both. You'll let me know?'

'Of course. I'll call you on Monday.'

Leah replaced the receiver and clasped her hands together. Sunday. The day after tomorrow. She must remember to get that flower. It was short notice. There wasn't much time to arrange anything. The first meeting with one's mother should be marked in some special way. Terry would have had ideas but he had already left for Lancashire. Her brain milling with a dozen half-formed plans, she burst in on Bill who was in the kitchen making himself toasted cheese.

'Bill, my mother's coming up to Town on Sunday. Would you mind if we came back here?'

He stared at her in astonishment. 'Good heavens, why would I mind? Your room is your own to do as you like in.'

'I know, but it's a bit special. I'd rather like to cook lunch – down here.' She looked at him. 'Are you in or out on Sunday?'

He laughed. 'What you're really saying is that you want the place to yourself.' His eyes narrowed. 'Wait a minute. Did you say your lover or your *mother*?'

'Mother.'

'So why all the excitement?'

She stared at him. 'Oh – I thought Terry would have told you. This is the first time I've actually met her.'

'Really? But I thought your parents were bigwigs on the town council of Much Fiddling on the Sludge or whatever it's called.'

Leah laughed. 'That's my *adoptive* parents. I'm talking about my natural mother. I've just located her and we're going to meet.'

'Right. Great stuff. Good luck with it then. As it happens I shall be out all day Sunday so be my guest. Do as you like.' He glanced at her, then looked again. It was as though he was suddenly seeing her for the first time. She looked as though someone had turned on a light inside her. She was incandescent; eyes glowing, cheeks pink. He felt himself stirred by a sudden irresistible urge to kiss her, and pulled himself up sharply. He was old enough to be the girl's father, for God's sake. He turned back to his toasted cheese in time to see it catch fire.

'Damn and *blast*!' He snatched the pan out from under the grill, blowing furiously at the flames. 'Oh, look at that. It's bloody burnt now.'

Leah took the pan from him. 'Tell you what, let me make you one of my famous Spanish omelettes.'

'It's all right. I like burnt cheese.'

Laughing, Leah tipped the burnt offering into the bin and pushed him out of the way. 'Don't argue. It was my fault anyway. And you have agreed to let me have exclusive use of the kitchen on Sunday.'

His eyebrows shot up. 'I *have*? First I've heard about it.' But he stood aside, watching her as she took eggs from the fridge and cracked them into a bowl. 'You'll – er – join me, won't you?'

'Naturally.' She looked at him. 'Well, don't just stand there propping up the worktop. The table wants laying. We'll need some crusty bread to go with these and I wouldn't say no to a nice glass of white wine with it either.'

'Certainly – right away, Madam.' Bill tugged an imaginary forelock. 'And would Madam be requiring the best silver.'

Ten minutes later as they sat together at the table Bill asked: 'So what made you decide to find this mother of yours?'

'It's something I've always wanted,' Leah told him. 'I had a twin sister too and I'd like to meet her. She was adopted as a baby, though, and may not want to rake up the past.'

He looked at her. 'Why weren't you adopted together?'

'No one wanted me. Apparently I was one of those ugly, whingeing babies.'

He grinned. 'I'd never have guessed.'

'I was in the children's home till I was seven. The people who finally adopted me expected . . .' She lifted her shoulders. 'I don't know. Something different. The relationship never really gelled.'

'And you always wondered if it would have done with your real mum,' Bill supplied. 'You can't help wondering if it was your adoptive parents at fault. Or if it might just possibly have been you.'

Leah stopped, a forkful of omelette halfway to her mouth, and looked at him. 'I never saw it quite that way before, but you could be right. The Dobsons lost their own child in an accident. Apparently she was my age and looked like me.' She shook her head. 'The whole thing was destined for disappointment from the start, wasn't it?'

'Poor Leah.' Bill gave her a rueful smile.

'Not a bit of it. I must have been a pretty obnoxious kid. I gave them a rough time. Once I knew it wasn't me they loved I hit back, though of course I didn't realise why I was doing it at the time. The one thing I did know was that I wanted to belong somewhere – to someone. That's when I decided to find my own mother as soon as I could.'

'And now you have.'

'Now I have,' she repeated triumphantly, raising her glass. 'And Sunday is the big day. Will you drink to it, Bill? Will you wish me luck?'

Oddly touched and infected by her excitement, he raised his glass and clinked it against hers. 'Here's to the two of you – maybe three. And to the end of disappointment.'

Chapter 15

Marie stirred from the kitchen window and drank the last of her tea. It was fully light now and she must begin to get ready for her trip to London. She tried hard to recapture the feeling of happiness and excitement she had felt ever since the arrangement was made, but the dark cloud of last night's nightmare still hung over her, laying a cobweb of gloom between her and the day she had looked forward to so much.

Once I'm on the train everything will be fine, she told herself as she padded softly through to the bathroom and turned on the shower. I'm going to meet Leah – my daughter. It's what I've dreamed of so often down the years. It's going to be wonderful. But somehow her heart refused to lift in response.

If only Ralph hadn't come home last night. His unexpected arrival late the previous evening had put everything else out of her mind. Sensing her dismay at seeing him, he'd perversely demanded that they retire early together, announcing that he'd had a hard week and was tired. But once alone in their room he'd resorted to his familiar cat and mouse tactics, claiming what he called 'his rights' and reminding her of how long it had been since they'd last made love. Annoyed and resentful over her obvious reluctance, he'd been even more sadistic than usual, mentally as well as physically. But this time Marie had made a stand, reminding him that although they were married he did not have the right to abuse her – that there was such a thing as rape within marriage. Her outburst had surprised him. For a brief, stunned moment he'd stared at her speechlessly, then he summoned his powers of denigration with more force than ever.

'Rape now, is it? And how would you set about proving it?' he asked her mockingly, his eyes glittering in the way she had come to hate. 'A case like that in the papers would be *really* good publicity for Evans Hotels, wouldn't it? And wouldn't Dad enjoy it all?'

She knew he was right and that she didn't really stand a chance but she stood her ground. 'Sometimes it's worth sticking it out,' she told him quietly. 'And I can tell you, Ralph, I've had enough of this marriage. I want it to end.'

He stared at her for a moment, then gave a bark of laughter. '*Marriage*. Is that what you call it? Did you really think I actually wanted to make love to you? To *you*, when I can have my pick. You must be joking!'

'I want a divorce, Ralph.'

'On what grounds?'

'Your infidelity. Cruelty – both physical and mental.'

'Proof?'

'You surely can't imagine that would be difficult. You've even taken your women to our own hotels. And heaven knows I've had plenty of bruises,' she added quietly.

He turned away from her. 'Try it if you like. You'll only end up the poorer. All the money is tied up in the hotels. You'll have no home and no job. Fancy the prospect, do you?'

'I can think of worse.'

Her determination and stoicism brought a flicker of uncertainty into the flinty eyes. 'And then there's Dad,' he said, playing his trump card. 'He wouldn't be able to stay here with no one to look after him. You realise that, of course. You'd have to take him with you. Either that or he'd have to go into a home.'

In spite of the warmth of the bathroom, Marie shuddered at the memory as she stepped out of the shower and wrapped herself in a towel. Rows with Ralph always left her feeling limp and drained. It was hardly any wonder that she'd slept badly, tortured by dreams of that other bad time in her life. And she had still to tell him that she was going to London for the day – unless she could get away before he wakened.

In the bedroom she saw with relief that he was still asleep. She opened the wardrobe as quietly as she could and took out the blue dress she'd decided to wear. Slipping it on she sat down in front of the dressing table to apply her make-up.

Would Leah be surprised to find her still quite young? She peered critically at herself in the mirror. She was still only thirty-seven though this morning she felt twice that. Her figure and skin were still firm and taut and her hair, which she now wore in a smooth, flicked-back bob, was as thick and naturally blonde as ever. She applied her favourite pink lipstick and clipped on the pearl earrings David had given her last Christmas. Almost ready.

'How nice of you to take so much trouble just for me.'

Ralph's mocking voice broke the silence, making her jump. Through the mirror she saw him watching her as he lay in bed, his hands clasped behind his head and his eyes gleaming malevolently. 'Oh, *dear*. Did I startle you?' he asked sarcastically. 'Have I spoilt the surprise?' He sat up suddenly and threw back the duvet, swinging his legs over the side of the bed. 'Or were you hoping to sneak off somewhere, leaving me to wake up and find you gone?' He crossed to where she sat at the dressing table and dropped large, heavy hands on her shoulders. As they gazed at each other through the mirror Marie saw that his face looked distorted, oddly lopsided. The mirror seemed to accentuate the lines etched by all his baser habits over the years.

'I have to go to London,' she said quietly, putting down her hairbrush. 'There was no reason to wake you.'

'Ah – what a considerate wife I've got,' he sneered. 'Going to London – on a Sunday? What for, I wonder? Or maybe I should ask *who* for?'

For a second she panicked. Could he possibly have found out? No, there was no way that he could. 'I've made arrangements with Hannah,' she said, mouthing the half-truth with a glibness that surprised her. 'It's months since I had a day off.'

He crossed to the table by the bed and picked up the telephone, slamming it down on the dressing table in front of her. 'Ring her,' he commanded.

She stared at him. 'Why?'

'Because I say so. Ring and tell her you can't go. Tell her your husband has come home unexpectedly. She'll understand. Any normal woman would.'

Marie's hand reached out, then she drew it back. 'Why should I ring her?' she said. 'I'm going to London as I've arranged. After all, you didn't let me know you were coming.' She began to get up but he pushed her down again.

'Do as you're told, damn you.' He lifted the receiver and thrust it into her hand. 'Dial the number.

Go on. I don't care whether you go or not. Confirm the arrangement if you like – anything. I just want to hear you speak to her.'

Marie dialled the number with trembling fingers. Hannah would understand. She would realise something unexpected had happened and go along with her. But at the other end the telephone rang out repeatedly – unanswered. She hung on in dismay for several minutes, trying to avoid Ralph's triumphant eyes as they burned into her. At last he said: 'Why don't you admit it? She isn't there. Who *are* you going to meet, Marie. It's that doctor, isn't it? The one you've been getting all cosy with these past few months. I hear he's moved down here too.' He laughed at her look of surprise. 'Oh, yes, I get to know more than you think.' His eyes narrowed. 'Have you been making a monkey out of me with him? Is it because of him you're so anxious to get a divorce? It'd give his career one hell of a boost to be named as co-respondent, wouldn't it? Or don't you give a damn whose life you screw up just as long as you get rid of me?' He stood over her, his eyes gleaming like hot coals and his fists clenching and unclenching at his sides. Marie knew that his violent temper was barely under control; she could feel the vibrations of it crackling the air between them like static electricity. She also knew that to give in to him now was out of the question. She had reached a point of no return. Slowly she got to her feet and turned to face him.

'I'm going to London, Ralph,' she said as levelly as the pounding of her heart would allow. 'I'm not meeting Doctor Hodges. There are no grounds for your allegations. The whole idea is absurd.'

'Absurd, is it?'

'Please stand out of my way.' Marie took a step

forward, but his hand lashed out with the speed of a cobra. It caught her across the mouth, making her head snap back with the force of the blow. Gasping at the pain, her hand flew to her lower lip and tears of humiliation sprang to her eyes. But when her fingers came away wet with blood from her split lip, blind anger suddenly exploded within her, blotting out the pain and the tears, letting her see only the years she had squandered in allowing him to use and exploit her. He was advancing on her again, but she squared her shoulders and looked him in the eyes.

'*Violence*! That's all you know,' she shouted at him. 'When insults and accusations won't work, you resort to fists every time, don't you? I know all about your past, Ralph – what your brutality did for your army career. It'll be your downfall again before you're through.'

He stopped in his tracks, eyes narrowing. 'Is that supposed to be some kind of threat?' His face flushed a dull crimson. 'Anyway, what can you possibly know?'

'I know why you were thrown out of the army. Hannah told me.' Marie dabbed gingerly at her lip with a handkerchief. Already she could feel it beginning to swell, making speech difficult. 'I even quarrelled with her over it. Can you believe that? What a joke – quarrelling with my best friend in *your* defence.' She pushed past him and made for the door. 'Well, this time you're not going to browbeat me into submission.'

'That's what you think.' He moved quickly to lock the door, slipping the key into the pocket of his bathrobe. 'All right, let's have it. What did that bitch tell you?'

Her chin lifted and her eyes blazed defiantly into his. 'That you were court martialled and sent to prison – for ill-treatment of prisoners and for beating up a girl. All people who were weaker than you, who couldn't defend themselves – because that's your way, isn't it, Ralph?'

'Lies,' he shouted. 'All lies.'

'No, it's true. Someone who served with you in Ireland at the time told Hannah. He was staying here and he recognised you. He thought you were with Hannah and he warned her against you.'

'It's a pack of bloody lies, I tell you. Just wait till I see that bitch. I'll . . .'

'You'll what? Are you planning to beat the daylights out of her too?' Marie asked him. 'You'll find yourself in trouble if you do. You can't go through life smashing hell out of everyone who sees through you, Ralph. In the end you have to come to terms with the fact that you're a loser. A loser through and through.'

His eyes bulged dangerously and the veins on his neck stood out like knotted rope. 'A loser, am I? We'll see about that.'

Marie's heart thudded in her breast but she knew she daren't show weakness to him now. 'Let me pass now,' she said. 'I've got a train to catch.'

He stood against the door, his arms folded. 'Tell me who it is you're meeting and I'll unlock the door.'

'I've told you.'

'So why isn't she answering her telephone?'

'I don't know. Maybe she spent the night away from her flat. She doesn't tell me all her movements.'

'Right then. If you're determined to go, we'll go together,' he said. 'As it happens, I've got a few things to say to Hannah Brown myself. She'll think twice before she blackens my name again.' He crossed the room, threw off his robe and began to get dressed.

Marie turned and caught sight of herself in the mirror. Her lower lip was still bleeding and the left side of her mouth and chin had swollen to twice their normal size. She sank wearily on to a chair. He'd won. In spite of her standing up to him, Ralph had won again. There was no way she dare let him know who it was she really meant to meet. And no way she could face her daughter for the first time looking like this.

Leah had never been on Waterloo Station before and she was impressed by its size and the cheerful music being played over the public address system. It gave the place a celebratory atmosphere that was just right for the occasion. She'd arrived early, having allowed more than enough time to change trains at Tottenham Court Road. Checking the arrival time of the Bournemouth train on the indicator she found that she had half an hour to spare. She wandered round the station, looking at everything of interest from the bookshop to the travel agency. Finally she finished up in the buffet with a cup of coffee and a Danish pastry.

At eleven o'clock she stood expectantly at the barrier of platform twelve as the train drew in. Adjusting the red carnation she had bought so that it was plainly visible, she scanned the faces and clothes of all the passengers disembarking. They passed her in ones and twos. People of all ages, shapes and sizes, all hurrying purposefully. There were several women wearing black coats, but none of them matched the description Hannah had given her of Marie. One woman even wore a blue Paisley scarf, but she was large and grey-haired. Finally, trailing behind everyone else, came a slim, blonde woman who just might have been Marie Evans. But she wore a dark green suit. Could she have changed her mind about what to wear? Leah stood firmly in her path, but the woman stepped aside with no more than the briefest of glances at her.

Leah wandered back to the indicator and was heartened to see that there was another train in ten minutes. She waited, walking up and down until the train slid alongside the platform. Once again her eyes eagerly raked the passengers. And once again she was disappointed.

After the third train had yielded its cargo of strangers she found a call box and dialled Hannah's number. There was no reply.

From the indicator she saw that there were no more trains for an hour. She stood gazing up at the revolving place names, chewing her thumb and wondering what to do. Eventually she decided to stay on the station. She would have a snack lunch and then meet one more train. Anything might have happened. And if Hannah was out for the day there would be no way that Marie could send a message through her either.

By three o'clock she was beginning to feel betrayed and disillusioned. It was always possible to get a message to someone who was waiting at a railway station if you really wanted to. Whilst she'd been here she'd heard several personal messages given out over the public address system. Marie could have made the effort, but it seemed she just hadn't bothered. She must be regretting the letter she had written. Or maybe she just didn't care. Why should she put herself out after all these years anyway? After all, she, Leah, was no more than a stranger to her. Angry and bitterly disappointed, she turned on her heel and headed for the Underground.

When she came out of the station at Notting Hill it was beginning to get dark. The street lights were already alight and a thin drizzle was falling. She turned up her coat collar, tears of anger and self-pity stinging her eyes. Why did people always let her down? What was wrong with her? I must be completely worthless, she told herself as she walked home, head down against the thin, cold rain. They all reject me. Even Terry sees me as a burden. He must have been really glad to get away from me. She swallowed hard at the tight knot of tears in her throat, determined not to give way. She'd missed Terry much more than she'd expected to since he'd left for Lancashire. Bill was kind and nice, but he wasn't Terry and never could be. They all had their lives to lead. They all had someone of their own who cared about them. Terry still had his father. Even Bill still kept in touch with his ex-wife. He'd told her so. There was even some talk of her coming to London to spend Christmas with him.

She turned the corner into Melbury Street and found it dim and murky after the brilliance of the main road. As she went down the area steps of number twenty-four she paused to search her handbag for her key, fumbling in the darkness. She was so preoccupied that when a figure stepped out of the shadows in front of her, she started violently.

'*Oh*! Who is it? Who's there?'

'It's all right. I'm sorry if I made you jump. You – wouldn't know if a Miss Dobson lives here, would you?'

'I'm Leah Dobson.' Leah peered at the stranger. She wore a skimpy raincoat but her head was bare. Her hair hung about her pale face in dripping strands. She was wet and bedraggled – and very pregnant.

'Have you been waiting long? You look soaked. Please come in and get dry.' Leah unlocked the door. 'Come through to the kitchen. It'll be warm in there.'

In the basement kitchen the table was laid for two. Leah had seen to it before she left for Waterloo. There was a bottle of red wine uncorked and 'breathing' on the dresser and the air was redolent with the aroma of the rich Norfolk casserole waiting in the Aga. The girl took all this in in one glance.

'Oh, look, you're expecting company. I'd better go.'

Leah reached out to lay a hand on her arm. 'No, it's all right. They – she's not coming now.' She smiled. 'Stay and help me eat it if you like. Somebody's got to.' She smiled apologetically. 'Look, I'm sorry, I'm obviously supposed to remember you but I'm afraid I still don't know who you are.'

Sally stepped forward and searched Leah's face, looking for some sign – some mirror image of herself. She found none. 'My name is Sally Payne,' she said softly. 'And I think I'm your sister.'

Stunned, Leah stared at her for a long time. This girl, this pregnant girl with the pale face and limp fair hair, wasn't at all what she'd imagined her twin sister to be like. What she had envisaged she didn't quite know, except that it wasn't this. 'You're my sister?' She said the words slowly, as a blind person explores the features of a stranger.

'You're – Sarah?'

'Sally. I've always been known as Sally. Hannah Brown gave me your address. Maybe I shouldn't have come like this – without letting you know,' she said hurriedly. 'I did try to ring this morning but there was no reply. I just came on the off-chance this afternoon. I thought . . .'

'You're cold and wet,' Leah interrupted. 'What am I thinking about? Take your mac off. I'll get you a towel for your hair.'

Sally looked better once the warmth had brought

the blood back into her cheeks again. Her hair, rubbed vigorously, began to dry and spring back into its natural curls, and Leah began to see that although pinched and peaky-looking she was really quite pretty. Sitting her down in the Windsor chair next to the Aga, she poured her a glass of wine.

'I don't know if I should really,' Sally said hesitantly. 'The baby . . .'

Leah shrugged. 'Surely one glass can't hurt.' She busied herself, taking the casserole and a dish of scalloped potatoes out of the oven. There were a hundred questions she wanted to ask – so much she wanted to know. It was agonisingly hard to be patient. But she knew instinctively that she mustn't rush things.

Sally tucked in hungrily and complimented Leah on her cooking. 'It's delicious. Where did you learn to cook?'

'My grandmother – my adoptive grandmother taught me,' Leah said, helping Sally to more. 'It's come in very handy since I left home. I worked in a pub for a time. Now I've got a job in a restaurant run by an Italian family. It's just round the corner from here and I've learned a lot of Italian dishes since I've been there.' She glanced at the other girl. 'I grew up in Norfolk. Where did you?'

'Leicester. I studied floristry there. Now I work in a florist's shop in Edgware.' She paused. 'Were you happy? Did you have any brothers or sisters?'

'No – to both questions. I was in the children's home till I was seven. My adoption never really worked out. But tell me about you. I can't get over meeting you like this.'

'It seems Hannah Brown contacted my parents,' Sally told her. 'They knew her from when they adopted me years ago. I think they were quite glad to see her. I've left home, you see. I took a job in London before they could find out about this.' She looked down at her expanding stomach. 'I didn't want them to know about it.'

Leah laid down her knife and fork. 'That's awful. Are they so terrible then?'

'No. That's just it.' Sally sighed. 'It's hard to explain and it makes me sound so ungrateful. But I wanted to take control of my own life. When this happened it changed me – made me think. I wanted time and space to discover . . . who I am, I suppose. I've been so shielded all my life, you see. I knew that if I didn't do it now, I never would.'

'I know the feeling,' Leah said. 'I left home too. I was sick of my parents trying to turn me into someone else. The more they pulled me one way, the more I pulled the other.' She looked at this girl who said she was her sister, trying to feel some bond – some empathy. 'Will you be all right? Is the baby's father helping you?'

'No. I'm having it adopted.'

'You're not serious?'

'Yes.'

Leah stared at her, her eyes round and very bright. 'But you *can't.*'

'What do you mean, I can't?' Sally's eyes were defensive. 'I've no choice.'

'You can't just give it away,' Leah said. 'Not after what happened to you and me. Why can't you keep it?'

'How could I? How could I work and support a child? Where would we live, and who'd employ me under those circumstances? As it stands I've got a job to go back to. With a child in tow . . .' She shook her head. 'It's impossible. Do you think I haven't thought it through?'

Leah was deeply shocked by the unexpected emotions that gnawed viciously at her insides. Suddenly she had found the bond she was seeking, but it was not for the stranger sitting opposite her, not for her sister, but for the child she carried and planned to give away.

'Look – if you told your parents, they'd help you,' she said. 'They sound like good people. I bet they'd hate the idea of your handing your child over to some stranger. The poor little kid might end up like I did. It's their grandchild, Sally. Don't you think they have a right to help it? If I were having a baby there'd be no one – nothing on this *earth* that could make me part with it.' In her earnestness she leaned forward so suddenly that she knocked over her glass of wine. The blood red stain spread slowly across the white tablecloth.

Sally jumped up. 'It's all right for you to talk like that,' she said. 'But it's not you who's pregnant. It's me. And I'll do what I want – what I feel is best.' She stood looking down at Leah, her cheeks pink and her eyes bright with tears. 'I might have known,' she said bitterly. 'I might have known you'd be just like all the others. You want to make me toe the line just like they did. I *won't* be told what to do with my life.' She snatched her raincoat from the hook behind the door and began to pull it on.

'Please – don't go,' Leah pleaded. 'Let me try to help. I want to. Please, Sally.'

'*No.*' She stood by the door, breathing hard and shaking her head. 'Leave me alone. I was wrong to come here, I knew it wouldn't work. I just wanted – I thought . . .' She ran out of the room and was out of the basement door and up the area steps before Leah could stop her. Following, she called her name:

'Sally – *Sally*!'

But Sally didn't look back. She just kept moving, as fast as her bulk would allow.

Standing by the railings Leah watched the stumbling figure of her sister hurrying through the rain towards the main road. And it was only then that she realised that she hadn't even asked her where she lived.

When Bill came in he found Leah washing up. The table was still spread with the wine-soaked cloth and the half-finished casserole stood on top of the Aga.

'Hi. Well, how did it go?' He stood warming his hands over the stove, rubbing them together. 'It's a pig of a day, isn't it?' When she didn't reply he turned to look at her. She was hunched over the sink, idly wiping the draining board. 'Uh-huh. I take it things didn't go as planned.' He peered at the casserole, lifting the lid and sniffing appreciatively. 'You haven't eaten much. What happened? Mum turn out to be a vegetarian?'

Leah turned to him, drying her hands on a teatowel. 'As it happened she didn't turn up at all. And if you want some of that you'd better get yourself a plate.'

'Oh, hard luck – about your mum, I mean. Hey, can I really have some of this nosh? It smells terrific and I'm starving.'

Leah fetched a plate from the cupboard and spooned a generous helping of meat and vegetables on to it, adding the remaining potatoes. 'There. That do you?'

'Fantastic.' Bill rubbed his hands together in anticipation and pulled out a chair. Leah sat down opposite and watched him for a few minutes in gloomy silence.

'Someone else turned up though,' she said at last.

He looked up. 'Oh? Who?'

'My sister. The one I was telling you about. She was waiting here when I got back from Waterloo. I couldn't believe it at first.'

'Great. So you had a reunion after all?'

Leah shook her head. 'I blew it, Bill. Messed the whole thing up. We had a row. Can you believe it? We meet for the very first time. Twin sisters. An auspicious occasion, you'd expect. And what do I do? I upset her – drove her away.'

'So you had a row.' Bill grinned. 'Sounds very normal to me. I never stop rowing with my sister. She'll be back.'

'No, she won't. You don't understand, Bill.' She laid her head down on her folded arms. 'I can't seem to hit it off with anyone. It's *me*. There's something wrong with me. There must be.' She looked up at him sideways, her dark eyes swimming with tears.

Bill sighed and laid down his knife and fork. 'Come on, girl. It's not like you to be depressed.'

She sat up. 'How would you know what's like me and what isn't? Sometimes I don't think I know myself.'

He nodded. 'Missing Tel?'

She shrugged. 'I'll bet he's glad to get away from me too.'

'Oh dear. We *are* feeling sorry for ourselves this evening, aren't we?'

Leah got up and walked straight-backed towards the door. 'If all you can do is make fun of me . . .'

He moved quickly, reaching the door before she did. 'Hey, come on, kid. Where's your sense of humour? It can't be as bad as all that.'

'It is. It *is*.' She bit her lip hard, hating the idea of weeping in front of someone as tough as Bill.

Laughing gently, he reached out and pulled her

against him. 'Go on – have a good howl on your Uncle Bill. You know you want to.'

She gave in and wept copiously into the shoulder of his plaid shirt, vaguely registering the fact that it smelled of a mixture of leather and tobacco, tinged comfortingly with the scent of male skin. Bill rubbed her back with one of his large paw-like hands, which turned out to be surprisingly gentle. After a moment or two he pushed a large handkerchief into her hand.

'Here, better have a blow,' he said. 'Otherwise your eyes'll puff up and I shan't fancy you any more.'

She did as he said, laughing – a little shamefaced. 'Thanks, Bill.'

'Feeling better now?' He tipped up her chin to look at her.

'I'm fine.'

'Tell you what,' he said cheerfully. 'You fed me. And incidentally, that was the best grub I've eaten since my old mum chucked me out. One good turn, as the saying goes. Come to the pub with me. We'll spend the rest of the evening drowning our sorrows together.'

Seated together in The Prince of Wales, Bill's favourite local, he confided in her that he'd spoken to his ex-wife on the telephone that morning. She'd told him she wouldn't be coming to London for Christmas after all.

'Some job she's been offered,' he said. 'At least, that's what she says. If you ask me it's some new bloke.'

'Why shouldn't she tell you if it's that?' Leah asked. 'After all, you are divorced.'

He gave her a wry smile. 'Some ties are not so easily severed, my angel.'

She winced. 'There I go again. You see. I'm always putting my foot in it.'

Bill leaned across and took her hand, pressing it warmly between both of his. 'No. You've just got some living to do, love. That's all.' He peered at her. 'What did you and your sister fall out over? You never did tell me.'

Leah sighed. 'She's pregnant. And she says she's having the baby adopted. It just seemed so awful. Like history repeating itself. I said . . .' She looked up at him ruefully. 'Well, too much anyway.'

Bill nodded understandingly. 'The guy responsible took off, I take it?'

'So it seems. Oh, Bill, I should have thought. She obviously couldn't manage by herself. I tried to tell her to go home. Can you imagine – *me* giving advice like that? And the rotten thing is, I can't put it right. She left without leaving me an address.'

'Maybe she'll come back again when she's had time to cool down.'

She shrugged. 'Not a hope. I know I wouldn't.'

They both drank a little more than was wise, though it seemed to have little or no effect on Bill, and at ten o'clock they walked back to Melbury Street hand in hand. The rain had stopped now and the sky was clear. There was a fine frosty moon and a sprinkling of stars.

'So you're not going home to your folks for Christmas?' Bill asked.

Leah gave an explosive little laugh. 'You've got to be joking. I'm the last person they'd want to see.'

'But would you like to see them – be honest now?' Bill bent his head to look into her face.

'The only person I'd like to see is my gran,' Leah confessed. 'She's the only person who was ever honest with me. The only one I've missed.'

'Well, why don't you go then?'

'I couldn't.'

'Why not? Just get on a train. Go for the day.'

Leah was silent, examining her own reluctance. 'Time off might be a problem.'

'You could get the morning off and be back in time for the evening rush.'

Leah pursed her lips. 'Mmm – Nenebridge is very small. Someone'd be sure to see me.'

'Okay, so they'd see you. Would it matter?'

Leah laughed. 'You're right. What the hell? Why don't I just do it? If there are trains running at convenient times, that is.'

In the kitchen at Melbury Street Bill made coffee while Leah did the rest of the tidying up. She was at the sink, still fussing over the wine stain on the table cloth, when he made a sudden exclamation. She turned to see him looking at his diary.

'How far from Nenebridge is Huntingdon?' he asked.

'Not too far – about twenty miles. Why?'

'Just that I have to go there next Saturday to interview a politician at his country home,' he said. 'It's to be a big double page spread with colour pics and the works, so I'll be taking a photographer. But there's room in the car for one more little'un. Why don't I drop you off at your gran's on the way – pick you up on the way back?'

Leah drew in her breath sharply. 'Oh, Bill. That would be marvellous. Thank you.' She launched herself at him, throwing her arms around his neck and kissing him soundly.

'Hey, no need to bust a gusset.' He laughed down into her eyes. Then, driven by some irresistible urge, he gathered her close and kissed her again. The feel of her slender body in his arms and her soft mouth on his made his cynical heart beat like a boy's again. Very reluctantly, he put her gently from him.

'That's enough of that. Next thing you know I'll be getting to like it.' He took her arms from around his neck and held her two hands firmly in his, kissing the fingertips. 'If you take my advice you'll get off to your room now, kid. Go on.' He turned her round and gave her a little push. 'Hop it while the going's good.'

She turned at the door and looked at him with shining eyes. 'Goodnight, Bill. And thanks again.'

Nenebridge looked much the same as before she left. The streets were busy with Saturday shoppers as they drove through the town. In the market place all the familiar stalls were there, the traders doing their usual brisk trade in fruit and locally grown vegetables. And Leah saw with a small pang of nostalgia that the man with the Christmas trees was in the same pitch he always had in the weeks before Christmas. He stood there just as he had every year since she could remember, his cap pulled down over his eyes and a dew drop on the end of his long nose. As they crossed the river she saw that the war memorial still wore its collar of weather-worn poppy wreaths and everywhere the festive decorations brightened the grey winter gloom.

Leah got out of the car outside Kate Dobson's bungalow and waved to Bill and his photographer friend as they drove away. She walked round to the back and tapped on the door. Inside, she could hear Kate muttering to herself and a moment later the door opened to reveal the familiar wrinkled face and springy white hair. Granny Dobson stared at her incredulously for a moment, then the blue eyes lit up and she flung the door wide with an exclamation of delight.

'Well, well. Look what the wind blew in. Come you on in, my old sugar. Don't stand out there freezing to death.' She held out her arms and Leah hugged her warmly.

'Oh, Gran. It's lovely to see you.'

The old women held her at arms' length, looking into her eyes. 'Have you come to stay?' she asked.

Leah shook her head. 'No. A friend was coming this way and he offered to give me a lift. I've only come for the day – to see you.'

'So you won't be paying our Jack a visit?'

'I'm sorry, Gran. I did ring Hilary a while ago, but she didn't seem pleased to hear from me. She hung up, in fact.'

Gran shook her head as she went about putting the kettle on. 'That Hilary. Stupid, shallow woman. Not that our Jack is any better, though I s'pose I shouldn't say it.' She smiled her mischievous smile at Leah. 'Well, never mind. All the more time for you to spend with your old gran then.' She patted Leah's shoulder. 'And you don't look so bad either, seein' as you live in that dirty old city. Come on then. Tell me all your news.'

They sat over the fire in the living room, drinking cup after cup of Gran's strong, scalding tea and exchanging gossip. Leah told about the time she spent at Cleybourn and worked at The Mermaid; her move to London and her job at Bella's; about the house she shared with Terry and Bill. She confided to Kate her disappointment over the broken appointment with her mother. And finally the surprise arrival of Sally. Shamefacedly, she confessed to the quarrel they'd had about the coming baby. Gran listened to it all gravely but impartially.

'Seems you've packed a lot into the time you've been away,' she said at last. 'But then that's modern life for you. It all moves much too fast for old biddies like me.' She shook her head. 'No wonder folks burn

307

themselves out so young these days. So you've had a setback with your blood relatives then?'

'It's more than a setback, Gran. More like a disaster. I've tried so hard to find them. I wanted so much to get to know them both, and now – through my own stupidity – it looks as though I never will.'

'This social worker person you mentioned, can't she tell you anything?' Kate asked. 'She must know how to get in touch with both your mother and your sister.'

'I've been trying to ring her all week,' Leah said. 'But she's not answering the phone. She must be away.'

Gran smiled reassuringly. 'Well – she'll be back, girl. And when you tell her what's happened she'll help you. It'll all come out in the wash. Just you see if it don't. I've lived long enough to see that everything works out for the best in the end, my girl.' She winked. 'Things haven't exactly stood still here, you know. It may not be London but it's not short of a bit of drama.'

Leah grinned. 'Tell me about it.'

'Well, we had a Royal visit in October. When they opened those new flats down by the river. The Queen Mother came. I went to see her. Got a lovely view.' She smiled. 'Aah, lovely, she was, in her blue hat and coat.' She chuckled. 'Caused quite a kerfuffle, among the councillors by all accounts; fighting over who should be presented to her and all. Then there was Bill Thompson – him that lived next-door to Jack and Hilary. He had a heart attack soon after. All the excitement I shouldn't wonder. Okay now, but touch and go for weeks it was.' She leaned forward. 'Then there's our friend Tom Clayton. Now, *he's* got himself into a real mess.'

'Tom has? How?'

Gran chuckled. 'Started runnin' round with a young married woman from over Kingsbury way. His missus found out and there was all 'ell let loose. She got in touch with the woman's husband. Now she's suin' Tom for divorce.'

'Really?' Leah said.

'They do say she's tryin' to get three-quarters of everything he owns,' Kate went on. 'Mind you – could be he thinks it's worth it. Ate, drank and slept them horses, that Angela did, so they say. Put them before everything. No wonder poor old Tom was lookin' for *his* oats elsewhere.' She chuckled as she helped herself to another biscuit. 'He come off a poor second this time though, in more ways than one. I heard that the woman's husband gave him a black eye. Waited for him leavin' his shop one night and dotted him a good fourpenny one. He had to wear dark glasses for a fortnight.' Gran slapped her knee and laughed, but the laughter developed into a fit of uncontrollable coughing, turning her face red and making her eyes water. Concerned, Leah poured her another cup of tea.

'Here, Gran, drink this. Have you seen the doctor with that cough?' she asked.

The old woman shook her head. 'Blasted biscuit crumb – went down the wrong way.'

Leah shook her head. 'It sounded more than that. You're quite chesty, aren't you?'

Kate waved a hand dismissively. 'Had a bit of a cold last month,' she said. 'Can't seem to clear it up. It'll go in its own good time.'

But Leah wasn't convinced. She'd been noticing things while they were talking. The layer of dust on the furniture, previously unknown in Kate's house. And the bottle of cough mixture standing in the hearth, a sticky spoon adhering to the tiles beside it.

309

In the kitchen too there were signs of neglect; the sink was stacked with dirty dishes, and there were unwiped spills on the cooker. Kate herself looked under par too.

'Does Dad come to see you?' Leah asked.

'Jack?' Gran shrugged. 'He comes when he can. The business and his council work keeps him busy.'

'All the same . . .'

'Don't you worry about me,' Gran said dismissively. 'Just you take care of yourself.' She looked into Leah's eyes and squeezed her hand. 'You are all right, my sugar, aren't you? You do get enough to eat – take proper care of yourself?'

'Of course I do. I've got a good job in a restaurant. I eat there mostly.'

'And you won't let the likes of Tom Clayton take advantage of you again, will you?'

'No, Gran. I promise. I've learned my lesson about men.'

Kate smiled ruefully. 'Women never learn their lesson over men. Oh, we always *think* we have. Then along comes another Jack-the-lad with his posh blue suit and Brylcreme on his hair and all the lessons are forgotten. Just you be careful, my lass.'

Leah laughed. 'I will, Gran. Don't you worry about me.' She looked at her watch. 'Tell you what – will you let me cook some lunch for us both?'

She'd expected an argument, but to her surprise Kate gave in graciously. After making her promise to stay where she was by the fire, Leah set to work on the kitchen, washing up the stack of dishes and scrubbing the floor till the place looked more like Granny Dobson's kitchen again. When it was done she slipped out to the local shops and bought the ingredients for a warming hot-pot.

The relish with which Kate ate made Leah suspect

that she hadn't cooked herself a proper meal for some days.

'That was real tasty, girl,' Kate said appreciatively, polishing her plate with a crust of bread. 'You've turned into a jolly fine little cook.'

Leah smiled. 'Thanks to you, Gran. It was you who taught me.'

The time went all too quickly and before Leah knew it, it was four o'clock and the hooting of Bill's car horn was heralding his arrival in the road outside the bungalow. Leah snatched up her coat and hugged Kate hard. She hated leaving the old lady alone. As she stood at the door, waving her off, she looked small and frail and Leah retraced her steps to give her another hug.

'Take care of yourself, Gran,' she said huskily. 'And if you need anything you mustn't be too proud to ask Dad.'

Kate waved away her concern with characteristic stoicism. 'Get along with you, girl. I'll not have that Hilary coming round here and lookin' down her nose at my bits and pieces. I might not have much but it's home to me and while I can polish my own door knob I'll be my own mistress.'

Knowing it was no use arguing, Leah gave her one more quick kiss and ran down the path to the waiting car. As they drove through Nenebridge's darkening streets the shops were closing and people were hurrying homewards. In the market place the traders were packing their unsold wares into vans and trucks. As Bill's car crossed the bridge the coloured lights strung out along the river bank were mirrored in the water, turning it from brackish grey to sequinned silver. A sadness settled over Leah; a sadness she didn't understand. She hadn't been happy here, so why this aching nostalgia? It felt as though a part of her life was coming to an end; a door closing behind her, leaving her to face the cold, dark night alone.

Chapter 16

The waiting room at the ante-natal clinic was crowded, overheated and stuffy. Sally's head ached. She had spent almost two hours sitting on the hard chair provided, listening to the tape of jolly Christmas music that played over and over and staring at the tired paperchains and shrivelling balloons that decorated the waiting room. She had exhausted all the tattered magazines on the table in the centre of the room.

Two bored and fractious toddlers were squabbling noisily over a toy tractor from a collapsing cardboard box in the corner while their mothers tried to placate them with sweets. Their shrill squeals grated on her nerves.

'Takes ages, doesn't it? How long've you been here?' the girl sitting next to Sally asked.

'Since two,' she said, glancing at her watch. 'I think it's my turn next though.' Her heart sank as she thought of the long bus ride she had to look forward to after her routine examination. The buses got so crowded in the late afternoon now, with the Christmas shoppers. At this rate she'd hit the rush hour and probably have to stand all the way. Not that anything wouldn't be a change from sitting here in this stuffy, noisy room with all the other pregnant women. We must look like a set of Toby jugs, she told herself, unconsciously echoing one of her mother's favourite sayings. Her mind lingered nostalgically over thoughts of a soft armchair, a blazing fire, and Mavis bringing her a hot cup of tea.

'When's yours due?' the girl was asking her chattily.

'Due? Oh, the baby, you mean. Not till the beginning of February.'

'Only another few weeks then?' The girl smiled. 'I bet you can't wait. Your first, is it?'

'Yes.' In an attempt to put the girl off, Sally buried her face in the magazine she had already read twice and tried to absorb herself in an article on varicose veins.

'My Darren wants a boy,' the girl went on, undeterred. 'But me and Mum'd rather have a little girl. Mum's already made me a pink pram set. It's my first too – Mum's first grandchild. Exciting, isn't it?'

'Very.'

'Have you thought of any names?'

'No.'

The girl's eyes widened. 'Haven't you? I like Tiffany, but if it's a boy – Darren wants Gary or Paul. Football mad, he is.'

'I see.'

'Haven't you got *any* ideas? You must have some favourites.'

Sally put down the magazine. 'I haven't thought about names at all,' she said with quiet deliberation. 'You see, I'm having mine adopted.'

The girl's mouth dropped open in surprise and her round blue eyes stared blankly. It occurred to Sally that she looked like a cod's head on a fishmonger's slab. It was all she could do not to tell her so.

'Oh . . .' the girl said inadequately.

'And if you're wondering why, it's because I've got no husband, right? No mum knitting pink pram sets either,' Sally went on brutally. 'Having a baby isn't at *all* exciting for me. In fact it's a disaster, a very bad mistake that I'm having to pay dearly for.'

'Oh, er . . .' The girl smiled nervously and moved away slightly.

'Oh, don't worry. Mistakes aren't catching,' Sally said waspishly.

'Miss Payne.'

A nurse holding a clipboard stood in the doorway looking round enquiringly. 'Come this way, please.'

Sally got to her feet, wincing slightly as she straightened the crick in her back. Without a backward glance she followed the nurse through the door leading to the examination cubicles. An older woman who had accompanied her daughter bristled visibly and tutted.

'Well, *really*. Young girls nowadays,' she muttered to no one in particular. 'No sense of responsibility at all. I blame the Government. Everything's handed to them on a plate nowadays.' She raised her voice in the hope that Sally would hear. 'And whose pocket does it come out of, eh? I'll tell you. The poor bloody tax payer's. Yours and mine.'

The obstetric registrar was tired. She'd been on duty since the previous night, having been called out to two emergency deliveries and a serious miscarriage on Casualty. She took Sally's blood pressure and palpated her abdomen. Glancing down as she did so she noticed the girl's puffy ankles and looked at her notes.

'Are you still working, Miss Payne?'

Sally nodded, heaving herself into a sitting position with difficulty. 'We're busy at the moment with the Christmas rush.' She rubbed at her fingers which were badly pricked and sore from making holly wreaths. 'In fact I've been staying on to do some overtime.'

'Mmm. On your feet for long hours. Any headaches or vomiting?'

Sally shook her head.

'Your blood pressure is on the high side and there's some protein in your urine sample this time. I think you'd be wise to stop work at this stage.'

'I can't,' Sally said. 'I need all the money I can get to pay my rent.'

'You've already worked long enough to qualify for the allowance, you know.'

'I know, but when my boss took me on it was on the understanding that I'd take as little time off as possible. I'll need the job after the – afterwards.'

'Your mind's still set on adoption, then?'

'There's no other way,' Sally said wearily. She got down from the examination couch and began to pull on her clothes.

'Think about what I've said,' the registrar said. 'You must think of your health, you know – the child's too. Even though the baby is going for adoption, you want it to be as healthy as possible.'

'I take the vitamin tablets and I drink milk.' Sally looked at her in alarm. 'It's all right, isn't it – the baby?'

'So far, yes. But I think you'd be wise to stop working now. If you really can't then try not to overdo it. You say you want to get back to work as quickly as possible afterwards.' The doctor smiled wearily. 'See you next month. And have a happy Christmas,' she added hopefully.

As Sally waited in the bus queue she thought about what the doctor had said. There was no chance she could stop work for at least another month. As for a 'happy Christmas', that was the least of her worries. In order to keep her mother from asking her to go home she had made up a story about being invited to a friend's home for the holiday, making it sound as though it was the one thing in the world she longed to do. Mavis had obviously been hurt and offended, but at least she had stopped asking.

The bus was crowded but an elderly man got up and gave her his seat. She accepted gratefully. But by the time she had reached her stop and walked the half mile back to the dingy Victorian house in Marshall Grove she felt exhausted. What a way to spend my half day, she mused wryly as she climbed the three flights of stairs to her room.

When she reached the top floor she saw to her dismay that she had a visitor. Someone was standing on the landing outside her room; a tall woman in a raincoat. She recognised the social worker who had come to tell her about her sister, Leah.

'Oh – it's you.' She leaned against the banister rail to get her breath. Another confrontation with long-nosed bureaucracy was all she needed.

'I'm sorry to come here, Sally. I went to the shop where you work. They gave me your address.'

'And I suppose you told them you were a social worker?'

'Of course I didn't. I'm not here officially anyway.'

Sally fumbled for her key and unlocked the door. 'I see. Then if it's a social call, I suppose you'd better come in,' she said dryly. She lit the gas fire and crossed to the curtained-off corner which served as a kitchen to plug in the kettle. 'You'll have to excuse me. I've been to the ante-natal clinic and I'm dying for a cup of tea. Perhaps you'd like one too?' She began to take off her outdoor things.

'Thank you. I'd love one.' Hannah sat down. 'I'm here because Leah rang me,' she said. 'I've been away for a few days. Apparently she's been trying to get hold of me.' She glanced at Sally's tired pale face, illuminated by the gas fire as she held her chilled hands out to its glow. 'She told me what happened on the evening you called to see her. She's sorry she upset you, and desperately anxious to make it up to you, Sally.'

'Really?'

'I'm glad you made the effort to go,' Hannah ventured into the silence.

'Much good it did me,' Sally turned to look at her. 'She's just like all the others – preaching – telling me what I should do.'

'I don't think so. You didn't really give her a chance, did you? After all, she had no idea that you were pregnant.'

Sally crossed to the steaming kettle and busied herself with making tea and getting out cups.

'To Leah, adoption is a traumatic subject,' Hannah went on. 'She wasn't as lucky as you in her adoptive parents.'

'I suppose it depends on what you call luck,' Sally said thoughtfully. 'What she'd see as a happy childhood I just see as a term of imprisonment.'

'Oh, surely it wasn't as bad as that. I think you're rather . . .'

'Ungrateful?' Sally spun round. 'Do you think I don't know that? Do you think I don't feel guilty about it? I know my parents made sacrifices for me, that they did their best – or thought they did. But all I really was to them was a possession. Something to hang on to and dominate for as long as possible. I was their *creature*, their *pet*. Not their daughter. They never prepared me for life. Just for living with them and following their rules, their code. In a way it's their fault that this has happened. Now all I want is to get it over with so that I can get on with my life. Make up for what I've lost.'

318

'What *have* you lost, Sally?'

'Freedom,' she said quickly. 'Freedom to think and decide – to be myself. Oh, I know children need guidance, and that's fine. But I was never allowed even to know the dangers – the risks. It's so *wrong* to bring kids up that way. It's like – like sending a blind man out for a walk on a cliff.'

Hannah was silent for a moment as she sipped her tea. 'Sally, on the day you visited Leah she'd just had rather a bad disappointment. For some time she's been trying to trace her – your natural mother. That Sunday they were to have met. She'd been waiting at the station for hours, but Marie – that's her name – wasn't able to make it.'

'Oh. She didn't say.' Sally fell silent, remembering the carefully laid table and the meal that Leah had invited her to share. 'That explains a lot.'

'It meant a great deal to her,' Hannah said. 'She must have been upset.'

'Yes, of course. I wish she'd said something.'

'So what will you do now, Sally?' Hannah asked at last. 'What are your plans for the future?'

For a moment Sally stared at her, then she shrugged. 'To get a better job. Save up and find somewhere nice to live. I don't want a lot. Just to be allowed to – to be myself.'

'What about friends – family?'

'Are we talking about my parents – or Leah?'

'Both. No one can exist in total isolation, Sally. We all need each other to some degree.'

'No man is an island, you mean?' Sally laughed. 'I've had enough of having my life planned for me, thanks.'

'Mavis and Ken may have got things a bit wrong, most parents do. But they care very deeply about

319

you. Don't turn your back on them, Sally. They don't deserve that.'

For a moment Sally's lip trembled. 'I'll ring them,' she said, turning away. 'I'll go and see them after the birth. I never meant to drop them completely, you know.' She rounded on Hannah angrily, her eyes bright. 'And I do love them, in spite of everything. And that's all part of the trap. It's the reason I'm keeping this from them. I'm still trying to please them as well as myself because I can't get out of the habit. Look, as soon as it's over I'll go and see them, okay?'

'And Leah?'

Sally turned away with an impatient frown. 'Oh – I'll see. I'll think about it.'

'Good.' Hannah stood up and began to button her coat. 'I'll go now and let you get some rest.' At the door she turned. 'Sally, what are you doing for Christmas?'

'Probably sleeping for most of it,' she said. 'At the moment that's all I want to do.'

'Leah told me to tell you that you're welcome to spend it with her at Notting Hill.'

'Thanks.'

When Hannah had gone Sally sat on for a long time. Engulfed in the familiar lethargy that made her brain feel numb and her body leaden, she stared into the red bars of the gas fire, her hands around her cooling cup of tea. She was vaguely aware that she was hungry but couldn't be bothered to get herself anything to eat. She was lonely too, though she refused to admit it to herself. 'If only it could all be over,' she said aloud. 'When I get myself back again I can really start thinking about a future. Everything will be all right then.'

The atmosphere in the kitchen at Bella's was electric.

Anna was slamming saucepans about, her sleeves rolled up and her black eyes flashing fire. Franco wore a morose, hangdog expression as he checked his wines for the evening and Joe had clearly been weeping emotional Latin tears.

'What's up?' Leah whispered to him as she took off her coat.

'Is Asunta,' Joe whispered back. 'Anna say she must go home to Italia.' He hunched his shoulders, spreading his hands exasperatedly. 'Nothing she do is right. My sister, she is evil bitch.' He gulped hard and rubbed at his nose with the back of his hand. 'I tell her – Asunta go, I go too.'

'What did she say?'

Joe's dark eyes swam. 'She say: "Go to hell. Get stuffed," she say.' He sniffed hard. 'I wish I never come to England.'

Leah patted his shoulder. 'Come on, Joe. You don't mean that. You're Anna and Franco's partner. It's what you always wanted.'

'Not no more.' Joe was openly weeping now, fat tears slipping down his olive cheeks, dripping on to his white shirt. 'I hate English winter. London is so cold and dirty. It make everyone bad – unkind. Not like Italy. In Italy the sun always shine and people are every day happy and smiling.' He pulled out a handkerchief to mop his face. 'Asunta go – I go too,' he announced firmly.

Leah left him to pull himself together and went into the kitchen to help Anna. She found her still muttering, and trembling like a small volcano about to erupt. They worked together in silence for a few minutes, then Anna suddenly threw up her hands and said: 'That *girl*. She drive me round-a-the-bend.'

'I gathered something was wrong,' Leah said tactfully.

321

'She is *slut*. She don't wash Paulo's nappies properly. He cry all day and all night. And you know what I find when I change him? I find he got a *rash*.'

'Look, why don't you let her work down here with me for a while so that you can take care of the baby?' Leah suggested. 'We'll manage. Just till Paulo is a little older.'

'That girl – work in *my* kitchen? You gotta be joking.' Anna's dark eyes flashed as she rolled down her sleeves and straightened her shoulders. 'No. She goes home,' she said firmly, thumping the table. 'I tell Franco – either she goes or I do. And if I go I take his son with me and he never see him again.'

'Oh dear.'

'I do it. I had-a-that girl up to here.' Anna's voice rose shrilly. 'She ruin my life, my son, my marriage and my business. My stupid brother, he is besotted, Franco, he stick up for her. Only Anna can see she no bloody good. So tonight I tell them.'

'But – if she goes and Joe goes too, what will happen here?' Leah ventured.

Anna threw up her hands, her eyes rolling. 'How I know that? I don't-a-care. Can all take running bloody jump and best of British luck. Anna go home too – to Mama.' She sank on to a chair, the floodgates of her stifled emotions suddenly breaking into an explosion of dramatic sobbing.

Somehow they all got through, but an atmosphere of threatening gloom like vaporised gunpowder pervaded the restaurant all evening. It seemed to permeate the building like a creeping fog. Anna's cooking was erratic and over-seasoned, either too hot or too cold. Joe sniffed audibly as he waited on the tables. He forgot to pull out chairs for the ladies and neglected to unfold their napkins for them, and his expression of monumental gloom was guaranteed to put the hungriest diner off his food. Franco was so silent and lugubrious that it might have been hemlock he was serving instead of wine. The clanging of Anna's saucepans kept up a continuous percussion, penetrating the stout kitchen door and causing the diners to exchange wary glances. No one lingered over their meal at Bella's Ristorante that evening.

They closed early, and with relief Leah left them to sort out their troubles among themselves. Bill put his head round the kitchen door as he heard her come in.

'Tel rang,' he said. 'He's ringing back.' He looked at his watch. 'Any time now.'

'Great. I could do with cheering up,' Leah said, taking off her coat. She glanced at Bill's expression. 'Why do I get the feeling that I'm about to hear something I'd rather not know?' she asked. 'Terry is all right, isn't he?'

'Ye-es.'

'Okay, let's have it.'

'Better let him tell it,' Bill said. 'I've just made coffee. Come in and have a cup while you wait.'

He'd only just poured it when the telephone rang. Leah went into the hall to answer it.

'Terry?'

'Ah, Bill told you I'd rung.'

'Yes. Are you all right? How's the frozen north?'

'Fine. Look, Leah, I'm going to have to stay up here for Christmas.'

Her heart sank. 'Oh, Tel, why?'

'It's Dad. He's not very well. He's going into hospital next week for an operation. I feel I ought to hang around. He hasn't got anyone else, you see.'

Leah gripped the receiver hard. She longed to say selfishly: Neither have I. Instead she said: 'Of course. It's nothing serious, I hope?'

323

'Not really. It's just that I don't like to think of him coming out of hospital to spend Christmas alone. I haven't seen as much of him as I might have done the last few years.'

'Of course. I understand.'

There was a small silence then Terry said: 'Leah? You're still there?'

'Yes, I'm still here.'

'You are all right, aren't you?'

'Of course I am.'

'How did the reunion with your mother go?'

'It didn't. I went to meet her train – hung around for half the day. She didn't show up.'

'Oh, God. Poor Leah. I'm sorry, love.'

'I've spoken to Hannah since. It seems she was unavoidably detained, as they say.'

'What a pity. I quite thought – hoped you and she would be spending Christmas together.'

'Never mind, Probably just as well,' she said, trying to sound philosophical. 'I daresay we'd both have been disappointed. Things have a way of turning out for the best. 'Bye then, Tel. Hope your father's better soon. See you sometime.' She. hung up quickly – before he could ask about Sally, before she found herself pouring out that particular tale of woe. Or relating to him the nerve-racking evening she'd just had at Bella's. Why should he want to listen to her troubles when he had enough of his own? She was getting to be a walking disaster lately.

As she walked back into the kitchen Bill glanced at her. 'He told you?'

'Yes.' She picked up her cup of coffee and sat down in front of the Aga with it.

'You're disappointed.' He pulled up a chair and sat down opposite her.

'There's no reason why Terry should feel obliged to

spend Christmas with me. I've taken advantage of his good nature enough.'

'I wondered if you might be going home for Christmas.'

She gave him a wry smile. 'You're joking.'

'I thought maybe your grandmother . . . ?'

'I expect she'll go to the Dobsons'. Jack is her son after all, and she's been poorly. It's about time they put themselves out.'

'I see. So what will you do?'

She shrugged. 'I did send a message to my sister inviting her to spend Christmas with me.'

'And?' He looked at her enquiringly.

'Nothing. But then I didn't really expect her to respond after what happened.'

'So it'll just be us. You and me?'

She gave him a rueful smile. 'Sorry, Bill.'

He laughed. 'Don't be sorry. Can't you see that I'm trying to keep the grin off my face? I've been dreading my own company.'

'I'll cook your Christmas dinner – try to make myself useful.'

He grinned. 'Thought you'd never offer. We'll have a great time, eh?' He watched her for a moment. 'Leah, I've never asked about you and Tel. What's the situation there?'

'We're mates,' she told him. 'I've known him since I was at school. He's always been a good friend. And as I said, I've taken advantage of him dreadfully. Time I stood on my own feet.'

'There's no romantic attachment then?'

Leah smothered the aching feeling that had been steadily growing over the past weeks. 'No. I rather suspect that Terry sees me as a tiresome younger sister.'

'And how do you see him?' he asked perceptively.

'I told you. As a good friend. One who's probably fed up with the sight of me by now.'

'Well, I can't quite believe that.' They sat in silence for a moment, then Bill asked: 'Ever been in love, Leah?'

She smiled a little wistfully. 'I thought I was – very briefly. But I know now that it wasn't the real thing. I don't believe in it really, Bill. Not the way it is in books and films. It's all a con trick, invented to keep the human race going. There's friendship and there's sex. Nothing else. People waste their entire lives looking for something that doesn't exist. They keep on looking till they're too old to care one way or the other.'

'What a depressing thought.' Bill gave a little snort of laughter. 'It's a very cynical observation for a young girl like you. Anyway, what about the love we feel for children – family?'

'Ah, well, I've no first hand experience of it, have I?'

'Sorry, I forgot.' He looked at her. 'Leah, that day that your sister came here – apart from the little disagreement you had – what did you think of her?'

'She wasn't at all what I expected. She's my twin, and yet she might as well be a complete stranger. She doesn't even look like me.'

'I suppose growing up together must make a difference.'

'Maybe.' Leah sighed. 'I doubt if we'll ever be close now. It's too late, isn't it? I should have known. Then there's my natural mother. I'd built up such a picture of her in my mind; dreamed for years of the great day when I'd find her. And then when she wrote me that letter I thought – I really believed it was all coming true. The social worker made excuses, said something unexpected had happened to prevent her coming that day, but I don't know.' She stared pensively into her cup and, touched by her lost look Bill reached out impulsively.

'Don't look like that, Leah.'

Kind words were the last thing she wanted. Getting up quickly she took the cups to the sink and began to wash them, acutely aware that Bill was standing hesitantly behind her. She felt his hands, gentle on her shoulders, and stiffened, biting her lip. 'Bill, please – I don't think I can handle sympathy just now.'

He turned her gently to him. 'Look, do you want to talk about it? I don't mind if you do.'

She shook her head. 'I just seem to be going through one of those phases when everything seems to go wrong. Everybody gets them, I suppose. It'll pass.' She swallowed hard in a desperate attempt to iron the wobble out of her voice. 'Oh dear, I despise feeble women. I'll be all right in a minute.'

'You know what? You're one of the strongest women I've ever known,' he told her.

She raised an eyebrow at him. 'What about all those tough career girls you work with on the paper?'

Bill shook his head. 'Ah, but you're not tough. There's a difference between strength and toughness. You've got guts and the determination to survive. But you're deliciously feminine too.'

Surprised, she looked up at him and for a moment his eyes held hers. Then he bent and kissed her. At first she pushed against his chest in a half-hearted effort to break loose, but his arms held her gently captive, drawing her closer. And suddenly the warmth and comfort of his masculinity were too powerful to resist. She capitulated, letting her body mould itself to his and winding her arms around his neck. With a little murmur she relaxed, letting her lips part in response to his kiss.

Bill was a thoughtful, considerate lover, taking the initiative in a firm, positive way and yet with an infinite tenderness. It was only later, as she lay watching him doze, that all the complications that this situation might contain began to occur to her.

'Bill.' She shook him gently. 'Bill, listen. I'm not moving in with you. I'm not saying I'm sorry that this happened.' She frowned, searching for the right words. 'We were just . . .'

He opened his eyes and watched her struggling. 'We were just two friends comforting one another,' he said with a smile. 'Is that what you were trying to say? There's friendship and there's sex, you said, didn't you? It's not a bad combination. Can't knock it, can you, Leah?'

'I'm not all that sure that they mix.'

He closed his eyes again. 'Don't worry. I'm not going to get all heavy and possessive.'

'You're more than just a friend though,' she said, tracing the line of his jaw with one finger.

He chuckled, catching at her finger and biting it gently. 'So I should bloody well hope.'

'I suppose we could call ourselves – loving friends.'

'So we could.'

She regarded him for a long moment as he lay on his back. His eyes were closed again and she noticed with faint surprise that his eyelashes were as long and thick as a child's. He was a strong man, perhaps twenty years or more older than her. He had a positive, analytical journalist's mind and a powerful muscular body, and yet seeing him in repose like this she saw that there was something vulnerable about him. Maybe we're all vulnerable, she told herself. All lonely, lost children at heart, needing comfort from each other. Maybe that was what Tom Clayton had needed when she had tried so ruthlessly and brashly to exploit him. She thrust the memory from her with a little stab of shame. In the months since Tom she'd done some growing up. In that kind of situation perhaps one partner always ended up exploiting the other. She shivered slightly as she said: 'I should really find myself somewhere else to live.'

His eyes snapped open and he looked up at her. 'Why, for God's sake? Look, Leah, it needn't make any difference. Tonight was a special occasion. A . . .'

'One off? A one night stand?' She raised her eyebrows at him.

He frowned. 'No. That sounds so sordid. I was going to say, a sort of celebration, a gift to each other.' He frowned. 'You don't really see it as sordid, do you?'

'No, and perhaps that's why I should go.' She sat up and began to wrap herself in his dressing gown. 'I may have to anyway. I've got a horrible feeling I'm going to be out of a job soon.'

'What makes you say that?'

'The Andrettis. They've started quarrelling. I suspect that home-sickness is at the bottom of it. It wouldn't surprise me if they were to pack up and go back to Italy.'

'What will you do if they leave?'

'Look for another job, I suppose. In another town perhaps. Maybe it's time for me to move on.'

He was silent, shaken by the knowledge that her going would leave a bigger gap in his life than he would care to admit. 'I know, why not start up on your own?' he said suddenly.

She turned to stare at him, in the act of rolling up the robe sleeves. 'Start up what?'

'Catering. A mobile service.'

'But that takes money. I haven't got any and the bank wouldn't be daft enough to make a loan to someone like me.'

'You wouldn't need a lot, surely? You could work from home, doing dinner parties, buffets, small functions.'

'Home? What home?'

'This one, of course.' Bill spread his hands. 'Look, before she left, Janet – my ex – bought a bloody great freezer. It's standing there empty. Then there's the Aga burning away like the clappers all day just to heat this place and boil the odd egg. You might as well be making use of it.'

Leah's mind was beginning to stir with interest. 'It's not a bad idea, I admit. But I'd need more than a freezer and a cooker. I'd need some kind of transport. And there'd be other things – equipment and stuff. It all costs. It'd come to quite a lot by the time you'd added it all up.'

'So – I'll lend you some money.'

Leah frowned. 'No, Bill.'

He sat up. 'Why the hell not?'

'All kinds of reasons. Suppose I failed – couldn't pay you back?'

'You won't. But if you feel like that you could make me a partner.' Seeing her doubtful expression he leaned forward. 'Look, Leah, you could do it. I know you could. One of these days I'm going to be too old and tired for journalism and when I finally chuck it I'm going to need something to fall back on. Why don't I set up the business and let you run it for me?' He reached out to grasp her arm, his eyes earnest. 'Look, there'd be no strings if that's what's worrying you.'

'It wasn't.'

330

'Well then?'

She laughed suddenly. 'How did we get into this? The Andrettis are an unpredictable lot. By tomorrow they'll probably have made it up and be all sweetness and light. I daresay I'm worrying for nothing.' She looked at her watch. 'It's late. We should both get some sleep.'

'You're welcome to stay here.'

She shook her head, smiling.

'Think how cold your bed must be.'

'Goodnight, Bill.' She leaned across and kissed him lightly, slipping out of the reach of his encircling arms. 'Sleep well. See you in the morning.'

At Petals the staff were rushed off their feet. Sally had been busy all day making up bouquets and arrangements as last-minute gifts, and although it was almost five o'clock she was only just snatching a tea break in the room at the back. It was Christmas Eve. One more hour and she could go home and put up her feet for four precious days. For a moment she allowed her thoughts to dwell on Christmas at home in Leicester. Mavis would have put up the decorations at least ten days ago. And trimmed the tree. It would be standing proudly in its usual place, in the window of the lounge, its coloured lights twinkling for passers-by to see. She wondered if the fairy doll was there on the topmost branch – and wondered wistfully who would have put her there this year. That had been her own special privilege for as long as she could remember, since the days when she had been too little to reach and Ken had had to lift her up to it. Putting the fairy on top of the tree had seemed to symbolise the start of Christmas for them all.

'Sally, there's a man at the counter waiting to be

served.' Mrs Greg the manageress put her head round the door. 'You'll have to come, I'm afraid, dear. We're rushed off our feet.'

He was good-looking and quite young, and his brown eyes were alight with excitement. 'I want some flowers,' he said.

'Well, we've got plenty of those,' Sally said dryly, catching Mrs Greg's frown out of the corner of her eye.

But the young man only laughed. 'I reckon you have. I want a-thingummy – decoration.'

'For an occasion, sir? Any idea what sort of flowers – any particular colour?'

'Well, pink and blue, I suppose,' he said thoughtfully. 'Jane, that's my wife, has just given birth to twins, you see. A boy and a girl. One of each,' he added, hardly able to keep the broad smile from splitting his face. 'I'm on my way to see them now.'

'Oh, I see. Well, if you'd like to wait I'll be as quick as I can.'

Suddenly filled with new energy, Sally went through to the back room and searched the cupboard for something she had seen weeks ago: a pair of baby's shoes in white and silver ceramic, resting on a satin cushion. Working quickly and creatively she made up a delicate arrangement of tiny pink and white dianthus, frothy gypsophila and miniature trailing ivy. When the young man saw it he was delighted.

'Oh, thank you. It's super. Perfect. Jane will be absolutely thrilled.'

'It's a pleasure. I'm a twin, actually.'

He looked up with a smile. 'Hey, you don't say. What a coincidence.'

Watching him write the cheque Sally suddenly realised that for the first time she had openly acknowledged the fact that she had a sister. Somehow it seemed to make it official. Very carefully she shrouded the arrangement in tissue paper and found a cardboard box to put it in. When he had gone, wreathed in smiles and thanking her profusely, Mrs Greg came across to her.

'You did very well there, Sally. It was clever of you to remember the shoes, and the little arrangement was quite exquisite – just right.'

But somehow the compliment was lost on her. Creating the arrangement seemed to have used up the last of her energy and she felt suddenly drained.

'It's almost closing time, why don't you get your things and go home now?' Mrs Greg was looking at her with concern. 'You look all in. Try to get some rest over the Christmas break, eh?'

'Yes, I will. Thank you, Mrs Greg.' Sally began to move mechanically towards the staff room.

The bus was crowded and she had to stand almost all the way to her stop. Most of the other tenants of the house in Marshall Grove had gone away for the holiday and the place seemed to echo with emptiness as she climbed the stairs. When she opened the door of her room on the top floor it looked depressingly dreary and cheerless, and the cold hit her like a wall of ice. As she waited for the gas fire to warm the room and the kettle to boil she thought of the young man; saw him proudly bearing her flower arrangement to his wife in the hospital. She could imagine the kiss and the loving look they would exchange. She saw him looking down at the two small babies in their identical cots, a tender smile on his face while his wife watched, her eyes full of pride and contentment. When her baby was born there would be no one to bring her flowers. No one to kiss her and tell her how clever she was or how happy she had made him. Suddenly it was more than she could bear and she sank down on the bed overwhelmed by loneliness and longing. Somewhere in the back of her mind a voice was saying, If I can only get through this Christmas everything will be all right. If I can stand this, I can stand anything.

The kettle boiled, spluttering over on to the shelf. Sally sat up. Hiccuping childishly and blowing her nose, she went to make the tea. As she passed the mirror she caught sight of her swollen eyes and blotchy face. How shall I bear it though? she asked herself bleakly. How shall I stop myself from going mad, alone in this place for four whole days – at Christmas?

It was on Christmas Eve that the blow fell. Anna had decided to open the restaurant at lunchtime only on that day and when Leah arrived at ten-thirty that morning she found Anna waiting for her alone in the kitchen.

'Asunta walk out this morning,' she said without preamble. 'She leave a note, saying she is homesick. Joe . . .' She threw up her hands, raising her eyes to the ceiling. 'I can do nothing with him. It seems he ask Asunta to marry him. She say no.'

'Oh dear. He'll get over it, surely?'

Anna shook her head. 'He don't take no for an answer. He say he follow her. He is already packing.'

'What will you do?' Leah asked, but she already knew.

'Franco and I, we talk. We make up our minds. We leave too. After Christmas we put the ristorante up for sale and we go back to our country.'

'I'm sorry to hear that, Anna. You won't change your mind?'

She shook her head. 'We try, Leah. We make good long effort. But London, it get us all down – make us

334

sick. Back home we don't quarrel and fight like this.'
She sighed and looked around her. 'We get money for
this place – buy a *ristorante* somewhere nearer home.
Cattolica, maybe. Nice holiday place – sunshine and a
beach for Paulo. Plenty tourists.'

'I shall miss you all – and the job,' Leah said. 'I've
been happy here. I've learned a lot.'

Anna hugged her. 'We love you, Leah cara, you
are like family. You come to Italy too?'

Leah smiled and shook her head. 'It's generous of
you to offer, Anna. But I think I might get as
homesick as you are.'

'You come for holiday then. On us – on house.'

'When will you go? Will you stay until the place is
sold?'

But Anna was shaking her head. 'We leave after
Christmas. As soon as we can pack and book a flight.
We pay you instead of notice, of course.'

'So soon?' Leah tried to hide her dismay. As from
midday she was out of a job. It had come sooner than
she expected.

At three o'clock, after they had cleared up and
washed the last of the dishes, Franco gave Leah an
envelope. It contained the wages she was owed, plus
two weeks' money and a generous Christmas present.
He opened a bottle of champagne and the four of
them toasted each other's future. They hugged each
other and said tearful emotional goodbyes all round,
promising faithfully to write and keep in touch. After
that Leah walked home to Melbury Street with a
heavy heart. Once again she was just another
member of the army of unemployed.

Bill was fixing the lights for the enormous Christmas
tree he had brought home with him the previous day
and erected in the corner of the kitchen. He turned,
screwdriver in hand, as she came in.

'There, how about that then?' he said, switching on the lights with a flourish. 'Ta-raah. I declare this Christmas officially open.'

'It's great, Bill.' Leah said flatly. She threw down her handbag and began to take off her coat.

'Oh dear. What's up?'

'It's happened,' she said. 'Just as I was afraid it would. The Andrettis are throwing in the towel. I'm out of a job as from this moment.'

Bill stood up, his face concerned. 'You mean they didn't even give you notice?'

'They couldn't,' Leah told him. 'They plan to leave for Italy right after Christmas.'

'Oh. I'm sorry, kid.' He took both her hands. 'There's always plan B.'

She smiled. 'Your mobile catering idea? I don't know, Bill. It needs a lot of careful thinking.'

'So – we'll carefully think.'

'Not now. Let's have Christmas first. Let's not think of anything at all until after Christmas.'

'What a good idea.'

'I've bought the turkey. I got it at cost from Anna's butcher. If we go to the supermarket now we can buy the rest of the stuff. Then I'll come back here and make a start on the cooking.'

'Tonight?'

'Of course. There are mince pies to make, stuffing and brandy sauce, vegetables to prepare.' She prodded his chest, laughing up into his eyes in the way that turned his knees to water. 'That's where *you* come in, you lazy slob. You needn't think you're going to sit there and watch me do all the work.'

'No, Ma'am – certainly, Ma'am.' He stood to attention and saluted. 'I'll get the car right away. Your word is my command.' He turned in the doorway. 'On one condition though.'

'What's that?' she asked suspiciously.

'That you let me take you out to dinner when it's all done. Strikes me we're both going to have bloody well deserved it if you get your way.'

'Right, you're on.'

Bill took her to a wine bar in the Strand that was a favourite among journalists. The lighting was dim and they sat at a corner table illuminated by a candle in a bottle. Leah didn't think much of the food, though she didn't say so. Bill seemed to be enjoying himself. He introduced her to several of his colleagues who eyed her with everything from admiration to speculation. She had the distinct impression that he was showing her off to them, but she didn't mention this either. They finished the bottle of wine Bill had ordered with the meal and then he insisted on ordering a second. He waved away her protests that they had had enough, reminding her that it was Christmas and that they had left the car at home.

When they came up into the street again the sky was clear and frosty. The lights of the street decorations were twinkling merrily and somewhere in the distance the sound of church bells could be heard. Leah looked at her watch.

'It's almost midnight.'

'So it is.' Bill drew her into a shop doorway and kissed her lingeringly. 'Happy Christmas, Leah, my love.'

'Happy Christmas, Bill.'

He smiled at her with eyes that were slightly unfocused and pulled her hand through the crook of his elbow. 'Come on, let's see if we can find a cruising taxi.'

In the taxi Bill was amorous and as she stood on the pavement waiting while he paid the driver she felt distinctly uncomfortable, knowing what was in his mind. He was expecting her to go to bed with him and she racked her brain in vain for an excuse that wouldn't wound his manly pride. As she followed him down the area steps she began:

'Look, Bill, I . . .' But he turned at the bottom and pulled her into his arms, his voice quivering with alcohol-enhanced emotion.

'Leah – I don't know what I'd have done without you this Christmas.'

'It's the same for me, Bill, but we mustn't get carried away. Please remember what we said we'd be for each other.'

But he wasn't listening. 'You're a lovely kid,' he murmured, burying his face in her neck. 'You make me feel so . . .'

'No, Bill.' She pushed him gently. 'Look, you've had a bit too much to drink and . . .'

'Oh, come *on*. Don't tell me you're going to . . .'

'*Excuse me*.'

The hesitant voice from the top of the steps made them both turn and look up in surprise. Peering down at them was a figure muffled in a voluminous coat, a scarf tied over her fair hair.

'I'm sorry to intrude, Leah, but Hannah Brown told me you'd very kindly invited me for Christmas. I know it's a bit late in the day but I've come to see if the invitation still stands.'

Leah went up the steps, her hands outstretched. She welcomed the diversion, but she welcomed her sister even more.

'Sally, how nice. Of course it still stands. We've got plenty of room and enough food to feed an army. You're welcome, isn't she, Bill?'

Looking acutely disappointed and slightly hangdog, he nodded, fumbling in his pocket for his latchkey.

'Of course. Come on in. Like Leah says, it's Liberty bloody Hall here.'

Chapter 17

'The Ocean' wore all its Christmas finery. The reception hall was decorated in romantic blue and silver, the centrepiece being a twelve-foot tree dripping with silver icicles and lit with blue and white lights to simulate moonlight. The dining room was bright with traditional evergreens and Christmas roses, and on the menu were some exciting new dishes as well as all the old favourites.

Marie had thrown herself into the preparations with extra energy this year. She had scoured the shops for special lighting effects and ideas on decoration; bought most of the food herself and encouraged the chef to try out new recipes. The small gifts that were to be found on each dressing table had all been chosen and wrapped by Marie herself. It had been hard work but she had enjoyed every minute of it. It had helped a little to make up for the crushing disappointment she had suffered in being forced to miss the meeting with Leah which she had looked forward to so much.

It also helped her to forget, just for a while, her increasing anxiety over the mess Ralph was getting them into over his inept running of the business. Keeping their position from David was a constant strain and she knew that her impossible situation could not go on for much longer. Very soon now she was going to have to face Ralph with the unpaid bills and threatening letters that now arrived with almost every post.

Philip Hodges had booked himself into a room on the first floor of 'The Ocean' for Christmas some weeks before. He had no close relatives, and since he'd moved to the Dorset practice he'd had little time for socialising or making friends outside his immediate circle.

'There's nothing nicer I can think of than spending the festive season with all of you at "The Ocean",' he said with a smile when he made the booking. 'The atmosphere is always so friendly and warm. Hardly like a hotel at all.'

But although Marie was pleased that he would be with them and flattered by his complimentary remarks she was also apprehensive. Ralph had taken a violent dislike to Philip. He had accused her, quite without grounds, of seeing him illicitly. He objected to David leaving his previous GP in favour of Philip too, and seized every opportunity to make snide remarks about everything from his appearance to the way he spoke.

Ralph had announced his intention of arriving late on Christmas Eve and remaining till Boxing Day, when he would move on to 'The Marina' in Norfolk which he had now made his headquarters. He told Marie that he was to go through the books with an accountant, but when she pressed him for more details he waved her questions away irritably, telling her as always that he had everything in hand and that it was not her province.

Philip checked in on the day before Christmas Eve. It happened to be his day off and he expressed his intention of having as many days as possible with his friends. Marie had asked the receptionist on duty to let her know when he arrived and to

340

send him up to join them for a drink.

When the girl rang to say that Philip was on his way up Marie felt a little thrill of anticipation. She replaced the receiver and turned to David with a smile.

'Philip has arrived. He's on his way up to have a drink with us.'

'Good.' David returned her smile. 'I haven't seen him since my last check-up. It'll be good to talk to him without a desk between us for once.' He looked at his daughter-in-law with a frown. 'You're looking tired, Marie. You work much too hard, you know. You have a good staff. You should delegate more.'

Marie, who had taken a long time over her appearance, smiled wryly. 'Thank you, David. There's nothing like telling a girl she looks tired for making her feel her best.'

He reached out to pat her arm. 'You know I don't mean to criticise, love. You still manage to look lovely. In fact, your tiredness adds to that, gives you that fragile air – like a piece of Dresden china.'

Marie laughed. 'You're a genius at putting the gilt back on the gingerbread. I'll forgive you this time.' She went to the table where she had set out glasses and Philip's favourite malt whisky as well as mineral water for herself and gin for David. She'd also made up a shaker full of dry Martini and put out plenty of ice and lemon slices. She was opening a jar of olives when there was a tap on the door and Philip walked in.

'Happy Christmas to both of you,' he said with a smile. 'They said in Reception that you wanted me to look in.'

Marie went to him with outstretched hands. 'Happy Christmas, Philip. We'd like you to have a drink with us before you go off to unpack.'

341

He drew from behind his back two parcels wrapped in Christmassy paper and handed one to each of them. Marie exclaimed.

'Philip! We didn't expect this.'

'I've had a lot of happy times here,' he said, waving away her protests. 'It's nothing – just a small token of my appreciation. Besides, you're a fine one to protest. When I dropped my things into my room just now I found this on the dressing table.' He held out the small parcel which Marie had wrapped herself. 'May I open it now?'

She laughed. 'Of course.'

Philip exclaimed over the slim gold cuff links nestling in their velvet-lined box. 'How clever of you to know I needed some.'

'Not really. It was when you stayed here for the medical conference that you lost one,' Marie reminded him. 'The first time you came – when David was taken ill. Remember?'

'I'm not likely to forget.' He smiled. 'You really do think of everything, don't you? No wonder your guests come back time after time.'

David found a smart striped tie in his parcel, but when Marie opened hers she found an exquisite silk Hermès scarf in scarlet and black wrapped around a bottle of Arpege perfume.

'Oh, Philip,' she said, breathing in the fragrance. 'This is lovely – but so extravagant. You really shouldn't.'

'Got it at the duty free shop at Heathrow,' he said dismissively. 'Last time I flew. I hope it's what you like.'

'I love it.' Marie had already opened the crystal bottle and was dabbing some of the perfume on her wrists. 'I'd never buy it for myself though. Thank you, Philip.'

He accepted the drink that she handed him and looked at them both. 'Well – here's to a happy Christmas. I take it you'll both join me for dinner this evening?'

David shook his head. 'I hope you'll excuse me, Philip. I'm having something up here on a tray. There's a programme I rather want to see on TV.'

'Well, of course, but . . .' Philip looked at Marie. 'I hope you're not too tied up.'

She smiled. 'I'd love to have dinner with you, Philip. I want to hear all about how the practice is doing and about your new house.'

Philip had recently bought himself a pretty little cottage in the New Forest and was in the process of having it refurbished.

When Philip had gone off to unpack and change for dinner, David looked at Marie as she collected the glasses on to a tray.

'I hope Philip didn't think I was rude,' he said. 'But I really don't feel like socialising this evening.'

'You're all right, aren't you, David?' Marie put down her tray and went to him. 'Not feeling poorly?'

He smiled and shook his head. 'I'm fine. Don't worry about me.' He couldn't tell her that he had used the TV programme as an excuse because he knew quite well that Philip would rather have her to himself. He could hardly help noticing that the good-looking doctor always brought a soft pink flush to her cheeks. God knew the girl deserved a little pleasure. She worked so hard and never went out anywhere. The hotel was her whole world. Although she hadn't complained to him, David knew that Ralph kept her short of money. He worried a lot about the way he treated her. He often heard him shouting at her when he was at home on one of his rare weekend visits. And he couldn't help but see the bruises and the tell-tale signs of tears that she tried so touchingly to conceal from him. They made him feel guilty. In a way he had engineered the marriage, thinking it would be good for them all. He felt helpless too, hating to think there was nothing he could do but stand by and witness her unhappiness. The least he could do was to see that she accepted a harmless invitation that would give her pleasure, he told himself.

In the dining room Marie had seen to it that a table was laid for them in a quiet corner. In the centre of the snowy damask cloth a green pine-scented candle floated in a bowl of Christmas roses, its gentle light making the waxen petals glow like pearls. Marie had changed into a plain black dress, and she wore the scarf Philip had given her stylishly draped over one shoulder and fastened on the other with a silver pin. The contrasting colours enhanced her fair complexion and made her look delicate and fragile. Philip smiled at her across the table.

'You look very nice. I was right about the scarf. It suits you.'

'Thank you.' She wanted to return the compliment but she was still a little shy. She thought that Philip looked very handsome in his dark grey suit. His dark hair was brushed smoothly back and there were grey wings over his ears that gave him a distinguished look. They ordered their meal and Marie leaned forward.

'Do tell me about the cottage. How is the work going?'

He smiled wryly. 'Slowly. You know what building is like in winter. And I'm afraid I shall have to wait for spring for them to begin landscaping the garden.' He leaned forward. 'I've been meaning to ask you, Marie. When I get to the interior decoration and furnishing, I'd very much appreciate your advice. Will you help?'

344

'I'd love to. Spending other people's money is such fun.' She laughed and he looked at her, his eyes gentle.

'I haven't seen you do that for some time,' he said. 'I'd like to see you do it more often. Laughing suits you.' He paused. 'By the way, why did you refuse to see me when I called round a couple of weeks ago?'

Marie's smile disappeared and she avoided his eyes, applying herself to the soup which the waiter had just put before her. 'I wasn't feeling very well.'

'Need I remind you that I am a doctor?'

He was teasing her and she shook her head. 'Oh, not ill. Call it an off day.'

'I thought we were friends, Marie. I'm not only here for the good days, I hope.'

'Of course you're not, Philip.' She put down her spoon and looked at him. 'Ralph was here. He came home unexpectedly. I'd arranged to go up to London to meet – for a rather special appointment, and I couldn't go. It was one of those times when everything goes wrong.'

'I see.' He looked at her thoughtfully. 'Marie, forgive me, but things are not all that they should be between you and Ralph, are they?'

'What makes you ask me that?'

'Forgive me for saying so, but all the signs are there.'

'Signs?'

'I've seen enough badly treated wives to recognise them by now.' Seeing her expression he said quickly: 'I'm sorry, Marie. That must have sounded awful. It's none of my business anyway. So you couldn't keep your appointment. Couldn't you have rearranged it?'

'I tried. It didn't work out. I told you – nothing went right that day. I wasn't even able to let my – let the person I was meeting know that I wasn't coming. I kept thinking of her, standing there at the station, waiting for me – thinking I'd let her down.'

Her eyes were looking past him, full of pained regret. He reached across the table to touch her hand. 'Marie, if there's ever anything you want to talk about, I'm always here, you know. Anything you tell me would be in complete confidence. I'm sure you know that.'

'Of course I do, Philip.' Her eyes focused on him and she let out her breath in a long sigh. 'Actually I would like to tell you. No one else knows. I didn't even tell David that on the day in question I was going to meet my – my daughter.'

'Your daughter?' He looked surprised. 'I didn't realise that you and Ralph . . .'

'Oh, not Ralph's child. She and her twin sister were born twenty years ago, when I was seventeen. Their father let me down badly. I gave them up for adoption at birth because I didn't know what else to do. One of them recently went to a lot of trouble to find me. A friend who happens to be a social worker arranged the meeting. But Ralph came home unexpectedly. I never told him about the babies, Philip, even though David had known from the first. Maybe I was wrong, but that's the way it was and if he found out now . . .' She shuddered.

'So you had to abandon your plans? That must have been very frustrating. But surely you can fix up something else?'

She sighed. 'I suppose I could, but since then I've been asking myself if it would be wise – or fair. I couldn't offer my girls any more now than I could then. You see, even now I'm still not free to acknowledge them openly as my daughters.'

'Would that matter? Perhaps they just want to meet you, Marie,' he said gently. 'After all, they're young women by now. I daresay they've become curious about their origins, and interested to know more about the woman who gave them birth.'

'And I would dearly love to see them,' Marie said longingly. 'Even if it was only once. Just to see how they'd turned out.'

'Well, at least one of them obviously wants to see you as badly or she wouldn't have tried so hard to find you. Don't let the chance go by, Marie.'

'I don't want to let it go by. It's just that Ralph . . .' She shook her head. 'There are other complications. It's very difficult. David is so easily upset and it's bad for him. And Ralph is his son after all. I'm sure there must be times when his loyalty is severely strained. I wouldn't want to make things worse for him.'

Philip smiled wryly. 'It's always saddened me that I have no family, but I have to admit that there are times when it seems a positive advantage. The complications seem endless.'

'Mine isn't exactly a normal, straightforward marriage.'

He touched her fingertips. 'Life hasn't been easy for you, has it, Marie?'

'No, not easy, but I've been lucky in many ways. If I hadn't gone to work for David . . .'

'You wouldn't have met and married Ralph?'

For a moment they looked at each other. Marie recognised that the conversation could, at this point, take two different directions. Immediately she was on her guard, unwilling to let Philip lead her into a confession she might regret.

'That's right,' she said carefully after a pause. 'And I'd never have come to Dorset.'

'Or met me?' he finished for her with a twinkle in his eyes. They laughed together and the tricky moment passed. Marie wished with all her heart that

347

she could have told him the whole truth about herself. But the idea of a respectable doctor wanting his name linked with a woman who had been in jail, convicted, albeit wrongly, of an act of terrorism, was unthinkable to her. As unthinkable as the prospect of losing his friendship.

They lingered over their meal then took their coffee in the lounge. It was quiet. Most of the guests who had booked in for Christmas would not arrive until tomorrow. A log fire blazed in the hearth and Philip ordered cognac with their coffee. Marie felt herself relax for the first time in weeks. They talked easily – about Philip's work in his new practice; about the cottage he had bought in a New Forest village, and his plans for it; about the guests who were expected tomorrow, some of whom Philip had met before. Finally Marie looked at her watch and was surprised to see that it was after eleven o'clock.

'Heavens, I'd no idea it was so late. I must go,' she said, getting to her feet. 'David will have gone to bed ages ago. I don't like to turn in without checking that he's all right.'

'He's lucky to have such an attentive daughter-in-law,' Philip said, rising with her. 'And he's looking very well at the moment. I'm sure it's all thanks to you. I'll say goodnight then. And thanks for your company.' He bent and kissed her lightly on the lips, then walked with her to the lift.

It was quiet as Marie got out on the top floor. She let herself into the flat and went immediately to David's room. Tapping softly on the door and getting no reply, she opened it and looked in. He was sleeping soundly, lying on his back and snoring gently. His book lay where he had dropped it on the floor, his tablets and a glass of water standing as usual on the bedside table. Marie picked up the book and drew the covers carefully up over his shoulders then tiptoed silently out and went to her own room.

When she opened the door she was surprised for a moment to see that the light was on. She must have carelessly forgotten to switch it off when she went down to dinner. Going to the dressing table she began to unpin the scarf Philip had given her, then she looked up into the mirror and was startled to see the reflection of Ralph's broad figure standing silently in the bathroom doorway.

'Ralph!' She spun round to face him and the silk scarf Philip had given her slipped softly to the floor.

'Startle you, did I?'

'I wasn't expecting you till tomorrow.'

'Evidently. I looked into the lounge on my way in but you looked so cosy with your doctor friend, sitting on the settee with your heads together, I thought I'd better not intrude.' The words were bland enough but his eyes were as hard as granite. She could see the dark malice in them from across the room and her heart turned to ice.

'Philip is staying for the Christmas holiday. He asked David and me to dine with him. He's a guest. I could hardly refuse.'

Ralph's mouth curved in a smile. 'Defensive, aren't we? I wonder why? Don't be a hypocrite, Marie. At least give me credit for recognising what I can see with my own eyes.' He looked past her at the open door. 'I do hope he isn't about to join us. That *would* be embarrassing.'

'Of course he isn't.'

He advanced towards her. 'Don't pretend to be so shocked at the idea. I daresay it wouldn't be the first time you've entertained him up here.' His eyes narrowed. 'You're not a patient of his, are you? I do hope he isn't behaving unethically with you?'

'I'm not his patient and he isn't behaving in anything but a perfectly proper and gentlemanly way. What you suggest is despicable.'

'Despicable, am I? Maybe *I* should have been a doctor. Is that what turns you on, Marie? The clinical touch? Does he wear a mask and rubber gloves when he makes love to you?'

'Stop it, Ralph. Please don't.' Sickened, she turned away, but he grasped her shoulders and jerked her round, forcing her to look at him.

'Don't turn away from me when I'm talking to you.' She caught the sickly-sweet smell of whisky on his breath.

'Ralph – your father is asleep. Please don't shout.'

'I'll shout if I bloody well feel like it!'

'What you're suggesting is completely untrue and I'm sure you know that I don't behave like that. Can we drop it, please? Ralph, I have to talk to you. I'm seriously worried. There have been more letters – and bills.'

He frowned. 'All bills are supposed to be sent to "The Marina".'

'These are final demands. Apparently they're tired of sending them to Norfolk. Why won't you let me deal with the business when you're away? Or at least engage a secretary to deal with things for you?'

'I've told you before. I won't have anyone else meddling with the business.'

'Then pay the bills. If we don't settle up soon, I'm afraid . . .'

'*Afraid*? You're always afraid, aren't you? You and Dad, you're like a pair of frightened rabbits, God knows where you'd be today if it wasn't for me.'

'Ralph, if we don't pay what we owe . . .' She went to her desk drawer and took out a sheaf of letters.

'Look – I've managed to keep them hidden from David so as not to worry him.' She leafed through them. 'They arrive every day. The stationers – the butcher – wine merchants – there's no end to them. The latest is from *Leisureways*, the holiday magazine we've always advertised with. If we lose our goodwill with them we'll lose a lot of business. So far your father knows nothing about them, but he'll have to soon.'

Ralph strode across the room and snatched the letters out of her hand. Tearing them in half, he tossed them into the wastepaper basket. 'There – that's what I think of petty tradesmen,' he said, dusting off his hands dismissively.

'They have to live too, Ralph. We're all in business to support each other. I paid as many bills as I could out of my own account, but there's nothing left in that now.'

'*Shut up*!' He rounded on her. 'For Christ's sake stop whingeing, woman. God knows why I bother to come home at all. I make time to come a day early to try and surprise you and what do I get? First I find you dining with another man; making a fool of me for all the staff to see. Then the moment you set eyes on me you start shooting off your mealy mouth about unpaid bills.'

Marie stood her ground. 'We have to talk about it seriously before you leave this time, Ralph. I insist. I have to live here and try to carry on. Since David's recovery he's trusted you to manage things.'

'Trusted me? Is that what he calls it?' Ralph snorted derisively. 'Why the hell can't he put the business in my name? Stubborn old fool.'

'One look at the unpaid bills would prove he'd been right all along on that account. Ralph, you owe it to him not to spoil the good name your father has built

351

for himself in business over the years. These people would have refused to supply us long ago if it hadn't been for that. Their patience won't last for ever though. What do we do then?'

'We go elsewhere.'

'We can't continue to do business on empty promises.' She went to him. 'Ralph, even though you keep me in the dark about the business, I know that we're doing well. "The Ocean" had a wonderful summer season. We've made a good profit. I'm sure the other hotels have too. There's plenty of money going into the bank, so why is there a problem? Where is it all going? Are you putting it into investments, shares or what?' He turned away from her in silence. 'Very well. If you won't tell me I'll have to . . .' She broke off, taking an involuntary step backwards. Ralph had turned swiftly, his face darkening with the danger signals she knew so well. His nostrils flared and she saw his hands clench white-knuckled at his sides.

'Are you threatening me?' He glowered at her. 'All right, so you know about my past and you think you can use it against me. You discovered that I'd signed one or two cheques in Dad's name. I had to do it, don't you see? I'm in an impossible bloody position. What do you think it makes me look like?' He banged his fist down hard on the dressing table, making the jars and brushes rattle. 'I'm made to look like a fool at every turn. By him – by you. I may not have much clout, thanks to Dad, but I'm still the one who's running this business, Marie, and don't you forget it.' He towered menacingly over her. 'Why should I be expected to know what's happening to the money when I don't have proper control? How could I buy shares or make investments when all the authority I have is a miserable power of attorney? You'd better

ask Dad. Maybe he's been making secret investments. You know how close to the chest he plays *his*
cards.' He glared down at her, his lips curling
scathingly. 'As for you, you're nothing but an
employee just like you've always been. If you're not
satisfied with the way things are here, you're at liberty
to leave any time you care to. See if your lover-boy
doctor needs a cleaning woman, why don't you?'

It was the same deadlock they arrived at every
time. As always Ralph was resorting to insults. First
came the verbal violence; any minute now he would
lose control and turn to physical abuse. Marie turned
wearily away. She was wasting her time as usual. She
should have known it would be no use.

To her great relief Ralph fell asleep almost as soon
as his head touched the pillow, but she lay awake long
after, staring into the darkness, her thoughts tor-
menting her. Where was all the money going? Even
his extravagant tastes and his womanising could
surely not use it all up so fast. Very soon now
something must happen. They'd be declared bankrupt. Maybe even worse, depending on what Ralph
was up to. One thing was certain: all three of them
would be out of work and homeless unless something
was done quickly. Yet Ralph persistently refused to
acknowledge that there was a problem. The burden
on Marie was becoming intolerable. If only he would
allow her access to the books. But they were locked
away at 'The Marina' in Norfolk now, and even if she
went there, there was no way she could get into the
safe. She wondered about the coming meeting with
an accountant that Ralph had spoken of. He'd been
hazy about that. Did he have some scheme up his
sleeve with which to save them? She desperately
hoped so. But when she'd asked, Ralph had refused
to tell her the man's name or even the name of the

firm he worked for. He was determined to keep her in the dark about their affairs.

Lying there in the darkness she went back in her mind to the day she had gone to see Father Jonathan at St Joseph's, to make her confession and to ask his advice about a divorce. She had confided in him about her past: about her conviction and the prison sentence she had served for a crime she hadn't committed; about the babies she had borne and given up; finally about her unhappy marriage. She had told him about Ralph's temper, his philandering and his cruel treatment of her. But when she tentatively mentioned divorce the priest had shaken his head.

'You are aware of the church's teaching on the subject, my child. Marriage is a holy sacrament. For those whom God has joined, the bond is for life.'

Marie's eyes had filled with despairing tears. 'But he's broken his vows, Father. He doesn't "love and cherish" me. He hasn't kept only to me either. I can't bear to think of spending the rest of my life with him.'

'And you, child, have you been entirely fair to him? You haven't been truthful with him about your past, have you? Maybe this is why God is punishing you.' Father Jonathan had smiled blandly and patted her hand. 'We all have our cross to bear, child. Your husband sounds a deeply unhappy man. Why don't you confess to him everything you have told me? I'm sure that if you show him love and consideration, if you prove yourself a good wife and work a little harder at your marriage, your prayers will be answered.' He looked at her. 'Why have you never had more children? There's nothing like a family to bind man and wife together.'

'I wanted us to have children, Father,' she told him, 'but Ralph didn't. He said they would interfere with the business.'

'In my experience women have ways of dealing with that situation,' he said, nodding with all the wisdom of the celibate priest. 'You're still quite a young woman. It could be your answer.'

Marie had come away from the Presbytery that afternoon with a heavy heart. She had pinned all her hopes on the advice of the priest but she had failed totally to make him understand her situation. If he only knew Ralph, perhaps he would see how impossible it would be to mend their differences by telling him her secret. Far from making him treat her more kindly he would use the knowledge to torture her further; throwing it in her face on every possible opportunity. No, it seemed there would be no help for her from any quarter – certainly not from the church.

Christmas Day was busy. In the morning there was the traditional visit from Santa Claus for the children and later cocktails for the adults in the bar. Marie, Ralph and David played host at Christmas lunch and later there was organised entertainment of various kinds: a guided walk for the energetic, video films in the lounge; a puppet show with clowns for the children in the games room, followed by a special festive tea and presents from the Christmas tree. Later there was a more sophisticated candlelit meal for the adults, followed by dancing till one.

Ralph behaved like the perfect host. He was charming to the women, courteous to the men and fatherly with the children. Watching him, Marie marvelled at his acting ability. He barely spoke to her or to his father and he had bought presents for neither of them, barely looking at the ones they had given him.

Noticing that David looked tired, Marie had seen

him up to the flat at half-past ten and waited until he was comfortably in bed with his book and a hot drink. When she went in to say goodnight to him he caught at her hand.

'You're very pale, love. Nothing worrying you, is there?'

She smiled and shook her head. 'It's only the extra work and the excitement. It's been well worth it though, hasn't it?'

He nodded. 'You've done marvellously. It's been a great Christmas. I'm sure they've all enjoyed it. You should have a holiday in the New Year though. Why not splash out and take yourself off somewhere nice and warm? Madeira perhaps. My treat. What do you say?'

Marie shook her head. 'I'm fine here with you. There'll be the summer season to plan soon anyway.' She bent and kissed his forehead. 'Don't you worry about me, David.'

On her way down in the lift to join the revellers she thought wryly about his suggestion. A holiday in the sun would be wonderful – if only she could be confident that the business would stand it. Little did David know of the knife-edge their financial situation balanced on.

In the small intimate ballroom the dance was in full swing. The lights were turned down low and the group they had engaged was playing a popular romantic ballad. She stood for a moment in the doorway, watching Ralph dancing with a young woman, the daughter of one of their regular family parties. He looked handsome in his dinner jacket, and perfectly relaxed as he laughed down into the girl's eyes. Just for a moment she wondered if all their troubles could be due to her. Did she bring out the worst in him? Did she irritate him beyond endurance?

Perhaps she made him as unhappy as he made her. It was a sobering thought.

'So there you are. Haven't had more than a fleeting glimpse of you all day.'

She looked up to see Philip smiling at her. 'Oh, I'm sorry if I've neglected you. It's been a hectic day.'

'Don't apologise. I know what it must be like for you – on duty every minute. I've had a wonderful time. Delicious food and good company. Renewing old acquaintances. Everyone here is always so friendly.' He held out his hand. 'But surely you can relax a little now? Dance with me?'

'I'd love to.' She smiled and put her hand into his as they moved towards the floor.

Philip was a good dancer and Marie found it easy and relaxing to match her steps to his on the small dance floor.

'Your husband seems to be in a good mood,' he said, looking over her shoulder to where Ralph shared a joke with his partner on the other side of the room.

'Oh – yes, he is.'

'David all right?'

'He's fine, just a little tired. I saw him to bed with a hot drink a little while ago.'

Philip looked down at her. 'Marie, you're looking so pale and worried. Is something wrong? Won't you let me help?'

She shook her head. 'There's nothing you or anyone else can do, Philip,' she said quietly. 'I only wish it was that simple.' She made herself smile up at him. 'It's Christmas. Let's forget it all for now, shall we?'

Leah had put Sally to sleep in Terry's room. It didn't take long to make up the bed and slip a hot water bottle between the sheets. Bill took himself rather moodily off to bed and Leah made cocoa in the kitchen where the two girls sat sipping it beside the Aga. Slowly, inch by inch, Sally began to relax.

'I hope it wasn't inconvenient,' she ventured. 'Dropping in on you like this. I haven't offended your – er – landlord, have I?'

'Bill?' Leah laughed. 'No. He's a dear really. I had already asked his permission to invite you to come for Christmas and he seemed to like the idea.'

'But I'd refused your invitation,' Sally said. 'And out there – when I turned up unexpectedly, you and he . . .'

'We'd been out to dinner and he'd had a few drinks,' Leah said lightly. 'I don't suppose he'll remember a thing about it in the morning.' She regarded Sally thoughtfully. 'Do you mind if I ask you what made you change your mind?'

Sally drained her cup before answering. 'I might as well be honest with you. I was lonely. I'd looked forward to the shop closing, to having four days to myself. But then, when I got home – to an empty house. Everyone had gone away for Christmas, you see. It was so silent, so cold and empty. All at once I felt . . .'

'Homesick?'

Sally looked up, her eyes bright. 'Do you get homesick too?'

Leah shook her head. 'Nothing to feel homesick for. My adoptive parents always gave me lavish presents. But Christmas was never really a homely family affair. Jack and Hilary were always too busy social climbing. It was one long round of smart parties, each one trying to out-do the others.'

'We used to have a lot of fun at Christmas,' Sally said wistfully. 'There was the Christingle carol service at Chapel, the Youth Club party, then we always spent Boxing Day with my Auntie Jean and my four cousins.'

'That sounds nice.' Leah tried to picture the cosy family party. 'When I was younger I usually got left with a baby sitter. If anything it was probably better fun in the children's home than at the Dobsons' – apart from Granny Dobson. She was the best thing about being adopted. But then, they didn't really want her either. We were two of a kind.' She glanced at Sally, remembering Marie's letter. 'Sally, have you ever thought about trying to find your – our – natural mother?'

The other girl shook her head. 'One mother per lifetime is quite enough for me, thank you. Besides, there doesn't seem to be much point after all this time, does there?'

Leah looked at the other girl's pale, tired face and decided to drop the subject. 'It's very late. Would you like to go up to bed now?'

'I would rather.' Sally held out her hand. 'Leah, I'm sorry – about the other time, I mean. We got off to a bad start. I understand how you feel about the baby. It's just that I can't keep it. I'd never manage, and anyway it would always remind me. I just want to . . .'

Leah took her hand and squeezed it. 'Please, don't – it's none of my business. I shouldn't have said what I did. It's late now. Maybe we'll talk tomorrow.' She smiled suddenly. 'Do you know, I've just realised something. This is the very first Christmas that I've ever spent with a member of my own family. That has to make it special, doesn't it?'

Bill had quite recovered his good nature by morning. He and Leah exchanged the small presents they had bought for each other and she wrapped up a bottle of perfume she had treated herself to and gave it to Sally. As she opened the little package the girl's eyes were misty.

'Oh. I wasn't expecting this,' she said. 'I haven't got you anything. I feel awful.'

'Well, don't,' Leah said as she whisked away the breakfast dishes. 'You brought yourself, after all. That was the best present I could have had. Tell you what, though, you can be my kitchen maid for the morning. That'll let Bill off the hook. I know he's dying to go off to the local and drink himself legless with all his mates.'

'Don't you believe it. That's just a nice way of telling me to get lost,' he said in Sally's ear as he passed. But when she looked up at him with anxious eyes she saw that he was smiling. 'You can come again, Sally,' he told her. 'I warn you, this long lost sister of yours is a positive slave driver when she's in the kitchen. You don't know what you've let yourself in for.'

The two of them worked happily together and when everything was under control Sally asked if she could lay the table.

Leah smiled. 'Please do. You'll find the table cloths in the dresser drawer.'

'Isn't there anything more festive than these seersuckers?' Sally asked after a few minutes' searching.

Leah turned thoughtfully. 'I don't know. You could have a look in the linen cupboard on the landing. I think I've seen some table linen stored away in there. Have a good rummage. Bill won't mind.'

Sally was gone for quite a long time, but she finally reappeared carrying a long lace curtain, a crimson

360

satin bedspread and a reel of red ribbon. When the white lace was laid over the red satin the effect was quite stunning. Leah gasped.

'What a clever idea.' She watched as Sally proceeded to gather up the edges of the lace at intervals, threading the red ribbon through and tying it in bows. Then she took three of the white chrysanthemums from the vase on the dresser, and, with the rest of the ribbon and a few pieces of ivy taken from the back yard wall, proceeded to make an effective little table arrangement. Leah's eyes were round with admiration.

'Hey, that's brilliant,' she said delightedly. 'Wait till Bill sees it.'

Sally looked doubtfully at the willow pattern plates Leah had put to warm beside the Aga. 'Isn't there any other china?'

Leah grinned, urged on by Sally's creativeness. 'Let's have a look. I'm sure there must be something more up-market somewhere.' Searching in the dresser cupboards together, they found an elegant white and gold Victorian dinner service stacked away at the back. It was incomplete, but there were more than enough dishes for the three of them. The vegetable tureens with their delicately scrolled handles and domed lids looked just right on the crimson and white cloth.

Leah stood back to admire her sister's work. 'It looks wonderful. We wouldn't have had anything as grand as this if it hadn't been for you.'

'It's my job,' Sally said. 'It's all I've ever wanted to do. The only thing I'm any good at. At the shop where I work now I'm not much more than a counter assistant, but once I've had the – when I'm free again, I mean to get something better. Maybe one day I'll even start a business of my own.'

Bill came back from the pub ravenous and waving a bottle of beaujolais. 'Got this at the pub. Find me the corkscrew, Leah.' He put down the bottle and rubbed his hands together. 'God, it's cold,' he said as he shrugged off his jacket. Then he caught sight of the festive table and stopped short. '*Wow*! Get that. If I'd known you were planning something on this scale, I'd have changed into something more formal.'

Leah beamed. 'Great, isn't it? You can thank Sally. She did it all, out of nothing too.'

'It's brilliant.' Bill walked round the table examining everything. 'Maybe we should have eaten in the dining room upstairs,' he said.

'Oh, no.' Leah put the steaming golden-brown turkey in the centre of the table. 'It's much more cosy and homely down here.'

Bill sat down at the table, fingering the lace cloth thoughtfully. 'You're a very talented pair, aren't you? When you start your mobile catering service, Leah, Sally here could do the table decorations or whatever you call them.' He looked in anticipation at the succulent white slices of turkey that Leah was expertly carving. 'That looks and smells wonderful.' He uncorked the wine and began to pour. Suddenly he jumped up from the table. 'We can't let this occasion go by without a photograph,' he said. 'Where's my trusty polaroid?' He took the camera from its case. 'Move in together. That's right.' The camera buzzed as the picture emerged. 'There, recorded for posterity.' He propped the photograph up on the dresser and returned to pouring the wine.

'What's this mobile catering service you mentioned?' Sally asked.

'It's just Bill's pipe dream,' Leah told her. 'Something he's planning for his old age.'

'Not at all,' Bill said with his mouth full. 'The

Italian restaurant where Leah's been working has just closed, which leaves her unemployed. She's a great little cook and she's got a real flair for catering. Now that she's had some experience I've suggested that she might start hiring herself out – dinner parties, buffets, that kind of thing.'

'What a good idea.' Sally looked enquiringly at Leah. 'Don't you fancy it?'

She shook her head. 'It isn't as simple as it sounds. There'd be all kinds of snags – least of which is the fact that I don't have the kind of money to get a project like that off the ground.'

Bill sighed. 'I've *told* you, I'll . . .'

'Bill.' Leah put down her knife and fork and shot him a warning look. 'Please. Not now. It's Christmas Day.'

'Okay, if you say so.' He held up his hands in surrender. 'But I still think it's a damned good idea.'

After they had washed up Leah made a pot of coffee and they carried the tray upstairs to the living room and sat talking. At least Bill and Leah talked. Sally felt silent and after a while asked Leah quietly if anyone would object to her going upstairs for a nap.

'Of course. Please do,' Leah said. 'Take advantage of all the rest you can get.'

Sally stood up, one hand in the small of her back. 'Are you sure you don't mind? I feel so rude and unsociable.'

'Off you go,' Bill instructed. 'Tell you what, I'll wake you about six with a cup of tea, then we'll all watch the telly like a really boring family. How's that?'

Sally smiled. 'You're very kind.'

After she had gone Leah was thoughtful. Three strangers, she told herself pensively. We're three misfits making the best of things. All of us would

363

probably rather be somewhere else if we had the choice. Or at least in the company of some*one* else. Bill would like to be with Janet, his wife, even if he won't admit it. Sally would clearly like to be with her parents. And I . . . She stifled a sigh, refusing to admit to herself how much she missed Terry. Deep inside an illogical voice insisted that as long as she didn't acknowledge what he had come to mean to her it couldn't hurt.

Bill dozed off in his chair, the effects of a morning's drinking followed by a heavy lunch. Leah watched him for a while, then wandered up to her room, combed her hair and renewed her make-up. She was on the landing and about to go down again when she thought she heard a faint sound. She stopped, inclining her head to listen. It came again, unmistakably this time – a muffled groan. Crossing the landing she pushed open the door of Terry's room and peered across the darkening room towards the bed.

'Sally, are you all right?' Reaching out, she found the switch and the next moment the room was flooded with light. Sally sat couched at the top of the bed, her back against the headboard and her knees drawn up to her chin. One clenched fist was pressed against her mouth and her face was deathly white. Leah's heart missed a beat.

'*Sally*! My God, what is it?'

'A pain – a bad pain – in my back.' Sally spoke with difficulty. 'It's been coming and going all afternoon. I thought it must be indigestion. I thought if I lay down it would go but . . . Leah, I'm sorry but I think – I'm afraid it might be – the – baby.'

Leah sat on the bed and took her hand. 'But surely it can't be? It's not time yet, is it? I mean, when's it supposed to be due?'

'Not for six weeks yet.' Tears began to fill Sally's huge frightened eyes and run down her cheeks. 'What do you think I should do?'

Although she tried to hide it, Leah was frightened too. She hadn't the slightest idea about childbirth – what it entailed or what one was supposed to do. It was Christmas Day. Suppose there were no ambulances? Suppose she couldn't find a doctor in time? Sally looked so ill, so racked with pain. Suppose it were to be born here with no medical help? Suppose they both died because of her ignorance? Swallowing the panic that pounded in her chest, she commanded herself: Calm down. She *needs* you. She's your sister and she's relying on you. The thought seemed to give her strength and confidence. Never in her life had anyone actually needed her before. Smiling, she laid cool fingers against Sally's cheek:

'Look, try to relax. And don't worry, Sally. Everything will be all right, I promise. Just trust me. I'll take care of you. Just hang on a minute while I get some help. I'll be right back. I won't leave you.'

Chapter 18

When Leah first wakened Bill and told him that Sally's baby was on the way he blinked at her uncomprehendingly. Then suddenly he was wide awake and leaping into action. Standing in the doorway of Terry's room he took one look at Sally and said: 'Right. We can't wait around for an ambulance. I'll get the car. Bring her downstairs.'

The journey to the hospital was tense. The roads seemed unreasonably full of traffic for Christmas Day. Leah sat on the edge of her seat, willing the car forward and chewing her nails with anxiety, whilst Sally half sat, half crouched on the back seat, rigid with pain and crying out pitifully at every bump and turn. It was with some relief that Bill drove on to the forecourt of the nearest hospital – only to find that the Accident and Emergency department was closed. As he made to get back into the car Leah put out a hand to stop him.

'We can't just go,' she said. 'At least it's a hospital. There are doctors and nurses in there. We have to get her some help, Bill – and quickly.'

They helped Sally out of the car and into the entrance hall. 'Please, can you help us?' Leah asked the receptionist. 'My sister is having a baby.'

'Are you booked in here?' The girl looked at Sally suspiciously.

Between chattering teeth she said: 'N-no. St Mary's, Edgware.'

'Then you'll have to go there.' Bill stepped forward, his face grim. 'Look, you can see the girl needs help. She's in no state to go anywhere. It's an emergency.'

'But if she's booked with another hospital, why didn't she go *there*?'

Bill glowered. 'Look, I'm not going to stand here arguing with you.' He produced his press card. 'I'm on the *Daily Globe*,' he said crisply. 'Do you want to put this hospital on the front page? It'd look good, wouldn't it? "*Christmas mother is told: Have your baby somewhere else. Shades of 'no room at the inn'.*"'

White with anger and muttering something about blackmail, the girl picked up the telephone. Minutes later the lift doors opened and a smiling porter appeared with a wheelchair.

'Any more for the skylark then?' he asked cheerfully.

Sally was helped into the chair and the four of them got into the lift. On the maternity ward a sister quickly summed up the situation and took charge.

'We've prepared that side ward.' She directed the porter. 'You can take her in there.' She turned to Leah and Bill. 'You can wait there.' She indicated a row of chairs.

'Will the baby be born soon?' Leah asked.

The sister gave a superior little smile. 'Good heavens, no. Not for hours yet.'

'Can I stay with her till it is?'

The sister frowned as she looked from one to the other. 'Are you the father?' she asked Bill.

'No, he's just a friend who helped us,' Leah explained. 'I'm her sister. Her *twin* sister,' she added.

The sister looked her up and down doubtfully.

'Well, it's unusual – but all right. You'll have to wait until the duty doctor has seen her though.' She bustled away.

'Starchy cow,' Bill muttered as he sank onto a chair.

Leah touched his arm. 'Bill – thanks for all you've done. I don't know what we'd have done without you down there in reception.' He looked huge and incongruous, sitting there on the flimsy plastic chair, his large feet spread out and his shoulders hunched into the collar of his leather jacket. 'Look, no need for you to hang around. Why don't you go home?'

'Might as well see it through now,' he said gruffly. 'Anyway, I'd like to get my breath back first if you don't mind. One minute I'm sleeping off my Christmas dinner, the next I'm practically delivering a baby.' He looked at her quizzically. 'You're not really going to stay with her while it's born, are you?'

Leah nodded. 'I promised, I can't let her down. She's only got me.'

Bill sighed and shook his head. 'I don't know. The more I see of life and human nature the more I marvel at it. Here you are, with a twin sister you hardly know – doing your best to have her damned baby for her.' He looked at her with a mixture of affection and exasperation. 'She's in good hands, you know. I don't suppose there's anything you can do – except get in everyone's bloody way. They won't thank you for it.'

'I don't care. She's just a body to them. I'm her sister.' Her face was pale, her lips set in a determined line. He guessed rightly that she was quaking inwardly, but apart from her pallor she showed no outward sign. 'She's all alone,' she said. 'I know what that feels like. I promised to stay with her and I will.'

'Okay.' He chuckled indulgently and slipped an arm round her shoulders. 'You've got guts, I'll say

369

that for you. Wild horses wouldn't drag me in there. One whiff of that antiseptic pong is enough to make my stomach heave.'

'Look, Bill, you heard what the sister said. It could be hours. Please go home.'

'Well, if you're sure.' He looked at her. 'Have you got any money for a taxi?' He slipped a hand into his pocket and pushed a note into her hand. 'That ought to take care of it. Well – see you later then. Good luck.'

When the sister finally allowed Leah into the side ward where Sally lay they were preparing to transfer her to the delivery room. Leah was relieved to see that she looked more relaxed.

'She's had an injection of something to help her,' the sister explained. 'She was very tired and stressed. But it won't last long. She's got a lot of hard work in front of her.'

'She will be all right, won't she?' Leah asked anxiously. 'The baby isn't due yet and . . .'

'It's premature and very small, but smaller ones than that have survived,' Sister told her briskly. 'Your sister isn't in very good shape, though. Looks as though she hasn't been taking proper care of herself.' She looked accusingly at Leah. 'Are there any other relatives you should contact – parents?'

'No.'

'A husband or partner then?' she added hopefully. When Leah shook her head again she gave an exasperated little shake of her head and turned her attention to her patient.

Walking beside the trolley, holding tightly to Sally's hand Leah began to pray.

Please God let her be all right. Please God . . . She repeated the words over and over mechanically inside her head, but they failed to raise any reassurance for her. They were like a useless litany, falling impotently into a void; unheard – unanswered.

In the sluice next door to the delivery room Leah was instructed to scrub up and given a gown and a mask to wear. As she rejoined Sally she saw that she was becoming restless again. The effects of the drug were wearing off and the pattern of her pain was undergoing a subtle change. Leah took her hand and smiled down at her.

'I'm here,' she said. 'Don't worry, everything will be all right.'

In the hours that followed Leah had never seen anyone work so hard or suffer so much. There were times when she was terribly afraid that it was more than Sally's frail body could stand, but the midwife and nurses were brisk and efficient. It seemed no more than routine practice to them as they instructed, encouraged and cajoled their patient. Leah tried hard not to reveal her shock and apprehension as she wiped the beads of sweat from her sister's agonised brow. She'd had no idea that childbirth could be so cruel and terrible. As the hours dragged by and Sally grew more and more exhausted she began to protest weakly that she could not go on. She begged them to let her sleep, to give her something to make it stop, but the process of labour ground on remorselessly; taking control of her tortured body. There was no turning back.

It was just after dawn when the tension in the delivery room suddenly reached a peak. At last the birth was imminent. First, to the midwife's delight, the crown of a small round head appeared. Her words of encouragement sharpened. Then, soon after the head, the child's body emerged, to be held up in triumph by the midwife.

'All over. It's a little boy.'

Deftly, she cleared the child's airway. There was a spluttering gasp and then a thin wail rose from the tiny mouth. A wave of relief in the form of a subdued flutter of laughter went round the delivery room. Leah swallowed hard at the lump in her throat and blinked at the tears that blurred her vision.

The midwife severed the cord as the final stage of the birth was completed. She wrapped the tiny wriggling morsel in a surgical towel and laid him in Sally's arms.

'Say hello to your son,' she said with a smile. 'Just for a minute then he'll have to go into the incubator. He's very small, but at least he's got a good voice.'

Propped up on pillows, her hair plastered damply to her face, Sally took the child and gazed numbly down at him. Her face still glistening with sweat and creased with the ravages of pain, she looked down at the baby for a moment, then held him out to Leah.

'Here, take him. You hold him too. It might be the only chance you get.'

From the end of the towel two minute, bluish pink feet emerged attached to touchingly skinny little legs that kicked feebly. Very gingerly Leah took the bundle from Sally and gazed down at the crumpled little face. Huge dark blue eyes were blinking at the glaring white light and the tiny rosebud mouth pouted pathetically. To Leah it was as though he was bewildered – wondering what he could possibly have done wrong to be so ignominiously ejected, naked from his warm, safe bed; torn from his mother and cast into a harshly bright, uncaring world. She cuddled him close, her heart overwhelmed with love and aching pity.

'Oh, Sally,' she breathed. 'He's so sweet and so *little*. You aren't really – you can't . . . ?' She turned to her sister, only to see that she had fallen into the fathomless sleep of the totally exhausted.

At Melbury Street Bill cooked Leah an early breakfast, then insisted that she got some sleep. When she awoke it was four o'clock. Daylight had come and gone and it was already dark again. Annoyed with Bill for letting her sleep so long, she dressed hurriedly and rushed back to the hospital. On the ward when she asked for Sally she was ushered into a room and asked to wait. Sitting alone in the bare little waiting room Leah grew more and more apprehensive as the minutes ticked by. What had happened? Why wouldn't they let her see Sally?

At last a man in a white coat came in and carefully closed the door. He was tall, with untidy dark hair, a long, thin face and wire-rimmed spectacles. He introduced himself as Doctor Gerald Freeman, the obstetrics registrar. He offered her his hand briefly and sat down. He shuffled the notes he held and jabbed at the bridge of his glasses with one forefinger. It was his first week on this ward and the first time he'd been given a job of this kind. He'd always been slightly afraid of women and didn't know how to make it sound better than it was.

'My sister . . .' Leah prompted, unable to bear the suspense. 'Is she all right?'

He looked up at her and cleared his throat. 'I'm – er – afraid your sister suffered a severe haemorrhage this morning.' He looked at her gravely over the tops of his glasses. 'We tried very hard but I'm afraid . . .'

'She's *dead*?' Leah leapt to her feet, one hand to her mouth. 'Sally's dead?'

'Oh no, *no*.' Appalled at his own clumsiness, he leapt to his feet and put out a hand to steady her. God, but he was making a hash of this. He'd known he would. 'Please – please don't worry. She's very poorly but not critical. The bad news is that we had to perform an emergency hysterectomy, which means that she won't be able to have any more children. It's very sad in someone as young as your sister. Naturally we would have avoided it if we could, but she was so weak after the birth. She was anaemic and rather undernourished too. She simply couldn't afford to go on losing blood like that.'

'I see.' Weak with relief, Leah sank down onto the chair again. She looked up at him. 'And – the baby?'

Doctor Freeman's tension relaxed a little. 'The baby is holding his own quite well for such a little fellow. He only weighed four and three-quarter pounds, you know.'

'She's explained that he is to go for adoption?'

He frowned. 'I didn't realise that. In that case he'll have to be transferred to the hospital where your sister was to have been delivered, but he isn't fit for that yet.'

Leah bit her lip. 'Good. What I mean is, I'm hoping to try and make her change her mind.'

He frowned. 'She really mustn't be worried with anything so traumatic at the moment.'

'No, of course not.'

'Later, of course, it will be up to you.'

'Can I see her?'

'She's in intensive care and still drowsy from the anaesthetic at the moment. But you can slip in just for a minute or two.'

Sally was asleep. Leah was awed and dismayed by the array of technology in the intensive care unit; the bleeping monitors and the various tubes that Sally seemed to be attached to. The pallor of her skin and the way she seemed to have shrunk and diminished in just a few hours shocked her. It occurred to her that

Sally's adoptive parents really should be notified whether she liked it or not, but she didn't have their address. Hannah would know it. Maybe she should get in touch with her. Even though Sally didn't want them to know it was only fair. The weight of responsibility was heavy on Leah's shoulders as she tiptoed out of the ward. In the corridor she asked a nurse if she could see the baby.

In the special care baby unit he lay in his incubator, naked except for a nappy that looked too large for him and something that looked like a doll's bonnet on his head. From time to time he made a little convulsive movement as though he were dreaming. As she looked down at him, he opened his enormous blue eyes and seemed to look straight up at her. One tiny fist waved like a sea anemone. It seemed to Leah as she stood there looking down at Sally's son that the tiny clenched fist challenged the world, announced his determination to survive – to hang on to his identity.

'The hospital chaplain would christen him,' said the nurse. 'Do you think your sister would like that?'

Suddenly it was desperately important to Leah that this was done. Sally's little son must have a name, an identity.

'Yes, I'm sure she would,' she said decisively. 'His name is to be James – Jamie.'

'Good. I'll make a note of it. The chaplain will be round later.' The nurse walked off and Leah leaned over the incubator. 'Hear that?' she whispered. 'Your name is Jamie. I hope you like it.'

In the hospital cafeteria on the ground floor she bought herself a cup of tea and searched her handbag for Hannah's number. Later, under the perspex hood of the public telephone, she listened to Hannah's recorded voice on the answering machine as it relayed its disembodied message. As she listened she caught sight of balloons and coloured paperchains decorating the hospital entrance hall and remembered suddenly that it was still Christmas. Hannah would be away somewhere, celebrating with friends. As she spoke the inadequate, unemotional words she wondered how long it would be before Hannah heard them. Certainly too late to be of any help now. She replaced the receiver and stood there chewing her thumb nail – until an idea that had hung shadow-like in the back of her mind all day, began to develop into a full-blown intention.

She was fairly sure that the envelope in which Marie Evans had enclosed her letter had borne a Dorset postmark. Branksome – that was it. And she remembered that Hannah had mentioned that Marie ran a hotel. If she were to look up all the Evanses in that area residing in hotels . . . She frowned and bit her lip. It could be that only the name of the hotel was listed. And the libraries were closed today anyway, so where would she find the appropriate directory? Then she remembered: Bill had them all. As a journalist he frequently needed them. She'd seen them, stacked on the bookshelf in the room he used as a study.

Outside it was raining. Icy needles whipped her cheeks as she waited impatiently outside the hospital for the bus.

As she let herself in at the area door, a murmur of voices came from the kitchen. Damn! Bill had a visitor. Still, she was sure he wouldn't mind if she slipped into his study and used his directories. Miraculously she found it almost at once. Evans, The Ocean Hotel, Branksome. The initial was 'D', but there was only one so it was worth taking a chance. She replaced the directory carefully and slipped downstairs again. In the hall she paused. Rather than risk interruption it would be better to ring from the kiosk on the corner. Thrusting her arms into the sleeves of her jacket she slipped quietly out of the house again.

'Ocean Hotel. Can I help you?' The voice was brisk and business-like. Leah swallowed hard, hoping she'd got the right number.

'I – er – can I speak to Mrs Evans, please? Mrs Marie Evans.'

'Who shall I say is calling?'

She was right then. In a few minutes she'd be speaking to her mother. 'Miss Dobson. Tell her, Leah Dobson.' Leah held her breath, listening to the drumming of her own heart as she waited.

'You're through,' the receptionist announced. Then a soft voice said hesitantly:

'Hello – Leah? I'm so sorry to have missed meeting you. I wish I could explain to you . . .'

'Look, I'm going to have to hurry. I'm in a call box and I don't have any more change. There's something I think you should know.'

'Please tell me,' Marie said.

Leah licked her dry lips. 'My sister, Sally – *Sarah*, I mean – is very ill. She had an emergency operation this morning. I haven't time to explain everything now, but I thought you might want to come and see her.' She paused for breath. At the other end she thought she heard Marie trying to say something, but she couldn't be sure. In any case she had to press on before the money ran out.

'Please – will you come?' she asked. 'I'm sure it would help.' She bit her lip hard, praying that the handful of coins she had fed into the box would be sufficient. Frantically, she tried to remember whether Boxing Day still carried cheap-rate all day.

At the other end Marie said. 'Quick, tell me the name of the hospital – and the address. I've got a pencil.'

Leah rattled off the address and her own telephone number. 'I thought maybe we should meet first,' she added. 'Then I could explain. There's a hotel near the hospital – "The Greenway". It's easy to find. Anyone will tell you.'

'"The Greenway". I've got that,' Marie said. 'I'll ring you back and let you know. But I'll come. Somehow. Don't worry, I . . .' There was a click as the money ran out and the dialling tone intervened. With a sigh of relief Leah replaced the receiver. Would Marie really come? She'd let her down that other time. But as she walked back down the street she felt buoyed up, suddenly sure that this time nothing would stop Marie Evans from making contact with her daughters.

As she let herself in at the basement door she suddenly realised how tired and hungry she was. Opening the kitchen door she stopped short on the threshold. She'd forgotten Bill's visitor. A woman sat at the table. Tall and blonde, she wore the glossy veneer that comes with success. Her expensively cut suit and flawless make-up skilfully concealed the fact that she was well past the first flush of youth. Her hands were exquisitely manicured and her aggressively blonde hair was coiffured into tortured perfection. She looked up in surprise, recrossing long, slim legs sheathed in cobweb-sheer lycra.

'Well, well, who have we here?'

Leah looked at Bill who got up from the table. 'This is Leah,' he said, looking slightly hang-dog. 'She's one of my tenants. Leah, this is Janet, my wife.'

'*Ex*-wife,' Janet qualified. Her shrewd grey eyes looked Leah up and down with frank appraisal, taking in the heavy wind-blown dark hair and

sparkling brown eyes; the perfect complexion, innocent of make-up and rosy from the cold air. With one
sweeping gaze she took in the girl's clothes; jeans and
a denim jacket, the badge of youth. But she saw that
she wore them with a grace and style that very few
young people possessed. Not a day over twenty, Janet
told herself wryly. Nubile – the kind who can exude
sexuality without lifting so much as an eyelash, damn
her. She glanced at Bill whose faint flush was as good
as a confession. Cynical, world-weary journalist he
might be, but he was still a total pushover when it
came to an attractive face and figure. And he'd never
been able to hide the truth from her.

'*One* of your tenants, did you say, darling – or your
only tenant?'

'I do have another actually – Terry – but he's up
north at the moment,' Bill stumbled.

'My sister has been staying here for Christmas,'
Leah said. 'She's in hospital.' She looked appealingly
at Bill. 'I came to tell you, Sally's had some kind of
relapse. She's had an emergency operation. She's
very ill – in intensive care. I was going to grab
something to eat before I go back to the hospital. But
I can see you're busy . . .'

Janet got up and took Bill's arm firmly. 'Don't
mind us, my dear. We can talk upstairs,' she said. 'Do
please have your meal. Bill and I have a lot to catch up
on, haven't we, darling? Even more than I thought,
by the look of things.'

Leah returned to Melbury Street that night, totally
exhausted. It was late when she finally left the
hospital and she had to wait for what seemed an
eternity for a bus. She was making herself a hot drink
in the kitchen when Bill appeared in the doorway
wearing his dressing gown.

379

'I heard you come in,' he said, closing the door. 'How's Sally?'

Leah sank into a chair by the Aga, her hands gratefully wrapped round her mug of cocoa. 'They say she's stable. She's still very ill though. I just sat there, watching her and holding her hand. I've never felt so helpless in my life.' She looked up at him. 'They had to perform a hysterectomy, Bill. That means she'll never be able to have another child.

He crossed the room to lay a large hand on her shoulder. 'That's rotten luck. I'm sorry, love. How's the kid?'

Leah's face relaxed a little. 'He's okay. They say he's making good progress. He's a tough little thing. It's as though all Sally's strength went into him. She gave him all she had. And now she's – she's giving him away.' She clamped her teeth over her quivering lower lip, determined not to let him see how much the thought affected her.

He squeezed her shoulder. 'Maybe it's best this way, love,' he said soothingly. 'Maybe it's for the kid's own good.'

'They must have said that about Sally and me,' Leah said angrily. 'But no one really knows, do they? No one can ever be sure. People who offload their kids just say that to make themselves feel better.'

'We're all guilty of self-justification, love,' he said. 'We can't always do the things we know we should do. Saying it's for the best is the only thing that makes life bearable at times like that.'

Leah sipped her cocoa. 'I know. That why *I* made a decision of my own today. I rang my mother.'

'Your mother? At Nenebridge, you mean?'

She stared at him. '*Hilary*? God, no. I mean my real mother.'

He pursed his lips. 'Was that wise?'

She shrugged wearily. 'Wise or not, I've done it. I can't cope with the situation on my own. I need someone to help – emotionally if nothing else. And so will Sally once she comes to properly. Our mother seemed the obvious choice.'

'But she's a stranger, Leah. You've never even met her.'

'She's also my mother – and Sally's mother too. She's been through all this herself, Bill.' She looked up at him. 'She said she'd come. She hasn't rung, has she?'

He shook his head. 'No.'

'She will. Tomorrow.' The look she gave him made it clear that the subject was closed. 'So – where's your – er . . . Where's Janet?' Did she have to go back?'

He turned away and pretended to warm his hands at the Aga. 'No. As a matter of fact she's – staying the night.'

'I see.'

He glanced at her, his eyes slightly defensive. 'We're still good friends, you know.'

'Of course. It must have been a surprise, her arriving like that, after she'd said she couldn't come.'

Bill shrugged. 'She likes to drop by when she's in Town – make sure I'm all right.'

To make sure you're still available, Leah wanted to say. She smiled up at him. 'What was it really – does she want something?' She shook her head. 'Sorry, Bill, that was a bitchy thing to say. Anyway, it's none of my business.'

'Her arrival was a surprise to me too as a matter of fact,' he said. 'I still don't know the real reason for it to be honest. I rather suspect that something went wrong with the new relationship. I expect she'll tell me eventually.'

'Pillow talk, eh?'

381

He put out a hand and touched her cheek. 'I'm sorry, kid. I'd really like to have been here for you tonight, Leah, like the loving friend I promised to be.'

'You've already been a great help, Bill. We'd never have managed without you.' She hid her face in her mug of cocoa. Why did men automatically interpret being friends as going to bed, and consider sex some kind of cure-all? At the moment it was the last thing on her mind. Nevertheless, she appreciated his concern.

'You'd better get back to Janet before she notices you've gone,' she said with a rueful smile. 'I can't afford to make any enemies right now.'

Leah was dreaming of Nenebridge. It was Sunday morning and the church bells were ringing. Suddenly she wakened and lay for a few seconds, drowsily wondering why the bells sounded so strange and different. Then she realised that what she was actually hearing was the telephone. She jumped out of bed and ran downstairs, but as she reached the bend in the stairs she saw that Janet Fenton had beaten her to it. She turned, looking up as Leah appeared.

'It's for you.' She held out the receiver. 'Someone called Marie Evans.'

Leah ran down the stairs to take the receiver from her. 'Hello. Leah Dobson here.'

'Leah, this is Marie, your . . . Marie Evans. I'm at the railway station. The London train leaves in a few minutes. I should be at the hotel by about ten-thirty. Shall I see you there?'

Leah's head was spinning as she tried to sort out whether she really was awake or still dreaming. 'Oh – er – yes, of course. I'll wait for you in the reception hall at half-past ten.'

'All right. Oh, here's the train. Goodb . . .' Marie's voice was cut off abruptly as she hurriedly dropped the receiver.

It was only after she had put the phone down that Leah realised that neither of them had much idea of what the other looked like.

'Not bad news, I hope.'

Leah turned to see that Janet was still standing behind her. She wore Bill's dressing gown, but Leah couldn't help noticing that she had taken the trouble to run a comb through her hair and apply some lipstick.

'No. It was my sister's – my . . . A relative who's coming to visit her today.' Leah hopped from one foot to the other, suddenly aware of the chill of the tiled floor on her bare feet and the fact that she wore only the baseball shirt she used as a nightdress.

For her part, Janet was aware of long, shapely legs and thighs, still lightly tanned from last summer's sun, and under the clinging cotton, a shape that owed nothing to an expensive bra and girdle. 'I'd put something on if I were you,' she advised pointedly. 'I hope you're not in the habit of running around dressed like that. You'll catch your death of cold.' She walked down the basement stairs to the kitchen and Leah followed her, grabbing a coat from the row of hooks by the door as she went.

'Actually I'm not in the habit of walking around in my underwear,' she said. 'The telephone woke me and I got straight out of bed to answer it.'

Janet smiled as she filled the kettle and set it on top of the Aga. 'Oh, don't worry. I'm not accusing you of corrupting Bill's morals. It's a bit on the late side for that. And, he's well able to take care of himself.' She gave Leah a quizzical look as she helped herself to a cigarette from the packet Bill had left on the dresser.

'Anyway, it'd take more than a flash of thigh to turn him into a Don Juan these days, poor old lad.' She drew hard on the cigarette and began to get mugs out of the cupboard. 'You might even be surprised to learn that I'm pleased he's got some feminine company.'

'Oh, really?' Leah watched warily as Janet went about the business of making tea.

'Yes, really. He'd turn into a slob without a woman around the place to keep him on his toes.' She smiled at Leah. 'We might be divorced but I'm still fond of the silly old sod.'

'Bill's a nice guy,' Leah said. 'He's been very kind to me – and to Sally.'

Janet smiled. 'Why shouldn't he? I'm sure you've been kind to him too.'

'I lost my job just before Christmas,' Leah told her. 'I was working at an Italian restaurant just round the corner, but the couple who ran it have decided to go home to Italy. Bill's been trying to encourage me to start up a catering service on my own.'

'That sounds like Bill. He's an old softie really, under that tough shell he hides behind.' Janet looked speculatively at Leah. 'And he's obviously fond of you. I've been hearing all about the marvellous Christmas dinner you and your sister prepared.' She picked up the polaroid snap that was still propped up on the dresser. 'I take it he took this?'

'Yes. On Christmas Day.' Leah took the photograph from her. It was the first time she'd actually looked at it properly. Sally looked so frail, with her blonde hair and delicate features. By contrast Leah's abundant dark hair and expressive brown eyes seemed to dominate the picture.

'You look happy,' Janet said, taking the photograph back.

'Yes. I think we were – just for a little while.' Leah met the cool grey eyes, trying to see beyond their unconcerned smile. She'd been wondering whether Janet was sincere or if her remarks carried an oblique accusation. Now she came down on the side of sincerity. Last night Bill's ex-wife seemed cold and brittle, with an acid edge to her tongue. But this morning she was softer and definitely more approachable. Perhaps it was the dressing gown.

There was a pause as the two silently assessed each other.

'I'm sorry if the phone woke you,' Leah said.

'It's all right, I was up anyway.' Janet exhaled another cloud of smoke. 'As a matter of fact I was half expecting a call myself.' She smiled. 'I'm sorry about your sister. I hope she's improving.'

'She's making progress. They don't tell you much.'

'Baby all right?'

'He's doing fine. No problems there, except . . .' Leah trailed off.

'I just wondered if things were worse,' Janet said, nodding towards the door. 'Early morning calls, relatives travelling from afar and all that.' She poured milk and tea into two mugs, watching Leah's face out of the corner of her eye.

'Oh, no. It was someone I asked to come. Sally's mother as a matter of fact.'

Janet's eyebrows rose. '*Sally's*? But surely, if you're sisters, she's your mother too?'

'Oh, yes, of course – our mother. We're twins actually.'

'Really? You surprise me. I hadn't realised you were twin sisters. You're not at all alike.' Janet smiled. 'Your mother must be very excited – looking forward to seeing her first grandchild. I take it this is her first?' She pushed one of the mugs across the table towards Leah. 'Here – have some tea. Come and get warm. Your feet are going blue.'

'Thanks.' Leah took the mug in both hands and sat down in the chair close to the Aga, tucking her bare feet up under her. 'Actually it isn't quite as simple as that,' she said. 'Sally and I were separated and adopted at birth, you see. As a matter of fact I didn't even know I had a sister till quite recently and neither of us knows our natural mother at all. This will be the first time either of us has met her.'

Janet's expression sharpened. 'Well, you certainly know how to choose your moment,' she said, her eyes glittering with interest. 'Talk about dramatic effect.'

'It's not just that. There's a problem and I'm at my wits' end. Sally keeps insisting that she's going to give up her baby for adoption, you see. I'm sure she's making the wrong decision and I want to get her to change her mind. I contacted our mother as a sort of last resort.'

'In an attempt to stop history from repeating itself, you mean? How fascinating. But you say you haven't met. How did you know where to find her?'

'I've been trying to trace her for some time. Recently I had some success. A social worker put us in touch.'

'Mmm, I always think that situation must be difficult,' Janet said thoughtfully. 'Years on like this, when the woman in question is married, probably with a new family and a whole new life.'

'I suppose it could have been awkward. As it happens she doesn't have any other children though,' Leah told her. 'We were to have met a few weeks ago, but something went wrong on that occasion and the meeting fell through.'

'Does she know about Sally's decision?'

'No. She doesn't even know about the baby yet.'

'I see. And what about Sally? Is she aware that she's about to meet her natural mother for the first time?'

'Well – no. She's been too ill to talk much so far. I arranged it rather on impulse.'

Janet drew hard on her cigarette, blowing out the smoke with an expressive hiss. 'Phew! Sensational surprises in store for them both then? Does your mother have far to come?'

'Not too far. From Dorset – Branksome. She runs a hotel there,' Leah finished her tea and stood up. 'I think I'd better go and get dressed. I've arranged to meet her at "The Greenway" in Kensington at half-past ten.'

'Look, tell you what,' Janet said hurriedly, 'I've got to leave around ten myself. 'Why don't you let me drop you off? It's on my way.'

'Well – thanks. That would be a help.'

As Leah released the seat belt in Janet's smart BMW sports car an hour later outside the hotel, she was suddenly stricken with nerves. 'Oh dear, I hope we recognise each other,' she said. 'I quite forgot to ask her what she'd be wearing.'

Janet smiled. 'That's no problem. Just ask the receptionist to page her,' she said. 'Tell them her name and yours and wait by the desk till she comes.'

'Of course.' Leah grinned. 'Why didn't I think of that? Thanks for the lift, Mrs Fenton.'

'Janet, please. I'm not Mrs Fenton any longer, remember?'

'Thanks anyway – Janet. Maybe we'll meet again.' Leah got out of the car and closed the door.

Janet sat watching thoughtfully as Leah ran up the steps and in through the smoked glass doors. She looked older this morning and more sophisticated. A white trenchcoat thrown casually over a short black skirt and red silk shirt replaced the denims, and she had disciplined the heavy hair into a sleek French plait, which accentuated her striking dark eyes and high cheekbones.

Janet drove around till she found a parking space. Locking the car she fed coins into the meter and began to walk back towards the hotel. On the corner she bought a newspaper from a street vendor, hardly even noticing that it was the early edition of her own old paper, the *Daily Globe*. Folding it under her arm she walked up the steps of 'The Greenway' to glance in through the doors. As she stepped into the dimly lit lobby and took a seat close to the door, her journalist's mind automatically pictured the headlines: *Mother and daughters reunited after twenty years*. If Leah managed to get things to go her way – or even if she didn't – it would make a fascinating human interest story. One of the more sensational tabloids would snap it up, especially if it were slanted in the right way.

Leah looked at her watch as she walked down the long narrow lobby towards the reception desk. She was early. It was still only twenty past ten. Marie might not have arrived yet. Better wait at least until half-past before asking for her to be paged. She sat down in the reception area and pretended to read a magazine, eagerly looking up every time anyone came in or stepped out of the lift.

Once she noticed a woman standing uncertainly by the desk. She was slightly built and fair-haired. It occurred to Leah that she bore more than a passing resemblance to Sally and her heart quickened in anticipation. But still she hesitated to approach her. As she watched, the woman looked at her watch and glanced around, then turned and walked off towards the coffee lounge.

After waiting another ten minutes Leah went across to the reception desk and asked: 'Could you page someone for me, please? I'm meant to be meeting her here at half-past ten but we haven't met before and I don't know what she looks like.'

She gave her own name and Marie's to the girl and a moment later the message was read out on the public address system.

'Would Mrs Evans please come to the reception desk where Miss Leah Dobson is waiting for her?'

She waited breathlessly, searching the faces of everyone who walked past. Then suddenly she turned and found herself face to face with the woman she had noticed earlier. So her instinct had been right. She opened her mouth to speak but found her voice had deserted her. Clearing her throat, she tried again.

'Mrs – Mrs Evans? Marie?'

'Leah!' The blue eyes filled with sudden tears as the woman held out her arms. 'Oh, Leah. It's so lovely to see you at last.'

The girl at the reception desk looked on with raised eyebrows. The girl had said they hadn't met before, yet here they were, the two of them, embracing for all the world like mother and daughter. It was odd the things people said sometimes.

From her vantage point at the end of the lobby, just inside the door, Janet lowered her newspaper a couple of inches. Well, they'd met all right. It looked like an emotional reunion. If only she could hear what was being said. Her eyes narrowed. There was something about all this that rang a vague bell somewhere. It made the hairs on the back of her neck tingle with a strange anticipation. All her journalist's instincts, coupled with her feminine intuition told her that she was on to something special. A bit more special than just a run of the mill human interest story. Maybe this one was worth probing deeper, doing some research on. If she found nothing – well, no harm done. It would still be an interesting story. On the other hand, if she was right and there was more to it, she might be on to a sensational winner.

Chapter 19

In the hotel coffee lounge Leah searched the face of the woman sitting opposite her, scrutinising every detail of her features. She had waited a lifetime for this moment. Leah found it faintly disturbing to see how incredibly like Sally Marie was, from the china blue eyes, fair hair and the slightly hesitant manner to the fine-boned, delicate build. She was well dressed and younger-looking than Leah had expected. In fact apart from the disappointing lack of resemblance to each other, they could almost have been taken for sisters.

'Does Sarah know I'm coming?' Marie asked.

'No, although I did tell her I'd been trying to trace you. She's still very ill, I'm afraid. I telephoned the hospital to ask if she could have two visitors this morning. They said yes, but to wait until after eleven. Something to do with the doctors' rounds.'

'I see.' Marie looked doubtful. 'But will she want to see me, do you think? Will it upset her?'

'Why should it?' But Leah was remembering Sally's words. 'One mother per lifetime is quite enough for me.' For the first time she was having misgivings about what she was doing.

'You haven't told me yet what is wrong with Sally,' Marie was saying. 'What happened? Was she involved in an accident?'

Leah swallowed hard. 'No. Sally gave birth to a baby boy on Christmas Day.'

'A baby?'

'Yes. He was premature and very small. He's still in an incubator at the moment, but he's holding his own. Unfortunately Sally suffered some kind of complication some hours after the birth and they had to perform an emergency hysterectomy.'

'Oh my God! Poor child.' Marie paused and Leah could see her trying to come to terms with what she had just learned.

'Is she married?'

'No.'

'I wish you'd told me all this before.'

'Why? Would it have made any difference?' Leah asked quickly.

'No. It's just that it's so hard to take in all at once. I haven't seen either of you since the day you were born. It seems so strange, sitting here with you – talking like this.' Marie leaned forward. 'I wish I knew more about Sarah,' she said. 'I feel so inadequate, knowing so little about my own daughter at a time like this.'

About Sarah? Leah felt resentment stab at her. It was she, Leah, who'd tried so hard to find her mother. She who'd day-dreamed as a child about the mother she'd longed to know; who'd made up stories about her and yearned to solve the mystery that surrounded her. Sally hadn't been the least bit interested in finding her real mother. She swallowed her resentment, telling herself she was being unreasonable. 'I hardly know her myself,' she said. 'We've only met a couple of times. I gather that the people who adopted her were very protective, but I don't know much more than that. All I do know is that she came up here to work without telling them she was pregnant. She 'hasn't been home since, so they still don't know.'

'So they don't know how ill she is?' Marie looked shocked. 'But surely you should have got in touch with *them*, not me.'

Leah bit her lip. 'I didn't know what to do. Sally is adamant that they mustn't know about the baby, you see. I had to talk to someone.'

'Oh, my God.' Marie's colour drained and she fumbled in her handbag for a handkerchief.

'I'm sorry,' Leah said. 'I hope I haven't upset you.'

'These people who adopted her – what would they do if they knew? Would they have disowned her?'

'Oh, no. They've been good parents. I think – I know she misses them a lot. I think it's just that she feels she's let them down.'

'But they'll have to know now, surely?'

'No. She wants the baby to be adopted.'

'I see.' Marie sighed. 'You really should have contacted her parents at once, Leah,' she said. 'She ought not to be making a decision like that alone.' She shook her head. 'Those poor people. If they knew, they'd be frantic. It's not right.'

Leah sighed. 'I know. But it didn't seem fair to go against her wishes. Especially when she's lying there so helpless. I tried to ring Hannah Brown, but she's away. Yesterday I suddenly felt overwhelmed by it all.'

'So you rang me?' Marie looked across the table at this young woman who, astonishingly, was her daughter. Sitting here like this, it seemed so unreal – almost dreamlike. She had a fleeting memory of the dark-haired, scrawny little baby who had screamed so furiously at birth. The tiny child she had held so briefly. And now, as she looked into the troubled eyes, she was reminded sharply of another face – of eyes and hair as dark as Leah's and of another full, sensuous mouth that had promised to love but had lied and betrayed instead. Liam . . . She was so like him – the traitorous father she would never know. Marie's heart contracted with a pain she had long since believed healed. She swallowed hard, her mouth and throat suddenly dry.

'You intended that *I* should talk her out of her decision?' she said awkwardly. 'Leah – I can't do that. Surely you must see that I can't?'

'No.' Leah's heart plummeted. She was on her own again. 'I'm sorry. I suppose I shouldn't have asked. It was just – there was no one else.'

Marie's heart ached for the girl. If only there was some way she could help.

Leah's eyes were clouded with reminiscence. 'I couldn't help remembering, you see. It's hard for a child to feel unwanted. I wasn't adopted till I was seven. And then it was only by a bereaved couple – as a replacement for the child they'd lost. It was a non-starter. I never came anywhere near to filling the gap for them.' She looked up at Marie, her eyes huge and dark with remembering. 'I don't think I've ever really mattered to anyone – not as *me*, not as myself. That's why it hurts so much to think of Sally's baby being discarded like a – like some little unwanted mongrel puppy – never knowing who he is or what he did to deserve rejection.' She looked at Marie, unable to keep the reproach out of her eyes. 'I know that feeling all too well. It's haunted me all my life.'

'Me too,' Marie said quietly.

Leah looked up at her sharply.

'Oh yes, Leah. I went through it too. I never knew who my parents were, never knew and can never hope to know. At the convent where I was brought up we weren't allowed to ask such questions. It was considered presumptuous to assume that one was in any way important.'

'Everyone's entitled to an identity,' Leah protested angrily.

'We were told: Go out and make your own mark in the world.' Marie sighed. 'But they never warned us about those who'd stand in the way; the people who would betray and deceive. Who'd lie and cheat and let us take punishment for deeds we hadn't done. They never prepared us for any of that.'

Their eyes met and Leah felt her heart soften. There was so much she didn't know about this woman. So much to learn, to discover and understand. Could either of them ever really make up to each other for what they had lost? And as for Sally . . . She bit her lip uncertainly. Marie was probably right. This wasn't the right time for a reunion after all. And yet again, it was the perfect time. 'I'm sorry,' she said quietly. 'I didn't mean to reproach you. Your letter. I should have known.'

Marie smiled. 'No. *I'm* sorry. You'll never know, Leah, how much I regretted letting you go. But I had no choice. No choice at all. One baby would have been difficult for a young girl alone in the world. But two . . . I've wondered about you both so often. There hasn't been a single day that I haven't prayed that you were both happy, and longed to see for myself how you'd grown up.'

'Sally's not alone like you were. She does have a choice,' Leah said. 'She has people who'd love and support her and the baby, if only she'd let them. But she'd rather give him away to a stranger.'

'But you see, it's *her* child,' Marie said quietly. 'It's her life and her choice. No one can make it for her. However much they might want to.'

Leah's heart turned cold. Marie wasn't going to help. She really wasn't. In spite of everything they'd just said to each other, she was going to turn her back and walk away from this. She felt bitterly let down.

'Well, let's hope she comes out of it as well as you have,' she said lightly. 'Let's hope she'll be able to pick up the pieces and make *her* mark in the world just like you did – with no child to hinder her. You'd be the perfect role model for her with your successful business, and your marriage.'

Marie's heart sank, dismayed by the girl's bitterness. 'I tried very hard to make a go of both those things. Maybe at one stage I almost succeeded.' She stopped. 'But we're not here to talk about me. Maybe one day I'll tell you all about that, Leah – if you want to see me again, and if you're interested enough to hear it. I'm afraid you'll find that it's not nearly as idyllic as you think.'

'Will you come to the hospital with me? Will you at least see her?'

An expression of regret crossed Marie's face. 'I think I'd better not,' she said regretfully. 'Not this time.'

'I see.' Leah stood up. 'I'm sorry to have wasted your time. It's my fault. I should have told you the truth on the phone, then you could have made some excuse not to come.'

Marie ignored the barb. 'If I hadn't come today I wouldn't have met you,' she said quietly. 'In spite of your disappointment in me, Leah, I wouldn't have missed meeting you for the world.'

She felt ashamed of her acid remark as the blue eyes held hers. 'I – it's been interesting meeting you too, Marie.' She forced herself to look away, picking up her coat and bag as she fought down the sudden rush of mixed emotions. Straightening up, she turned to take a last look at the stranger who was her mother.

'Well, goodbye then.' Slinging the strap of her bag on to her shoulder, she turned and walked purposefully away, leaving Marie looking wistfully after her.

When she arrived at the hospital she found that Sally already had a visitor. Hannah looked up as she came in.

'Leah, I got back this morning and found your message on my answering machine. Sorry I wasn't here when you needed me.'

'That's all right. It's good to see you, Hannah.' Leah was relieved to see that Sally looked a little better. Today she was propped up in bed, a little more colour in her cheeks. The drips and tubes had all been removed and there was a little more life in her eyes. Leah smiled at her.

'You're looking much better.' She unwrapped the fruit she had brought and put it on the locker.

'I feel it,' Sally said. 'Though when they had me out of bed this morning I was as weak as a kitten. My legs felt like jelly.'

'It'll take time,' Hannah said. 'Sally, have you thought where you'll go when they discharge you?'

'I'll manage,' she said dismissively. 'I'll be fine.'

'But you won't. You've just said you're weak. When you come out of hospital you'll discover just how weak you really are. You'll need nursing for weeks yet. Will you let me get in touch with Mavis?'

Sally's eyes widened and her cheek flushed with anxiety. 'No. Look, thanks, but I'd really rather you didn't.'

'I'm only facing facts, Sally. Someone has to,' Hannah went on, pressing the point. 'If you don't want to go home, maybe I could get you into a Council-run place for a while.'

'*No!*' Sally began to look panic-stricken. Leah turned to Hannah.

'It's all right. I'll take care of her. She can come to me.'

Hannah turned to her impatiently. 'Be sensible,

Leah. How can you? You haven't even asked your landlord. Then there's your job.'

'Bill wouldn't mind. As for my job, that's not a problem. I've lost it.'

'For heaven's sake, be realistic, Leah.' Hannah shook her head impatiently. 'What you're suggesting is just plain irresponsible. Apart from anything else, I really believe that Ken and Mavis Payne should be contacted. They're bound to find out eventually and when they do they're going to wonder why I've neglected to put them in the picture.'

'Oh, well, if it's your own squeaky clean image you're worrying about . . .' Sally winced with sudden pain and the hot colour drained abruptly from her cheeks. 'Look, could you go now, both of you? I don't want to discuss this any more.'

In the corridor they looked at each other. Hannah groaned.

'I handled that well, didn't I? You'd think with all my years of experience . . . It's just that she gets under my skin so with her stubbornness. Why won't she face up to the fact that she needs someone to look after her?'

'Hannah . . .' Leah interrupted her. 'Look, I've got to talk to you. I think I might have made a serious mistake. I've done something really impulsive and stupid.'

'Oh, dear.' Hannah took her arm with a resigned sigh. 'We'd better find somewhere to eat. Confessions always come easier on a full stomach, I find.'

Facing Hannah over the formica-topped table of the nearest fast food place, Leah poured out the details of her disastrous meeting with Marie.

'It was such a let-down, Hannah,' she said. 'I thought she was just the person to make Sally change her mind. She admits she's always regretted giving us up, yet she won't lift a finger to stop Sally making the same mistake.'

'How could she?' Hannah's face was stern. 'Put yourself in her shoes, Leah. I daresay she feels she has no right to advise Sally. She gave up that right twenty years ago. As for Sally, she's adamant about what's right, so she's not likely to take advice from a woman who is virtually a stranger. And quite honestly, in all fairness, it's no one else's business.'

'You want to make her tell her parents though,' Leah pointed out. 'Isn't *that* her business?'

'Yes, it is. She's an adult and it's her decision. I have to respect it, I agree. But I've tried to persuade her to tell them for her own sake, and for theirs. They don't deserve to be kept in the dark. I feel badly about the Paynes personally too. They asked *me* to sort this out for them. It puts me in an impossible position.'

They looked at each other for a moment, then Leah said: 'Marie wouldn't even see Sally.'

Hannah lifted her shoulders helplessly. 'You can see her point, can't you? Look, I'll do what I can. Is she staying up over night? Do you know where she is?'

'I met her at "The Greenway",' Leah said. 'But she's probably left there. By now she's probably on her way back to her neatly ordered lifestyle in Dorset.'

'That's not quite fair, is it, Leah?'

'What are we going to do, Hannah?' she asked bleakly.

'I wish I knew. I just wish to God I knew,' Hannah said wearily. 'I'm not worried about the baby. He'll be all right. It's Sally.'

Leah's dark eyes flashed. 'Have you even *seen* the baby?'

'No.'

'I saw him born. I stayed with Sally right through the birth. I've been to see him in the special care unit. He looks so little, clinging to life up there, all by himself. He's called Jamie. They wanted the chaplain to christen him so I named him. I wanted him to be real, you see. A person in his own right. Not just a few impersonal notes scribbled on a record card.'

'Oh, Leah.' Hannah touched her arm. 'Don't take it to heart so much. Things are so much better now than when you and Sally were born. His new parents will be matched perfectly to him and everything will be done to . . .'

'She'll never have any more, you know,' Leah put in. 'She's going to wish and *wish* she hadn't let him go.'

'Leave it, Leah,' Hannah said sharply. 'She's made up her mind.' Then, more softly: 'My dear, you have your own life. You must try to let go and forget about it.'

'You're as bad as all the others.' Leah sprang to her feet, her eyes bright and her cheeks burning. 'You don't give a damn really, do you? None of you gives a tuppenny bloody damn.' She ran out of the cafe, snatching up her coat and bag as she went. People turned to look at the striking dark girl running down the street as though the hounds of hell were at her heels. Finally out of breath, she came to a halt at a bus stop and clambered aboard a bus heading for Notting Hill. Throwing herself into a vacant seat she fumbled with trembling fingers in her bag for the fare, hot tears scalding her eyes and blurring her vision. Is there anyone left in the world who knows what love means? she asked herself. Is there anyone who really cares?

As Hannah pushed open the smoked glass door of 'The Greenway' she had very little hope of finding Marie still there. Her quick glance round the discreetly lit reception foyer revealed nothing. She walked across to the reception desk.

'A Mrs Marie Evans was here earlier this morning,' she said. 'I wonder – is she still here? She may have booked in for the night, or she might be having lunch.'

The girl smiled. 'I'll just check for you, Madam.' She ran a finger down the register and shook her head. 'She hasn't booked in.' She picked up the house telephone. 'I'll get them to see if she's in the restaurant.'

As she replaced the receiver she said: 'I think I remember the lady. Someone was asking for her this morning – a young lady. I paged her.'

'That's right. She's probably left by now,' Hannah said. 'I didn't even know she was in Town today, but when I heard I thought there might be a chance she was still here.'

The girl looked past Hannah, her face brightening as she saw someone crossing the foyer. 'Ah, you're in luck,' she said. 'I think this is the lady you're asking for now.'

Hannah turned and saw Marie coming towards her. '*Marie*! So you are still here. I'm so glad I caught you.'

'Another moment and I would have gone,' Marie said. 'I've just finished lunch. I was planning to catch an early train home. It's lovely to see you, Hannah. But how did you know where to find me?'

'I saw Leah at the hospital. She told me she rang you, and that you and she met here this morning.'

'Ah – yes, I see.' Marie looked depressed. 'I'm afraid it all went wrong, Hannah. When she telephoned me yesterday she sounded so desperate, but she told me nothing except that Sarah was very ill. I came without knowing what she expected of me. It was all such a shock. I'm afraid I disappointed her.'

'It was wrong of her not to put you in the picture.'

Marie shook her head. 'She was worried, poor girl. At her wits' end. I was very touched that she should call on me. And now I'm afraid she feels I've let her down badly.'

Hannah took her arm. 'Look, do you have to catch that early train? Have you got time for a talk?'

'Oh, yes please. I'd like to,' Marie said gratefully.

An hour later the two women arrived at the hospital and went up to the women's surgical ward. Sally was out of bed this afternoon and sitting in a chair. She looked small and frail, almost childlike, and when Hannah appeared her eyes clouded with dread.

She put out a reassuring hand. 'Sally, it's all right, I haven't come to nag you again,' she said. 'I've brought someone to see you. This is my friend, Marie Evans. She is in London for the day. I ran into her and I thought you two might like to meet. I can't stay so I'll leave you together.' She hurried off, leaving Marie and Sally looking warily at each other.

Sally was the first to speak. Clearing her throat, she said: 'Do please sit down. It's good of you to spend your day out visiting me. I'm afraid I'm not very good company at the moment. I'm sure you'd rather be looking at the shops.'

'Not at all.' Marie could hardly take her eyes off the girl. Looking at her, she saw herself twenty years ago. Her heart turned over and she felt her throat constrict. It was as though her own tragedy were being replayed right before her eyes. She reached out a hand to the girl in the chair.

'Sarah – Sally, how are you?'

'I'm improving, I think.' Sally frowned, puzzled at the woman's use of her formal name, and her emotional reaction. 'Hannah didn't introduce us properly. She said you were a friend of hers?'

'A friend, yes. A very old friend.' Marie moistened her dry lips and felt her heartbeat quicken as she said: 'Sally – I'm someone who knew you a very long time ago. You won't remember but I wonder – can you guess – do you have any idea who I am?'

'You're – you're not my *mother*?'

'Yes.'

For a long, stunned moment they stared at each other, then Sally said with a nervous little laugh: 'It's funny, I've never been in the least curious about you. Not till a few days ago. Not since . . .'

'Since you had the baby,' Marie completed the sentence for her. 'That's very natural. You're having him adopted, I hear.'

'Yes.' Sally looked away, her eyes troubled. 'They all think I don't want him – don't care,' she said. 'They think I'm being selfish. It isn't like that.'

'I understand.'

'Do you?' Sally looked up. 'I thought it all out a long time ago, you see, when I first knew. I'd have had an abortion if I hadn't cared, but no one seems to see that. No one need ever have known if I'd been allowed to do things my own way, but once they knew they started pulling me this way and that. Trying to make me change my mind. Trying to talk me out of it. I've always known what was right, both for me and the baby. This way no one need be hurt. If only they wouldn't interfere so.'

'I know, I know,' Marie said soothingly. 'I imagine it must be even harder for you than it was for me. I had no other option, you see. I had no family – no one at all to turn to for help. All along I'd been determined to keep my baby, but when I had two instead of one I knew I was defeated. There was

403

nothing else I could do. But for you the decision must have been agony.'

'It's the first decision I've ever made for myself,' Sally said slowly. 'My parents – the couple who adopted me – refused to realise that I'd grown up. They insisted on making all my decisions for me. When I discovered I was pregnant I knew that this was something I had to handle alone, get through in my own way.' She searched Marie's eyes. 'You think I'm doing the right thing then?'

'The baby's father,' Marie said tentatively. 'Does he know?'

Sally shook her head. 'There's no question of involving him. It was all a horrible mistake. Please don't ask me about it.'

Marie nodded. 'Well, you've obviously thought it out in a very adult way. Now you must stick to your guns and do what you think best.'

'It *is* best, isn't it?' Sally said, her eyes imploring.

'If you believe it's best, then it is. After all, those who want you to re-think won't be affected, will they? It's the next twenty years of *your* life, Sally. Maybe even longer. You must choose. But having said that, I do think that your parents have a right to know about it at some stage though.'

'I'll tell them,' Sally promised. 'Sometime. Later.' She reached out a hand. 'Thank you.'

Marie looked surprised. 'For what?'

'For your support – for being on my side – for taking away some of the guilt. They wanted me to see the baby. To have him with me for a week before the final decision. Can you imagine what that would have done to me?'

'Yes,' Marie nodded sadly. 'Oh, yes, I can.'

'All I want now is to be well enough to get out of here and back to work. To start again.'

'But you mustn't go back too soon, my dear,' Marie said. 'You should really have a holiday first. Get your strength back. You've had major surgery.'

'That's not possible, I'm afraid.'

'Oh, but it is.' Marie was seized with a sudden impulse – one which excited her as she explained: 'Listen. I run a hotel down in Dorset. We aren't busy at the moment. You can come and stay if you like when they let you out of hospital. Even a week would make all the difference, but two would be even better.'

Sally looked doubtful. 'But your husband – family? What would they say?'

Marie had already thought of this. 'There's only my father-in-law,' she said. 'My husband doesn't get home very often. We have several other hotels, you see. In any case, if you agree we'll pretend you're a friend. Would you mind that?'

'No. I'm sure it would be best,' Sally said.

Marie smiled. 'So it's arranged then? I'll drive up and collect you if you let me know when you're coming out.' She opened her handbag and produced a card. 'This is the address and my number.'

Sally took the card and glanced at it, her cheeks growing pink with pleasure. 'Well, if you're really sure?'

'Believe me, I've never been more sure about anything.'

'All right then – yes. I'd love to come.' Sally paused. 'Could we – could we keep this to ourselves?' she asked. 'I've a horrible feeling that if we tell anyone they might start trying to talk us out of it again.'

'Just as you say. It will be just between ourselves.' Marie got up and bent to kiss Sally's cheek. She'd dreamed so many times of something like this happening. 'I can't tell you how happy this makes me,' she said softly. 'I know we're going to be good friends, Sally.'

She smiled up into Marie's face. 'I know we are too,' she said.

As Marie left the hospital and headed for Waterloo station she felt happier than she had for a long time. Sarah, her own daughter, was coming to stay with her. She could hardly believe it. She was actually going to be able to help her after all. It was like the answer to all her prayers. At home, in the peace and quiet, she could tell Sarah her story – about Liam and his betrayal, about her struggle to live down the stigma of her unjust conviction and prison sentence, and her heart-wrenching decision to part with her babies. Together they would forge a bond that would last a lifetime.

When Leah had walked out of the hotel earlier this morning, her face sharp with bitterness, and anger in every movement, Marie had felt such an acute sense of failure. She would have left the hotel immediately and set out for home if it hadn't been for a chance encounter with a stranger, a woman who had spoken to her just as she was about to get up from the table.

'Excuse me, but are you all right?'

Looking up in surprise she'd seen an attractive blonde woman standing at her side. 'Yes, thank you. I was just . . .'

'Forgive me for asking, but I couldn't help seeing your – friend leave.' The woman slid into the seat that Leah had vacated. 'Or was it your daughter?'

Marie nodded. 'Yes. My daughter.'

'They can be so headstrong at that age. My sister has three so I know what I'm talking about. They can break your heart at times.'

'I'm sure you're right.'

The waitress appeared and the woman ordered a

gin and tonic. She looked at Marie. 'Please, will you join me? You look as though you could do with something stronger than coffee.'

Marie looked at her watch. She had missed the twelve o'clock train anyway. She looked again at the persuasive, smiling face. 'Well, all right, thank you. Perhaps I will.'

The gin, and the woman's relaxing conversation, seemed to ease her tension and Marie slowly began to unwind. She found herself talking – about Evans Hotels and how she had helped David to start the business. She had touched briefly on the unhappiness of her marriage after the woman had confided that she was divorced. It was so easy to talk to this friendly stranger. She told Marie that she'd had bad luck with her relationships with men. Her divorce had been devastating and a recent affair had ended in heartbreak. They talked on. The woman had drawn her out and Marie had even found herself hinting at those dark years in her past when she believed there could be no future for her. It helped so much to tell someone she would never see again about the illegitimate twin daughters she had given up at birth and found again only today. Found and lost, it seemed, all in one fell swoop.

By the time the woman, whom she knew only as Janet, had left, Marie felt so much better. Their brief meeting had lifted her spirits far more than Father Jonathan's biased counselling. Her uncertainties and doubts smoothed out, she decided to write to Leah again and try to explain to her why she had felt unable to offer help. Then, as she was leaving, she found Hannah waiting for her in Reception. Yes, the day that had begun so badly had ended well after all.

Leah ran up the stairs and closed the door of her

room. Throwing her coat and bag into a corner she threw herself on to the bed and rolled into a ball. She'd made such a mess of it. The same mess she made of everything. 'You have your own life,' Hannah had said. It was just another way of saying, 'Keep your nose out of other people's business.' When would she learn that she wasn't needed? Getting yourself into a state like that, she said through clenched teeth. Making a fool of yourself about something that doesn't concern you. Then she thought of the baby again and her throat constricted. What would become of him? Poor little scrap. Why was it so wrong of her to feel responsible for him – to want him to have a future?

Suddenly the sound of music made her start. She had thought she was alone in the house. She sat up and listened. It was coming from Terry's room and she recognised the familiar opening track of A New Flame, his favourite Simply Red album. Getting off the bed she went out on to the landing. The door to the room Sally had occupied until Christmas Day was ajar. Holding her breath she pushed it open.

'Terry?'

He turned, a broad grin splitting his face. 'Hi. I didn't hear you come in.' The sight of him made her heart leap with joy.

'Oh, *Tel*!' She launched herself at him, throwing her arms round his neck till her feet left the floor. 'Oh, Tel, I've missed you so *much*.'

He held her close, flattered and touched by her exuberant welcome. 'I've missed you too. Manchester has been bloody cold, in more ways than one.'

She leaned back to look at him, then kissed him full on the mouth. 'Terry Grant, you're the best Christmas present I've ever had. Are you here to stay?'

He shook his head, holding her away from him.

''Fraid not, love. I worked over Christmas so I've got a couple of days off due. I thought I'd like to spend them with you.'

'What about your father?'

'He's fine now. Gone off with some friends to relax in the sun. One of those senior citizens' winter sunshine trips, which left me free to succumb to this irresistible urge to come and see you.'

'It must have been telepathy.' She laughed. 'You must have guessed how much I needed you.'

He sensed an underlying note of desperation in the words. 'What's wrong, Leah?' He searched her eyes.

She began haltingly to relate the events of the past days – her aborted meeting with her mother and her row with Sally the first time they met, the closing of Bella's Ristorante, rendering her once more unemployed. As she reached the climax, Christmas Day and the birth of Sally's baby, the words tumbled over one another and her bruised emotions threatened to get the better of her. When she had finished he shook his head.

'But why have you never mentioned any of this on the phone?'

She shrugged. 'What was the point? There was nothing you could do. And you were worried about your father too.'

'I think you're about due for some better luck.'

'I thought I was getting it when Hannah managed to persuade Sally to spend Christmas with me here and it all began so well. When the baby was born I tried to get hold of Hannah, but she was away so in desperation I rang Marie yesterday.' When he looked blank she added: 'Marie Evans. Our natural mother.'

His eyebrows rose. 'Really? That must have taken some heart-searching.'

'Not enough, as it happened,' she said wryly.

Terry took her hands and drew her down to sit beside him on the bed. 'So there's more? Go on, tell me what happened?'

Leah shrugged. 'She agreed to come at once – today. I was so pleased about it. But it was awful, Terry. All my fault. I blew the whole thing, as usual. I just naturally assumed she'd agree with me about the baby, but she didn't. I thought she'd help me convince Sally not to give him up, but I was wrong. Then later, when I went to see Sally at the hospital, Hannah was there. She agreed with what Marie had said. The sum of what they were both saying was that I should mind my own business.' She looked up at him appealingly. 'And now I expect you're going to tell me they were right?'

'Oh, Leah.' Terry looked down at her with exasperation tempered with tenderness. 'What am I going to do with you?' He pulled her close. 'I daresay they *are* probably right, you know, love. It's not your problem really, is it?'

She leaned against him, relieved to be able to give in just for a moment – grateful for his strength and masculinity. 'No. But the point is, if we'd ever been a proper family it would have been, wouldn't it?' she said. 'I'd have had a right to my say then.' She looked up at him. 'All my life has been geared to finding my mother. It isn't easy now that I've found her and Sally to acknowledge the fact that they're just two ordinary people that I might meet in the street; that they don't – perhaps never will – see me as daughter or sister. I thought that finding my mother would give me a sense of identity. It was all going to be so wonderful. But now that it's happened, I don't feel I belong to her any more than I did to Jack and Hilary.'

'Did you really expect to after all these years? If you're to have a real relationship with her it will be

410

something to be built and worked at. Anyway, have you asked yourself if it's what you really want from life, Leah – to belong to someone? I always thought you were very much your own woman. Little Miss Independence.'

'And so I *am*. There's just this little bit of me, deep inside, that needs – needs . . .'

'Love?' He caught at her shoulders. 'No, don't turn away, Leah.' He cupped her chin and turned her face towards him. 'We all – every one of us – need that. It's the simplest, most basic, need there is. There's no need to feel apologetic about it.'

'For most people it's there from birth so they never even have to think about it.' She sighed. 'Do you know, I realised something today. No one has ever once, in the whole of my life, told me, "I love you".'

'And what about you, Leah – have *you* ever told anyone you love them?'

She was silent for a moment. 'There was a time when I thought love was just something to barter with,' she said softly. 'Something you only parted with if the price was right. I suppose love and sex and friendship were all hopelessly muddled up in my mind.' Inwardly she was remembering Colin Mays, the one person to whom she had given her love freely and unconditionally; the reckless words she had murmured feverishly during their ecstatic summer afternoons of lovemaking. The humiliation of that brief episode was painfully rekindled as she shook her head slowly. 'Now I'm not sure I know what it is, Terry, or even if it *exists*.'

'Oh, it exists all right.' He smiled at her wistfully.

'Does it?' She smiled tremulously. 'Then maybe I've got it to look forward to.'

'Oh, Leah . . .' Very gently he took her face between his hands and kissed her. 'Don't you know

411

how much I love you? Haven't you realised what hell it's been for me, being close to you – knowing that you didn't feel the same? That was why I jumped at the chance of going up north.' She opened her mouth to speak, but he put a finger against her lips. 'No. Don't say anything now. But if you really want to know if love exists, Leah, you don't have to look very far.'

'Oh, Terry. You're the best person in the world. I've missed you so much.' She looked at him for a long moment, her eyes huge and luminous. He paused, recognising her vulnerability, and although it was agony, he forced himself to wait for her to make the first move.

'I've been a fool, haven't I?' She reached up to wind her arms around his neck, pulling his head down to hers. 'An idiot not to see what was under my nose. I *do* love you, Terry. I suppose I always have.' For a moment her lips trembled beneath his, then they opened for him and her arms tightened around his neck. He swept her close, kissing her with all the hunger he'd kept at bay for so long, and Leah responded with all of her heart and soul, wondering how it could be possible that she hadn't seen before how much Terry meant to her. When they drew apart they were both a little shaken.

As she began to undo the buttons of his shirt, Terry looked down at her. His eyes wary, he caught both her hands in his. 'Look, you're upset and emotional at the moment, darling. You are sure this is really what you want? You're sure it's right this time?'

She laughed softly, burying her face against his chest. 'I've never been more sure of anything in my life, I promise you.'

Janet felt more cheerful than she had for weeks. She'd had a busy and productive day. The last two months had been hell. When she drove down to London on Boxing Day she'd been desperate. She'd intended to throw herself on Bill's mercy; to ask him to try to get her old job on the *Globe* back for her.

Her relationship with Mike Tessler, her boss, had ended disastrously when his wife had discovered they were having an affair. In spite of all their plans to be together he quickly forgot his promise to ask for a divorce and dropped Janet like a hot potato. Suddenly he saw his wife as a 'human being' and protested that he couldn't cause her any more pain. Janet wasn't fooled. She'd always suspected that Mike's wife had money, and there was no stronger tie than that of the purse strings. After that it became impossible for her to work at Pennine. There seemed no other course but for her to give up her job. And just when she'd been tipped for promotion. But even after she'd handed in her resignation she couldn't believe they'd actually let her go. They had. Mike had gone to the powers that be with his story first, and he was clearly more valuable to them than she was.

After the initial anguish she'd quite looked forward to coming back to London, to the familiar house and to seeing Bill again. But the moment they set eyes on each other she'd known it wasn't going to work. She couldn't admit her defeat to him, much less ask him for any favours. At best she would find herself beholden to him, at worst she would have to endure his pity. It would almost have been easier if he'd despised her, but he didn't. He was the same old Bill who'd driven her mad throughout their unsatisfactory marriage; tough and hard hitting as a journalist, but tolerant and forgiving to the point of stupidity when it came to relationships. He might even start nursing hopes that she'd come back to him. No, she would have to get another job under her own steam. And until she got one there was nothing for it but to fall back on freelancing.

Little had she thought that Bill's attractive young tenant would provide her with the story she needed to get started. After spending some time at the British Museum and St Catherine's House, checking records, she called in at the *Globe* offices on the pretext of looking up some of her ex-colleagues. Before leaving she paid a visit to her old friend Reg Jeffries who looked after the archives down in the basement. She spent an hour going through back numbers of the paper preserved on microfilm and meticulously catalogued by Reg, checking back over the past twenty years and further.

Finally, there it was, the story she'd been looking for. The date was 23 September 1970. The front page headline leapt out at her: *Pregnant Girl Held on Terrorism Charge*. Janet felt a charge of excitement surge through her. As she read her excitement intensified, sending the adrenalin tingling along her veins like liquid fire. She'd been sure the powerful gut feeling she'd had about this all along wouldn't let her down. Something about Leah and her twin sister, their connection with the Evans woman, had been niggling insistently at the fringes of her memory since early this morning. Now here it was, the whole story – everything she could have hoped for.

Opening her bag, she drew out her notebook. Tucked inside was the polaroid photograph Bill had taken of Leah and Sally on Christmas Day. All she needed now was a good contact and with a bit of luck she'd be on her way.

Chapter 20

It was dark by the time Marie arrived home. She was tired and hungry, but before going to the kitchen to make herself a snack she looked into the living room. David sat in the unlit room, slumped in his chair, his ashen face illuminated by the light of the fire.

'David, what is it? Are you ill?' Alarmed, Marie switched on the light and went to him, dropping to her knees by his chair.

'This came this afternoon,' he said numbly.

He took a letter from the table beside him and handed it to her. Her eyes widened with dread as she took in the stilted, legal phrases.

Looking up at him she said: 'Oh, David, I'm so sorry. I must admit that I've half expected this. I did my best to keep it from you – maybe I shouldn't have kept it back. Ralph hasn't been paying the bills. I've spoken to him time and again, but he just wouldn't listen.'

'I should never have agreed to give him power of attorney,' he said between tight lips. 'He confused me so – made me believe in the end that I really wasn't fit to handle things. I should have insisted on taking over the business again. That overdraft – those cheques. For a while I began to wonder if my mind was going, but I know now that it wasn't me.'

'Maybe you should have handed over to Ralph at

the beginning,' she said with a sigh. 'He's been so resentful and restless all along. Maybe if he'd had control from the start . . .'

David suddenly gripped her hand. 'How could I just hand over all that we'd worked for, you and I? I intended to, eventually, once he'd proved himself, but when I saw the way he was treating you I made up my mind.' He looked at her. 'Do you think I didn't see how unhappy he was making you? Do you think I didn't hear the rows? I blamed myself. If it hadn't been for me you'd probably never have married him.'

'You mustn't blame yourself, David. It won't help now. Perhaps I was wrong to keep you in the dark about the mounting debts. I kept hoping it would all sort itself out. Ralph has kept me in complete ignorance about the business.' She looked at him. 'What are we going to do, David?'

'The first thing is to get that solicitor up here.' David's voice was strong. It was as though he had suddenly been given a new strength. 'I've been trying to find his number but it doesn't seem to be in the directory.'

'I'll do it. It's too late tonight. First thing in the morning I'll get on to it. Don't worry, David. We'll sort it out one way or another.'

Later, after he was in bed, Marie telephoned 'The Marina' and asked to speak to Ralph. When he came on the line he sounded irritable.

'What is it, Marie? I was there only yesterday. Can't you leave me alone for five minutes?'

'It's happened, Ralph,' she said without preamble. 'We've been served with a writ. If we don't find the money quickly to pay our debts we'll be made bankrupt.'

'And you wait till this time of night to tell me?'

'I've been out all day,' she told him. 'David received the writ while I was out. He's out of his mind with worry.'

'Tell him he can leave it all to me.'

'I think he's heard that before, David,' she said tartly. 'He wants the power of attorney reversed. Can you tell me the solicitor's number? It doesn't seem to be listed.'

'I *said*, leave it to me,' he thundered down the telephone.

'We've been leaving it to you, Ralph, and look at the mess it's got us into. The solicitor's number, please. This can't wait.'

'I'll come back,' he snapped. 'I'll drive down first thing tomorrow.' Before she could argue further he'd rung off.

Marie spent a sleepless night. Unless they could pay off all that was owing before the date of their court appearance everything would be put into the hands of the trustees to be disposed of. If only she had some idea of the extent of their debts. Could they salvage anything out of the mess? More than anything else, she worried about the effect of it all on David's health.

Ralph arrived at midday. He looked tense and grey but his manner was as brash and defiant as ever. Marie insisted that they all three ate lunch before they got down to discussion though none of them had much appetite. Finally the table was cleared and David looked expectantly at Ralph.

'Right, how do you propose to get us out of this mess?' he asked.

Ralph shrugged. 'To be honest, I don't know if I can.'

Marie stared at him. 'But surely if we sell . . .'

417

'Selling takes time,' he interrupted. 'They might not give us the option. And we're mortgaged up to the hilt anyway. It'll depend on how much more time we can persuade our creditors to let us have.'

'Have you brought the necessary papers with you?' Marie asked. 'I think it's time the cards were on the table. Just how much do we owe? And to whom?'

Ralph opened his briefcase and drew out a sheaf of papers, spreading them on the table in front of her. Her expression of horror deepened as she leafed through them. 'My God. How could you let things go this far?' she said accusingly. 'Have you had advice? What about the accountant you were meeting at "The Marina" – does he know about all this? Is that what your meeting was about?'

'He advises voluntary bankruptcy,' Ralph said dispassionately.

'I can see his point.' Marie said ironically. She glanced at David as he rose unsteadily to his feet.

'You've ruined us,' he said in a low, growling voice she had never heard before. 'You've *ruined* us, and all you can do is sit there and talk about voluntary bankruptcy. Well, let me tell you that you don't have any say in this. It's *my* decision, just as everything should have been all along. Get that solicitor here at once.'

'There is no solicitor,' Ralph said coolly. 'The man who drew up the power of attorney was a friend of mine, a solicitor's *clerk* not a solicitor. The power was never registered. I did it to keep you out of my hair.'

David grasped the back of the chair and Marie saw the colour drain from his face. 'You – you *what*? You mean that all this time you've been pulling the wool over our eyes. I've been letting you – when all the time . . .' He swayed and Marie was on her feet instantly.

'David, don't upset yourself. We'll work something out. Come and lie down.'

'I'm all right.' He shook her hand away and straightened his back. 'I can't believe what a fool I've been. I should have done this years ago. I'd like you to leave, Ralph. From now on I don't want to see you unless I have to.'

Ralph laughed shortly. 'Don't kid yourself, Dad. We're all in this together. Besides, in case you've forgotten, I happen to be Marie's husband. What's she supposed to do?'

David glanced at Marie. 'That's entirely up to her, of course.'

Marie laid a hand on David's arm. 'Ralph is right in a way. We're all in this. We're going to have to see it through together.'

'Spoken like the loyal wife we all know and love,' Ralph jeered.

David took a deep breath and rallied himself. 'There's something you should both know. My Will is made out entirely in Marie's favour.' He held up his hand as Ralph half rose. 'I *know* you're not my true son, Ralph. I've known for a very long time that your mother deceived me when we married. But when you came back into my life I told myself that it wasn't your fault. You weren't responsible for her lies. You were the closest I'd ever had to a son of my own and I was flattered that you took an interest in me. I was prepared to give you a chance, but I couldn't have made a more disastrous decision. You've wrecked the business Marie and I built, and our lives with it.'

Ralph gave a callous shrug. 'So you've cut me off without a shilling, have you? Marie gets the lot.' His eyes glinted with malice as he looked at Marie. 'Congratulations. You'll be lucky to be left with the clothes you stand up in once the receivers get their hands on everything. Look, all business is a gamble. It was Marie's idea to have a chain of hotels. Why don't you blame her? If it had come off I'd be the hero of the day. Now that it hasn't, I'm just the son-of-a-bitch who lost your money. Well, tough. But don't run away with the idea that it bothers me, because it doesn't. Marie's my wife. What's hers is mine anyway, whether it's debts or riches. Like she said, we're in this together.' He began to shove papers back into his briefcase. 'Right, I'm off now. But I'll be back to stay once I've cleared my things out of "The Marina".' At the door he turned with a defiant smile. 'See you later.'

'Janet, how nice to see you.'

Harriet Marsh, the editor of the *Recorder*, looked up as Janet was ushered into her office. She took off her glasses and pushed back her chair. 'What can I do for you?'

She'd heard, of course, on the grapevine that Janet Fenton had been forced to resign her promising and coveted job at Pennine TV. She and Janet went back a long way. They had met when they were trainee reporters on the same provincial newspaper twenty years ago. But if Janet was expecting to be given a job on the strength of their longstanding friendship, she had another think coming. The paper was already overstaffed. Only last week she'd had a directive from above to decide on six redundancies.

'Coffee?' Harriet's beaming smile masked her reservations as her hand hovered over the intercom.

'No thanks, I haven't really got time. Look, Harriet, I won't beat about the bush. I've given up my job with Pennine. TV wasn't really me and I didn't want to waste any more time going in the wrong direction. I've decided to go freelance,' she added quickly, guessing at Harriet's thoughts and forestalling the rejection she saw looming. 'I've had an idea for a series and I'm already working on the first story. It's pretty sensational stuff and as we're old friends I thought I'd give you first refusal.'

Harriet relaxed a little. So she wasn't after a job on the staff after all? Janet was a good journalist and if she was really on to something it might be worth looking at. 'What's your idea?' she asked.

'It's a sort of "Where are they now?" thing.'

Harriet pursed her lips. 'It's been done.'

'Not like this though,' Janet put in. 'These are sensational cases. Women who hit the headlines some years ago.'

Harriet looked unimpressed. 'We-ell . . .'

'Women who got a raw deal from life – who were judged guilty when many thought them innocent,' Janet went on. It was proving harder to sell than she thought. 'For instance, does the name Marie O'Connor mean anything to you?'

'Mmm.' Harriet frowned. 'Rings a dim and distant bell somewhere. A long time ago, wasn't it?'

'Twenty years ago. An young Irish girl arrested at Paddington Station with a bloody great bomb concealed in her luggage. She went down for a five-year stretch for terrorism. Much public sympathy was on her side but she was convicted just the same.'

'That's right, I remember now. Some thought the so-called boyfriend used her as a human bomb. It was while you and I were on the *Clarion*. Wasn't she also pregnant?'

'She was.' Janet was trying hard to keep the triumphant smile off her face, Harriet was biting nicely now. 'She gave birth to twin girls in the remand home before the trial.'

'So what's the angle? Where is she now? And what

happened to the kids?' Harriet leaned forward expectantly.

'The twin girls were adopted at birth. I've located them too and I can tell you that they've recently found each other again. But if you want to know the rest it's up for grabs,' Janet said. 'I can promise you, it's well worth buying.' Harriet's hesitant expression encouraged her. 'Oh come on, Harri. You know you can trust me.'

Harriet examined her immaculate fingernails. 'Suppose we run this first one as a pilot – see how it goes?'

Janet shook her head. 'It has to be a firm commission or nothing,' she said. 'And I'd have to have an advance. There'll be travelling and more research to do. And I have to get myself a permanent place to live, now that I'm back in London to stay.'

'Well, I don't know.' Harriet was thoughtful. 'Care to give me a little bit more on it first?'

Janet laughed. 'Not a chance. I've already given away more than I should. Do you want it or not?'

'I suppose you'll want a by-line?'

'No. At least, I'd prefer not to do it under my own name. I thought I'd like to do the series under the name of "Pandora".'

Harriet looked at her for a moment, one eyebrow raised, then she laughed. 'Pandora, eh? Very apt. You know, if it was anyone but you I'd tell you to get lost, but seeing we go back such a long way – okay, you're on.' She pressed the buzzer on her desk. 'You'd better have that coffee while we negotiate a fee. Then you can fill me in on the rest of the story.'

Sally was feeling better. Her stitches were out now and she was able to get up a little each day and walk down to the day room where there were magazines and a television. Most of the other patients were older women. There was no one with whom she could hold a conversation other than to pass the time of day. They all seemed to enjoy swapping symptoms and exchanging details of their operations – the last thing Sally wanted to indulge in. Sometimes it seemed to her that they looked at her with curious, speculative eyes. As far as she knew none of them knew about the baby but these things had a way of getting around. The sooner she could get out of here and get on with her life again, the better she'd like it.

Although she refused to admit it, even to herself, she thought about the baby constantly, trying to remember what he looked like, wondering how he was alone up there in his incubator. Often as she lay awake late at night she'd been tempted to get up and creep upstairs to the baby unit to take a peep at him. She had never once allowed herself to ask about him, but there was one nurse, an older woman with children of her own, who insisted on bringing her snippets of news. He was breathing unaided now – and taking his feed from a bottle. Did she know that her sister had given him the name of Jamie? When Sally heard this she felt a stab of resentment. So Leah was interfering again, was she? What right did she have to name her child? Knowing that he had a name made him much more real somehow – made the unexpected pull even stronger. Half of her longed to hold him, to protect him, or at least be reassured that he was all right, whilst the other half shrank from any knowledge of him. Once she'd left the hospital, she'd be able to make herself forget all this, she promised herself. Forget the long and painful birth, the terrifying haemorrhage and operation that had followed. When she was away from all the associations she'd find it much easier to shut out the memory of the tiny face with its fuzz of soft hair and the wide blue eyes that she had looked into just the once. Maybe then her arms would stop feeling so empty and her heart stop yearning.

Meeting Marie had been quite an experience. She'd neither expected, nor wanted to meet her natural mother, but in some strange way on the day she'd arrived unannounced with Hannah, Sally had known instinctively who she was. She'd seen at once her own resemblance to Marie, and she found herself drawn to the warmth of her personality and the soft voice that still retained a trace of the musical lilt of her native Ireland. There had been an instant rapport between them. Marie was the only person who truly understood how she felt in all this, and her invitation to go down to Dorset was like the answer to all Sally's problems. She'd so dreaded the thought of returning to the cold, lonely little bedsit and coping alone.

When she told Hannah about the invitation, the social worker's eyes had clouded with doubt. 'What about your parents, Sally?' she asked. 'Do you really think it's fair, the way you're treating them? Surely *now* you could go home and reassure them that you're still their daughter?'

Sally had turned her face away. 'I will, Hannah. In my own good time. I've promised you, and I *will* go. Just give me time.' Deep inside she couldn't stamp out the feeling that if they hadn't sheltered her so closely while she was growing up it would never have happened. If she'd been more like Sharon, streetwise and able to look after herself, she wouldn't be where she was now. She couldn't count the nights she had lain awake, thinking of the manner in which her child had been conceived; shuddering with revulsion and self-disgust. After the operation, when they'd broken the news to her that she would never be able to have

424

another child, she'd been glad. She'd never marry – never give herself to a man again, so what did it matter?

'What am I to tell them?' Hannah asked.

'Tell them I'm fine and that I'll be in touch. You could say I've gone away on a course or something if you like.'

'So I'm to lie for you?'

Sally frowned impatiently. 'Oh, tell them what you like.'

'As long as it's nothing like the truth, you mean?'

'I don't see why you should have to tell them anything,' Sally protested. 'You're not my social worker and you're not theirs either. Haven't you got enough work of your own to do?'

'They asked me to help as a friend, Sally. To my way of thinking that makes me doubly committed, but maybe I shouldn't expect you to understand that.'

'Because I'm so selfish, you mean? Because I want a life of my own? Is that so wrong?'

'Are you really so hard that you feel you owe them nothing?'

'I owe them *this*,' Sally said, spreading her hands to encompass the hospital ward. 'When I've come to terms with that I'll try to forgive them.'

'They tell me they're taking Jamie – the baby – to St Mary's tomorrow,' Hannah said. 'And when he's reached an acceptable weight he'll go to the home from which he'll be adopted.'

'Really?' Sally's eyes refused to meets hers.

'If you like he could go to a foster home until you . . .'

'I'm *not* going to change my mind,' Sally interrupted. 'It's no use your keeping on at me.' She swallowed hard. 'I'm tired. I'd like you to go now if you don't mind.'

Hannah stood up and laid a hand on Sally's shoulder. 'I won't come again,' she said quietly. 'But you know where I am if you want me.' She waited, but when the girl didn't reply or look up she walked away. She'd tried her best, she told herself. She could do no more.

Sally watched Hannah go, making sure that she was quite out of sight before giving way to the tears that threatened to choke her. Hiding her head under the bedclothes she stifled the sobs that tore at her throat and chest. Hot, salt tears scalded her cheeks and soaked into the pillow.

The letter came by the first post next morning. Most of the other patients in the ward had a host of 'get well' cards displayed on their lockers, but Sally had had no cards or letters. She turned the envelope over in her hands, looking curiously at the unfamiliar writing and wondering who could have written to her. Then she saw that it was postmarked Dorset and guessed that it was from Marie. Eagerly she tore the envelope open. It was brief and barely filled one side of a single sheet of notepaper.

My dear Sarah

It is so hard for me to write this letter to you after inviting you to convalesce at 'The Ocean'. Since my visit to you we have had a serious business upset which means that the coming weeks will be difficult and very busy. I'll write to you again, my dear, as soon as I can see my way clear to having you with me for a visit. I hope you will forgive me and believe that I would not have let you down like this unless it were unavoidable. Please keep in touch. I do hope you are feeling better.

My loving thoughts and good wishes for the future go with you.
Marie

Sally crumpled the letter into a ball and pushed it into the waste bag taped to the side of her locker. She might have known. Marie had let Leah down, hadn't she? Quite clearly her first impression had been wrong. Marie Evans was not a very reliable person. She took a deep breath, trying to ignore the crushing disappointment. Well, so much for that. If she was to live an independent life she must learn to stand on her own two feet. If she accepted no help, then she would have no one to be grateful to. It was what she wanted after all, wasn't it? All the same, she couldn't help feeling disappointed. She'd been so sure that Marie Evans was sincere.

Leah and Terry spent three idyllic days together. They went window shopping in Regent Street and sight-seeing at Hampton Court and Kew. They treated themselves to a fiendishly extravagant lunch at L'Escargot and Terry even managed to get tickets – through a friend-of-a-friend – for *Aspects Of Love*. Leah could not remember ever being so happy. Since he'd been away she sensed a certain change in Terry. She approved. He seemed suddenly older, more positive and confident in his outlook. Since he'd moved up north he had traded in his old 2CV for a smart little Spitfire sports car; second-hand but fast and racy. Clearly he loved his new job and was learning fast. He told Leah about the photography course the group was sending all their reporters on.

'The old idea of having to drag a photographer along on a story is cumbersome,' he explained. 'So much better if we can take our own.' He laughed. 'I can't believe how naive I used to be, snapping away with my old Instamatic for the *Nenebridge Clarion*. One of these days I'll hit the front page with the biggest scoop there's ever been,' he said with a laugh.

'Oh, yes? Do they let junior reporters loose on front page stuff?' she'd asked teasingly.

'If I stumbled on a really hot story I could always sell to another paper under a trade name,' he told her. 'It happens all the time.'

She was fascinated, hearing about his job. His enthusiasm was infectious. He made it all sound so exciting that she almost wished she could work for a newspaper too. Terry's new self-assurance had made a subtle difference to the way she saw him. In the old days she'd been the dominant one, but now there were times when she was almost shy with him. Somehow he seemed so much wiser. The boyish charm had gone, replaced by a new assertiveness that she found irresistibly attractive.

'Successful newspaper reporters have to be hard and ruthless sometimes,' he told her when she teased him about it. She'd laughed, unable to see the old Terry as either of these things. All the same, she found herself looking at him speculatively after that. Terry was ambitious. She recognised his determination and single-mindedness and admired him for it. The only cloud on her horizon was the fact that he would be back in Manchester by the end of the week.

'Shall I come back with you?' she asked suddenly as they were eating supper in the kitchen at Melbury Street on their last evening together.

Terry looked up in surprise. 'There's nothing I'd like more. But London is where you've always wanted to be. Aren't you going to look for another job? And what about Sally and Marie?'

'Let's face it – they don't really want to know me,' she said, pushing her plate away. 'That's a fact I've just got to face. Hannah keeps telling me to let go and I can see now that she's right.' She looked up at him. 'I can get a waitressing or a bar job up there as easily as down here. And you'd like me to come, wouldn't you?'

He laughed gently and reached out to take her hand. 'You know I would. I'm just afraid you haven't really thought it through. Leah, you're a very bright girl. You've wasted so much time chasing rainbows. You've been doing it half your life and I'm not convinced that you aren't still doing it. There's nothing I'd like better than to take you back up north with me tomorrow. I'm more tempted than you'll ever know. But I've got this horrible feeling that you'd regret it in the long run.' Seeing her crestfallen expression, he turned his chair towards her and took both her hands in his. 'Listen, Leah, find yourself first before you make a commitment. There's so much you could do with your life.'

'Oh, yes?' Hurt that he hadn't accepted her offer eagerly, she pulled her hands away. 'Like what?'

'I don't know – *anything*. You mentioned that Bill had suggested going into business on your own.'

'I couldn't do what he suggested. I don't want to take chances with someone else's money. Anyway, I don't fancy a mobile catering service.'

'Then why not take over Bella's?'

'*Bella's*?' She stared at him, then gave an ironic laugh. 'It's for sale. Where would I get that kind of money?'

'The bank.' When she shook her head, he added: 'Well, you could at least try. Reach up, Leah. Set your sights high and do your darnedest to reach them. You can do it.'

'What you're really saying is that you're afraid you'd get bored, having me hanging around.'

He got up from the table and began to clear the dirty dishes. 'If you only knew how wrong you are, Leah. What I am afraid of is catching you when you're vulnerable. You've got a lot of thinking to do; thinking you should have done long ago. You've let your search for your mother eclipse everything else. It's been your only motivation. Take some time to find out who you are and what you really want from life.' He pulled her to her feet and put his arms around her. 'Believe me, having you around permanently is just about the most desirable thing I can think of. But I'll still be here when you've made up your mind, you know.'

'You might not be,' she said ruefully. 'You might meet someone else and fall in love with her.'

'And so might you.'

'I won't.'

'Good, then neither will I.' He laughed and kissed the tip of her nose. 'Now come and help me do the washing up. This is my last night, remember?'

Much later, after they had made love and Leah lay with her head in the hollow of his neck, she said: 'Suppose I asked you to marry me – would that convince you that I'm serious?'

'It'd convince me that you think you are. That's not the same thing.'

'So what would you say?'

His arm tightened round her but he didn't open his eyes. 'I'd say you were feeling ever so slightly insecure.'

'Don't hedge. Would you, Tel? Would you marry me?' When he didn't reply she tugged hard at the hair on his chest.

'*Ow!*' He sat up and looked down at her. 'Listen to me, Leah Dobson. If you think I'd marry a girl with sadistic tendencies you've got another think coming.'

He kissed her and then wrapped his arms around her, pulling the covers up warmly around them both. 'Are you going to let me get some sleep now? I've got an early start in the morning, remember?'

She snuggled close. 'Okay, you win.' After a moment she murmured into his neck: 'I'm going to miss you, Tel.'

'Mmm. Me too.'

'And I *do* know what I want, you know.'

'Right. I'll ask you the same questions a year from now and we'll see, shall we?'

'Oh, all right.' Her lips moved against his skin, tickling his neck. 'I love you, Tel.'

He squeezed her. 'I love you too.'

''Night.'

'Goodnight.'

She fell asleep almost at once but Terry lay for some time, listening to her regular breathing. Being close – making love with Leah had been very special; something he'd dreamed about, wondering often how it would be, but never really believing it would ever happen. Because he loved her it was even more wonderful than any of his dreams; passionate, yet tender and poignant. But perversely, part of him wished now that it hadn't happened. He was pretty sure that Leah had a long way to go before she became a whole person and if she tired of him or changed her mind, it would be so much harder to bear now that they had taken their relationship a step further. He raised himself on one elbow to look down at her in the soft moonlight that filled the room. With her dark hair spread out on the pillow and the vibrant features in repose she looked happy and at peace. If only he could take her at her word when she said she loved him. If only they could stay like this, he thought wistfully.

It was still dark when he was packed and ready to leave next morning. He hadn't wakened Leah, snatching a quick breakfast of toast and coffee downstairs in the kitchen. Now he stood by the bed, looking down at her as she slept. A strand of dark hair lay across her forehead and her cheeks were rosy with sleep. One arm lay across his pillow as though she had reached out for him. It was so tempting to wake her for one last kiss, but he knew that if he did their parting would be almost impossible. Tucking the brief note he had written under the edge of her pillow, he lifted his case and tiptoed out, closing the door softly behind him.

Ralph had returned from Norfolk the following day, his mood still unrepentant. In his absence, David had enlisted the help of an independent accountant and a solicitor and the Evanses had spent all day with the two men, trying to untangle the crippled finances of Evans Hotels. The accountant went through the books that Ralph had brought with him from Norfolk. From time to time he glanced up with a sigh and at the end of his examination his advice was the same as that given by Ralph's accountant. Voluntary bankruptcy.

The solicitor agreed. 'You can file your own petition and it will be heard in the County Court,' he explained. 'The hotels and effects will be sold off to pay the outstanding debts.' Looking at Marie's worried face he added: 'Don't worry, Mrs Evans, you won't be left destitute. The law is not as harsh as it once was. It now requires that you have enough left to provide you with a home. I suggest that we file as soon as possible.'

When Marie had shown the man out David sat in

silence for several minutes, his face like carved grey stone. 'As far as I'm concerned that's the end,' he said at last. 'I'm finished.'

Ralph got up from the table and walked to the window. 'Oh, come *on*, it's not as bad as all that,' he said lightly. 'Within quite a short time we can start up again.'

'What do you mean, *we*?' David asked, his voice like gravel. 'I'm too old to begin again, and even if I intended to carry on, any further business with you would be out of the question.' He looked across the table at Marie. 'What you do, my dear, is up to you of course.'

'I shall be filing for divorce,' she said quietly. 'As soon as all this is over.' She turned to look at Ralph. 'I take it you'll have no objection now?'

He shrugged. 'Do what the hell you like.'

Later that night, when Marie returned from taking David a hot drink, she was surprised to find Ralph preparing for bed in their room.

'There are plenty of rooms vacant downstairs, Ralph,' she said. 'I'd be grateful if you'd sleep in one of those from now on.'

'Yes, I daresay you would.' He continued undressing. 'You may be filing for divorce, but as long as we're married we'll share a room.'

'Then I'll go myself.' She picked up her things and made to walk past him but he caught at her wrist, swinging her round. 'You'll bloody well stay here. There'll be enough for the staff to gossip about soon without giving them some more.' He looked down at her, his lip curling. 'Oh, don't worry. I won't touch you. The very sight of you makes me puke. When I think of the way you've been oiling round Dad – getting him to leave you everything in his Will.' He gave a harsh laugh. 'What a pity there'll be nothing left.' He pulled her towards him to glower intimidatingly down into her face. 'I wonder just how much you've had to do for him to get what you want?'

'You're disgusting.' She tried to turn away but he held on to her wrist with a grip like steel.

'I can't say I've ever found you that exciting myself,' he went on. 'But then, he is an old man. At his age I suppose you have to be grateful for what's on offer.'

Her free hand came up to slap him in the face. All her fury was behind the blow. It was almost a reflex action, surprising herself as much as him. Her fingers throbbed with the impact and for a second he just stood there looking at her, rocking slightly on his heels, his eyes blank with shock. Then, as his hand came up slowly to finger his cheek, he said: 'You'll wish you hadn't done that, Marie. You're going to have to pay for that little bit of self-indulgence.'

'*Pay*?' She laughed hysterically. 'I've already paid everything I have, Ralph. You've had it all – money, position, dignity, and finally self-respect. There's nothing more you can take.' She turned, and picking up her night things from the floor where she'd dropped them, she walked to the door. 'I'll sleep on the couch in the living room. I'd rather sleep on a stone floor than share a room with you again.'

It was six a.m. when the newspapers arrived. The local newsagent delivered a selection to 'The Ocean'. They were taken in by the night porter whose job it was to lay them out on the reception desk before going off duty. Three were always laid aside for the Evanses, to be sent up later along with the mail. They were the *Daily Mail*, the *Independent* and the *Recorder*, a paper Marie liked because of its human interest stories.

434

Chapter 21

Ken Payne still hadn't returned to work after the bout of 'flu he'd had just after Christmas. He looked pale and drawn and the cough that was the result of an additional chest infection still bothered him. Mavis's nerves were stretched to breaking point. What with sleepless nights and worrying over Sally *and* Ken, she was almost at the end of her tether. It was her private opinion that Ken's illness had more to do with Sally's rejection of them than with any virus. His refusal to discuss the matter, or to speculate on the reason for Sally's prolonged silence, frustrated and angered her beyond words. He behaved almost as though he had written the girl off.

Looking across the breakfast table at him this morning she saw that as usual he was absorbed in his newspaper. There was a time when they had chatted companionably to each other over breakfast, but since Sally had left home Ken had wakened each morning in a morose, taciturn mood and usually remained so until well into the morning. Mavis felt hurt and excluded. The most she could get out of him at breakfast these days was a grunt and she had grown accustomed to anticipating his wishes, accepting his silence with resignation.

Pouring him a second cup of tea, she turned her attention to her own paper, the *Recorder*. Ken had always disapproved of it, labelling it a 'rag', but Mavis liked the fashion and the gossip pages. There was more to interest women in the *Recorder*, she argued.

On the front page of today's edition a new series was advertised: 'Yesterday's People'. She saw that it was about women who had made the headlines in the past and what they had done with their lives since. That should be interesting. Mavis refilled her own cup and turned eagerly to the page indicated.

She found the page and then stared in disbelief as her own daughter's face looked up at her from the page. She glanced up at the headline, *Tragic Marie is Reunited with her Lost Twins*, and the blood froze in her veins. As she read, the words seemed to dance before her eyes and her heart began to beat sickeningly fast in her chest. The full page-article resurrected the twenty-year-old story of a young teenage girl, brutally betrayed by her heartless lover. Marie O'Connor's trial and conviction for terrorism, and how she had been forced to give up the twin girls, born in a remand home before her trial, was recounted from newspaper articles printed at the time and transcripts from the trial. Transfixed, Mavis read on:

Marie always protested that she was the innocent victim of a cruel plan to use her as a human bomb, but in spite of her protestations a jury convicted her of conspiracy to cause an explosion. When she came out of prison she built herself a successful new life, but she never forgot the two daughters she was obliged to give up. A few days ago her dream of meeting them again came true when one of them gave birth to a child herself in a London hospital on Christmas Day. As history threatened to repeat itself the girl's sister, who had recently succeeded in her long search for her natural

mother and sister, contacted Marie, begging her
to visit unwed Sally and persuade her not to give
up her baby son.

As Mavis laid down the paper her hands trembled
uncontrollably. So that was it! The reason for Sally's
refusal to come home or even to see them was crystal
clear now.

'Ken.' Her voice sounded high and unfamiliar as
though it belonged to someone else. 'Ken, look.'

'Huh?' Glasses on the end of his nose, he lowered
his own paper a fraction to peer in irritation at her.
'What is it?'

Mavis cleared her throat. 'There's something in
here I think you should see.'

He rattled his newspaper irritably, turning the
page. 'That rubbish? You won't catch me reading the
gutter press.'

'Ken, for heaven's *sake*, I'm serious. Look what it
says – here. It's about our Sally.' She pushed the
paper at him across the table.

'What are you talking about? It can't be.' With a
look of concern he took the paper from her. He read
the article quickly, his lips moving as he read. When
he had finished he pulled off his reading glasses and
looked up at her, his face flushed.

'So that's why she wouldn't come home or let us
go and see her. It wasn't because she didn't want
us. Oh dear God! Our girl – bearing a burden like that
all on her own. She did it for us, to shield us, poor
child.'

Mavis stared at him. 'Do you know what you're
saying? She must have been pregnant before she left
home. She could have married Jason too. He asked
her, and now we know why, don't we?' Her eyes fell
on the newspaper again. 'And now there it all is in the

paper for everyone to see.' She gave a short, hiccuping sob and clasped her hand to her mouth. 'I'll never hold up my head again.'

'For heaven's sake, pull yourself together, Mavis,' Ken snapped irritably, frowning at her. 'This is no time for reproaches. You should be thankful that the girl's all right.' He shook his head, frowning. 'Maybe we should take some of the blame for this. Maybe we should ask ourselves where we went wrong.'

'Where *we* went wrong?' Mavis stared at him.

'We must go to her at once and tell her we forgive her,' Ken went on. 'We must make her see that we don't blame her – that everything will be all right and she must come home. Above all, we can't let her part with that little baby.' He got up from the table, dropping the forgotten newspaper on the floor. 'Where's that Miss Brown's telephone number? I'll ring her. She'll be able to tell us which hospital Sally's in.'

Mavis was stunned into silence by Ken's liberal attitude. What about the morals they'd tried to instill into Sally? Did it count for nothing that she'd clearly ignored them? Was that what he called their 'going wrong'?

'Hannah Brown promised to see Sally and find out if anything was wrong,' she said. 'She's let us down badly in all this, if you ask me.'

'I daresay Sally wouldn't *let* her tell us,' Ken said.

'She should have let us know anyway. It was her duty to . . .'

But Ken wasn't listening. He was muttering to himself as he leafed through the address book they kept beside the telephone. 'B – Br – Ah, here it is,' he said triumphantly. 'I'll ring her, shall I?'

Mavis nodded grudgingly. The initial shock was

wearing off a little now. Ken was right in a way of course. It was a relief that Sally was safe, and that her reason for not coming home had been to save them from shame. A sudden thought made her heart flip with a dizzying stab of excitement. I'm a grandmother. For the first time she wondered what the baby was like. Did he look like Sally? She'd been such a pretty, contented baby. It would be so lovely to have a child in the house again. Her mouth began to soften into a smile 'Oh – all right,' she said, trying to sound casual. 'Talk to her if you like.' But I'll have something to say to Hannah Brown myself later, she added under her breath. She's got a lot of explaining to do.

Leah walked up and down outside Bella's Ristorante. She'd taken her courage in both hands that morning and telephoned the estate agent. She was meeting someone here at eleven to view the place, but in her eagerness she'd arrived ten minutes early. Not that she needed to be shown the place. She was familiar with every nook and cranny of Bella's. It was just that she wanted to see how it would feel to have it belong to her – a bit like trying on a garment for size. It would be fun to look around with fresh eyes and visualise the changes she would make. She had lain awake till the small hours, ideas buzzing through her brain. She'd call it Country Fare or something like that, and specialise in traditional regional dishes using fresh fruit and vegetables – organic maybe if she could find a supply. Perhaps there was a course she could go on to increase her repertoire of dishes? She could turn Alfredo's bar into a carvery, provide snack lunches like the ones she'd served at the Mermaid in Cleybourn – even take-away meals for business folk. She might have a delivery service once she could afford a vehicle and a person to drive it, she told herself, excitement building.

At five past eleven a car drew up and a young man got out. 'Miss Dobson?'

'That's right.' She held out her hand.

He shook it and took the key from his pocket. 'Right then, shall we go in?'

An hour later she was on her way home, her head spinning. Owning Bella's would be a dream she hardly dared to believe could come true. First she would have to get that loan. Terry had seemed fairly optimistic about it, but she still felt doubtful. Why should a bank manager who had never even heard of her provide her with the wherewithal to take such a gigantic risk? Well, she wouldn't know till she had tried, would she? She'd go round and make an appointment this afternoon.

She ran down the area steps and let herself in. The morning papers were still on the kitchen table where Bill had dropped them on his way out. She put the kettle on for coffee and opened the first one, flipping over the pages and scanning them quickly for anything of interest. Then she saw it. Staring up at her was her own likeness, with Sally beside her. It was the photograph that Bill had taken on Christmas Day. And beside it, a picture of a much younger Marie, looking, apart from the out-dated hairstyle and clothes, uncannily like Sally. It was taken from an old newspaper at the time of her trial.

Ignoring the whistling kettle Leah bent over the paper, reading quickly. It was all here; the harrowing story of Marie's betrayal and the reunion brought about by the birth of Sally's baby. But who could have written it? There was no by-line on the story. The new series was credited to someone called 'Pandora'.

Obviously a pseudonym. Her thoughts went immediately to Bill, but she quickly reasoned that it couldn't have been him. He didn't know about Marie's conviction for terrorism. She'd shown only one person the letter Marie had sent her. There was only one person who knew this much about them all and who could also have had access to the photograph. *Terry*. Hadn't he told her when she showed him Marie's letter that he'd discovered the story of her trial and conviction when he went through the newspaper archives on her behalf last autumn?

How could he do this to her? She recalled something he had said: 'If I came across a really hot story I could always sell it to another paper.' No wonder he'd talked her out of going back up north with him. He'd known the story would be published almost immediately and that when she saw it she'd realise it must have come from him. Clearly that hadn't bothered him. He cared much more about his career than about her. Her eyes smarted, remembering their three days together, and at the realisation that all the time he was making love to her he was planning to capitalise on her story. She went upstairs and tried to put through a call to him, but they said at the Manchester office that he was out and wouldn't be in for the rest of the day.

By the time that Bill came in at one o'clock, looking for a quick sandwich and a coffee, she had worked herself into a state of impotent fury.

'Hi,' he said, breezing into the kitchen. 'How did the viewing go?' He stopped short at the look on her face. 'Oh God – as bad as that, eh?'

Leah passed the crumpled copy of the *Recorder* towards him. 'Have you seen this?'

'What is it? The *Recorder*?' He laughed. 'Come on, surely you don't expect me to read a thing like that . . .' He stopped in mid-sentence as his eyes fell on the photograph that he himself had taken. He scanned it quickly, then looked up at her. 'My God. Is all this true – about your mother?' She nodded. Suddenly he looked at her. 'Leah, you didn't think it was me, did you?'

'No. I know who wrote it. It was Terry.'

'No.' He shook his head. 'Tel wouldn't do a thing like that. He doesn't work for this group, and anyway he thinks far too much of you to put you through something like this.'

'He's changed, Bill. He's fiercely ambitious these days. He's determined to get on. He told me only the other day that if he came across a good story he'd sell it to another paper.'

Bill shook his head bemusedly. 'Nothing wrong with ambition, but I can't believe he'd do this to you, Leah. When I rang him on Boxing Day and told him about your sister he sounded so concerned, he . . .'

'*You rang him?*' She stared at him. Terry hadn't come back because he was missing her but because Bill had prompted him to.

'Well, yes.' He looked slightly abashed. 'I was worried about you. I felt you needed a friend with you – someone you could talk to, who knew you really well. He agreed to come at once. And the two of you have seemed so happy these past few days, I thought it had worked.'

Leah felt sick. There was a huge lump in her throat that threatened to choke her. 'Oh, it worked all right,' she said thickly. 'For Terry, it worked.' She stabbed at the paper with her finger. 'Will they have asked Marie for permission to print this? Surely they aren't allowed to publish without?'

'If it's all true and there's nothing libellous in it, yes, they are.'

'I see.' Leah flung herself into a chair. 'Well, that's that then.' She looked up at him with an expression that wrung his heart. 'I've got to make a go of Bella's now, Bill. I've wasted too much time. At least Terry was right about that. He was telling me to stand on my own feet and that's what I intend to do from now on.' She got up. 'I'll go and make an appointment to see the bank manager right away.'

'Leah – wait.' Bill put out a hand to stop her. 'Look, love, I don't want to discourage you, but you haven't a prayer of getting a loan from a bank.' Seeing her defeated look he drew her towards him. 'I'm only telling you because I don't want to see you face another disappointment. Think about it. You don't have anything to offer in the way of security. And although I've every faith in your ability to succeed, you're very young. A spell as a barmaid and another few months as a waitress isn't going to impress any bank manager I know – not in the present economic climate.'

Her shoulders slumped. 'Thanks. So what do you suggest I do next? Dig a hole and jump in?'

'Why don't you let me put up the money?'

'That's not standing on my own feet, is it? Besides, if the bank won't lend me money, why should you?'

'Because I believe in you. Look, I'm no fool, Leah. If the restaurant did well for the Andrettis, it'll do well again for you – better even. If I didn't believe that I'd tell you to forget the idea.' He glanced at his watch. 'Hell, look at the time. I've got to go. What d'you say we sit down and work something out tonight, eh?' Already he was on his way out.

'Okay – thanks, Bill.' Leah sat staring at the door after he had gone. She'd no choice really. She had to have some kind of job and it really was a good opportunity. At least she could work hard and pay Bill back. She'd make a go of it or die in the attempt, she told herself determinedly. At least it was a chance to prove that she could do something

It wasn't until mid-morning that Marie had time to look at the papers. All morning as she went through her routine she wondered with a numb detachment how many more times she would plan menus with the chef, check supplies with the housekeeper and attend to all the other daily routine matters? How long before the loyal members of her staff must be given notice? How long before the doors of 'The Ocean' closed for the last time and the property was placed in the hands of trustees to be disposed of? It was a relief to go upstairs to the empty flat for her coffee break. Ralph was out and David had gone for a further talk to the solicitor. She made her single cup of coffee and carried it through to the living room. When she opened her copy of the *Recorder* and saw the photographs her heart contracted with shock. Who could possibly have got hold of all this information? Who was 'Pandora'? It was all so long ago. She'd thought her story must be long forgotten, but it seemed she was to go on paying the price in spite of everything she had already sacrificed. With a sinking heart she read on:

On her release from prison Marie O'Connor went into the hotel business, marrying her boss's son a few years later. An odd twist of fate decreed that her husband Ralph was newly home from Northern Ireland where he had served with the military police. He, like so many others, must surely have believed in her innocence. Now together they own and run several hotels around the British coast; popular hotels that carry a reputation for luxury combined with personal service and a family atmosphere.

444

Twenty years on, reunited with her daughters and established in her successful new life as a businesswoman, Marie is living proof that it is possible to overcome the worst of disasters.

She closed the paper with a sigh. This was the last straw – all she needed just now. Could this Pandora person know what anguish it would cause her, or the harm it could do to the business? She'd be viewed very differently by staff and guests alike now that her past life had been laid bare for all to see. Did any of these people give a damn about the result of their work? Surely they should have asked her first for permission to print this kind of information about her?

The secret she had kept from Ralph all these years was out in the open now. It was only a matter of time before he picked up this paper and read about it. What would his reaction be then? Marie sighed resignedly. What did it matter any more? Their lives were falling apart anyway. There was nothing more he could do to hurt her, and Evans Hotels were finished too now that he'd bankrupted them. None of it mattered really. Then her heart plummeted as she remembered Philip. What anyone else thought didn't really matter – but Philip . . . She valued his opinion of her. And the girls – Leah and Sarah. They'd never forgive her for drawing this kind of attention on them. She laid her head down on her folded arms. I might as well have died in prison, she told herself despairingly. I'm never going to shake off the stigma of my conviction – never going to be able to prove my innocence. I'll never get to know my daughters now.

Ralph had spent the morning driving round, waiting for the pubs to open. If ever he had needed a drink it was this morning. The past few days had been trying in the extreme, testing his nerve almost to breaking point. The sooner all this could be got through and he could make his escape, the better he would like it. He thought of the coming weeks. He would have to part with the Merc and a few of the other luxuries he had become accustomed to, but that was a small price to pay for the future he had planned. The thought buoyed him up. Warm sunshine and a life of leisure, money in his pocket to spend as he chose. Not long to wait now.

There had been times when he had seriously questioned if it was all worth it. David Evans, the man he'd called Father all these years, was nothing more than a boring old fart, and Marie had gone from placid compliance, irritating him sorely with her sanctimonious whining, to stubborn defiance. There'd been a time when he could control her. One smack across her quivering mouth had been enough to stop her nonsense in the early days. He had to admit that there had been times when he'd enjoyed bullying her into line. But more recently she'd started standing up to him. Instead of bowing under his dominance, she seemed to have become stronger. No doubt wheedling her way successfully into a firm promise of the old man's money had given her a feeling of security.

In the bar of his favourite hostelry he sat alone with a double whiskey. He'd acquired a taste for Irish during his service days. He tipped back his head and relished its fiery solace, feeling it slide smoothly down his dry throat, warm and relax his jangled nerves. The corners of his mouth lifted in a smile at the thought of Marie buttering up David to get what she could out of the old fool when all the time he'd been there before her, milking the business for all it was worth. The thought of the money, salted away out of harm's way, warmed him. He liked the picture of Marie wheedling and cajoling away for nothing. It was rich; something to remember and savour in the years to come. They'd be all right, those two. The solicitor had said that they wouldn't be left destitute. And she was still young and fit enough to earn a living for them both. They deserved each other. Bloody good luck to them.

The bar was almost empty but someone had left a newspaper on the table where he sat. He drew it towards him and began to leaf through the pages. The *Recorder*. A popular paper though not one he normally read. But he was bored enough this morning to have read the telephone directory if there'd been one handy. When he got to the centre pages he paused. The photograph of the fair-haired woman looked a bit like Marie. He looked closer, frowning. It was Marie – twenty years ago when she was a very young girl. What the hell was it doing in the paper? Surely they couldn't have got wind of the bankruptcy.

Leaning forward, he began to read rapidly. So they'd dug up the stuff about her prison sentence? But the bit about her having twins by the bloke who'd ditched her – that was news to him. His eyes narrowed as he wondered just how much of this story his father knew. No wonder he'd been so keen to get the two of them hitched. God, but they'd taken him for a mug.

He read on – about the bomb found in her suitcase and her arrest on a charge of 'conspiracy to cause an explosion'. He shook his head, speculating on how much *he* could have squeezed out of a newspaper if only he'd thought of selling the story.

It seemed that Marie had protested all through that she was innocent – that she'd been the victim of a plot to cause an explosion. All through the trial she'd persistently named a man, but her alleged lover could not be traced and it was believed that the man she named as Liam Costello was a figment of the girl's imagination, dreamed up in the hope of procuring a sympathetic acquittal. Ralph laughed to himself. A likely story. He began to wish he'd used his knowledge of her terrorist connections to bring her into line earlier.

Then suddenly a thought occurred to him and the sneer left his face. He sat back in his chair, one finger nervously loosening his collar. Marie couldn't have picked a worse time to get herself into the papers. Before you could say 'knife' some nosey sod of a journalist would be sniffing round *his* past too. Knowing how deep they were capable of digging, it wouldn't be long before the finger of suspicion would point in the direction of his business practices. And that wasn't all. He felt the sweat break out under his collar as another, more sinister thought occurred to him. Suppose some of this Costello's cronies began to get touchy? Suppose they found that he – the former Sergeant Ralph Evans – had married Costello's woman?

Shaken, he bought himself another double whiskey and returned to his corner to think. There might well be old scores to settle. Costello understandably hadn't come forward at the time. Presumably there'd been more at stake for him than the discovery of a few pounds of explosive in a suitcase.

Ralph's face took on the colour of putty as his imagination worked overtime. Clearly the time had come to make himself scarce. He'd intended to brazen it out – see the bankruptcy through as though everything was above board. He was pretty sure he'd cooked the books convincingly. At least he was confident that nothing could be proved. He'd cleverly planned to come out of it with his name clean, even with a few quid to spare. But this newspaper article changed all that. He couldn't afford to hang around now and wait for the press to make mincemeat of him. His lying bitch of a wife and the old man were going to have to battle it out on their own. But he couldn't just disappear. He chewed his lower lip. What to do and how to make it look convincing enough to keep them all off his back – that was the question.

He tossed back the remainder of his drink and ordered another. Then in a flash of inspiration the idea came to him. Of course, why hadn't he thought of it before? He'd use the Merc. He smiled to himself, the irony of the idea appealing to him. It was a fitting twist. After all, if he couldn't have it, why should they?

When Sally saw Hannah coming up the ward that afternoon along with the other visitors, her heart sank. She'd promised to leave her alone. What did she want now? Then she saw that Hannah was not alone and her heart missed a beat. Behind her, walking on tiptoe as though they were in church, came Mavis and Ken Payne. Speechless, she stared at Hannah, then at her parents as they reached her bed to stand awkwardly at the foot. Ken was the first to speak.

'Sally, love. Why on earth didn't you *tell* us?' There was no hint of reproach in his voice but the wounded look in his eyes brought a lump to Sally's throat. 'Couldn't you trust us not to fly off the handle at you? Did you think we'd blame you?'

Mavis said nothing but her eyes spoke volumes. The hurt and disappointment she had felt since reading the newspaper article showed clearly in them, but in spite of this she pushed Ken impatiently out of the way and stepped up to Sally.

'How are you feeling then, lovie?' she asked gently. Hannah had told her the shocking news about Sally's operation. Contemplating a life of childlessness was something Mavis knew all about. She bent and kissed her daughter, giving her a motherly hug. 'Don't you worry about it any more, lovie. Your daddy and I are going to take that little baby home and bring him up ourselves. He's not to go to strangers – not your little son.'

Dumbfounded, Sally stared into Mavis's eyes. How did they *know*? How had they found out? Had Hannah told them after all? Suddenly all the resentment and the blame she had attached to them evaporated. The joy and relief of seeing them – touching them – of having them here with her after all these months overwhelmed her. Tears of weakness poured down her cheeks.

'Mum – oh, *Mum*!' was all she could mutter as she clung to Mavis. Ken moved to the other side of the bed and joined in the embrace.

'There, there, pet. Don't take on like that. You'll have me at it in a minute.'

Hannah quietly pulled the curtains round the bed and withdrew, leaving them to have their reunion in private.

When the emotion of the moment had subsided and Mavis sat in the chair provided for visitors, dabbing at her puffy eyes, Ken drew the tightly folded paper out of his pocket.

'This is how we found out, love, in case you're wondering,' he explained. 'I don't suppose you've had the chance to see it.' He spread the centre sheet of the *Recorder* on the bed in front of Sally and she read, her eyes growing round with astonishment. Did Leah know about Marie's past? If she did she had never mentioned it. According to what the newspaper article said, Marie Evans had overcome her disastrous past and now had everything she wanted from life. Obviously she had had second thoughts

450

about taking up with the daughter she had long since given away.

'You can carry on with your work if you'll only come home,' Mavis was saying. 'You don't have to do anything you don't want to.' She smiled. 'I expect you thought we'd insist that Jason married you?'

Sally stared at them in dismay. '*Jason*? But Jason wasn't – isn't – the baby's father.'

Mavis's jaw dropped with surprise.

'But he was so fond of you,' Ken said. 'He *asked* you to marry him, didn't he?'

'Yes, he did, but he knew the truth of it. He was just being kind. I couldn't let him. You do see that?'

Mavis was frowning. 'Well then, who . . . ?'

Slowly and painfully, Sally told them about the night of Sharon's party. She owed them the truth. There must be no more lies. 'I deceived you,' she said softly. 'But it was because I felt smothered – overprotected. All the same, I shouldn't have gone to Sharon's without telling you.'

'I never liked that girl,' Mavis muttered. 'Always said no good would come of knocking around with her kind.'

'You shouldn't have left home without telling us what it was all about either,' Ken said sadly.

'If I'd stayed it would have been awful for you, Dad,' Sally said. 'The shame would have half killed you. There'd have been all your friends at Chapel to face – the neighbours. I wanted to save you that. I wanted to handle it on my own. I thought I could, at the time. Later, I wasn't so sure.'

'Silly girl. There's not the stigma there used to be,' Ken said dismissively. 'This sort of thing happens all the time nowadays. Anyway, as if we *care* about any of them. What matters is that we've obviously failed you, and we want you to come

451

home so that we can make it up to you.'

Mavis was frowning at what she saw as Ken's over-indulgent reaction. 'You *did* do wrong, Sally,' she put in with a shake of her head. 'There's no getting away from that.' She gave Ken a reproachful look. 'But you've paid a terrible price for it. Like Daddy says, we want to help you start again.' She leaned forward to take Sally's hand. 'We've been to St Mary's to see the baby. You didn't really want to give him up, did you?'

Sally shook her head, her eyes brimming. 'Everyone seems to think I'm hard, but it isn't that. There seemed no other way. I didn't see how I could manage to keep us both on what I earn. It would have been such a miserable existence for both of us.'

'He's lovely, Sally,' Mavis told her. 'The image of you were when you were tiny. I can't wait to get him home and love him. He's had such a sorry start, poor little mite. What do you say? Will you let us take him? Will you come too?'

Sally considered. 'What I'd like is to keep my job here and maybe come home for weekends. Is that all right?'

Ken patted her shoulder. 'Of course it is, love. Just as long as you know it's your home, you can come whenever you like.'

That decided, Mavis considered that she could safely mention what had been nagging at her ever since she had read the article. 'It says in the paper that you've been reunited with your mother and sister,' she said.

Sally nodded. 'Yes, Leah got in touch with me when I came to London. We've seen each other a couple of times. She invited me to her place for Christmas and I was there when the baby started. I don't really know what I would have done without her.' She paused, trying to assess their reaction. 'Marie – my natural mother – came later, after the baby was born. Leah was so against me giving the baby up for adoption and when I wouldn't listen she asked Marie to try to persuade me to keep him.'

'So we gathered from the paper.' Mavis and Ken exchanged glances. 'What was she like?' Mavis asked, unable to contain her curiosity. What must a woman who had mixed with terrorists and been in prison be like? She couldn't possibly imagine. All she hoped was that Sally had made no plans to see the woman again.

Sally smiled. 'She was nice, and very kind. She didn't try to persuade me either way. She really understood how I felt.' She covered Mavis's hand with hers. 'But she was a stranger, Mum. That's all she'll ever be, a stranger.'

Leah and Bill sat opposite each other at the kitchen table. He had laid his plan before her in some detail.

'I could take out a mortgage in my name. I'd get one easily. This house is mine, you see, my parents left it to me. Or, alternatively, I could sell it and buy Bella's outright. These houses are very popular nowadays. The agents can't get enough of them. After all, there's quite a large flat over the restaurant, isn't there?'

Leah's heart sank. Was that to be a condition – that he moved in with her? Better to get it out of the way once and for all. 'I'm sorry, Bill,' she said. 'But if that's part of the deal you can count me out.'

'Okay, okay.' He held up his hands. 'It was only an idea. What I was planning was to give up my job once the restaurant was established and help you run it. If I'm to do that it would seem to make more sense if I sold this place.'

'But suppose it didn't work out?' Leah said. 'Wouldn't it be better to keep your house on for a while, just in case? You could always let the rooms to help with the overheads.'

'I suppose you're right.' He looked at her. 'We would be partners though, wouldn't we?'

'Business partners, yes,' Leah said guardedly. 'Nothing else, Bill.'

He studied her face thoughtfully for a minute. 'This business with Terry has hit you hard, hasn't it?'

'I suppose it has.'

'I always knew you were in love with him,' he said a little ruefully. 'Even if you didn't know it yourself.'

'If I was, it's over,' she told him firmly. 'There'll be no more men in my life. I'm sick of them if you want to know.' She stopped to smile at him apologetically. 'Present company excepted, of course.'

He shrugged good-naturedly. 'Maybe it's a father figure you're looking for. And much as I hate the idea, I'm old enough to be it, I suppose.'

'I've had two fathers already, thanks,' she said. 'The first one tried to have me blown up before I'd even seen the light of day and the second one despised me simply for being me. I don't think I'll be looking for any more fathers.'

'Well, I won't say I'm not relieved to hear it.' He reached across the table and touched her hand. 'Leah, I'm still your friend, you know. I won't let you down, I promise. You do trust me, don't you?' He stood up and drew her to her feet. 'I'll never make any demands on you. We said we'd be loving friends for each other once, didn't we?'

She allowed him to draw her close, letting her head rest against his shoulder. It was good to feel his strength flow into her, to lean against his shoulder and relax. But then he turned her face up to his and kissed her and when she felt his tongue probe her lips apart to explore her mouth, when she felt his arousal beginning, she stiffened, suddenly hurt and angry. What did he think she was? What did *any* of them think she was? Bill had sent for Terry when he thought she needed help. He knew how it had been between them yet now . . . He thinks I'm an easy lay like they all do! Angry tears sprang to her eyes and she pushed him away.

'Bill, don't. I'm sorry, I can't.'

He let her go, his hands dropping to his sides. Under his breath he swore softly. Not because of her refusal but because of his own clumsiness. 'Sorry, Leah. I shouldn't have done that. I won't again, I promise. Strictly business from now on.'

She turned away, shaking her head, unsure now. A few months ago she would have seized the chance to capitalise on Bill's desire for her, but now . . . He had been right about one thing: Terry's betrayal certainly had got to her. And, yes, she couldn't deny that she was in love with him. The knowledge was deeply humiliating – like looking her own weakness in the face. But weakness could be overcome.

'Well?' Bill was looking at her anxiously. 'Am I forgiven? Do we go ahead with the restaurant?'

She turned to him. 'Look, I'd like some time to think about it. I think I'd like to go away for a while.'

'Where?'

She searched her mind for the answer. She could go down to Cleybourn. Stay at the Mermaid with Dick – work her passage. But Cleybourn held memories of other past mistakes. No. There was only one person she really wanted to see; only one person with whom she could truly be herself. 'I think I'll go and stay with Granny Dobson for a few days,' she said.

He nodded, forcing himself to smile. 'That sounds

like a good idea, and you could do with a break after all that's happened. But don't stay away too long, will you? Bella's might be snapped up by someone else. Besides,' he added with a sheepish, lop-sided grin, 'I'll miss you.'

Sally was in the day room when Leah arrived. She couldn't leave London without seeing her sister – finding out what her reaction to the article in the *Recorder* had been. She found her sitting by the TV set, watching one of the daily 'soaps' whilst a gaggle of middle-aged female patients gossiped over their knitting at the other end of the room.

'Hello there.'

To her surprise Sally looked up at her with a welcoming smile. 'Leah, I'm so glad you've come. I think they're going to let me out of here in a few days and I was hoping to see you before I left.'

'It's nice to see you looking so much better.' Leah drew up a chair close to her. 'I'm sorry I haven't been in for a few days, but a friend has been down for a visit. Besides, we haven't exactly seen eye to eye, have we? I didn't want to hinder your recovery.'

'I've got lots to tell you.' Sally's eyes shone and her cheeks were pink with excitement.

'Before you go any further – did you see the article about us in the *Recorder*?'

'Yes. That's what brought it all about,' Sally said. 'My parents saw it and they rang Hannah at once. They came up to London to see me yesterday and everything is going to be all right, Leah. They want to take the baby and bring him up for me. And I'm to keep my job here in London and go home to see him every weekend.'

Leah felt her heart lift with relief. Reaching out she took both of Sally's hands and squeezed them. 'That's great news. I'm so happy for you, and for little Jamie too.'

'They like the name you chose for him,' Sally told her. 'Except that they're going to call him James instead of Jamie.'

'Sally, was it a shock, reading about Marie's past – the circumstances in which we were born? I suppose I should have told you before. I found out when I was trying to trace her. I'm sorry you had to find out like that.'

'It's all right. I shan't be seeing her again,' Sally said. 'She came to see me, you know, invited me to go down to Dorset and convalesce at her hotel. I thought she was so kind. But I had a letter from her the other day, putting me off. She said something about being too busy.' She shrugged. 'I was hurt and disappointed at the time, but maybe it's all for the best. I'll be going home now anyway.'

'I'm going home too,' Leah said. 'At least, I'm going to stay with my grandmother for a while. I'm thinking of going into business with Bill. We're going to buy the restaurant where I used to work. His cash and my know-how. At least, that's the plan.'

'But you're not sure?'

Leah lifted her shoulders. 'I'd rather be independent, but beggars can't be choosers, can they? Anyway, Granny Dobson will put me right. She's the wisest person I know.' She stood up. 'I'll have to go now. You will keep in touch, won't you, Sally? Maybe when we're both back in London we could meet occasionally.'

'That would be nice.' Sally walked to the lift with her. They turned to each other and Sally held out her arms. 'Thanks for everything, Leah.'

Leah hugged her. 'What for? All I did was nag you. If I'd been you I'd have told me to get stuffed.'

'You were such a help when Jamie was born, staying with me like that, not letting me go through it alone. If it hadn't been for you and Bill . . .'

Leah shook her head. 'That's all over. Take care of yourself. Give little Jamie a cuddle for me.' To her great relief the lift doors opened at that moment. She got in quickly with a bright smile at Sally. ''Bye. Take care.' The doors closed and she was left with the image of her sister, still pale and fragile-looking in her pink quilted dressing gown, her hand half raised in a wave. As the lift plunged downward she swallowed hard at the lump in her throat, fumbling in her pocket for a handkerchief. Damn! Why was she so easily moved to tears lately? She must be getting soft in her old age.

Leah stood in the hall at Melbury Street, listening to the telephone ringing out at the other end. In her mind's eye she pictured Granny Dobson getting up stiffly from her chair and going into the hall of the bungalow to answer it. Could it be that she was in her beloved garden, picking winter greens for lunch? Whatever the reason, she always took some time to answer the telephone so Leah hung on, a smile of anticipation on her face. Wait till Kate heard that she was coming up to stay for a few days. She'd be so pleased. They'd have such a lot to tell each other and laugh over. They might even . . .

'*Hello*.' Her thoughts were abruptly interrupted by a strident voice. It wasn't Kate's.

'Oh – hello. Can I speak to Mrs Dobson please?'

'I take it you mean Mrs *Kate* Dobson.'

God. It was Hilary. 'Yes. Is she there?'

There was a pause. 'Is that you, Leah?'

'Yes, it is.'

'This is your . . . This is Hilary. It's odd that you

458

should ring. I was going to ring you later this morning. I'm afraid your grand . . . I'm afraid that poor Kate died early this morning.'

Hilary's brutal abruptness hit Leah like a mule's kick. Groping behind her for a chair she sat down heavily. 'She – she *died*? How? What was the matter with her?'

'Pneumonia – among other things,' Hilary said in a detached tone. 'She'd had a series of bad colds all winter and she never would take proper care of herself. The doctor put her into hospital towards the end.'

'I wish you'd let me know.' Hilary didn't reply. 'When – when is the funeral?' Leah asked.

There was a pause, pregnant with meaning. 'You mean to come then?'

'Of course. Granny Dobson meant a lot to me.'

'*Evidently*. I understand you were here shortly before Christmas.'

Hilary's voice sounded shrill and slightly accusing. Surely she wasn't annoyed because Leah hadn't visited her and Jack? 'That's right.'

'Then you won't be surprised to know that she made a new Will.'

'Did she?'

'Yes, she did. I think you certainly *had* better come, Leah, and as soon as you can make it,' Hilary went on. 'More especially in view of the fact that you now appear to be her sole beneficiary. But of course you already knew that, didn't you?'

'No. Of course I didn't know.'

Hilary gave a dry, disbelieving little laugh. 'But don't think for one minute that you're going to get away with it, Leah. Jack and I will contest the Will. We're going to see our solicitor as soon as we can. I'll expect you some time tomorrow – right?' And

without waiting for a reply she rang off abruptly, leaving Leah staring numbly into the receiver.

Chapter 22

Hannah didn't see the article in the *Recorder* until she got home from work late in the evening. The moment she had finished reading it she telephoned Marie.

'How did the press get hold of the story?' she asked. 'Has anyone been to see you?'

But as soon as Marie began speaking it became clear that the re-emergence of her past was only one of her problems.

'We're bankrupt, Hannah,' she said bleakly. 'It's what I've been afraid of for a long time. We're having to wind up the business and get out. Everything we've worked for over the years has been wrecked by Ralph's mismanagement. The newspaper story was a blow but it's not the worst thing that's happened.'

'How is David taking it?' Hannah asked.

'Surprisingly enough, he seems to be coping quite well,' Marie said. 'He's doing all he can to try to salvage as much as possible out of all this. As for the story in the *Recorder*, he's more worried for me than for himself.'

'And Ralph?'

Marie's sigh was audible at the other end of the line. 'It seems he read the story in a bar somewhere. He came back here blazing with fury, accusing me of deception – justifiably, I suppose. But it was all he needed to deflect some of the blame for the crash from himself. He actually accused David and me of setting him up. Then he stormed out, saying that we'd wrecked his life between us and that he'd got nothing left to live for.'

'And now?'

'I don't know. I haven't seen him since.' Marie's voice caught and trembled. 'Oh, Hannah, it's all such a mess. And after I tried so hard – after I thought I'd lived it down.'

'I'll come right down,' Hannah said decisively. 'I'm due a few days off. A colleague will take over anything that can't wait. Just give me time to fix things at this end and I'll come.' She paused. 'If you want me, that is.'

'Oh, Hannah, of course I want you,' Marie said. 'You're just about the only real friend I've got left now.'

The following morning Hannah spent an hour on the telephone, rearranging her work schedule. The last call she made was to Leah. She listened to the phone ringing at the other end for a few minutes, but when there was no reply she replaced the receiver and scribbled a quick note. Putting it into an envelope and addressing it to Leah, she posted it on her way to collect the car. It was only right that the girl should know about Marie's trouble.

She arrived at 'The Ocean' late that afternoon and found Marie exhausted. She had spent the morning talking to the managers of each of the hotels on the telephone, explaining the situation and instructing them to dismiss staff and cancel all bookings. Advertisements for the coming season had to be cancelled and tradesmen notified. The painful business of winding up seemed endless, and Ralph clearly had no intention of doing any of it. It had been a traumatic day and at the end of it Marie looked pale and drained of energy.

David, on the other hand, seemed oddly buoyant. Talking to him, Hannah had the impression that the demise of Evans Hotels would be something of a relief to him.

'Things started to go wrong almost as soon as Ralph joined us,' he told Hannah after they had packed Marie off to have a hot bath before dinner. 'We were doing well up till then – keeping the business on an even keel, being careful not to overreach ourselves. Marie was good at the business side. She made sure we kept our heads well above water. But when Ralph came in with us he wouldn't let her touch it – insisted on having it all his own way.' He looked at her. 'I don't know whether she told you, but Ralph isn't my true son.'

'Marie hasn't told me anything.'

David nodded. 'No. She wouldn't. My first wife let me believe that Ralph was mine when all the time he was another man's child. It didn't really surprise me, to be honest. I'd suspected it for some time. She lied to me in other things too, you see. She wasn't like Meg, my second wife. Now there was a woman for you . . .' He smiled reminiscently to himself and Hannah could see that his mind was drifting. She looked at her watch.

'When will Ralph be back? I don't imagine that he's going to be exactly overjoyed to see me.'

The smile left David's face as his eyes darted to the clock. 'I've no idea. He doesn't tell us when to expect him. He might even have gone back to Norfolk for all I know. Between you and me, Hannah, I hope he has. He came back here after he'd seen the newspaper article yesterday, raving and shouting at poor Marie –

as if she hasn't enough to bear. He flung off somewhere afterwards, left her in a shocking state and didn't come in all night. We haven't seen him since.'

The three of them ate dinner together and afterwards David went off to his room, saying he was tired and would appreciate an early night.

'What will you do now?' Hannah asked when they were alone.

Marie shook her head. 'I haven't thought much about it. At the moment it's a question of taking one day at a time. David is my priority though. I'll have to make some kind of home for him. Maybe we'll be able to afford a little flat. After I've sorted that out I suppose I'll have to find a job – start trying to pick up the pieces.'

'And Ralph? Where has he gone, do you think?'

Marie shrugged. 'Who knows? Over the past few years we've seen very little of him anyway. And when he was here he usually made trouble. I'll be filing for divorce,' she added. 'I would have preferred to have done it with the church's blessing but we can't possibly stay married now so it seems I'll have to do without.'

'Have you spoken to Philip?' Hannah ventured.

'I wrote to him last night and told him everything,' Marie said. 'I thought it was the best way. I have to face the fact that a man in his position can't be associated with this kind of thing. Not only having my lurid past spread all over the newspapers, but bankruptcy as well. It'll only be a matter of time before the press gets hold of that too. I told him not to contact me for a while. And that I shall understand if he wants to drop our friendship permanently.'

'Oh, Marie.' Hannah hesitated. 'Look, something's been bothering me in all this. Do you blame me? I'd understand if you did. I mean, if it hadn't been for Leah asking me to put her in touch with you again none of it would ever have come out.'

'Blame *you*?' Marie smiled and shook her head. 'You're my best – my only real friend, apart from David. Of course I don't blame you. We don't know that my meeting with the girls triggered this off. Heaven only knows how the story got out. But whatever it was, I'll always be grateful that I had the chance to see them again. I'm sorry that Leah and I couldn't agree. Even sorrier that I had to let Sally down without explaining properly. But at least I saw them.'

'Sally is keeping the baby,' Hannah told her. 'At least, her adoptive parents are going to bring him up for her. They saw the newspaper article and it brought them all together again.'

Marie sighed wistfully. 'I'm glad it did some good. And I'm glad she won't have to go through the years wondering about her child as I have.'

They went to bed just after eleven o'clock and Hannah went to sleep almost immediately. She was awakened some time later by movement outside her door in the passage. Switching on her bedside lamp she saw that it was a little after one o'clock. There were voices, Marie's and another, male and unfamiliar. Not Ralph's or David's. With a sudden feeling of foreboding, she got up and put on her dressing gown, then opened the door and looked out. The light in the hallway was on and she could see that the door of the living room was ajar. Walking across she pushed it open to look in. A tall policeman stood by the fireplace. He was looking anxiously at Marie who sat on the settee, looking numb and dazed. As Hannah opened the door he glanced up and saw her standing in the doorway.

'Are you a relative, madam?'

'No, a friend. What's happened?'

'I'm afraid there's been an accident.' The policeman walked across to her, easing her out into the hallway and pulling the door to behind him. 'Earlier this evening a car went over the cliffs at Lulworth,' he said quietly. 'The cliffs are very high there and very rugged. It's a total wreck. It exploded on impact, but one of the number plates was thrown clear. We've established from that that the car belonged to Mr Ralph Evans.'

'And you're sure he was in the car when it crashed?'

'As I said, it was blown to bits,' he said. 'There's very little left and what there is is in the sea, but we'll have frogmen out at first light and forensics will be going over what there is as soon as possible. We understand Mr Evans has had some financial difficulties,' he added quietly. 'I'm very much afraid that everything points to suicide.' He nodded towards the door. 'Will you be staying on tomorrow or shall I send a WPC along?'

'I'm staying.'

'So you'll look after Mrs Evans? I don't think the shock has really sunk in yet. She'll be needing someone when it does.'

Hannah nodded. 'Of course.'

Leah walked from the station. She had only a small case and it hardly seemed worth waiting for a bus or getting a taxi. At Acacia Grove Hilary opened the door to her. When she saw Leah standing on the doorstep her mouth seemed to set in an uncompromising line. Leah wondered detachedly whether she realised how old it made her look.

'So you've come?' she said superfluously. 'I've prepared your old room. I think you know where it is.' She walked through to the kitchen and closed the door, leaving Leah to make her own way upstairs.

She found that her old room had been completely refurnished and redecorated. It was as though they had tried to erase any trace of her. She unpacked the few things she had brought with her, washed and renewed her lipstick, then went downstairs. There seemed to be no one about, so she tapped on the kitchen door and looked in. Hilary was making tea.

'I suppose you'd like a drink,' she said grudgingly over her shoulder.

'Thank you.' Leah shut the door and took a seat on one of the breakfast bar stools. 'Look, I'd like to get one thing straight,' she said. 'I came to see Gran before Christmas but I had absolutely nothing to do with any change she may have made to her Will. She has never, at any time, mentioned it to me. Anyway, I'm pretty sure she had no intention of dying for years yet.'

Hilary made no reply. Pouring a cup of tea, she pushed it towards Leah along the worktop. 'I'd prefer not to discuss the matter of Kate's estate until Jack is here,' she said. 'I told you we were seeing our solicitor. Jack is with him now.' She took her green Barbour from behind the door where it always hung and put it on. 'I'll leave you with your tea now, if you don't mind,' she said, zipping the front with an air of grim determination. 'I've got some work to do in the garden.'

'Aren't you worried I might ransack the house while you're gone?' Leah muttered under her breath as the door closed. It looked like being an uncomfortable few days. In fact, by the look of Hilary it was going to be bloody impossible. Picking up her cup of tea, she made her way back to her room with it.

When Jack came home he was in a black mood.

Hilary met him in the hall and held a finger to her lips, nodding towards the stairs.

'She's arrived. She's upstairs.' She raised an eyebrow at him. 'Well – what did he say?'

Jack drew her into his study and closed the door. 'It's no use,' he said. 'There isn't a thing we can do.'

Hilary's jaw dropped, her mouth forming a silent oval. 'But there *must* be. She isn't even a real relative.'

Jack lifted his shoulders. 'Makes no difference. Mother was entitled to leave her money to whoever she chose. And she chose Leah.'

'Surely we can still contest it, under the circumstances?'

Jack shook his head. 'It seems we wouldn't stand a chance unless we could prove that without Mother's money we would be seriously deprived financially. I'm sure we don't want *that* kind of publicity.'

Hilary shuddered at the thought. 'What about her state of mind? Can't we plead that she didn't know what she was doing?'

'No. Apparently the Will was drawn up and signed in the presence of her solicitor and witnessed by a member of the office staff. Both were completely satisfied that she was totally compos mentis at the time. And by the way, it seems that it was all done *before* Leah's Christmas visit.'

'I see.' Hilary bit her lip. 'There can't be much money, of course, but there's the bungalow and about half an acre of land. It won't fetch a great deal, but it annoys me to think of Leah getting it after all her ingratitude and – what she did.'

Jack gritted his teeth. As a member of the Town Council and chairman of the planning committee, he knew that there was more to his mother's Will than a clapped out bungalow and a bit of land, but he wasn't going into that with Hilary now. He'd had enough for one day. 'Nothing more we can do about it.' He glanced towards the ceiling. 'I suggest we encourage her to leave as soon as possible after the funeral.'

Hilary nodded in agreement. 'Leave it to me.'

Dinner was a strained affair. No one spoke unless they were obliged to. Jack passed Leah a piece of paper on which he'd written the name of Kate's solicitors and advised her to visit their offices first thing in the morning.

'And Hilary and I would appreciate your silence on the matter of the Will,' he added. 'Thankfully, we managed to keep your last little escapade quiet. We do still have to live here, remember.'

After coffee Leah excused herself and went gratefully up to her room, glad to escape.

Kate's solicitor turned out to be a woman called Jane English. She was the junior partner in an old established firm whose offices were tucked away in a narrow street behind the market place. When Leah was ushered into her office, Jane rose and came round her desk to shake her hand.

'How nice to meet you, Miss Dobson. I've heard so much about you from your grandmother.' She smiled and indicated a chair. 'Do please have a seat. I've ordered some coffee. It'll be here in a moment.'

'I wasn't Kate Dobson's real granddaughter,' Leah said. 'Her son and daughter-in-law adopted me when I was seven.'

Jane smiled. 'I know.'

'I'm telling you because I'm afraid this Will of hers is causing some bad feeling. I left home a few months ago, you see – after a row. My parents don't approve of Gran leaving everything to me.'

Jane nodded. 'Mrs Dobson senior foresaw that and

warned me to make sure everything was tightly sewn up with no loopholes. But her message to you was to take no notice. She said you'd earned it and she was sure that you were well up to sticking it out and fighting for what was rightly yours.'

Leah's lips twitched. The words were typical of Kate, she could almost hear her saying them as she signed the document; chuckling to herself, her bright eyes glinting with glee at the mischief she was about to cause. 'I won't be living in the bungalow, of course,' she said. 'I'd like you to handle the sale of it for me if you would.'

'Just as you wish.' The coffee arrived and a secretary brought in Kate's file. When the girl had withdrawn Jane opened the file and took out Kate's Will. 'It should be relatively simple,' she said. 'As the Will is very straightforward and you are the sole beneficiary, probate should take no longer than a couple of weeks, after which we can begin to dispose of the property on your instructions.'

She took off her reading glasses and looked at Leah. 'Now – under normal circumstances the bungalow would not fetch a very great sum. It's in need of extensive modernisation and is lacking most of the amenities that people take for granted nowadays. But for some time past Wonderbuy, one of the giant supermarket chains, has been trying to buy the small estate on which it stands in order to build a large hypermarket and car park. All the other owner-occupiers have agreed to sell. Your grandmother was the last to hold out.'

Leah's eyes opened wide. 'She never mentioned this to me. What price are they offering? Should I accept? Would you say it was fair?'

Jane smiled. 'Oh, more than fair, Miss Dobson – *much* more.' The figure she named took Leah's breath away. She could see now why Jack and Hilary were so annoyed.

'All *that* – just to pull it down?'

'Ironically, your grandmother's stubbornness has increased the price,' Jane told her. 'But believe me, if they didn't feel it was worth it they wouldn't have made the offer. If I were you I'd accept at once before they give up and look for a site elsewhere.' She opened a drawer and took out an envelope and a labelled key. 'Your grandmother left you this letter,' she said. 'And this is the key to the bungalow. You'll probably want to go along and sort out her belongings.' She passed them across the desk. 'I can give you the name of a good firm of house clearers if you like. They'll dispose of the contents for you and forward the money to us to add to the estate.'

Out in the fresh air Leah felt stunned. She was going to have more money than she'd ever imagined possible. She was actually going to be quite rich. She did a quick sum in her head. If she were to invest the money she could probably live modestly on the interest for the rest of her life without ever doing a stroke of work. But she certainly wasn't going to do that. She would use it to make something of herself. If she couldn't have love, then she'd build respect; she'd make people admire and look up to her. She and the money would work together to make a dream come true. And even as the thought occurred to her, Leah knew without any shadow of doubt that it was for this that Kate had left her the money.

The funeral that Jack Dobson had arranged for his mother appalled Leah. It was ostentatious to say the least and Leah knew that Kate would have hated it. It was well attended, mostly by Jack's business colleagues, fellow Rotarians and Councillors. Hardly any of them knew Kate personally, and those who did hated and feared the old woman's outspokenness and the knowing tongue that could blow their pompous pretensions sky high.

As Leah followed Hilary and Jack into church behind the flower-laden coffin she glanced discreetly around at the dark-clad figures. Tom Clayton stood alone in a pew near the back of the church. He caught her eye and gave her a sly smile. She ignored him. The sooner she could get away from here, the better.

Sorting through Kate's meagre possessions the day before had been painful. She'd asked Hilary to go with her, but she'd refused adamantly.

'Nothing to do with me any more,' she'd said with a sniff.

'But there might be things you'd like to have, if only for sentimental reasons,' Leah had urged, but both Jack and Hilary stubbornly refused to have anything to do with the bungalow's clearance, each of them determined to make Leah feel guilty about her inheritance.

As she worked it had touched her deeply to see how frugally the old lady had lived, especially in comparison to her son's opulent lifestyle. If she'd sold out to Wonderbuys she could have bought herself a nice little ground-floor flat in the new block by the river. She would have been close to the shops, with central heating and no maintenance worries. She could have had a much needed holiday in the sunshine which would have helped her bad chest, and still had plenty left over. But the reason she hadn't sold became apparent when Leah read the letter left for her at the solicitor's office. It was brief and typically to the point, written in the spidery copperplate of Kate's generation on lined notepaper torn from a shopping list pad.

My dear girl,

I'm leaving you everything – it's what the legal folks call my estate. Sounds grand, don't it? Maybe it'll help you make something of your life. That new start you been wanting. Anyway, I know you'll do your best, my old sugar. I know you won't want to live in my old place. The lawyer lady will tell you about the offer I had from the grocery people. Jack wanted me to sell to them some time ago and got real mad with me when I wouldn't. But I'm not daft. He wanted me to sell, bank the money and move into an old folk's home. Catch me doing that! He was after the cash himself and I'll be damned if he'll have it now. That's when I made up my mind to leave it all to you.

Take care of yourself. Be a good girl.

Your loving Gran,
Kate Dobson (Mrs)

Sitting in Kate's old chair, the letter in her hand, Leah could imagine the situation. As chairman of the planning committee Jack would have realised that eventually he stood to gain substantially from the sale of the land and pushed the plans through. How embarrassed and irritated he must have been when Kate refused to sell; even more so now that she – Leah – had been named as sole beneficiary.

There had been a postscript at the end of the letter that had intrigued her:

P.S. If you look in my underwear drawer you'll find some cerstifercats in an envelope. They was given to my Albert by a P.O.W. who worked for him on the railway in the war. He sent them to Albert as a thank you gift after he went back

home to Germany after V.E. Day. They might
be worth a few bob. Ask the lawyer lady.

Leah had found the brown envelope tucked away in a
drawer under Kate's fleecy-lined winter underwear.
In it was a bundle of share certificates. As Kate
said, they were in German and the name of the firm
was unfamiliar to Leah, but she left them with
Jane English who had promised to pass them on
to a broker who would check the value and advise
her.

The vicar intoned his eulogy, creating a picture of
Kate, obviously passed on to him by Jack, which
seemed to Leah totally inaccurate and hypocritical. It
made Kate sound like some upper-class dowager.
Part of her wanted to laugh whilst the other half
stormed inwardly at a son who clearly neither knew
nor wanted to know the worth of the down-to-earth,
gritty character who was his own mother.

At last she rose with the rest of the congregation to
sing the final hymn, Abide With Me. Hilary had
chosen the hymns and Leah knew that Kate had
particularly disliked this dirge-like tune. She would
have preferred a quiet ceremony in the village church
at Smallfield, attended by a few friends and neighbours, with the sound of the rooks in the elm trees for
music; a few of the simple spring flowers she loved
instead of the expensive, out of season roses and
orchids that smothered her coffin and the waiting
hearse. The whole thing was a circus, put on for the
benefit of the Dobsons' social standing. As she
mouthed the words of the hymn, Leah's throat
tightened and her eyes stung with tears. Sorry about
this, Gran. I'll do my best not to let you down, she
promised. I'm going to miss you so much. As the

ceremony came to a close the bearers lifted the coffin and began to make their way out of the church, Jack and Hilary behind, followed by Leah. To her horror, when they reached the back of the church Tom Clayton slipped out of his pew and fell into step beside her.

'How are you, Leah?' he asked quietly.

'I'm well, thank you.'

'Angela and I have parted. We're getting divorced.' He glanced at her out of the corner of his eye, trying to assess her reaction.

'I'm sorry to hear that.'

'Come off it. You don't care any more than I do. I thought we might have dinner while you're home.'

She turned to glare at him. 'We're here to bury my grandmother, not make social arrangements.'

He shrugged unrepentantly. 'Maybe later. I'm invited to the house after the interment.'

So Tom was back in favour? Leah sighed. But of course, he would have to be *seen* at least still to be a friend of the Dobsons so as not to attract speculation. How much more of this charade could her patience stand?

At Acacia Grove the funeral tea was waiting. Hilary had engaged a firm of caterers to do it. White-jacketed waiters moved among the so-called mourners with trays of sherry and canapés and Leah reflected that it was more like a cocktail party than a funeral. Tom Clayton cornered her in the hall as she was trying to escape upstairs.

'Hello there.'

'Oh – hello.'

'You weren't trying to avoid me, were you?'

'Whatever gave you *that* idea?'

'Don't be sarcastic, it doesn't suit you.'

She turned the full force of her most withering look

475

on him. 'Get lost, Tom. You've caused me enough trouble. I don't want to see you or have anything to do with you. Right?'

He reached across her shoulder to lean one hand against the wall, cutting off her escape. 'You blackmailed me, Leah,' he said softly. 'You left me no choice. I had to protect myself. I'm sorry if it made things difficult for you, but you brought it on yourself. Won't you let me try to make amends?'

'No.'

'Listen, I might be selling up shortly, taking early – very early – retirement and going off somewhere warm and sunny to spend the rest of my life in luxury. Doesn't that appeal to you?'

'Why should it? Anyway, I thought you were all set for the Mayoral chain.'

'I resigned from the council. Got fed up with it.'

Leah said nothing. Could it be that Jack had made it impossible for him *not* to resign after what had happened?

'I daresay you won't have enough left to live anywhere sunnier than Hunstanton once you've given Angela her share,' she couldn't resist saying.

'*Hunstanton*?' He laughed dryly. 'Good God, no, I've got much more exciting plans than that. Some luscious tax haven – haven't decided which yet. You see, strictly between ourselves, there's this big supermarket chain that's been trying to buy a parcel of land out at Smallfield. I've heard on the grapevine that they can't get it all. I'm going to offer them Clayton's. I reckon they'll jump at it. After all, they won't even have to build. They can have the other shop too if they're interested. I'm like you, Leah. I'm sick of Nenebridge.'

'I suppose you would be.' Leah smiled to herself, remembering what Gran had told her about Tom's come-uppance on her last visit. But she knew something that he didn't. She'd heard just that morning from Jane English that Wonderbuys had clinched the deal for the parcel of land at Smallfield. They'd asked her to call in to sign the contract. Once probate had been granted the money would be hers, but she'd leave Tom to find that out for himself. 'Well, congratulations,' she said, ducking under his arm and up the stairs. 'It all sounds great. I hope it keeps fine for you.'

Hilary and Jack had already made it clear that she wouldn't be welcome in the house once the funeral was over but Leah didn't need prompting. She had no intention of hanging around in Nenebridge once her business there was over. On the other hand she wasn't ready to go back to London yet either. She decided to go to Cleybourn and stay with Dick at the Mermaid for a few days after she'd made her last visit to the solicitor's office. Her unhappy memories of the place didn't seem so important now. She was starting again, wiping the slate clean. There was a lot of thinking to be done, plans to be made, and for that she needed the peace and quiet that only Cleybourn could offer.

She got up early next morning and packed her case. When she came down, ready to leave, she was surprised to find Hilary already up and in the kitchen, making early morning tea.

'I'm just off,' she said. 'Thank you for putting me up.'

'That's quite all right.' Hilary flushed and pulled her dressing gown around her, one hand going self-consciously to her cheek. Her face was devoid of make-up, her hair soft and tousled. Leah sensed that she was feeling resentful. She hated to be caught like this. It made her feel vulnerable, which was a pity. If she only knew, she looked more human without the polished veneer she wore for the outside world.

'I've arranged for Gran's bungalow to be cleared the day after tomorrow.' She handed Hilary the key. 'If you wouldn't mind opening up for them – and locking up again afterwards? And then maybe you would drop the key into Jane English's office for me?'

'Very well.' Hilary took the key with a grudging nod, aware that she could hardly complain, having made it impossible for the girl to stay on herself.

'And if you change your mind and decide there's anything you'd like to have of Gran's, I hope you'll help yourself.'

'Thank you. Very generous, I'm sure.' Hilary's tone was sharp and her eyes flashed as she applied herself to the tea tray she was preparing.

'Well, I'll go,' Leah said, picking up her case. 'Say goodbye to Dad for me, will you?'

'I'll tell him you've gone. Goodbye.'

Leah paused in the doorway. 'Oh, by the way, he asked me not to tell anyone about Gran leaving everything to me. But I'd have thought it better for *me* to be seen to be selling out to Wonderbuys than him. It wouldn't have looked good for him as chairman of the planning committee, would it?'

The look on Hilary's face betrayed the fact that the Wonderbuys bid was news to her. 'I'm afraid I haven't the slightest idea what you're talking about.'

'Oh, I'm sure Dad will explain if you ask him.' Leah closed the door behind her, realising as she did it that this was one door she would not be opening again.

She ate a breakfast of scrambled eggs and coffee at the little cafe by the bus station, the one that catered for out of town folk who came in on the early bus for the market. It was hot and steamy, smelling of wet overcoats and burnt toast, but the food was good and the formica-topped tables clean. As soon as it was nine o'clock she went along to the solicitors' office. Jane greeted her with a smile.

'I've got the Wonderbuy contract all ready for you to sign,' she said. 'And I've also got some rather good news. Those shares you found . . . They were in a German pharmaceutical firm that was very new in 1938 when they were purchased. It seems that it prospered during the war, and since then the firm has gone from strength to strength.'

'So the shares are worth something then?'

'I'll say they are.' Jane smiled. 'Not only that, the dividends have been building very substantially over the years. Your grandmother never bothered to have them transferred. She couldn't have realised that she was sitting on a valuable source of income.'

Leah sighed. To think that Kate had a businessman for a son yet she hadn't felt she could show him the shares and ask his advice.

'You're looking rather dazed,' Jane said. 'I take it you'd like me to sell the shares for you?'

'Not yet,' Leah said after a moment. 'A steady income might come in useful, you never know. I'll wait till I see how things go.'

'I'll have them transferred to your name then, shall I?'

'Thank you.'

After completing the necessary formalities Leah walked out into the street again. The town was fully awake now and the air was crisp and clear. There was almost a hint of spring in it. She breathed deeply. In the space of a few days she had become an independent woman with money to invest and a readymade income. A woman of means. She tried the words experimentally inside her head. A woman with money. Money and no friends, a silent voice mocked

479

in reply. No one who cares. Ironically, the one person who had truly cared in her own inimitable earthy way was gone for ever. But that was just one of the new things she was going to have to learn to adjust to. God only knew, she ought to be used to it by now.

In the days that followed Ralph's accident the reception hall of 'The Ocean' was packed with newspaper reporters from morning till night. If Marie had hoped to keep the collapse of Evans Hotels secret it had been a forlorn hope. On the day after the accident the local papers and some of the nationals carried the headline: *Failed Businessman in Death Crash*. There followed the story of Ralph's financial crisis, coupled with the renewal of Marie's own recently published story. For Marie herself the whole thing was a living nightmare. Whenever she emerged to go out to the shops or for fresh air, they were waiting. And the questions relentlessly fired at her sickened her heart and made her head spin.

'Was your husband aware of your past, Mrs Evans?'

'Did he ever meet your daughters?'

'Could the shock have been the final straw for him?'

'Did it tip the balance of his mind, do you think?'

Whatever replies she made would be reported, twisted and distorted out of all recognition in the next day's papers. Finally she was reduced to sneaking in and out by a rear door, disguised in dark glasses and a headscarf.

Hannah would have liked to stay with her but her own work demanded she return to London. She stayed as long as she could, supporting Marie through the daily police and press visits, the results of the forensic examination and the pathologist's report. It seemed that the sea, which carried strong currents at that point of the coastline and was particularly turbulent at this time of year, had swept away most of what was left of the body. It was hoped that some identifiable matter would eventually be washed up. But – although the police declined to say how they were able to tell – there clearly had been a body in the car when it went over the cliff and that body was assumed to be Ralph's. The verdict at the ensuing inquest was one of 'death by misadventure'. Apart from Ralph's financial troubles there was no proof that he had taken his own life; no suicide note – no life insurance.

Marie, on the other hand, was convinced of it. She kept silent about the row they had had over the newspaper story. Ralph's last words echoed constantly in her mind and filled her with guilt. She could not rid herself of her firmly ingrained Catholic belief that suicide was a mortal sin from which there was no absolution. And the thought that she might have been the cause of it disturbed her deeply.

On the night of the inquest Marie had an unexpected visitor. Philip Hodges rang the bell at the rear of the hotel where the flat had its own entrance. Marie answered the entry-phone, her voice cautious and apprehensive.

'Who is it?'

'It's me, Marie – Philip.'

Her heart quickening, Marie released the door lock and went out to wait by the service lift. When the doors opened and she saw him she caught her breath. 'Philip, you shouldn't have come. If any of those reporters were to see you . . .'

'It's all right. I made sure there were none about.' He took her hands. 'My dear, what must you have thought of me, letting you face all this alone?'

She shook her head. 'You got my letter?'

'I did. And I'm ashamed that I didn't come to stand by you at once. I was away at a conference when the story broke.'

'You mustn't come here, Philip. You have your partners and the practice to consider. That's why I wrote to you. You must go. Go now. It's sweet of you to come but . . .'

'I had hoped you might ask me in.' He was smiling. 'After all, I'm here now, aren't I? It can't make much difference if I stay a while.'

Marie smiled uneasily and opened the door, standing aside for him to enter. There was so much she wanted to say to him. She had no idea where to begin; no idea how much he knew. If he'd been away he mightn't have read everything. It would be better – easier for her – if he were to go now, saving her the further trauma of having to see the horror and disappointment on his face when she told him.

It was after ten and David had gone to bed. In the living room Marie switched off the television and they faced each other across the silent room.

'First, let me say that I've read everything that's been in the papers,' Philip said. 'I don't know how much truth there is in it, I daresay some of it has been twisted, but that doesn't concern me. I want you to know that I'm so sorry, Marie. And if there's anything I can do – anything at all . . .'

'There's nothing anyone can do,' she said. 'What's past can't be undone. Now Ralph is dead and the business is bankrupt. Nothing can alter that either.' She looked up at him and saw the compassion in his eyes, and for the first time she felt the ice of her guilt and defeat begin to melt into tears. 'I – I blame myself for all of it,' she said quietly.

'*Yourself*? But why?'

She shook her shoulders as though trying to free herself of some intolerable burden. 'I should have stood up to Ralph years ago – refused to let him take the finances out of my hands – should have seen that he was letting things run away with him. I should have known that he wasn't up to running a business of this size. I'm not sure that I would have been either – not alone. I should have told him about my past – the babies. When he read about it in the paper he was so angry.' Her voice broke on the first of the sobs she had held back too long. 'But I can't believe it caused him to do such a terrible thing, Philip. I feel so *guilty*.'

He said nothing. Stepping forward, he took her into his arms and held her close, letting her cry out all the pent-up torment of the past.

'I'm here now,' he said softly against her hair. 'If you'll let me, I want to take care of you.'

She looked up at him. If only she could let him. It would be such a relief, such sheer luxury, to be able to give in and let someone else take all the strain, do all the worrying. But it wasn't possible. 'You have your career to think of, Philip,' she said. 'I've already made a mess of my own life and wrecked David's and Ralph's – not to mention the children I gave away.' She shook her head. 'I'm bad news, Philip. Sometimes I feel there must be some kind of curse on me.'

He shook her gently. 'That's superstitious nonsense. You're tired and overwrought. You've had more than your share of bad luck, that's all. But that's going to change. To begin with, I think you should leave here. Why don't you move into my cottage?'

She stared up at him, lost for words.

'It's tucked away in the New Forest,' he went on. 'No close neighbours. No one need know where you are, except your solicitor. You'd be free of the press –

able to breathe again. And if you want something to do, you can plan the new decor for me. You promised to help me with that anyway.'

She shook her head. 'I couldn't. There's David.'

'He must come too, of course. I'm still his doctor, don't forget. I'd be able to keep an eye on him there. It couldn't be better.'

'But – why should you do all this for us, Philip? Especially now that you know – about me.'

'I knew you before all this, Marie,' he said softly. 'The important things about you, not some lurid story dredged up by a newspaper reporter who has never set eyes on you. I know that you're caring and loyal and that you're incapable – and always have been – of committing any act that might hurt innocent people. No, not even for a man you loved. I know that as surely as I know I'm standing here in this room with you now.' He cupped her face with his hands and looked into her eyes. 'And you ask, why am I here – why am I doing this? Because I love you, Marie. I feel free to say it now. It's been true for a long time and nothing can change it.' He brushed the tears from her cheeks with his thumbs and kissed her, gently at first, then, as he felt her warm response, more deeply, wrapping her closely in his arms and holding her close. At last he released her and looked down into her misty eyes.

'So – what do you say? Will you come to the cottage?'

She bit her lip in an agony of indecision. 'Someone would be sure to find out, and what about your reputation – your standing as a doctor? If you lose the respect of your colleagues and patients . . .'

He was shaking his head. 'I won't. But even if I did it wouldn't be nearly as disastrous to me as losing you. Marie, I know how unhappy you were with Ralph. I know how cruelly he treated you. How do you think I felt, standing helplessly by and letting it happen to you? I don't intend to let anything hurt you again. Once all this is over I want to marry you.' He paused, a rueful smile on his face. 'If you'll have me, that is.'

Her heart full, she wound her arms around his neck. 'Oh, Philip. It all sounds so tempting, but I can't run away. I must stay here and face it. And we mustn't meet again until all this mess is sorted out. You know as well as I do that the press have ways of finding out even the best kept secrets and I don't want anyone else dragged into all this. I don't need anything else on my conscience.'

For a moment he looked as though he were about to argue, but common sense told him that she was right. 'I'll wait then, if you insist. It can't take that long,' he said. 'Nothing lasts for ever. We'll write letters – talk on the telephone,' He took her hands. 'And David is still my patient, so I have a perfectly valid excuse for visiting.' He looked into her eyes. 'As long as I know you love me, I can wait.'

She stood on tiptoe to kiss him. 'Of course I love you, Philip. I thought I'd lost you too, but now that I know I haven't I can face anything.'

Leah caught the bus to King's Lynn and then took a taxi to Cleybourn. It seemed terribly extravagant and she had to keep reminding herself that she could afford it now. Jane English had arranged for her to have some money from Gran's estate to tide her over until probate was granted.

It was just after lunch when she arrived at the Mermaid and Dick had just called 'time'. He was just about to lock up for the afternoon when she walked into the bar.

He stared at her in surprised. 'Well, *well*. Look

what the tide's washed up. How are you, m'love?' He lifted the bar flap and came through to hug her. 'What brings you down 'ere at this time o' the year?'

'I'm fine, Dick. And I'd like to stay if you can put me up for a while.'

He scratched his head. 'Well, now, I don't know about that. Rooms ain't aired. How long did you reckon to stay?'

'Don't know really,' she said with a shrug. 'A few days – a week or two. I'll give you a hand in the bar – and I'll pay, of course.'

He chuckled, 'An' what about my reputation, eh? An old man and a smashin' young girl like you, all alone together?'

She winked at him. 'Do your reputation no harm at all, I'd have thought. Come on, Dick, I've come all this way, and I really need a quiet place to stay for a while.'

He peered at her. 'Not in any kind of trouble, lass, are you?'

'You mean you haven't read about me in the papers?'

He shook his head. 'Don't have a lot of time for readin' papers, an' as you know, I got no telly. I has the wireless on, but the feller on there never mentioned you.' He grinned and nudged her arm. ''Ere – you're 'avin' me on, aren't you?'

'No. But I'll tell you all about it later. I haven't done anything wrong, though, so don't worry about that. Well, do I get to stay or don't I?'

'Have to make up the bed and dust the room yourself,' he said. 'Better put a couple of 'ot water bottles in the bed too, 'less you want pneumonia.'

She grinned. 'I'll see to it right away, Dick, then how about a cup of your famous tea? I'm parched.'

Over the tea and a doorstep cheese and pickle

sandwich, Leah told Dick about her mother and sister and how the story had broken in the *Recorder* about Marie's conviction and prison sentence. He listened patiently, nodding from time to time. When she had finished he said: 'I reckon the way we come into this world don't matter, girl. It's what we do with the life we've been given once we'm got it. Thass the important thing. It's how we proves we've got the right to be 'ere, if you asks me.'

Leah nodded. Dick's philosophy might be earthy and homespun but it was right on the button for her money.

Chapter 23

With a baby in the house Mavis was in her element. Caring for an infant again after so long seemed to have taken years off her. In spite of his precarious beginning, little James had developed into an easy, contented baby. He took his feeds eagerly, slept soundly and put on weight almost before their eyes. Under Mavis's loving care and Ken's smiling indulgence he flourished visibly. At six weeks old he was already smiling, seeming to recognise the proud faces that bent over his cot. His little arms and legs grew firm and rounded and his cheeks glowed with rosy colour. When Mavis wheeled him out in the shiny new pram that Ken had bought him, she positively beamed with pride.

To their relief, the Paynes had managed to get Sally and baby James away from London before the press could get on to them. Ken had sworn the hospital staff to secrecy, making them promise not to reveal Sally's whereabouts to anyone. And when the story of Ralph Evans' death had appeared in the papers he and Mavis had decided to keep the news from her. The less the girl had to do with her natural mother's shady affairs, the better in their opinion. Sally had promised them that she would remain at home until the doctor pronounced her fully recovered and fit to go back to work, and they were determined to shield her from any more traumas for as long as she remained with them.

In the early days when she still felt weak after James's birth and her illness, it was bliss for Sally, being pampered again; not to have to worry about getting up in the morning, struggling to work on the overcrowded bus or planning what she would have to eat when she got home in the evenings. But as her strength returned the inactivity began to pall and she soon felt the reawakening of the restlessness that had once made her rebel. Life was very different now. She was a girl no longer, but a woman. A woman with a purpose to her life. It was time she took control of her own life once again.

She telephoned Mrs Greg at Petals to let her know that she was on the mend and would soon be fit enough to come back to work. But to her dismay she was told that her job was no longer available. The business hadn't been doing too well and Mrs Greg had decided to sell up and retire. Immediately she saw the danger of the trap that beckoned. After the miserable discomfort of the past months it was good to be comfortable again, and although Mavis hardly let her do anything for James, Sally had grown to love her small son more as each day passed. It would be all too easy to give up and stay. And the longer she stayed, the harder it would to be leave. But after only one month of having James in the house she could already see that Mavis and Ken had become reconciled to the idea of her living away from home. In fact, she had the distinct impression that they were looking forward to having James all to themselves. He had taken Sally's place in their lives. He had become the child whose loss they had been mourning ever since she'd grown up and away from them.

Aunt Jean came to visit one Sunday afternoon, soon after Sally and James came home. She admired the baby, bringing him a present of a teddybear and leaning admiringly over the cot to coo at him. But she was unable to conceal her curiosity as to the identity of his father. All afternoon she dropped little hints into the conversation, which all three Paynes studiously ignored. Later, alone with Sally in the kitchen as they shared the washing-up after tea, she broached the subject more directly.

'Jason wanted to come with me today, but I told him to wait until I'd asked if you wanted to see him first.'

'Whatever for?' Sally laughed. 'Jason doesn't have to ask if it's all right to come and see me. We've been friends for as long as I can remember.'

'Mmm, exactly.' Jean dried a plate thoughtfully. 'Sally – there's something I have to know. I didn't like to ask Jason outright because he's very loyal and I might not have got the truth from him, but was – is . . .'

'Is the baby his?' Sally finished the question for her. 'You can put your mind at rest, Auntie Jean. Jason isn't Jamie's father.'

Jean couldn't hide her relief, 'I hope you don't think I'm prying, dear, only, I mean – you know what he's like. If he thought he had a child – and he *did* ask you to marry him before you went away. When I heard about the baby it seemed obvious – well, I mean, you *were* sort of engaged, weren't you?' She looked expectantly at Sally, the unasked question in her eyes.

'Jason knew about the baby and he offered me marriage as a way out,' Sally said. 'You're right. He is very loyal, which was why I couldn't let him do it.'

Jean looked relieved. 'It was very brave of you to go away like you did,' she said. 'Jason was quite upset at the time but he never let on, you know. He never said anything about you being pregnant.' She paused, avoiding Sally's eyes. 'As a matter of fact, he's met this girl now – Paula. I think things are getting to be quite serious between them. She's a lovely girl and I know she thinks the world of him. She told me so.' She glanced at Sally out of the corners of her eyes. 'I – um – wouldn't like anything to spoil things for them.'

Sally got the message. 'It won't, Auntie Jean. Not if I can help it. I hope they'll be very happy,' she said. 'All I want for myself, apart from knowing that James is well looked after, is to get on with my life again.' She smiled as she tipped out the washing-up water and wiped the draining board. 'But tell Jason I'd love to see him – *and* meet his girlfriend – any time he likes.'

'So the baby's real father – you're not planning to . . . ?'

Sally gritted her teeth as she took the damp teatowel from Jean's hand and hung it up to dry. 'No, I'm, not,' she said. 'Shall we join the others now?'

The following week she began scanning the Situations Vacant column in the local papers for a job, but there didn't seem to be anything at all in the floristry line. The little house with its neatly ordered rooms and immaculate garden was beginning to feel claustrophobic. Even the presence of a young baby didn't seem to have disrupted it much. Grateful as she was to Mavis and Ken for making it possible for her to keep James, she grew more certain as the days passed that she had to get away and make a life for herself. Apart from anything else, the Paynes were not young. By the time James reached his teens they would be too elderly to be expected to cope with him. She must begin now to prepare for that time; to make a home and start saving for the day when she must take over James's upbringing herself.

At last, as a desperate last resort, she rang Hannah one afternoon when Ken was at work and Mavis was out shopping.

'Can you help, Hannah? Petals is closing down and I need a job,' she said. 'There's nothing here. Anyway, I can't live with Mum and Dad for ever.'

Hannah laughed dryly. 'You're hardly alone in needing a job, Sally. You and a couple of million others.'

'I am a trained florist, remember. The field is pretty wide and I'm willing to take anything. If necessary I'll take some other kind of job. I really need to get away.'

'How do Mavis and Ken feel about it? Have you discussed it with them?'

'No, but it was understood from the beginning that I'd work away once I'd recovered. I'm sure they'll be quite happy for me to visit at weekends.'

'Nevertheless, I feel you should pay them the compliment of talking to them about it. No more skipping off, Sally.'

She swallowed her resentment, realising that in a way she deserved Hannah's mistrust. 'I've no intention of skipping off this time, Hannah. Everything's changed now. I've done a lot of thinking over the past weeks. Mum and Dad are happy to help bring up James now while he's little, but it can't last for ever. I have to start building some kind of future for us both as soon as I can. Besides, grateful as I am, I don't want him to grow up in the rarefied atmosphere that I did.'

Hannah was surprised and impressed. All Sally's blinkered resentment seemed to have disappeared. She'd got things into perspective at last. Motherhood seemed to have brought out a new, pragmatic side of her. 'I can see your point,' she conceded. 'I don't know of any jobs going, but if you want to come up to London and have a look round, you're welcome to stay with me at the flat for a couple of nights.'

'Thanks, Hannah, Actually I had thought of asking Leah to put me up.'

'She seems to be out of town at the moment,' Hannah said. 'I've been trying to get in touch with her myself, but her landlord tells me that her adoptive grandmother died and she went home to Norfolk for the funeral. It must have come as a blow, especially on top of that awful newspaper exposé about Marie. I've spoken to Bill Fenton but he hasn't heard from her since either.'

'Oh, I see.'

'Sally, I take it you've read about Marie Evans's husband in the papers.'

Sally frowned. 'Her husband? No. What about him?'

'His car went over a cliff. They suspected at one point that it was suicide. The hotel chain they own has gone bankrupt, you see – which must have been her reason for asking you to postpone your visit.'

'Oh, Hannah, how awful.' Sally drew in her breath sharply. She'd been so preoccupied with her own problems that she hadn't given a thought to other people's. She'd taken Marie's letter at face value, seeing her in the worst possible light. 'And poor Leah,' she added. 'Is there anything I can do?'

'I doubt it,' Hannah said. 'I just thought I'd put you in the picture.'

'I'll write – to them both,' Sally said. 'Will you give me Marie's address?' She scribbled down the details that Hannah gave her, and, promising to let Hannah know when she decided to come up to London, she rang off.

For a long time she sat staring out of the window. In the neat front garden firmly disciplined rows of spring flowers were all coming into bud in unison and a robin was chirping in the flowering cherry tree. It would soon be spring. One more spring, just like all the ones she had known in the past. In a place like this, where everything followed an unchanging, clockwork pattern, one grew so insular, so complacent and self-centred. It was what she'd always been so afraid of. The outside world – people, with all their problems – seemed so far away and unreal. She felt ashamed – and so selfish.

'I've *told* you, Tel, she went home for her grand-mother's funeral. I haven't heard a thing from her since.' Bill sounded slightly irritable. He'd lost count of the number of times Terry had telephoned for news of Leah.

'But where can she *be* then?' he asked. 'I've tried ringing her parents in Norfolk. They don't know where she is either. What's more, they don't seem to care.'

'I'm sorry, old son, I can't help you. I don't understand why she didn't come straight back after the funeral or why she hasn't been in touch. She was interested in trying to get a mortgage on the restaurant round the corner. We were thinking of going into partnership.'

'Then where the hell is she? Bloody hell, Bill, *anything* could have happened to her. Doesn't anybody give a damn?'

'I reckon she's old enough to take care of herself,' Bill said tersely. 'I think she's proved that. But I do know one thing. She was pretty fed up about the article in the *Recorder*.'

'I can imagine. It was one of the reasons I rang her.'

'So what made you do it, Tel? I thought you were a friend of hers. Christ knows I'm a hardened enough old hack, but even I wouldn't pull a stroke like that on a mate – however tempting it might have been.'

There was a stunned silence at the other end of the line. '*Me*? My God, you don't think that *I*. . . Are you out of your head? Bill, let's get this straight. Are you telling me that Leah thinks I wrote it?'

Terry's raised voice crackled down the line, vibrating against Bill's eardrum. Wincing, he said, 'Come off it, Tel, who else could have written the story? Who else knew enough to do it?'

'God knows. Anyone who wanted to take the trouble to research it, I suppose. It didn't have to be me and you bloody well know it. Even *you* could have written that article if you'd put your mind to it.'

Bill laughed shortly at the back-handed compliment. '*Thanks*, pal.'

'All I do know is that it wasn't me,' Terry went on. 'Christ, what do you think I am, Bill? What's worse, what does Leah think I am? Surely she knows me better than that?'

'To be honest, I don't think the poor kid knows what to think. There's this business about her real mother's husband driving over a cliff and the hotels going bust. That hit the tabloids right after the other story, right on top of her grandmother dying too. My guess is that she's either gone down to Dorset to see if she can help, or she's taken off somewhere to get away from the lot of us. And I can't say I blame her, frankly.'

There was a pause at the other end of the line then Terry said, 'Of *course*. Why didn't I think of it before?'

'Think of what?'

'Nothing. Look, I'll be in touch. If you do hear

anything give me a ring, eh? And I'll do the same for you. Right?'

'Right.' But the word scarcely had time to leave Bill's lips before Terry had rung off.

The wind that came off the North Sea was icy and relentless. It whipped the grey-green water of the saltings into angry peaks, and in the little harbour wavelets dashed themselves against the wall and tossed the moored fishing boats about like corks. Unequipped for the weather, Leah had borrowed a bulky fisherknit sweater from Dick and wore it with her jeans, topped with the waxed jacket he wore when he went fishing. Both came past her knees, but they kept her snug and warm as she walked out to the point, her hair streaming and her cheeks whipped pink by the wind.

Cleybourn had been just what she needed and she was beginning to feel better for her stay; stronger and almost ready to go back and face the new beginning she was determined to make for herself. She would buy a restaurant; not Bella's but another, somewhere away from London, in a completely new place where the new Leah could start again. Maybe she would take a holiday first. Perhaps go to Italy and visit the Andrettis. Anna had left her mother's address and begged Leah to keep in touch. Now that she had money there were any number of options open to her. Secretly she believed that if she engrossed herself in work she would be able to put Terry out of her mind.

Forgetting was proving more difficult than she had thought. Out here, with only the wind and the seabirds for company, it was possible to look at the future as a viable proposition. It was at night, lying in the bare little room at The Mermaid with the sound of the sea crashing against the harbour wall, that her mind became tortured by doubts and thoughts of the past. Waiting for sleep she would find herself thinking of Terry, remembering things they had said and done together, wondering how it was that she hadn't realised long ago that she loved him. Lying in the darkness she was forced to come face to face with herself. It was like looking into a magic mirror which reflected not only her face but her faults – her darker side; all the things she disliked about herself and which she'd refused to acknowledge. If she had been used and betrayed it was little more than she deserved, for she had been guilty of using people too – on the assumption that what she hadn't been given, she would take. What had happened to her was no more than what Granny Dobson would have called her 'just deserts'. But it hurt unbearably that it was Terry who had dealt her the final blow that forced her to face it. She thought of the days they had spent together just after Christmas and winced at the memory of her own vulnerability, laid bare for him to see. She'd even asked him to marry her.

Angrily, she tried to tell herself that all that was over – in the past; that she was putting it all behind her and beginning again. She would never see Terry again. Because of some serious flaw somewhere deep inside her, it would be better if she made no more close relationships. In the bright new future she planned she would build an impenetrable wall of defence around herself so that she could neither hurt nor be hurt. She would trust only the signed and sealed – give and take only in business matters. Emotionally, from this day on, her heart was a closed book.

The days she spent at Cleybourn were busy and satisfying. She helped Dick in the house and pub, using all her spare time to cook enough meals to stock up his freezer. In the afternoons she walked by the sea and in the evenings she helped in the bar, enjoying the company of the locals and providing them with tasty and popular ploughman's suppers to eat over their darts matches.

Dick watched her wistfully. Since last summer she had changed. She'd told him a bit about herself – how she'd found her long lost mother and sister. And about the windfall inherited from her grandmother. It was bad luck, the papers getting hold of the story. He assumed at first that it was this that had upset her and caused her to be so restless. But often when she didn't know he was looking he caught her with that sad, wistful look on her lovely young face and he wondered about the part she hadn't told him – the thing that had hurt her so deeply. But he didn't ask. If she was here to forget something she wouldn't want a nosey old codger like him ferreting out her secret pain. Best let the poor lass heal in her own good time, he told himself wisely.

One bright morning in early March, Leah found the pantry at The Mermaid almost empty. She suggested to Dick that she might drive into Sheringham to the supermarket and stock up for him. Taking his old Cortina she left Cleybourn soon after breakfast and did a month's shopping at a superstore on the outskirts of the little seaside resort. Stowing it all in the capacious boot, she found it was still quite early so drove the rest of the way into town, intending to look at the shops and maybe have a coffee.

Parking the car, she walked through the streets to the clifftop. When she was a child Jack and Hilary used to bring her to Sheringham sometimes for a weekend, but she'd never seen it at this time of year. In summer it was a cosy, family resort, slightly old-fashioned like the seaside towns in story books.

Today the sky was grey with heavy, lowering clouds. The tide had swallowed the beach whole and white-capped waves leapt and crashed against the sea wall, throwing up plumes of spray that filled the air with salty droplets that stung her face and beaded her hair. The wind was so strong that it almost took her breath away. She looked around for somewhere to get coffee but, understandably, most of the hotels on the seafront were still closed for the winter. There was a shuttered, unwelcoming look about them, except for one which still had its 'Vacancies' sign hanging out. It swung wildly in the wind, creaking on chains rusted by the salt air, attracting her attention as she passed. She stopped to read it and found that 'The Haven' was 'Open to non-residents for lunches, teas and morning coffee'.

Inside she ordered coffee at the reception desk and wandered through to take a seat in the shabby little lounge with its faded carpet and sagging armchairs. The windows looked out on to the furious grey sea and deserted promenade. As she drank her coffee she looked around, amusing herself by imagining what she could do with the place if it were hers. Mentally she refurbished and redecorated it. Remembering Sally's skills at floristry she visualised her luscious floral arrangements in each of the arched alcoves on either side of the fireplace. What fun it would be. But Sally had gone home to Leicester with her baby son, she reminded herself wistfully. It would be a long time before she was ready, or inclined to pick up the threads of her career again.

On her way back to the car she spotted freshly caught local fish at a small fishmonger's shop and decided to buy some for lunch. On the counter was a neat stack of newspapers. The fishmonger saw her looking at them.

'Nuthin' like newspapers to keep the moisture in,' he told her. 'Let's the fish breathe too – not like your plastic rubbish. That only . . .' He broke off, looking at her white face with concern. ''Ere – you feelin' all right, m'dear?'

The large black headlines of the paper on top of the pile seemed to leap up at her: *Failed Businessman in Death Crash*. Swiftly she read the opening sentence: 'Ralph Evans, part owner of Evans Hotels died last night when his blazing car crashed over a cliff at Lulworth Cove, a Dorset beauty spot'. She looked at the man. 'I – I'm sorry, but would you mind if I had that paper?' she asked, pointing.

Puzzled, he handed it to her. 'O'course you can, love. *Hey!*' he called, holding out her parcel as she hurriedly left the shop. 'Don't forget your fish.'

In the warmth and seclusion of the car she unfolded the paper and looked at its date, horrified to find that it was more than a month old. She read the rest of the story about Ralph Evans's death crash. Its reference to the failure of the hotel chain carried thinly veiled implications of suicide. Leah folded the paper and stared unseeingly out through the windscreen. How terrible for Marie. She'd lost her business and her husband and presumably her home – everything she'd built over the years out of the ruin that was her life. And it had all happened soon after the damning article Terry had sold the *Recorder*.

All this could be because of me, she told herself with growing horror, remembering the abysmal failure of their one and only meeting. I might have brought all this disaster down on her. Why did I only think of myself when it happened? I should have got in touch – told her I was sorry and tried to help put things right.

501

Over lunch she was quiet. Dick finished the last morsel and pushed away his plate with a sigh of satisfaction.

'Aah, that was good. Nuthin' like home-cooked fish 'n' chips. Good of you to think of it, love.' He looked at her barely touched plate and pensive face. 'Nuthin' wrong, is there, my 'andsome? Not feelin' poorly, are you?'

She shook her head. 'No, Dick. And you're right. The fish is good. I'm just not very hungry.' She gave up all pretence of eating and pushed her plate away, looking at him across the table. 'Dick, I think I'm going to have to leave tomorrow.'

He shrugged resignedly. 'Well – can't really say I'm surprised. I guessed it wouldn't be long before you'd be itchin' to be off again.'

She reached out to touch one of his large brown hands. 'You've been a wonderful help. Thanks for letting me stay and for everything,' she said. 'You're a real friend.'

He shook his head, grinning self-consciously. 'G'on with you. It's you what's the friend. Look how you've worked. Shan't need to cook meself nuthin' for weeks to come now.' He rose and began to clear the table, mainly to hide his embarrassment. 'Always a room for you at The Mermaid, girl,' he muttered. 'Told you that a'fore, didn' I? Long as I'm 'ere you'll be more'n welcome.'

He insisted on driving her into King's Lynn next morning to catch the train. She was sharply reminded of the last time he had seen her off. It had been autumn then. Now it was almost spring. There was a gentler feel to the wind this morning and a honeyed scent to the air. Buds were bursting on the trees and the birds had begun to sing again. Perhaps it was an omen, she told herself hopefully.

'Don't wait, Dick,' she told him as she got out of the car. 'I hate railway station goodbyes. Anyway, you'll be wanting to get back for opening time.' But he insisted on carrying her case on to the platform for her and giving her a bear-like hug.

'Just you look after yourself, girl,' he said. 'An' don't forget, you can come back any time. No need to write or phone.'

'I'll remember.' She kissed his rough cheek. 'Goodbye, Dick.'

The little sports car was standing outside when Dick arrived back at the Mermaid. Terry got out as soon as the Cortina came into view. Dick recognised him at once and guessed why he was here. 'If you're after Leah, she's gone,' he said before Terry could ask. 'You've just missed her. Took her to Lynn station meself.'

Terry sighed. 'Oh no. It's desperately important that I see her. Do you know where she was going?'

Dick shook his head. 'Never asked. Back to London, I s'pose.'

'Damn. Oh, well . . .' Terry flexed his long back and winced a little at the stiffness in his spine. 'I've been driving all night,' he told Dick. 'All the way down from Manchester. I'd appreciate a bit of a rest before I start out for London again. Not much point in hurrying now. I suppose you couldn't rustle up a bit of lunch?' He looked at Dick hopefully and the inn keeper chuckled.

'*I* can't, but Leah can.' Seeing Terry's puzzled expression he explained: 'She stocked up my freezer for me while she was 'ere. Homemade steak and kidney pie do you?'

Terry grinned. '*Would* it? Just try me. No rush now that I know where she is.'

503

It was evening by the time he arrived at Melbury Street. He found Bill in the kitchen eating fish and chips out of their newspaper wrapping. By the chill in the place it was clear that he had let the Aga go out. He sat huddled in his leather jacket, with what looked like two days' stubble darkening his jowls. When Terry walked in he looked up without enthusiasm.

'Oh, it's you. More time off?'

Terry looked around at the squalor with distaste. 'Not really. I'm supposed to be working. I drove down to Norfolk to look for Leah. Set out in the small hours. I should be back in Manchester by now. I feel like I've been driving for about a week.'

'More fool you,' Bill said. 'Obviously she wasn't there.'

Terry nodded. 'Got there to find I'd just missed her. The paper's sending me to Sarajevo and I wanted to put things straight about this *Recorder* thing. I'm off first thing in the morning.'

Bill whistled softly. 'Yugoslavia, eh? Hot stuff. Well done.'

'I know. I'm looking forward to my first big assignment, but I wanted to see Leah before I went.'

Bill shook his head. 'Sorry, old son. Unfortunately you've just missed her here too.' He pushed the last of the chips into his mouth, screwed up the newspaper wrapping and threw it at the Aga. Pushing a note across the table to where Terry sat, he said: 'Found this when I came in just now. Seems she came in while I was at work. By the time I got home she'd packed and gone. She left her door key and a month's rent in lieu of notice – but no forwarding address.' He watched Terry's crestfallen face as he read the hurriedly scribbled note. 'Sorry you've had a wild goose chase, mate. Let it be a lesson to you. Women are all the same.' He glanced round the cold, neglected kitchen. 'Let you get used to them, then bugger off without so much as a goodbye. D'you know what? I found out today that Janet is back here in London permanently. Been here freelancing since Christmas and didn't have the decency to tell me, blast her. I tell you – they're all the bloody same.'

The house had been built in the early nineteen hundreds and had originally been intended as a comfortable family home for some wealthy business-man. It had been converted into three apartments soon after the war. Marie and David occupied the ground-floor flat, which consisted of a sitting room, two bedrooms, a small bathroom and a kitchen. Half of the small back garden went with it too, where David liked to potter whilst Marie was at work.

She'd found the job easily enough. There was always plenty of domestic work in the off-season. Most of the small hotels and guest houses were spring cleaning just now and glad of a good worker.

'La Mer' was one of a row of modest guest houses in a tree-lined road which advertised itself as being 'five minutes walk from the sea and shops'. It reminded Marie nostalgically of 'Homeleigh', the small private hotel in Cromer where she had first gone to work for David. It was ironic that fate had deposited her unceremoniously back where she had started. She seemed to have come full circle. Philip had begged her to let him help financially, but she wouldn't hear of it. With David's pension and what she earned, they could just about manage. She still believed that the bankruptcy was partly her fault. Now it was up to her to make reparation to David in whatever way she could.

John and Mary Weaver, the couple who owned 'La Mer', had realised who Marie was soon after they had employed her, but they decided not to mention it to her. She was a hard worker and a nice person. It was obvious that she was down on her luck and they saw no reason to make things even worse for her.

Marie liked the Weavers. They were young and as enthusiastic as she had once been. Looking round the flourishing small hotel she envied them a little, and longed to warn them not to overreach themselves. She hoped they'd have better luck than she'd had. Her work was hard and tiring but she enjoyed it. And though it was a step backwards, Marie tried stoically to see it in a more positive way. At least it helped to take her mind off her present position and all that had happened. It stopped her wondering about the future too. She could not expect Philip to wait for ever, yet she was determined that when she agreed to marry him it would be on an equal footing. No one, least of all Philip himself, must ever feel that she was opting for marriage as a last resort.

Ralph's funeral had taken place soon after the inquest. The enquiries seemed to have dragged on for weeks and she was relieved when at last the body was released for burial. She still shuddered when she thought about it, trying not to imagine what had been in the coffin. The police had already told her that there was very little left after the explosion. She was just grateful and relieved to have the whole thing over and done with, more for David's sake than her own. The trauma had aged him considerably and Philip was keeping him carefully monitored on his weekly visits to them.

Now the receivers had taken over, Evans Hotels had come under the auctioneer's hammer along with everything else they had worked for. Two hotels had already been sold and 'The Ocean' with all its contents was to be auctioned next. Marie secretly dreaded seeing the place she had loved as both her home and her career for the past eight years pass out of her life for ever.

One afternoon she arrived home to find that David was entertaining a visitor. She could hear voices in the sitting room. Sighing wearily, she slipped into the bedroom to change and put on some lipstick. Whoever it was, she hoped they wouldn't stay long. Philip was coming for dinner this evening and she wanted time to cook a special meal.

In the sitting room she found her father-in-law giving tea to a young woman. She was smartly dressed in a dark blue suit and crisp white shirt. The briefcase at her feet suggested she was some kind of sales person and Marie felt slightly irritated. A double glazing rep' perhaps? David should have known better than to ask her in, let alone give her tea. He knew very well that they couldn't afford to buy anything.

The young woman was slim and attractive, her shining dark hair cut in a short, gamin style which accentuated her shapely head. She had high cheekbones and dark, expressive eyes. Marie frowned. Surely they'd met before? There was something familiar about the way she held her head and the timbre of her voice. As she stood in the doorway the girl looked up.

'Good afternoon.' She stood up and turned towards her, holding out her hand tentatively. 'How are you – Marie?'

She checked, peering uncertainly at the girl. 'It's – Leah, isn't it?'

'Yes, it's me. I hope you don't mind me dropping in on you like this.'

'Not at all.' Marie's heart quickened with shock. She'd told herself after their first meeting that it was most unlikely they would ever meet again. She opened her mouth to ask 'Why are you here?' but bit back the question. It sounded abrupt and unfriendly. Instead she asked: 'How did you find us?'

'Hannah gave me your address.' She saw Marie's expression and held up her hand. 'Oh, but not until after I'd spent ages talking her into it. I did have a good reason, you see.'

'I see.' Marie licked her dry lips, apprehension making her wary. 'Is – is there some kind of problem?'

'No, nothing like that. Please don't worry. As a matter of fact I've come to talk business with you.'

'Business?' Marie shook her head, watching as Leah unzipped her briefcase and took out a folder. 'Look, I'm sorry, I don't think . . .'

'Please – it's very important that I talk to you.' Seeing Marie's hesitation she said: 'Of course, if it's inconvenient I could come back . . .'

'Oh, no.' Marie made up her mind. She couldn't imagine how she could be of help but she was touched that the girl had come to her for advice. 'Stay to dinner,' she said impulsively. 'We're expecting a friend. He's a very close friend and I'm sure he can offer you far better advice that I could.' She smiled ruefully. 'I'm hardly the ideal person to advise anyone on business matters. I only wish I could offer to put you up . . .'

'It's all right, I've booked into a hotel,' Leah interrupted. 'Look, I think I should explain, Marie, it isn't just advice I need, it's *you*. You see, I'm here for the sale.' She opened the folder and took out the estate agent's brochure. 'I want to buy "The Ocean" and if I get it I'd like you to help me run it. In fact everything hinges on what you say. If your answer is no the deal is off, so you can see how important it is to me. You see, I know nothing about the hotel business except the catering side.'

On her return to London Leah had gone to see Hannah. She'd told her about the money Kate Dobson had left her and what she intended to do with it. Then she asked Hannah to tell her the truth behind the newspaper story – about Marie's bankruptcy and the death of her husband. At last, in confidence, Hannah had told her everything – about Marie's early struggle and her unhappy marriage. She added, at the risk of appearing callous, that Ralph's death was perhaps the best thing that could have happened for Marie.

'But how could she let him treat her like that?' Leah asked, horrified. 'No woman has to put up with treatment like that in this day and age. Why didn't she leave him years ago?'

'It was a little more complicated than it might seem,' Hannah explained. 'Marie felt trapped – by her religious beliefs and also by her loyalty to David, to whom she owed so much. Ralph recognised both these facts and exploited them to the full, holding them over her head to get his own way.' She smiled wryly. 'It's a piece of cruel irony that she and David are in the position now that they would have been if she'd divorced Ralph years ago.'

'So it's all been for nothing?'

'One would have thought that at least she had peace of mind now,' Hannah said. 'But the last time I spoke to her she was blaming herself for the whole disaster.' She shrugged. 'That's Marie for you. Being a victim at an early age seems to leave a deeply ingrained mark.'

Leah was appalled. At their one meeting she'd seen her mother as smug and complacent. A woman who'd worked hard to get what she wanted from life and was now determined to hang on to it. 'It was weeks after the accident and bankruptcy before I saw the newspaper story,' she told Hannah. 'I saw an old copy of the paper quite by accident. It was soon after that that I got this idea. I'd been thinking of buying a restaurant,' she said. 'But I know that with Marie's help I could make a go of a hotel. After all, "The Ocean" already has a good reputation behind it. How can we fail – if she agrees, that is?'

Hannah looked doubtful. 'You realise that you might have to sink everything you've inherited into it and maybe borrow more?' she said. 'It's an enormous risk for someone your age. If you invested the money wisely you'd be sitting pretty.'

'But I don't want to sit pretty,' Leah said vehemently. 'All my life till now I've been drifting. If I do this I'll be making something of myself – a real career. I'll be someone who counts, Hannah. Granny Dobson would have wanted me to do it. I know she would.'

'Are you sure you've taken enough advice – thought it through carefully enough? Marie is bankrupt, remember. She could make no contribution herself.'

'But she *could*. All her experience, her contacts and the knowledge she's built up over the years. That's the most valuable contribution of all.'

Hannah looked at the earnest young face and made up her mind. 'All right,' she said. 'I'll give you her address. But I warn you, she's a very independent woman. Don't be surprised if she refuses.'

But Marie did not refuse. Over dinner that evening the four of them discussed the idea. Philip and David patiently pointed out all the pitfalls, but even they had to agree that the business would have a good chance of success with Leah's money and Marie as advisor.

'All the same, I'd hate to think of you risking your entire capital,' Philip said, echoing Hannah's fears.

But Leah's face wore a look of determination. 'I had nothing before. If I lose, which I've no intention of doing, I can't be any worse off than I was, and at least I would have tried. I could always get another job in a restaurant. I want to do it. I'd already decided to start some kind of business with the money anyway. Surely there couldn't be anything better than this?'

Philip smiled. 'I can see that you've made up your mind. It looks as though there's nothing more for me to say than to wish the two of you good luck.'

He promised to go along to the auction with Leah, to lend his support and help her bid.

'I have to admit that I'm almost as excited as you,' he admitted as he drove Leah back to her hotel later that evening. 'And although she may not show it, I know Marie is too. She deserves a lucky break. I'll be keeping my fingers crossed.'

'I haven't said anything to anyone about it, but I'm hoping to offer my sister a job too,' Leah confided. 'I had a letter from her recently. She's looking for a job so that she can support herself and her baby son.' She smiled at him. 'So you see, a lot depends on my getting "The Ocean".'

The hotel was being auctioned as a whole, complete with furniture, equipment and other effects. Leah had already been to view it and had loved the place the moment she walked in through the glass entrance doors. It was just right to be run as a family concern; larger and more up-market than a guesthouse, yet

511

small enough to give personal service and retain an informal, relaxed atmosphere.

It was a very nervous Leah who stood with the other interested parties in the large reception hall, waiting for the auctioneer to begin. If the hotel didn't reach its reserve price as a whole, it would then be split up into separate lots. Leah wondered nervously just what that reserve price was.

The bidding was slow to start, but once it got under way the speed accelerated alarmingly. It was clear from the beginning that there were two other seriously interested parties. Philip had warned Leah not to jump in too quickly and she let the others bid against each other till one looked likely to drop out, then, with a nod of encouragement from Philip, she made her first bid. There was a flurry of surprise as heads turned to look at her. Her main opponent upped his offer – she bettered it, holding her breath. One more bid and she would be out of her depth. Suddenly it was the most important thing in her life. Her heart pounded. She wanted 'The Ocean' more than she had ever wanted anything. The auctioneer glanced across at the other party who hesitated then shook his head and turned away.

A moment later the gavel came down with a loud bang and the sale was over. Slightly dazed, Leah turned to look at Philip.

'Is it me? Did I get it?'

He laughed. 'You certainly did, my dear. And at quite a reasonable price for all that's included.' He slipped an arm around her shoulders. 'And all my best wishes go with you. You'll never know what you've done for Marie today. I'm sure you won't regret it.'

Marie had waited restlessly all afternoon. When Leah

and Philip arrived back at the flat she could hardly bring herself to look at them, let alone ask about the outcome of the sale. But the moment she saw the broad smile on Leah's face she knew that she'd pulled off the deal.

'There's so much to do if we're to open for the summer,' Leah said excitedly. 'I must write to Sally at once and offer her the job. I'll have to apply for a licence and then there'll be the advertisements to insert in the papers and magazines. We're going to have to hurry.' She looked at Marie. 'And I'm sure you can think of a million other things. I suggest that we move in as quickly as possible.'

Marie looked at Philip and laughed. 'I'm seriously beginning to wonder if this girl really needs me,' she said.

'Of course I do,' Leah told her gravely. 'Don't for one minute imagine this is some kind of charitable act, Marie. Without your promise of help I'd never had dared to think of embarking on something so ambitious, and don't you forget it.'

In spite of Leah's suggestion that they should all move into the hotel, Marie decided that it would be better if she and David remained where they were at the flat. David had settled well there. It was on the ground floor which made it easier for him. He enjoyed the garden too, it gave him something with which to occupy himself when she was at work. But apart from all that, she wasn't sure that going back to live at 'The Ocean' was a good idea for him. The place held too many traumatic memories for them both. She was still young enough to put them behind her and start again, but they had left marks on David that nothing could ever erase.

'If Sally comes to join us you'll be needing the room

for her,' she told Leah. 'It'll give the two of you a chance to get to know each other.'

When Sally had first received Leah's hurried letter explaining what had happened and offering her the job she'd had mixed feelings. After weeks of searching for a job, both at home and in London, all in vain, she was almost ready to take anything, but she hadn't visualised going as far away as Dorset. Clearly it would be impossible to get home every weekend to see James. In the summer season, maybe not for weeks on end. She hated the thought of all she would miss: his first words, the first wobbly, faltering steps. But worst of all she hated the thought of his not recognising her when she came home on infrequent visits. Already Mavis filled the role of mother for him far more than she did. If she spent even less time with him he would hardly know her at all.

She re-read the letter wistfully. Even with this snag, it would be mad to pass up such a good chance. With her lack of experience and the shortage of work it wasn't likely she'd get another opportunity like this. She told Mavis and Ken about Leah's offer that evening after supper.

'First of all, would you like to take the job?' Ken asked practically. 'Is it what you want? Because you're going to be spending a lot of time doing it.'

'Leah says we'll all have to be prepared to do a bit of everything to begin with,' Sally said. 'But I'll be in charge of all the floral work, of course. Leah even suggests that I might take on some freelance floristry work too, going round to other hotels to do their flowers on a weekly basis. It sounds wonderful.' She sighed wistfully.

'Where would you live?' Mavis asked.

'There's a flat on the top floor of the hotel,' Sally told her. 'Leah and I would share that, so I'd have no expenses. It's just that it's so far away. I'd miss James terribly – and you two, of course.'

Ken looked thoughtful 'Well, if it's what you want . . .' He cleared his throat. 'I'll be retiring in a few months' time. Mother and I have been talking about what we'll do. We'd already discussed buying a little place near the sea, somewhere healthy for young James to grow up in. It might as well be Dorset as anywhere else.'

Sally looked from one to the other. 'You mean – you'd move too? You'd leave this house that you've lived in all these years, just for me?'

Ken shook his head. 'Not just for you – for all of us. Leicester is getting too hectic for us now we're getting older. Somewhere sunny by the sea with a warm climate sounds just the job, eh, Mother?'

Mavis wasn't as sure as Ken. She didn't trust the Evans woman after what she'd read in the papers. She was torn two ways, visualising her dream cottage and long walks along the beach with James, then at the same time imagining the bond that would grow between Sally and her natural mother if they were to work together. But then she reminded herself that she held the trump card; James. As long as she and Ken had him Sally would be theirs too. 'It sounds very nice,' she said with a smile.

Chapter 24

To Leah's relief 'The Ocean' needed very little in the way of refurbishment. By the time she had paid all the bills run up in the course of the sale there was perilously little cash left over in her bank account. Everything hung on the coming season. It was a gigantic gamble, but deep in her heart Leah felt sure that her investment would pay off.

She had written to Bill, telling him what she had done and explaining her reason for not taking up his offer of help to buy Bella's. It had been hard not to sound arrogant and selfish but she had done her best, thanking him for his help and support. She had hesitated as she concluded the letter, wondering whether to ask him to tell Terry where she was, but she decided not to weaken and quickly sealed the letter into its envelope. Better to leave things as they were. She could not stop loving Terry, but neither could she forgive him for what he had done.

Marie threw herself wholeheartedly into her new job as Leah's mentor. It was wonderful to be working at 'The Ocean' again and she was enjoying working with the girls and getting to know them. They were so unalike, both in looks and temperament. It was difficult even for her to believe that they were twins. Leah reminded Marie of herself when she had first become interested in the hotel business, full of drive, inspirational ideas and enthusiasm. Already she was talking about building a larger ballroom that could be let out for functions in the off-season, a swimming pool and larger car park. Marie was delighted and inwardly excited by Leah's enthusiasm, but she felt obliged to exercise cautious restraint, knowing from bitter experience what could happen when ambition overtook reality.

In Sally she recognised the vulnerability and stoicism that she herself had possessed as a teenager, and the girl resembled her so much in appearance that at times it was almost like looking at herself through the wrong end of a telescope. It was as though her daughters had inherited the two sides of her own personality, neatly divided down the middle.

The three of them worked very hard preparing the hotel for its reopening. There was very little time to spare before the onset of the season and from the beginning it was clear that Leah could not afford to employ a full complement of staff until they were on their feet. They shared the work, allocating the jobs according to each one's capabilities. Marie was to handle the bookings and secretarial side, Leah the organisation of kitchen and dining room, whilst for the time being Sally was to act as temporary receptionist and general assistant. Apart from a couple of daily cleaning women, they managed the domestic chores between them.

Marie was an invaluable source of information about the hotel business as Leah had known she would be. She reminded herself again and again that she couldn't possibly have taken on anything of this magnitude without her. They worked harmoniously together and as the weeks went by they grew not only to know but to like and respect one another as well, each of them looking forward to their first summer season with a sense of adventure born of Leah's infectious zest and ambition. The advertisement they had prepared carefully between them began to bring results and as the first of the summer bookings began to trickle in, a feeling of nervous excitement pervaded the atmosphere.

Occasionally, when she was unable to sleep at night, Leah would panic, frightened by the sheer magnitude of the task she had set herself. She would ask herself how she'd had the effrontery to imagine that she could run a hotel. But the clear light of morning usually brought calm and reassurance. And if she was nervous and lacking in confidence, Marie was always there to quell her doubts. In quieter moments she often amused the girls with anecdotes about her own first foray into the hotel world, and of the time she'd persuaded David, against his better judgement, to buy the almost derelict 'Marina'. She described the pleasure she'd had in the refurbishment of the rundown place and her youthful audacity in throwing a dinner to celebrate its reopening. It was this story that stirred Leah's imagination and gave her an idea.

'Why don't *we* give a reopening dinner?' she suggested one morning as the three of them were taking their coffee break.

Marie looked doubtful. 'You haven't engaged a chef yet,' she said. 'And when you do it'll be a week or so before you could spring a dinner like that on him. They're notoriously temperamental, you know.'

'Then I'll cook it myself,' Leah announced.

'*You*?' Marie and Sally looked at her. 'Are you sure you're up to it?'

Leah laughed. 'Thanks for the vote of confidence. We won't invite too many people. No more than thirty, say, mainly the press. We'll have some advertising people and a few civic dignitaries. I want

519

them to see that women are perfectly capable of making a go of things on their own, and that you're not beaten, Marie. Well?' she looked at them with bright, enquiring eyes. 'Are you game?'

Marie and Sally looked at each other, then back at Leah. 'All right,' Marie said at last with a smile. 'I can hardly veto the very thing I once did myself, can I?' She smiled. 'So I suppose we'd better start making plans, hadn't we?'

'God – this place stinks.'

Janet stood in the middle of the kitchen in her elegant suit and wrinkled her nose in disgust. Piles of dirty dishes covered the draining board and filled the sink. The table was covered with a stained table cloth, and ashes from the Aga had been spilled on the hearthrug. Bill sat in his dressing gown in the rocking chair, eating canned tomato soup from a cracked basin. He looked up disinterestedly at his ex-wife.

'What brings you out of the woodwork?'

'I rang you at the office. They said you were off sick.'

'So you thought you'd come round and gloat.' Bill returned his attention to the soup; lifted the spoon to his lips, then grimaced and dropped it back into the bowl.

'What's the matter with you?' Janet asked abruptly, taking in the pallor under a week's growth of beard. 'You look like shit.'

'Thanks. I've had a touch of 'flu, that's all.' He glowered at her with bloodshot eyes. 'Seen what you came for then?'

Ignoring his deliberate boorishness she began to fuss round the room. 'If it's like this down here, God only knows what your bedroom is like.'

'Since when have you been interested in my bedroom?'

She stopped and looked at him. 'Have you seen a doctor?'

'*No*. How many more times do you need telling? It's a bit of 'flu. I'm over the worst. Bugger off and leave me alone, can't you?'

Janet sighed. 'I suppose I'd better go up and see what I can do.' In the doorway she paused to look back at him. '*Men*,' she said scathingly. 'You're pathetic, the lot of you.'

An hour later she had changed his bed, dusted and swept the room. Downstairs, she washed up and made the place more comfortable generally. The whole time she worked, Bill grumbled.

'I'm perfectly capable of looking after myself. Why do women always think they know best?'

'Because we do,' Janet said, scrubbing at the layer of grease on the sink. 'When I've shifted this gunge I'll get you something to eat. I suppose there's no point in asking if there's any food in the house?' Bill shrugged. 'That's what I thought. Why don't you go up and have a sleep while I do some shopping?'

'For Christ's sake, stop bossing me about,' he snapped. 'I don't *want* you doing my shopping for me, and I don't want to sleep either. Over the past week I've slept my brain to a jelly.'

Finding some eggs in the fridge and a loaf of sliced bread sitting in solitary state at the bottom of the freezer, Janet rustled up a poached egg on toast which Bill ate with an air of disgruntled indifference. 'Why are you *really* here?' he asked suspiciously over his second cup of tea. 'I didn't even know you'd left Pennine TV until someone mentioned it in passing. Can you imagine what a prat I felt, having a comparative stranger tell me my own ex-wife was back in London?' He peered at her. 'Why didn't you tell me at Christmas? You must have known then.'

Janet avoided his eyes. 'I meant to. I really did. I came here to tell you I'd split with Mike. Then I realised that your interests were elsewhere.'

He frowned. 'Would you mind telling me what you're talking about?'

'Don't pretend you don't know. That girl. The dark one with the eyes.'

'Leah?'

'Yes, Leah. And don't come the innocent.' She shot him a challenging look. 'Don't bother telling me you haven't slept with her because it won't wash. I know you too well.'

Bill lifted his shoulders helplessly. 'I've no intention of arguing with you. I haven't the strength. It wasn't the way you make it sound. Anyway, you're the one who's always pointing out that we're not married any more, so why should you care?'

She chose not to rise to that particular bait. 'Anyway, I take it from the mess that she's gone,' she said. 'And your other paying guest too?'

'Yes to the first – partly yes to the second. Terry's due back soon. He's been sent to Yugoslavia on a special assignment.'

'Yugoslavia, Eh?' Janet raised an enquiring eyebrow at him. 'Why is it they never send you on any of the exciting jobs any more, Bill?' She smiled smugly. 'And what happened to Luscious Leah? Get fed up with your slobby habits? Or did she find someone younger and better-looking?'

'Neither. As a matter of fact, she came into some money,' Bill said. 'I had a letter from her not long ago. She's gone down to Dorset – bought a hotel and gone into business with her mother and sister.'

Janet was immediately alert. 'The sister who had the baby?'

'She's only got the one, as far as I know.'

'And the woman whose husband topped himself when they went bankrupt?'

He stared in horror as she pulled a notebook out of her handbag and began to scribble furiously. 'Hey, all that was in confidence. You're not going to start bothering her, are you? She's had enough hassle.'

'Not *bother* her, no. I should think some high-profile publicity is just what she can do with right now. Besides, it'll make a super follow-up for the article I did about the three of them in the *Recorder*.'

Bill stared at her as the realisation of what she had just said sunk in. 'Wait a minute. Are you telling me *you* wrote that?'

She looked up at him in surprise. 'Yes – well, it was too good a story to pass up. Cropped up just when I needed something really dramatic to get me back into free-lancing.' She met his blistering stare unflinchingly. 'Don't tell me the tough old Bill Fenton we know and love is going soft in his old age?' She laughed. 'Has the old Tiger of Fleet Street lost his teeth then? Oh, come off it, Bill. We're both journalists, for Christ's sake. There's no sentimentalism in newspaper work. Not if you want to get to the top, that is. You of all people should know that.'

'Did it bother you at all that your article was probably responsible for the Evans guy topping himself, as you so delicately put it?'

Janet shook her head. 'I was right, you have gone soft. You know, I worry about you, Bill. You've never been the same since you reported on that MP's blackmail case a couple of years back, have you? You really blamed yourself for his suicide, didn't you? It's our job to . . .'

'*Get out*,' Bill growled. 'Get out before I throw you out. And I'm warning you, if you hassle Leah again I'll . . .'

'Oh, all right.' Janet stuffed the notebook back into her bag. 'That's all the thanks I get for coming round here and mucking out for you. If you really want to know I was going to offer to move back in. God knows why. You certainly don't deserve it. I must need my head examining to worry about someone as boorish and cantankerous as you.' She thrust her face close to his. 'Your trouble is that you're getting old, Bill.' She smiled mockingly. 'Old and washed-up.'

'Well, I bow to your superior knowledge there.' Bill rose unsteadily to his feet. 'As for moving back in – don't make me laugh. I might have known there was something more behind the Florence Nightingale act. Let me tell you, Janet, I wouldn't have you back if you were the Queen of bloody Sheba. Sod off, and don't show your face here again unless you want it slapped.'

He listened, unmoved, to the stream of obscene invective she flung at him; winced as she slammed the door so hard it almost left its hinges; and watched dispassionately through the basement window as her five-inch heels tapped their way furiously up the area steps. As her footsteps died away he sighed. That was that then. Any hopes of repairing his broken marriage were well and truly laid to rest now – and probably all to the good. Even in the beginning, when they were in love, he and Janet had always fought like cats. In those days her aggression had fascinated and excited him. It had been stimulating – fun even. Now he found it tiresome and irritating; their arguments merely bored and exhausted him. Perhaps she was right. Maybe he *was* old and washed-up.

When he'd received Leah's letter he'd been somewhat mollified. At least she'd had the decency to write. But he was more disappointed than he'd cared to admit about the collapse of the restaurant venture he'd had such hopes of sharing with her. Janet was right there too, damn her. He'd lost his zest for journalism, unable to see it nowadays as anything more than preying on other people's misfortune. If wanting a quiet life, if caring about screwing up other people's lives, was going soft then it was something he'd known he was guilty of for some time. If nothing else, Janet had made him face it – at least from now on he wouldn't have to despise himself.

Ten days later Marie had received replies to most of the invitations she had sent out. She and Leah went through them one morning in the office so that Leah could get some idea of the number she would need to cater for.

'I did think of sending one to the *Recorder*,' Marie said. 'After all, if they were interested in the bad things that happened to us then maybe they'll be interested in the good things. And they're more likely to get things right if they come and see for themselves.'

Leah shook her head, her heart quickening with alarm. 'Oh, I'd rather you didn't. Anyway, I'd have thought he – or she – would have been the last person you'd want under your roof.'

'But it isn't my roof, Leah,' Marie reminded her. 'It's yours now. And it's not just a roof, it's a business. If they can print what we don't want, they can print what we *do*. They owe us one and I don't see why we shouldn't call in the debt.'

Leah sat down. 'Marie – I've never asked you, but do you think that article was the cause of your husband's . . .'

'The inquest verdict was accidental death, Leah,' Marie interrupted.

'And you believe it?'

'I believe that Ralph would never commit suicide,' she said. 'He was a calculating man, Leah, a violent one too. It still puzzles me that he could have got into such deep financial trouble. But suicide – definitely not.'

'I see.' Leah took a deep breath. 'Marie, don't send an invitation to the *Recorder*. You see, I have reason to believe that a friend of mine wrote the article. He was someone I trusted. I can't forgive him and I don't want to see him again.'

'Someone you cared for a great deal?' Marie saw the pain in Leah's eyes and smiled sympathetically. 'I see. And of course I understand, dear. In that case we'll leave it.'

Leah had planned a fairly simple menu. Cream of celery soup, saddle of lamb with baby spring vegetables, followed by a special *bombe surprise* she had created herself, with coconut liqueur, pineapple and kiwifruit.

Marie had organised the temporary staff they would need and Sally had excelled herself with the floral arrangements. They were spectacular and would have cost them a small fortune if they'd engaged an outside florist. Banks of lush tropical green plants would welcome the guests in reception, whilst the dining room was aglow with colour and fragrant with the delicate perfume of spring flowers. To add to the occasion, Sally had made each of the female guests a dainty posy to be laid beside their place at the table. Each one was different, varying from a single rose or a fragile spray of pastel freesias to gardenias or violets.

On the day of the dinner the atmosphere at 'The Ocean' was electric. All Leah could think about was whether everything would be ready on time. Marcus, the new chef she had engaged just one week previously, good-naturedly donned his white overall, rolled up his sleeves and helped, assuring her that all would be ready on time.

In spite of his name, his short, stocky figure and dark, Gallic looks, Leah had been amused to hear him speak with a broad Yorkshire accent. He told her at his interview that his father was French but his mother was from Halifax. Despite Marie's prophecy he didn't seem in the least temperamental. He admired Leah's culinary ability and her willingness to turn her hand to any job. He even displayed his approval by teaching her some of his favourite tricks of the trade – special garnishes he had devised himself and little short cuts that made life in the kitchen easier and less fraught. She soon discovered to her delight that he was an inspired genius when it came to exotic decoration. Going to work on her *bombe surprise*, he made it look like something from a Caribbean banquet.

At last everything was ready. The dining room looked elegant and the waiters had arrived and been inspected and briefed by Marie and Marcus. Marie came into the kitchen to tell Leah that their guests had begun to arrive and, confidently leaving Marcus to take charge, she slipped up to the flat to change and join them for a pre-dinner drink.

The reception area was quite full when she stepped out of the lift in the slim-fitting garnet red dress she had bought specially for the occasion. She hoped that the new sophisticated short hairstyle made her look older. She badly wanted to be taken seriously as the new proprietor of 'The Ocean'.

Looking around her and trying hard to look self-assured and confident, her eyes searched the room.

She spotted Doctor Philip Hodges, looking handsome and distinguished in his dinner jacket, and David Evans, smiling proudly as he stood beside Marie. Mavis and Ken Payne were there, talking to Sally. They had left baby James with Ken's sister, Jean, and were combining the occasion with a weekend of house hunting. Leah was particularly pleased to see that Hannah had managed to make it. She stood in the far corner, looking attractive in a black dress, talking to Bill Fenton. Leah wanted to go at once to them, take refuge in the familiarity of people she knew well, but she knew she must first give her attention to the local guests. There were journalists from the local press and radio stations; even the Mayor and Mayoress had arrived with their little entourage. Everyone she had invited was there, yet now that her moment of triumph had arrived she felt curiously lost and insecure. Sally had her adoptive parents for support; Marie had her father-in-law and her handsome doctor friend. She, Leah, had no one close to reassure her and bolster her confidence. For the moment she was just an anonymous young woman in an eye-catching red dress.

She stood for a minute, part of her clinging to her anonymity and putting off the moment when she must step forward and accept the responsibility for her new role. She fought hard not to think of Terry, and how perfect this moment could be if he were here to share it with her. Then she shook off the negative feelings and straightened her shoulders. Taking a deep breath, she assumed her new mantle and moved forward, smiling, to introduce herself and welcome her guests.

The dinner went without a hitch. Marcus had taken charge in the kitchen, proving his worth by serving everything to perfection and keeping the staff firmly in order. As they reached the coffee stage Leah drew a sigh of relief. She had never prepared a meal for so many people before and now that it was safely over she felt a glow of achievement. The editor of the local paper, with whom she had earlier had a long chat, stood up to propose a toast and make a small speech of thanks. He praised the food, the service and ambience of the new 'Ocean', and wished its new young owner every success. His compliments were echoed by the applause that followed and Marie nudged Leah, signalling to her with her eyes that it was up to her to respond. She rose shakily to her feet.

'Ladies and gentlemen,' she began. 'Thank you all for coming this evening to share with me the beginning of what I hope will be a great new adventure. Most of you will have read in the press of some of the tragedy and misfortune that has dogged "The Ocean" in the past months. Also you will probably know that although I have the help and support of my family, we three are as yet comparative strangers. But I like to think that my joining together with my mother and sister will mark the beginning of a new era for all of us as well as for this hotel. All three of us have put a great deal into this project and we intend to make a success of it. Our aim is to make it a place for families.' She smiled. 'It's only when you have been deprived of your family you appreciate how precious it is. We want "The Ocean" to be somewhere where families can relax and be together.' She turned to smile at Marie and Sally, holding out a hand to each of them. 'Once again, we thank you all for coming. I hope you enjoyed your evening.'

She sat down to applause and reached with some relief for her glass of wine. Marie took a sip of her wine too, but in her case the action was to mask the gleam of moisture in her eyes. Leah had referred to her as 'my mother' – and she clearly hadn't even realised she had said it.

'Thank you for inviting me, Leah. I'm impressed.'

She had been mingling with her guests. Now she turned to see Bill smiling at her. '*Bill*! How lovely to see you.' She kissed him. 'Thank you for coming. I'm glad you've enjoyed it.'

'I have. It's good to see you and Sally doing so well together. I do wish you all the very best of success.' He gave her a rueful smile. 'I can't say I wasn't disappointed about Bella's though, and I miss you too. The place isn't the same without you.'

She looked more closely at him. He'd lost weight and there was a weary dullness about his eyes. 'Are you taking proper care of yourself?'

He laughed. 'Don't you start. I've had Janet round fussing. I had a bad bout of 'flu a few weeks ago but I'm fine again now.' A hand on her arm, he drew her to one side. 'Leah – can I have a word with you?'

'Oh dear, you do look serious. What can I have done now?'

'I wouldn't press it now when you have guests,' he said apologetically, 'but I'll have to go soon and it's important. It's – er – it's about Terry.'

'Oh.' The smile left her face. 'Do I really need to hear this, Bill?'

He grasped her wrist. 'Yes, I'm afraid it's vital that you do.'

He looked so grave that she felt a sudden chill. 'He – he's all right, isn't he?'

'Is there somewhere we can talk in private?'

She looked around her and, satisfied that everyone was happily occupied, turned back to him. 'We can go into the office, if you like.'

Closing the door, she turned to face him. 'Bill, if you've come to make excuses . . .'

'Listen – Terry didn't write that guff in the *Recorder*, Leah.'

She shook her head. 'It couldn't have been anyone else, Bill.'

'*Janet* wrote it. She told me so when she came round the other day. It was after she met you at Christmas. She was looking for a good story to get herself started in free-lancing. It seems she hung around at the hotel where you met your mother. After you'd left she somehow contrived to speak to her. They had lunch together and for Janet the rest was child's play. She always was good at coaxing people's innermost secrets out of them.' He looked at her. 'I'm not making it up. It's true, Leah. Terry had nothing whatever to do with it.'

Leah's heart was thumping sickeningly in her chest. 'Oh, God. But why didn't he get in touch with me?'

'He tried to. He went to Norfolk to look for you; unfortunately he arrived on the day you left, then he just missed you at Melbury Street too. He was frantic to put things right with you before he went to Yugoslavia.'

Her eyes opened wide. '*Yugoslavia*? Is he still there?'

'As far as I know.'

She bit her lip. 'Oh, God, Bill, it must be horrendously dangerous.'

He shrugged. 'There are bound to be risks.' He leaned forward. 'The point is, Leah, when he does get back he'll be coming back to London, to the *Globe*. Do I have your permission to tell him you know? Shall I ask him to come down and see you?'

'Yes – though what I'll say to him I don't . . .'

'You'll think of something. You'll be fine.' He

looked at his watch. 'I suppose I'd better go and look for Hannah. I came down by train but she's very kindly offered me a lift back.'

She stepped forward to catch at his wrist. 'Bill – is Terry – what does he think – about me blaming him?'

He shrugged. 'I don't know, love. All he wants is to put things straight. He loves you, Leah. But of course you know that.'

She bit her lip. 'Why couldn't I have trusted him? I should have known.'

He looked at the anguish in her eyes and squeezed her hand. 'Trusting is something you're going to have to learn, Leah.' He smiled. 'It's not easy for some of us. But I'm sure you and Tel are going to be all right from now on.' He kissed her cheek. 'Good luck, m'love. You deserve it. It'll all work out, you'll see.'

It was much later, upstairs in the flat when everyone else had gone home, that Leah and Sally sat drinking coffee and talking about the evening's success.

'Mum and Dad told me that they've sold the house in Leicester,' Sally said. 'And they've seen a place they like here. It looks as though it won't be long before I can see James every day again.'

'You've missed him, haven't you?' Leah asked.

Sally nodded. 'More than I'd ever have imagined I would.' She looked at Leah. 'When I think that I almost let him go . . . I've got you to thank for all that, Leah, as well as the job here. Marie and I owe you a lot.'

'Rubbish,' Leah said dismissively. 'We all owe it to Kate Dobson really. I couldn't have done any of it without her.'

'That's not quite true and you know it. But we won't argue. It was good to see Bill, wasn't it?' Sally said. 'I was pleased to be able to introduce him to Mum and Dad. Did you notice how well he and Hannah were getting along together? It'd be great if those two got together, wouldn't it?'

Leah nodded abstractedly. 'Yes. I think Bill needs a strong woman like Hannah. His wife was certainly strong, but it was the wrong kind of strength.'

Sally looked at Leah's pensive look and asked: 'Did he bring you some news? I saw you take him into the office and you've been very thoughtful since he left.'

'Yes.' Leah sighed. 'He wanted to tell me that it was his ex-wife who wrote the article about the three of us. All this time I've blamed Terry for it.'

'That article did a lot of good in many ways,' Sally said.

'Not for Marie. Up until then her husband never knew about us. It can't have done their relationship much good.'

'But surely it wouldn't have caused him to commit suicide?'

Leah looked thoughtful. 'I'm beginning to wonder about that. Marie seems to think it was totally out of character. Maybe it was just accidental as the inquest found. But caused because he was so furiously angry and driving recklessly.'

'Well, at least now you know that Terry wasn't responsible for the article,' Sally said. 'Are you going to get in touch?'

Leah sighed. 'I only wish I could. At the moment he's in Yugoslavia on an assignment for his paper.'

'You must be worried about him.'

'I just wish I'd had the chance to sort things out with him before he went.' Leah bit her lip. 'I should have trusted him, Sally. I should . . .'

'You're in love with him, aren't you?' Sally asked gently.

Leah shook her head bemusedly. 'I've tried not to

believe in love. I've always mistrusted it. I've always thought you had to snatch what you wanted from life before it kicked you in the face, and most of the people I've met seemed to confirm that belief.'

'Until Terry?'

'I believed he was different – till that article in the *Recorder*. He was the only person I'd confided in, you see. I couldn't see who else could have written it. I felt so *betrayed*. Now I wish I hadn't jumped to such hasty conclusions.'

'You could always write to him,' Sally suggested. 'You could tell him you were mixed up at the time – that you weren't thinking straight.'

'Bill asked if he could send him down to see me,' Leah told her. 'I said yes. And now I'm wondering what on earth I'm going to say, and if things can ever be the same between us again.' She looked up. 'If he comes, that is. He may not even want to see me again now.'

'He will,' Sally said softly. 'And if you really love each other, everything will be all right.'

David was tired when they got back to the flat. He rarely stayed up this late. Marie made him a hot drink and took it to him in his room, but when she got there he was already in bed and fast asleep. Smiling affectionately, she tucked his arm under the covers, switched off the light and picked up the untouched cup. She was in the hall when the telephone rang. Afraid that the noise would waken David she lifted the receiver hastily. Who could be ringing at this hour?

'Hello? Marie Evans speaking.'

'Hello, Marie.'

The sound of his voice sent a tremor though her body, turning her blood to ice. For a moment she stood there, numb with shock. Someone must be playing a cruel trick on her. As though from somewhere a long way off she heard her own voice say shakily: 'Who – who is this?'

The voice at the other end of the line chuckled softly. 'Oh, come on, Marie. I think you know who it is.'

With a cry she slammed down the receiver and stood there as though frozen to the spot. *Ralph was still alive*. Somewhere deep inside a part of her had always known it. But how had he found out where she was? And what did he want? Her knees suddenly too weak to hold her, she groped for the nearest chair and sank on to it. One thing was certain: having contacted her, he would ring again. What if he rang when David was here alone? The shock would kill him, she was sure of that. If – *when* – he rang again she would have to talk to him, find out what it was he wanted and strike some kind of bargain. Whatever happened, David mustn't know.

She didn't have long to wait. It was an hour later when the telephone rang again. She'd been lying awake, staring into the darkness. At the first ring she was out of bed and through the bedroom door instantly, snatching up the receiver.

'Hello?'

'Ah, you were waiting for me. How touching,' he said mockingly.

'What do you want?' she demanded. 'It's a criminal offence to fake your own death. I only have to call the police . . .'

'But you won't do that, will you, Marie?'

'Why shouldn't I? You've caused me enough trouble and pain, Ralph. I thought . . .'

'You thought you'd got rid of me. And now you're nicely set up with your daughter. Back at "The

Ocean". You've really landed on your feet, haven't you?'

'How do you know all this? Where are you?'

'I know everything. And I'm nearer than you think. But never mind any of that for now. I'll come to the point. I need some money, Marie.'

'You're mad. You left your father and me penniless.'

'But this daughter of yours has money. She must have. You can get it from her. Get it for me and I'll get out of your life for good.'

'There's no way I can ask Leah for money. And even if I did, how do I know you'd keep your word?'

'You don't. You'd have to trust me.'

'Trust you – *you* of all people?' She laughed dryly.

'I'm trusting you, Marie. I'm trusting you not to go to the police. I know you won't because the stakes are too high for you to do that.'

'Stakes?' Her mouth dried.

'For one thing, Dad wouldn't be too pleased to see me back, would he? I've an idea he'd take it badly. Then there are your two daughters to think of. You wouldn't want anything to happen to either of them – or some nasty upset to occur that would ruin the reopening of "The Ocean", would you? Then there's this baby grandson . . .'

She caught her breath. 'You *wouldn't*! Even you wouldn't stoop to that.'

'I wouldn't bet on it. They're nothing to me, Marie – any of them.' He paused to let the full implication of his statement sink in. 'Well, do we have a deal?'

She bit her lip hard, seriously frightened now. 'I've told you, Ralph, I can't get any money, whatever threats you make. Leah's spent everything on reopening the hotel. Anyway, how could I ask her? What reason could I give?'

536

'You'll think of one if you know what's good for you,' he said roughly. 'I don't need all that much. A grand would do it. Cheap at the price to see the last of me, eh, Marie?'

'I don't know – I'll have to think about it.'

'Twenty-four hours, and I want it in cash – used notes,' he said. His voice was as hard and sharp as steel, cutting into her like a knife. 'I can't give you longer. After that I'll have to start proving to you that I'm not playing around over this. I'll call you this time tomorrow.' There was a click as he rang off abruptly.

Leah found every aspect of the work fascinating and absorbing and with Marie's help she was quickly getting the hang of the business side of it as well as the catering. It was as she was opening the mail in the office on the morning after the reopening dinner that Marie arrived. She looked up in surprise.

'I told you to take today off. After all you did yesterday, I thought . . .' She broke off, seeing the look on Marie's face. 'What is it? Has something gone wrong?'

'No.' She cleared her throat. 'It's just – just that I've got something to ask you and – and I don't quite know where to begin.'

Leah laughed. 'How about the beginning? Don't look so worried. You know I'll help if I can.'

Marie's legs threatened to buckle under her and she sat down in the chair opposite. 'The fact is, I need some money. And, things being as they are, there's no one else I can ask.'

'How much money?'

'Rather a lot.' Marie took a deep breath. 'A thousand, in fact.'

'I see.' Leah looked at Marie's white face and realised that she wouldn't be asking if her need wasn't

537

desperate. 'Do you mind if I ask what it's for?' she asked gently. 'Is there some kind of problem?'

Marie had spent the remainder of the previous night racking her brain for a convincing answer to this question. After all, people didn't hand out a thousand pounds without wanting to know what it was for. 'I still owe some money – to a friend,' she said. 'I borrowed it when we were in difficulties. It was a friendly agreement so it wasn't covered by the bankruptcy. Now I hear that her husband is ill and he's had to give up his job. I – I feel terrible about it. I know she needs the money and I want to pay it back.'

'I see.' Leah nodded. 'I understand how you feel. It's just that I've spent so much. Preparing to reopen has cost more than I'd thought. The bookings are rolling in nicely now, though. If it could wait just a couple of months more?' She broke off, seeing Marie's anguished look. Then she remembered the shares Kate had left her. The income from them had been useful, helping to cover her expenses. But soon 'The Ocean' would start to make money. She could probably afford to sell some of them. She would ring Jane and ask her advice. 'Look,' she said, 'can you leave it with me?'

'For how long?' Under the cover of the desk Marie's fingers laced and twisted, the knuckles white with tension.

'I could probably let you know after lunch.'

'I'll ring you, if I may?'

'Of course.'

Marie stood up and backed towards the door, her face unnaturally flushed. 'Oh – one more thing. Could I have it in cash?'

'In cash? It's a lot of money. A cheque would be more convenient – and safer.'

'I know but – since my trouble I feel awkward about giving people cheques.'

'Of course. I should have thought.'

Marie stood by the door. 'Thank you, Leah,' she said. 'I wouldn't have asked you if it wasn't important. I'm sure you know that.'

When she had gone Leah sat for a moment, considering the request. There was something about it that didn't quite ring true. She hadn't known Marie very long, but she'd have staked her life on it that a request for money – especially this kind of money – was the last thing she'd do willingly. But whatever her reason it was clearly important. She lifted the telephone and dialled Jane English's number.

Marie had been waiting for the call but when the telephone rang, shrilling through the silence like a banshee's wail, she started violently. Snatching up the receiver she said breathlessly: 'Hello?'

'Marie?'

'Yes, it's me.' She clutched the receiver. She'd been on edge ever since she arrived home this evening, praying that he wouldn't call until David was asleep. Now it was a quarter to two in the morning and she was almost dropping with exhaustion.

'Well, did you get it?'

'Not yet. I'll have it the day after tomorrow.'

'Not till then?' He sounded agitated. 'If you're up to anything, Marie I warn you . . .'

'It takes time, Ralph. Be reasonable. People don't carry that sort of money around with them.'

'Right. The day after tomorrow. No longer, okay?'

'Yes, all right. Where do I send it?'

'You can't. I want you to bring it to me in person.'

'In person?' Her mouth dried at the thought of

seeing him again – of being alone with him, maybe in some isolated place. 'I don't see how I can do that.'

'Then you'd bloody well better think of a way. Remember what I said – mixed notes, used ones. Tell no one and come alone. If you bring anyone with you or contact the police you can expect the worst. I'm not making idle threats, Marie. I'm not alone. The people who are helping me are quite ruthless. They'll know what to do if anything happens to me.'

She swallowed. 'All right – all *right*.' She clamped her teeth together to stop them from chattering. 'Tell me where to bring it.'

'You've got a car?'

'Yes.'

'Good. Drive out to the New Forest. About a mile north of Ringwood on the main Salisbury road there's a clump of trees in an open space. Park the car out of sight behind the trees and wait for me there. I'll ring to tell you when it's safe to come and I'll be waiting and watching for you, so remember – don't try anything clever.

He was about to hang up when Marie said: '*Ralph*, wait – where can I contact you in case anything goes wrong?'

'You can't,' he said shortly. 'And I warn you, Marie, nothing had better go wrong. I'm relying on you to make sure it doesn't.'

Chapter 25

Jane had agreed reluctantly to sell some of Leah's shares for her.

'Are you sure you want to sell?' she'd asked. 'They're doing particularly well at the moment.'

'I need a thousand pounds quickly, Jane,' Leah explained. 'And as it's an emergency, is it possible to let me have the money by the day after tomorrow?'

'Probably not, but if it's that important I'll make it available for you.' There was a pause then Jane asked: 'There's nothing wrong, is there?'

'No. Everything's fine.'

'You're sure it's nothing I can help with?'

'No, really, but thanks for asking, Jane.'

'Okay, I'll have the money transferred to your account. It should be available for you in a couple of days.'

When Leah told Marie about the delay the following day she thought she looked anxious, so she made a point of ringing the bank next morning to check that the cash was available. Told that it was, she decided to telephone Marie at home to reassure her.

'I'll go the bank this afternoon,' she said. 'And I'll bring the money round to the flat if you like.'

'Oh, thank you.' Marie sounded grateful. 'I'll pick it up later this afternoon, if that's all right.'

'Of course, if that's what you want.' Leah was

replacing the receiver when Sally slipped into the office. Closing the door behind her, she said: 'You have a visitor.'

Leah looked up. 'Can you handle it for me, Sally? I haven't started on the mail yet.'

'Afraid not. This is something only you can deal with.' Sally seemed to be trying hard not to smile. 'I – er – think you're going to have to see this particular guest yourself, as soon as possible.'

Leah sighed. Clearly the mail would have to wait. 'All right,' she said resignedly. 'Send her in.'

'It's not a her, it's a *him*. And I've sent him up to the flat.' Sally gave up the battle and allowed her mouth to stretch into a grin. 'As a matter of fact, it's Terry Grant.'

'*Oh*!' For a moment Leah felt as though all the breath had been knocked out of her.

'Well, is that all you're going to say? He's driven all the way down from London overnight just to see you. Look, I've given him my key and told him to go up. The mail and telephone calls will wait for an hour or so and I'll cope if anything important crops up.' Sally grabbed her hands and pulled her to her feet. 'Go on. He's waiting.'

As she went up in the lift Leah had an odd feeling of unreality. She felt as though she were moving in a dream – or watching some stranger going through the motions. Letting herself quietly into the flat she stood for a moment in the empty hall, her heart thudding. The living-room door was open and she moved towards it apprehensively, realising that nothing could ever in her entire life be as important to her as the next few minutes.

He stood by the window, looking down at the sea view, his back towards her. He looked thinner and somehow older, and was wearing unusually formal clothes – a dark grey suit. She looked down at her own clothes; the neat businesslike skirt and jacket she always wore for work. The same might be said for her. It was a far cry from the casual clothes they had both favoured in the past. Suddenly it struck her that they'd both grown up over the past eighteen months. Had they grown away from each other in the process? It would be a strange irony if, having recognised that she loved him, he had grown out of her like some childhood habit.

She spoke his name very quietly. 'Terry?'

He turned to look at her and neither of them spoke. In the long silent moment that they looked into each other's eyes across the room, she knew that in spite of her misgivings nothing had changed for either of them. Without being aware of moving they were suddenly in each other's arms. Leah felt the wetness of tears on her cheeks and heard the crazy jumble of words that tumbled incoherently from her lips. Terry covered her mouth with his, smothering the garbled sentences, replacing them with something that said far more. She closed her eyes and gave herself up to his kiss and for a long moment neither of them spoke. Finally she pushed him away, shaking her head and brushing impatiently at the tears on her cheeks.

'Look what you're making me do,' she said, half laughing, half crying. 'You know how I hate weeping women. I never cry.' She thumped his chest. 'Oh, Terry, I've missed you so much.'

'I've missed you too.'

'And I'm sorry – about . . .'

'Don't.' He covered her lips with his fingers. 'You don't have to say anything. Bill has explained it all. I can't blame you for thinking I wrote that article. I did a lot of showing off last time we were together.'

'No, you didn't. You've done well and . . .'

He shook his head. 'No more. Look, I can't stay long and we've got some catching up to do. We won't waste time talking about that. It's history – right?'

'Right.'

He looked at her. 'I was sorry to hear about Kate.'

'I know. I went home for the funeral.'

'Was it awful?'

She nodded. 'Jack and Hilary wouldn't believe I hadn't wheedled round her to make her Will in my favour. It must have come as a shock to them to know that a supermarket chain wanted to buy her bungalow and land.'

'And you decided to put the money into this place?'

She nodded. 'I haven't regretted it so far. I'm determined to make a success of it, Terry. It's my whole future now.'

'Not quite your whole future, I hope.' He tipped up her chin to look into her eyes. 'I'd like to be part of that too.'

'Terry, last time we were together I made a fool of myself. I'd like you to forget that.'

'Are we talking about your proposal?' His eyes teased her.

'I was hoping you'd forgotten. You turned me down.'

'To be honest, I wasn't sure you really knew what love was about,' he said gently. 'I wanted to be sure you knew what you were letting yourself in for before I let you commit yourself.'

'I *was* sure, Terry. I was then and I still am,' she told him earnestly.

He pulled her close. 'In that case I accept – if the offer's still on the table.' He smiled. 'This time I'm not pushing my luck.' He looked at his watch and groaned. 'Damn. Look at the time. I shouldn't really be here at all, but after I heard what Bill had to say I just had to see you.' He looked at her. 'I've only got a couple of hours. Can you take a little time off?'

She smiled. 'I've got a feeling Sally would kill me if I didn't.'

He scooped her into his arms and crossed the room, shouldering the door open. 'Great. Show me which room is yours.'

Leah wakened with the sound of the sea's roar far below in her ears. For a moment she thought it was early morning and that what had happened was a dream, then she turned her head and saw Terry beside her. He lay on his back with one arm flung out and she felt a rush of love for him that almost took her breath away. With one finger she traced the line of his jaw. Then, leaning across, she kissed him softly. He stirred and opened his eyes.

'Don't wake me,' he mumbled, looking at her with slightly unfocused eyes. 'I'm used to the dream, but I'll never get used to the waking.'

She kissed him again. 'You *are* awake.'

Putting his arms around her, he pulled her down to him. 'You're right,' he murmured, his mouth against hers. 'I am awake. The dream was never this good.' He studied her thoughtfully. 'I miss your hair. Why did you have it cut?'

'It's my new image,' she told him. 'After – everything that happened I wanted to make a completely new start. This is the new me.'

'I liked the old you.'

'She's still there, Terry,' she said softly. 'Inside I'm the same.' She put up her hand to the new short hair. 'I realise now that changing your hairstyle doesn't really alter anything. I never had any real sense of identity till now. In the children's home I was just another kid; at the Dobsons' I was a disappointing replacement for Fiona. But now I know who I am and where I want to go.' She looked at him. 'And who I want to be with.'

He kissed her. 'I admire this new self-assured businesswoman.' He raised himself on one elbow to look down at her. 'But it's Leah I love – the Leah I know as no one else does.'

'Even after what I accused you of?'

'Shhh.' He covered her lips with his fingers. 'What did we promise?'

'When I heard about Marie's bankruptcy and her husband dying in a car crash, I suddenly saw the perfect use to put Kate's money to,' she told him. 'It wasn't just a question of finding myself. It was a way I could make a career and help Marie and Sally over a bad time too.' Her eyes shone. 'And it's going to work, Terry. It's really going to work. For once in my life I've done something that's worthwhile, and it's actually going to come off.' She laughed suddenly. 'But that's enough about me. I want to hear what you've been doing. Bill told me the paper sent you over to Yugoslavia.'

'Yes, to Sarajevo.'

'Was it dangerous?'

He avoided her eyes. 'Looking back, yes, it was. When you're in the thick of it, you tend to forget the danger.'

'What was it like? Tell me, Terry.'

There was a pause then he turned to look at her, his eyes clouded. 'It was terrible, Leah. So stupid and futile. Such a waste of human life. Until you've seen suffering like that, you haven't really lived.'

'Oh, Terry.' She held him close.

For a moment they were silent. Then, taking her face between his hands, he looked at her. 'Leah, there's something I have to tell you.'

She pulled a face. 'You look serious?'

'I am. You'd better prepare yourself for a shock. Leah – Ralph Evans is still alive.'

She gasped. 'Alive? But he *can't* be. His car . . .'

'It looks very much as though he faked his own death.'

'How do you know this?'

'A guy I work with on the paper has a contact – a relative over in Northern Ireland. He got in touch a few weeks ago. There had been reported sightings of Evans over there more than once since the accident.'

Leah gripped his hand. 'But how did they know it was him?'

'It was him all right. This guy persuaded the editor to let him go over and make a few enquiries.'

Leah frowned. 'But – I don't understand. What's the connection?'

'It seems Evans was an ex-army man; served in Northern Ireland for some time. He was kicked out of the military police some years ago – suspected of double-dealing, though nothing could be proved at the time. He was court martialled for other offences, violence amongst them. Obviously, having faked his own death Ireland was the only place he could run to. The theory is that his friends over there were quick to cash in on his dependency on them, making him work for them in exchange for a forged passport and a ticket to somewhere he'd never be found.'

'A bombing campaign, you mean?' Leah asked.

Terry nodded. 'About a week ago there was a raid on the house where he was staying. A huge arms and explosives cache was discovered and several arrests were made. Unfortunately, Evans escaped.'

Leah looked at him, her eyes wide with fear. 'God, Terry, he could be anywhere. We must warn Marie. Suppose he comes here?'

'I don't think you should tell her. At least, not yet.'

'Why?'

'There's no point in frightening her unnecessarily. I don't think for one minute that he'd be foolish enough to come here, but if that is his plan, it wouldn't do to have him warned off.'

'She *wouldn't* . . .'

'She might. After all, he is her husband.' He took both her hands. 'Don't look so scared, Leah. I'm sure she's in no danger. A careful watch is being kept on all ports and airports. It's my guess that it won't be long before he's caught.'

She was shaking her head. 'But if your paper is on to it, surely the story will soon be common knowledge? Marie will know then.'

He shook his head. 'There's a press black-out in force till he's caught,' he said. 'Which is why I'm going to have to ask you to promise me not to breathe a word.'

'Of course I promise, but it's worrying all the same.' She put her arms around him. 'Oh, Terry, when I think of you out there in Yugoslavia – in the middle of all that fighting. You might have been killed,' she whispered. 'I might never have seen you again.'

He kissed her. 'Well, I wasn't. I'm here now and we're together. I'm back in London to stay now. And due for some time off next week.'

'Then you'll come back – spend it with me?'

'Just try and stop me.' Over her shoulder he caught sight of the clock. 'I'm sorry, darling, I'll have to go now.' He got up and began to dress hurriedly.

'And I have to be at the bank before they close.' She broke off, biting her lip as she suddenly remembered her reason for going to the bank. Was it possible that Marie's request for money had a more sinister motive? She opened her mouth to mention it to Terry, then, without quite knowing why, she closed it again.

Marie sat by the telephone, waiting for his call. The money was in a sealed envelope in her handbag, on the hall table next to her coat. When the phone began to ring she snatched up the receiver quickly.

'Hello – Ralph?' At the other end of the line she heard him gasp.

'You *fool*! Suppose it hadn't been me?'

'No one else rings at this time of night.' Her voice was thin and tight with tension. 'I've got the – what you asked for. Do I come now?'

'Yes, as soon as you can. I'll be waiting. Sure you know where to come?'

'Yes. One mile north of Ringwood on the Salisbury road. Open ground with a clump of trees.'

'Right.' He rang off without waiting for her reply.

It was beginning to rain as Marie backed the car out of the garage. A thin drizzle misted the windscreen, obscuring her vision. She hadn't wanted to attract attention by switching on the lights until she was on the road. As she drove she was acutely aware of the envelope in her bag on the seat beside her; money she had borrowed from Leah – lied to obtain. She despised herself, and hated Ralph for forcing her to do it. Should she have called his bluff and gone to the police? She shuddered, remembering his words: 'I have friends – ruthless friends.' She believed him. He would have paid her back. Maybe not right away but later, sometime when she least expected it, and in the subtly cruel way that Ralph was so good at. She'd never have had any peace, wondering – looking over her shoulder.

The roads were almost empty of traffic and after

she left the lighted streets of the built-up area she found the darkness oppressive. It was a relief to get on to the brightly lit by-pass. She reached the small town of Ringwood and followed the signs for Salisbury, her heart beginning to beat dully. She was almost there. Soon she would have to face him.

It was still raining when she found the place and carefully parked the car so as to be out of sight. The night was so black that once she had switched the car lights off she could see nothing – hear nothing but the patter of rain on the car's roof and the trees rustling in the wind. A sudden tapping on the window made her start violently and her heart almost stopped beating when she turned to see Ralph's face peering in at her. At first she hardly recognised him. He had grown a beard, and his hair – normally cut short, military fashion – was long and unkempt. She wound down the window.

'The money's here.' With trembling fingers she opened her bag, but he was wrenching the door open.

'Get out.'

'Why?' Cold with fear she thrust the envelope at him. 'Here's your money. I've kept my side of it. I have to go now.'

'You haven't finished yet. There's something else I need you to do.' He reached into the car and grasped her arm. 'Get out. Do as I say and be quick about it. There's no time to lose.'

Her heart thudding and fear rising in her throat, acid as bile, she followed him. Deep into the trees they went. His fingers round her wrist were as cold and relentless as steel. As her eyes became accustomed to the darkness she saw that they were approaching a disused hut, its roof made up of sheets of corrugated iron on which the rain beat a noisy tattoo. Ralph opened the door and pushed her unceremoniously inside. In the dim light coming in through the one dusty window she could just make out that it was furnished with a table and two chairs. On the table was the remains of a hurried meal and a black leather briefcase. She spun round to face him, trying to hide the fear that had turned her legs to water.

'What do you want?' she asked breathlessly. 'I've done what you asked. There's nothing else I can do for you.'

'Yes, there is.' He pulled out one of the chairs from under the table. 'Sit down there and listen. You'll have guessed that the money is payment for a passport and a ticket for – a place where I can fade into obscurity. It's to be handed over early tomorrow morning at Waterloo Station.'

'So . . . ?'

'The man who is to do the swap will be waiting in the buffet,' he went on. 'I'm taking no chances on anything going wrong, so you are going to drive me to London – to Waterloo – and you are going to do the swap for me.'

Her mouth dried. 'That doesn't make sense. He won't know me – won't trust a stranger. I won't know how to recognise him.'

'He'll be waiting in the buffet. All you do is go in and buy a coffee, sit down at a vacant table and put the briefcase on the table. He'll join you – ask if the seat opposite is free and sit down. He'll put a folded newspaper on the table. Inside will be an envelope for me. After a moment or two he'll get up and take the case, leaving the newspaper. You bring it to me. That's simple enough, isn't it?'

'I can't, Ralph. You don't know what you're asking.' Her knees were shaking. 'If I were to do this I'd be implicated.'

He grasped her coat collar and pulled her to her feet. 'You think you're not *already* implicated? Let me down now, Marie, and you'll wish you'd let Costello finish you off all those years ago.' He thrust his face close to hers. 'You'll do as I bloody well say or you'll be sorry. It only takes one phone call from me and . . .'

'It won't work, Ralph. If this person is expecting a man – *you* . . .'

'He isn't. All he knows is that he'll pick up a briefcase in exchange for the envelope. Once you've delivered it to me you can go. And you'll never see me or hear from me again. You can go on pretending you think I'm dead.' His eyes glittered in the dimness. 'Isn't that worth going to a little trouble for?'

'Why did you do it, Ralph?' she asked. 'If I'm to do this for you, I think I have a right to some answers. Why did you fake your own death?'

He shrugged. 'I thought it would make things easier for everyone. Don't pretend you and Dad didn't wish me dead often enough.'

'You opted out,' she said scathingly. 'Because you knew you'd get help from – from the people over there; people you helped in your army days?'

'Something like that.'

'So it was true – all that?'

'Yes. It was true.'

'So what went wrong?'

He turned from her to pace the tiny room restlessly. 'It would have been all right. I'd have been long gone by now, only there was a tip-off about – what was being planned. Some bastard must have blown the whistle – informed. If I ever find out who . . . Some of them were arrested. I got away though. As far as I know no one saw me so I'm still in the clear.'

552

He turned to face her. 'That's why I have to have that passport *now*. There's no time to lose.' He took a threatening step towards her. 'No more questions. Give me the money.'

'One more thing, Ralph. Who was it in the car?'

He gave an impatient snort. 'No one.'

'There was a body. We had a funeral.'

'He was *no one*, I tell you. Some old wino – a drunk. I picked him up off the street and bought him a few drinks.' He shook his head. 'He was old and sick. He wouldn't have lasted much longer anyway. I did him a favour.'

'You *murdered* him – used him,' Marie said quietly. 'Just as you used David and me, just as you're using me now.'

'Just as *you* used *me*, you mean – keeping quiet all those years about your bastard brats. Just hand over the cash and shut your lying mouth.'

Resignedly, she handed him the envelope and he pushed it into an inside pocket.

'Right, if you've quite finished moralising, we'll go.'

Dawn was breaking when they reached the outskirts of London, but already the traffic was quite heavy. Ralph barked out directions to her in a sharp, staccato voice that told her how nervous and jumpy he was.

The drive had been like a bad dream. Marie had longed desperately for some miracle that would save her; a breakdown – an accident even. As she drove she made wild, impossible plans. If he would only fall asleep she could drive straight to the nearest police station. She glanced at the petrol gauge, cursing herself for filling the tank only the previous morning. She couldn't even plead that she had run out of petrol.

At last they reached Waterloo and Ralph directed her to a place where she could leave the car, in a tense silence, Ralph holding her firmly by the arm, carrying the briefcase in his other hand. On the station's huge concourse the bustle of the day had already begun. They were just two more travellers – anonymous faces in the crowd. No one gave them a second glance.

As they walked on to the station he whispered to her: 'Don't get any clever ideas, Marie. I'm a dead man, remember? I'm not wanted by the police. I'm not missing. If you show the smallest sign that anything is wrong it'll be the worse for you. From now on you're in this with me, right up to your neck, remember?'

She could feel her legs trembling beneath her. Now they'd arrived and the worst part of her ordeal was yet to come. She was aiding a criminal – a murderer – to escape. She would be as guilty as he was if she allowed it to happen, yet what else could she do? As they moved among the morning travellers every bone in her body ached and her eyes burned with fatigue. Nothing could prevent it now. Oh, God, let it soon be over.

Ralph nudged her. Since they'd arrived at the station he'd grown even more edgy than before. She could feel the tightly coiled tension emanating from him like a vapour. 'Over there, look' he said. 'The buffet bar.' He rammed a fist painfully into her back just under her shoulder blade. '*Well* – do you see it or don't you?'

'I see it.'

He pushed the briefcase into her hand. 'I'm not all bad, Marie. There's a little reward waiting for you when you've helped me out. Something to make you happy.' His eyes smiled enigmatically into hers as she looked up at him. 'Go on then,' he said. 'What are you waiting for? And remember what I said. Do as I say and everything will be fine.' When she hesitated the smile left his lips and his eyes began to gleam dangerously. His voice was sharp and raw with tension as he snapped: 'Oh, go *on*, woman. For Christ's sake get on with it. Once you've done it you're free, understand. *Free*.'

I'll never be free now, she thought despairingly. If I help him to freedom I'll never know when he might come back. If I fail I could go to prison again. On legs that threatened to buckle beneath her, she began to walk slowly towards the buffet.

It wasn't busy. Only a handful of people sat at the tables. There were plenty of empty seats. She bought a cup of coffee and chose a table near the door. Her heart hammered as she placed the briefcase where it could clearly be seen. She sat down. The minutes ticked by. Nothing happened. Her heart pounding, she watched as people came in and out of the buffet. She took a sip of her cooling coffee in a vain effort to appear relaxed. She watched as commuters hurried past outside on the station, each one intent on their own business. All of them blissfully unaware of the drama being acted out just feet away.

He isn't going to come, she told herself. And if he doesn't, what then? She lifted her cup to her lips and realised that it was empty. Should she get another? Should she remain doggedly where she was? Should she leave?

'*Is that seat taken?*'

She started violently as the quiet voice spoke at her shoulder. Strange that she hadn't seen anyone come in. Perhaps he'd been here all the time, just watching her.

'No – no, it isn't.' Her voice sounded thin and

strange as she turned to look up at the man. Then her heart almost stopped beating. Her stomach churned sickeningly and she felt her eyes widen and her mouth drop open in shocked surprise. The dark hair was now streaked with grey and the face was heavier and more mature, but nevertheless unmistakable. She would have known it anywhere. It was a face etched on her memory for all eternity.

Incredulously, she breathed his name: '*Liam*?'

For a second their eyes locked in stunned mutual recognition. Then she remembered Ralph's leering smile and his promise of a reward and instantly she knew he had planned all this to pay her back for her deception. She opened her mouth to speak, but suddenly, without warning, Liam snatched up the briefcase from the table and made swiftly for the door. She sprang to her feet. The *newspaper*! The newspaper with the envelope hidden inside. He'd gone without leaving it. She leapt to her feet.

'*Wait*!' She heard her own voice, unfamiliar and shrill with panic. Without that envelope God alone knew what Ralph would do. The heavy door of the buffet swung back in her face, stopping her – delaying her from following. She struggled through it and stood for a moment, her eyes frantically raking the crowd for him. She saw him. He was moving fast, his open trenchcoat flapping behind him. He was making straight for the station exit. If she didn't catch him – if he got into a taxi or a bus . . . Then she saw Ralph, standing in the place where she had left him, his back towards her. Liam seemed to be making straight for him, yet so far Ralph hadn't seen him. Was he going to give Ralph the envelope himself?

She stopped, her hand flying to her mouth as a sudden fearful possibility occurred to her. The briefcase . . . had Ralph really put the money into it or did it contain something else – something more deadly.

The thought barely had time to form in her mind when suddenly it was as though all hell had been let loose. The explosion lifted her off her feet, tossing her aside like a rag doll. She was aware of the flash and the deafening report – a fearful noise that grew louder and louder inside her head like the rushing of a great wind. Her ears seemed to swell to bursting point and pain ripped savagely at her legs. She heard screams, some of which she knew were her own. Confused shouts mingled with the din of breaking glass, pounding feet and falling masonry. They merged into a single high-pitched sonic whine – then the merciful black curtain of oblivion came down, blotting it all out.

Chapter 26

The little church nestled in the heart of the woods. It was reached by an ivy-covered lychgate leading to a long drive bordered by ancient yews. Inside the pews were filling fast and already the organ was playing softly, its sound drifting out through the open door to mingle with the singing of the birds.

Sally got out of the car with Mavis and Ken. Between them trotted her small son, James. At three and a half, he was a sturdy, fair-haired little boy, perhaps a little solemn for his years. Mavis and Ken adored him. They had not regretted moving to Dorset and were happy in their new home. Ken had even joined the local gardening club through which they had quickly made a new circle of friends. It was almost as though they had lived here all their lives.

For Sally it had been a fortunate move. Two years ago, after running her floristry business from 'The Ocean' for a year, she had taken her courage in both hands and gone to the bank for a loan. Now she had her own premises from which she provided floral decor for many of the local hotels, as well as being in demand for wedding bouquets and flowers for all kinds of festive occasions. The little white van with Ocean Blooms in bright colours on its sides was a familiar sight and her business was growing daily.

She had spent most of the previous day in St Mark's

doing the flowers; even this morning she had driven round to the church before breakfast to freshen her arrangements with a fine mist of water and to put the finishing touches to her work before going home to change.

As they reached the church porch the mixed scents of rose, lilac and jasmine drifted out on the spring afternoon air. Mavis turned to her.

'Dad and I will go in, shall we?'

Sally nodded. 'Save a seat for Jason. He shouldn't be long parking the car.'

'I want to wait for Jason too, Mummy.' Sally looked down as her small son slipped his hand into hers.

'All right. We'll wait for him together, shall we?'

It was just a year ago that she had met Jason again. At first he had come to Dorset with Aunt Jean, driving his mother down to spend a week's holiday with Mavis and Ken. He and Sally had renewed their acquaintance a little warily at first, but Sally's small son had no such inhibitions. It had been James, toddling on fat little legs, who had made them laugh together and captured Jason's heart. Soon, Sally found that she too could relax in his company. She confided in him about her plans for the future and asked his advice; took him to 'The Ocean' and introduced him to Leah.

After that first visit he asked if he might come again. The occasional visits had become monthly, then fortnightly, till now everyone seemed to have accepted them as a couple. Sally found this a little irksome at first, but now even she had accepted the situation, slipping easily into the relationship. She felt comfortable and contented with Jason. Almost without realising it, she found herself looking forward eagerly to his visits.

From the first he had been frank about his broken engagement to Paula.

'We weren't right for each other,' he told her. 'We were drifting. Our relationship had become a habit. Because everyone accepted that we'd get married, we just sort of went along with it.' He smiled wryly. 'For months before it ended I had the feeling she was trying to think of a way of letting me down lightly. Neither of us wanted to see the other hurt, you see, so it came as a relief to us both when I finally grasped the nettle and called it off.' He looked at Sally. 'But it had to be done. Marriage is for ever. At least, that's how I see it.'

'I agree,' Sally said. 'Which is why I made up my mind after James was born that I wouldn't marry. I'll never have another child, you see. It wouldn't be fair.'

'Surely that depends on the man.' Sally had been aware of his eyes on her but she had refused to meet them. He would want a child of his own one day whatever he might think now. Quickly she changed the subject and Jason let the moment pass. I can wait, he told himself patiently.

'Here's Jason.' James pointed excitedly. When she saw him walking towards her, tall and upright in his dark grey suit and sober tie, her heart lifted. He joined them, lifting James on to his shoulder with a smile.

'Do you think you can be quiet for a whole half hour, ragamuffin?' he asked teasingly.

The little boy squealed with delight as Jason took a bag of jelly babies out of his pocket.

'Maybe these will help,' he said.

'You spoil him,' Sally chided him. She looked at her watch. 'Mum and Dad are saving you a seat. I think you'd better go in now. It's almost time.'

He bent to brush his lips softly across her cheek. 'Anyone tell you how beautiful you look this morning?' he whispered.

Leah took a last look round the poolside lounge. She had hoped so much for a fine warm day so that they could hold the reception out of doors beside the new swimming pool, and although it was still early May her wish had come true. The sky was a clear azure blue and the sun was as warm as July. Marcus's sumptuous buffet, crowned by the superb cake, was laid out in the new lounge with its glass doors overlooking the pool. Sparkling glasses were waiting on their trays near the door and the champagne was on ice. Everything was ready. At last it was time to go to the church. Suddenly Leah was aware of a pang of nervousness.

'Almost time we were going.'

She looked up to see Terry standing in the doorway looking at his watch. She went across to him and slid her arms around his waist, hugging him tightly. He laughed gently.

'Hey – what did I do to deserve this?' he asked, looking down into her misty eyes.

'It's nothing, I'm nervous, that's all. Oh, Tel, it will be all right, won't it?'

He kissed her. 'Of course it'll be all right.'

'You're sure she'll be able to make it?'

Terry laughed and kissed her. 'I've never seen anyone as determined as Marie. I'd put my last pound on it.'

Reassured, she smiled at him. 'Right. I'll go up and get her then, shall I?'

He nodded. 'If you need me just ring down. I'll be waiting in Reception.'

As she went up to the flat in the lift Leah thought

back over the past three years. This was the day none of them had thought they would ever see, and now, miraculously, it was here.

She remembered the terrible morning when the police had arrived to tell her about Marie's involvement in the Waterloo bombing. Looking back now it seemed unreal, like a bad dream.

They had already heard about the explosion on the early morning news, but as far as any of them knew Marie had been at home in her own flat that night. The news that she had been injured in the explosion that had caused two deaths and many more injuries had been hard to take in.

Later, at the hospital, she and Sally had been shocked to learn the extent of Marie's injuries. Her legs had been so badly shattered that at first it had been feared that the surgeons might not be able to save them. Even when the first of the operations had proved successful it was thought that she might never walk again. Many months of painful surgery and treatment had followed. And the shock and trauma of what had led up to it took its toll on her health too.

As soon as she was well enough to make a statement she had told the police about Ralph's reappearance; his demands for money and the nightmare drive he had forced her to make to London that night. The rest only Leah knew. It was when she was sitting at her bedside one evening, about a month after the bombing. Thinking Marie was asleep she had picked up a book and begun to read. The sound of Marie's voice coming suddenly out of the silence had startled her.

'It was him, Leah – Liam, the man who was your father. He did it to save me. I realise that now.'

She put down her book and took Marie's hand.

She'd been delirious at times and at first Leah thought she was rambling again. 'Don't try to talk. You must rest.'

'But it's true. I wanted you to know.' Marie turned her head on the pillow and Leah saw that she was fully awake and in command of her senses. 'Ralph had planned it all. He did it to punish me – for not telling him about you and Sarah. He must have arranged it all with his associates – over there.' An expression of pain clouded her eyes. 'Seeing him again, suddenly like that, face to face – I can't tell you what it was like. We never spoke – just looked at each other. Then all at once Liam picked up the case and ran. I believe that in that moment he too guessed what Ralph had done. He did it to save my life.'

Leah pressed the frail hand. 'Surely even Ralph wouldn't plan something so – so *sick*?'

Marie shook her head. 'You never knew him. It was typical – his own special twisted kind of joke – just the kind of irony he enjoyed. The bomb was meant to go off in the buffet. To take us both. Liam knew it too. I saw the realisation dawn in his eyes in that moment when we looked at each other. What he did was for me, Leah; to save me, to wipe out that other time.'

'If the man really was Liam, why didn't you tell the police?' Leah asked. 'Don't you see, Marie, you could have cleared your name – proved that you were innocent all those years ago?'

'What good would it do now? Marie turned her head from side to side on the pillow, tears trickling down her cheeks. 'Nothing could give me back the years I lost – make up for all I went through.' She looked at Leah, her eyes glazed with the memory. 'I'll never forget that morning, Leah. Ralph had his back turned. He never even saw Liam coming. Then . . .'

564

She shuddered. 'It was so sudden – so violent. They were both . . .'

'*Don't*!' Leah urged, pressing her hand. 'Please, Marie. Try not to think about it. It's all over. No one can hurt you any more. You must concentrate on getting well again.'

'Yes,' Marie murmured. 'Yes, I must, because if I don't it will all have been for nothing, won't it?'

Leah watched her fall into an uneasy sleep again. No one would ever know whether her interpretation of Liam's action was the true one. But if it brought her comfort . . .

All through Marie's long illness Philip had been a tower of strength. As soon as she was fit enough he had had her transferred to a hospital closer to home where he could keep a special eye on her. When she first came out of hospital Marie had been confined to a wheelchair. Philip had engaged a nurse and a housekeeper and cared for her himself at his cottage in the New Forest. Then, just as she was making good progress, David had died suddenly. He'd been staying at the cottage too and had seemed to cope well with all that had happened, but the past months had been too much for his frail heart. He died peacefully in his sleep early one morning the following October. His loss set Marie back. She seemed to blame herself and for months she was listless and depressed.

From the first Philip had persistently begged Marie to marry him, but she had been adamant. She would not agree to marry until she could walk normally again. And as the doctors held out little hope of that, marriage seemed unlikely. Nevertheless, Philip insisted that he would propose regularly at least once a month until he wore down her resistance and they could reach some kind of compromise.

Leah and Terry were married the following spring.

Terry had been appointed editor of a regional daily newspaper. Sally moved out to make room for the newly-weds and into the flat over her own premises. 'The Ocean' was flourishing and life was changing. Leah tried hard to involve Marie in the improvements she was planning. Her efforts paid off; being given *carte blanche* on the furnishing and decorating of the new extension seemed to arouse some of the old enthusiasm in Marie. Slowly she began to take an interest in life again.

With a new task to occupy her, encouragement from Philip and daily physiotherapy her legs grew stronger daily, and when he proposed again for the hundredth time she surprised him by hesitating, a smile making her eyes dance in a way he had thought he would never see again.

'When I can walk down the aisle,' she said quietly, 'when I can make it on my own, then I'll marry you, Philip.'

He looked at her in astonishment. 'Would you mind saying that again, please?'

She reached out to put her arms around his neck. 'Darling Philip. You've been so patient and so good to me. When I can walk down the aisle – walk normally mind, not stumble – I'll marry you. I love you so much. You deserve better than a useless invalid for a wife and I intend to see that you get it.'

That had been eight months ago and since then Marie had worked hard. With Leah's help, she swam daily in the new pool at 'The Ocean' and worked with the physiotherapist to strengthen her legs. Each day she walked a few more steps – at first with the help of crutches, then sticks, then at last unaided, until finally the day came when she was sufficiently satisfied with her own progress to agree to set a date for the wedding.

Leah got out of the lift and went into the bedroom where Hannah was helping Marie to dress.

'Well, it's time. Are you ready?' She stopped in the doorway, catching her breath. Marie stood in the middle of the room. In the long dress of palest primrose she looked only half her forty years. Her blonde hair was cut short in a halo of soft curls and the simple dress with its full skirt flattered her slender figure. When she turned to look at Leah her smile was one of radiant happiness.

'Yes. I'm ready,' she said. 'And you look lovely too. That shade of apricot is wonderful for you.'

Hannah carefully placed the wide-brimmed picture hat with its single white rose on Marie's head and handed her the bouquet of white and yellow roses. 'There,' she said, standing back. 'You look quite beautiful.'

In the church porch Sally was waiting as the car drew up outside the lychgate. Terry got out and helped Marie out of the back. As Hannah carefully arranged the folds of her dress Terry whispered: 'The folding wheelchair is in the boot if you want it. It's a long walk from here to the church.'

Marie smiled and shook her head. 'I'll be fine,' she said, taking his arm firmly. 'No walk could be as long or as hard as the one I've made to be here. I'm so lucky. Two lovely daughters as matrons of honour and a handsome son-in-law to give me away. What more could I ask?' She smiled up at him. 'The best man in the world is waiting for me in there this morning and I'm going to him on my own two feet.'

Together they set out towards the church. Marie

faltered slightly at first then became steadier as she held her head high and took her first proud steps into the future.